I0671706

BLOOD

and

BELLADONNA

BLOOD

and

BELLADONNA

WESTWOOD
ORIGINS

J.D. CAREN

Blood and Belladonna: a Westwood Origins novel
www.jdcaren.com

© 2023 J.D. Caren
All rights reserved. No portion of this book may be reproduced
in any form without permission from the author, except as
permitted by U.S. copyright law. For permissions contact:
authorjdcaren@gmail.com
Ebook ISBN: 978-1-7339206-3-6

CHAPTER 1

E IRNEN WESTWOOD STOOD over the last of three bodies. Well, *bodies* wasn't precise as it insinuated the crumpled figures were dead when the persistent twitches and mewls of misery suggested otherwise.

"Abel's forces increase by the day. His power grows by the night," he shouted. The sight of the cringing male incensed him. "You had twohundred wolves adding to your power and still you are useless!"

He kicked what used to be Blacke, alpha to the werewolf pack, hard enough to splay his nose open across his face. The once vicious male whimpered and yipped like a pup, slinking away. Eirnen stomped forward, intent on kicking until the disgusting display of weakness ceased.

"But, my love, those same twohundred are still yours to command," Marceline interrupted from the door.

"You know you are not permitted here," he snarled without sparing her a glance. "Blacke was useless alive and whole. At least his current state garners a lesson, but you, Marceline, are below either of his forms in terms of purpose. Purpose, as you know, is the requirement for admittance to this room," he said and finally turned to face her.

"You have visitors, my lord," she said with a slight bow and an unaffected curl to her lips. "Shall I summon Riley to put these in the gardens?"

"By all means clean the mess," he spat and stepped over yet another useless body.

The long robe hissed across the stone floor as it trailed behind him, his harried steps echoed in the corridor. Weeks wasted on Blacke and his two companions, not only time but power and energy. Some of his own and now all of theirs had been depleted from the collective, but he would not relent. He couldn't afford to, not now. Not with Abel set on destroying everything he'd built. He needed creatures of more power. More strength and resilience, just…more. One time, one perfect moment when all the right pieces fell together, and Abel would not be alone in falling under the warriors at Eirnen's command. He'd be unstoppable, unopposable. For that reason alone he'd continue to search until every last creature in this kingdom was shriveled to nothing if that was the cost.

The sound of agitated footsteps coming from the great hall gave Eirnen a reasonable idea of who his guests were before they came into view. There were three of them, each as feral-looking as the next with long hair tangled into ropes and dressed in naught but thread-bare trousers stained with gods knew what. These beasts were one of many reasons his precious Camilla did not roam the castle. Seeing them only solidified the rightness of his decision. She was fragile, delicate, naïve, and had to be protected from such things.

They smelled of sweat, a stench the lead male was determined to continue feeding with his fevered pacing. His head snapped up and his lips peeled back to show human teeth, but the animal gesture was not lost on Eirnen.

"Where—" the male growled and Eirnen flicked his fingers.

Rowan's glaive sang as it sliced the air and was followed by the wet thud of a head connecting with the floor. Rowan, Eirnen's ever-faithful guard, was back at attention, blood rolling down the staff of his glaive before the body completed its fall.

"No one speaks until I am seated and have given consent." Eirnen stood before his throne, daring the other two men to even squeak. The blood of their packmate pooled, seeping ever closer to the two men, but they didn't step back to avoid it touching their bare feet. They stared at the dead animal but said nothing. These two were smarter or they learned faster. Both attributes would be instrumental to them leaving Westwood Castle. Eirnen lowered onto the seat and laid his palms flat on the golden arms. "Speak."

The man to the right was the first to regain composure. His companion seemed determined to take up the anger of the fallen. "Your Majesty, my name is Grayson Quinn and this is Thomas Birch. We have come to inquire about our alpha."

"Your Majesty?" Thomas said and stopped pacing to gape at Grayson. "You speak to him as if *he's* your alpha," he accused before turning eyes so heated he was a heartbeat from shifting form. "You sit on your throne of gold, declare yourself a king—though you have no claim to such a title—and condemn the rest of us to suffer at your whim. We owe you no allegiance. Blacke is our alpha, *our* king, and we demand you present him to us, now."

"All who live to reap the reward of making a home in Calame owe fealty and they owe it to me. I am the reason your pack has free hunting range and are not hunted yourselves. Does that not earn me your loyalty as well?"

"You talk about loyalty, you expect our gratitude, but we know what you are. We hear your creations howling in the night. Their cries are wordless pleas to end their suffering, yet you show them no mercy. We know the only motivation for allowing us passage onto your lands is for your own purposes in syphoning from us. For this you want loyalty?"

"I borrow from your pack as you take from the bounty of my lands. Bounties, I might add, which have allowed your pack to grow from no more than a defenseless twenty to over two hundred. Would you prefer I left you as I found you? Is your memory so short that you forget I'm the reason you're not lapdogs for Master Shaughnessy? Or perhaps you would have me halt my endeavors in seeing that the amarok, beasts of your design, are kept in the confines of Chesslain Wood? My memory is not short. Shaughnessy demanded servitude for his aid, I ask only that you do whatever is necessary to preserve what I have given you."

"We haven't forgotten," Grayson said, taking Thomas by the elbow to silence his next words. "And we are indebted," Grayson dropped to one knee in the congealing blood and bowed his head. "Our alpha, my lord?"

"Is no longer available," he said with a wave of his hand. Eirnen thought, drumming his fingers on the arm of the throne as an idea formed, a potential opportunity for strategic maneuvering. "Blacke proved to be less than he presented himself, neither I nor the pack have need of such weakness. This alpha, the next, will be one we choose together. Yes, I've made my decision," he said, adjusting in the chair. "You will present me with ten of the best your pack has to offer two nights from this. From those ten we will choose."

Eirnen left the great hall and Thomas, protesting his decision, to find his son. The wolves were unruly and defiant, which was, in part, why Eirnen prodded them by inserting himself into what was traditionally a private matter. Forcing them to allow him to partake in their rituals would also drive them further under his thumb.

Henrik was neither unruly nor defiant. Eirnen had seen to it that his oldest, his legacy, was fit to take reign and be the ruler Eirnen himself was, a perfect replica in personality if not in appearance. It was no surprise when Eirnen found him in the study, poring over the parchments detailing the night's events and this latest failure.

Eirnen had other sons, three of them, and four daughters. His first wife, Delia, had served the spousal purpose and bore them all before dying with the child that would have been the ninth and another son. Henrik resembled his dear mother, his daughter, Camilla, more so. Fair of eyes, hair, and skin, delicate. In Henrik, the beauty had been a hindrance and perhaps motivated Eirnen to mold him with more harshness to compensate. Henrik had seen the purpose in what those of ignorance in such matters may call cruelty and used similar tactics with his own son, Ian. In Camilla, the same beauty was an asset to be used with care and wisdom.

Henrik needed skills and lessons that would not be of value to the rest, which was the reason he was the only other person Eirnen allowed as collaborator on this all-important venture.

"Three essences are too many," Henrik said, not for the first time.

"I tire of this argument and what it insinuates." To say three were too many was to say Eirnen hadn't the power to place them. He did. He was the single most powerful caster alive. No other could match him. Those that challenged him in the past, including his own father, had learned. Abel would soon have those same lessons taught to him, as would Henrik if he didn't speak with more care.

"There was no insinuation intended," Henrik said, humbled. "If one were inferred, I offer apologies. Perhaps the number is inconsequential. Perhaps it's the essences of the creatures we have attempted to use. I still believe the vampire to be the cause of deterioration, it simply cannot be harnessed into another being without a bite."

"The bite negates all else, all the essential elements needed. A turned caster loses all ability to cast, wolves become the vrykolakas, and so on. Lessening is not the goal."

"Yes, but would it not be a step forward if we were to successfully merge caster with wolf? The wolves are fast, strong—stronger than most vampires—and they're vicious. To have them gain casting ability with the way they work as a cohesive unit would make them quite formidable."

"Formidable, yes, but it takes them far too much time to heal wounds a vampire can heal in moments if fed well, time we don't have in the midst of battle. Vampires have little sense of loyalty, and my warriors wouldn't be proper warriors if defeated by nothing more than dawn. We need the cohesiveness and inherent loyalty of the wolves, the strength and resilience of the aged vampire and our ability to defend against casts."

Henrik paced, rubbing his forefinger along his bottom lip. It was a gesture he did often when lost in thought. "The wolves have proven unable to withstand the conversion, caster hosts as well no matter the age or level of power. Perhaps that's the problem, the hosts were too weak of body. Perhaps we should *start* with vampire. The older the better, but that would make capture difficult."

"My thoughts precisely and I have one in mind."

⁓

"I've seen them again," Camilla said the moment Callum appeared in her quarters.

"Ah, the heavenly lads. Gifts of the Gods," he shouted and threw his arms wide while she shushed him. He continued to crow and her attempts to quiet him were ineffective, especially as she started to laugh with him.

"Stop laughing at me," she chastised and pulled her shoulders back into some semblance of a dignified position. He, on the other hand, lay across the bed on his side, smiling like a devil. "Callum, do you truly believe they are real?"

"Yes," he said, losing all signs of jest in his features. "My power is not one of imagination. They are real beings sharing this world with us at this moment. My fear is *you* have imagined them as something more than they are. They are men and nothing else,

Camilla. Be they caster, wolf, vampire or other, they are but men. Don't allow your expectations to exceed their abilities."

"I can't help myself. They're outside these walls, outside this castle, and outside Calame. With my James, there's peace and comfort, warmth, an ease of love that is pure of heart. But the other, Dorin, he is an adventure, potent, and passionate. Fire." She ducked her head to hide the heat creeping up her face. "I should not speak to you so."

"If not me, then to whom would you confess? We're both prisoners, you and I, birds in cages we cannot escape. Yours gilded and mine infinite, but cages none the less."

"What of you, Callum, have you ever had a lady to love?"

"Aye. Ana"—he said, his eyes lighting—"and quite a lady she was. Sweet and gentle, and so beautiful she set my heart to try to break from my chest with nothing more than a glance in my direction." Camilla watched a serenity and shyness come over his face, neither of which she'd ever seen on him before, but then he blinked and came back to himself and Westwood Castle. "We were to be wed."

"I'm sorry, Callum. If I knew how to free you, I would."

"I know, love," he said.

Callum was trapped, a prisoner just as he'd said, and she, his jailor. But she didn't know how to find the key to his cell, if there even was one. He was a ghost, a lost spirit she'd somehow summoned to her side, and then she'd stolen his ability. All of this without intention and yet here they were, she with all the benefit and his only reward her company. Poor Callum.

She stiffened as he sat upright, both at attention and casting wary eyes around the room. *Not again.* There was nothing to see, but a presence was here with them. It was a weight, an invisible vice squeezing and pressurizing until the room was smaller. The air heavier, harder to breathe. A dull ache started in Camilla's head and marched down her spine, touching every nerve pathway on its trek. A voice whispered and although she couldn't make out the words, the tone was confused, afraid, but also angry.

Her pulse quickened and her skin tingled with the sensation of being aerated, like stepping out of a bath with mentholated oils. She patted the bedding next to her until she found Callum's hand.

"Don't go," she whispered with the first brush of power. "Please don't leave me."

The ache eased. Every tense muscle relaxed. Between one blink and the next, a film that she'd not known was there was wiped from her eyes. Prisms of glittering light made by the flame of a candle reflecting off tinted perfume bottles caught and held her eyes. It was beautiful, a galaxy of color with millions of multihued stars, colors she had no name for. A more splendid sight she'd never beheld. She held her breath for fear of scattering the little motes to the wind.

Her ear twitched with the sound of a raised voice, one she didn't recognize. "...Blacke is our alpha, our king..." Scents swirled—cooking meat, dust, perfumes, sweat, and copper.

Nausea churned her gut. Blood. The copper smell was blood and it made her mouth water and her teeth ache with the desire to bite, to tear flesh. She squeezed her eyes closed tight and clapped her hands over her ears. Sights, sounds, and smells this crisp did not come with being a caster, neither was the smell of blood an enticement. The presence with them was a wolf, a dead one, and she was scavenging the poor creature's remains. Some part of her reveled in it, in the flood of energy that was the reward offered up by the bounty called by her power. Even now, as her stomach heaved, the desire to open up and drink in all the dead had to give was near undeniable.

James. Think of James. The added shame of picturing his gentle face was enough to dampen the craving further. He would never have to fight to be decent, to not delight in pain and torment. He'd be disgusted by her if he had the capability to watch her as she watched him. He'd have found a way to stop this and that's what she had to do if she ever wanted to be worthy of a male such as him.

She sat with her eyes closed, mind focused on James, hand squeezing Callum's like an anchor. In the early hours of the morning, she'd watched James place himself bodily between a musket and young female wolf. The musket had been in the hands of the man James claimed as father, no less. If he could find the courage to do that, she could find the will to abstain from gorging herself on the loss of someone else's life. This man, this wolf, did he have a mate, young that were even now awaiting his return? The wolves were allies of Grandfather's. Did he die fighting to defend this castle? Her family?

The scents faded and her ears felt like she'd stuck her fingers in them to muffle the sounds. When she allowed her eyes to crack open, the chamber looked once again as it always had. Gone, the poor wolf was gone.

"Camilla," Callum said and shook her hand. "It's over."

"No, it isn't. Others will follow, maybe even another will become a prisoner here with me as you are. I can't stand it, Callum, but I'm helpless to stop it if everyone around me continues to keep me ignorant. It's time you stop lying to me and calling it protection."

"And what do you suppose you can do from here, Camilla? Nothing. You can do nothing but sit in here with this new knowledge barbing you. Knowledge you wouldn't have if I didn't exist as this shadow. I can't do that to you. I won't," he said and shook his head.

"If not you, then who?" she challenged, using his own words. "I'm not stupid, Callum. I know the addition of a second master power means I've grown stronger than Grandfather anticipated. He will be hurt, perhaps even angry that I've kept such a secret from him."

She was a Westwood and that meant something important. Her lineage, one of immense power, was rumored to be descended directly from the gods and goddesses that once ruled the world. Which meant they bore a responsibility to those of lesser power.

To do their best to keep them safe, provide for them when they couldn't provide for themselves, offer protection when needed.

Callum was not a Westwood but was an upper-level caster. Born with the power to conjure the present in a reflective surface, he could show anyone who looked upon the surface—a mirror or still water—anything or anyone they wished to see at that moment. Once the image was past, it was gone and Callum could not call it forth again.

Camilla had been born with the ability to recreate anything she had seen with her own eyes. Like most casters, she had shown hints of her primary power from a young age. A second power was rare, but not unheard of—one of her aunts had two primary powers. Developing a power this late in years was odd and casters with no ability by the onset of puberty were labeled latent. Camilla was in her sixteenth year when this second ability, over death, presented itself.

"Should I bang on my door until someone comes to take me to Grandfather so he can give me answers? He'll ask how it is I know of the death tonight and I will tell him if that's what I have to do to get his aid in ridding myself of this revulsion. There's a reason you advised me to keep these secrets about this power. Tell me what it is or you leave me no choice."

"You know as well as I there is no way to purge this ability. It's yours, a part of you as much as the illusions, as your heartbeat. Besides that, there are benefits, yes? Don't make a decision on the heels of something that caused you enough fright to forget that."

He was right, she knew he was. Hadn't she just moments before been waxing romantic about Dorin and James, her fairytale princes? Months before Callum's arrival, she'd dreamed of them in visions so real she could still smell their skin when she woke. She'd recreated those dreams here in her chambers over and over again, but they were naught but illusions. Re-creations created by her gift. She couldn't touch them, nor them her, couldn't speak to them. If she tried the illusions dissipated. In many ways, having the taunt of what she was missing was worse than the loneliness she'd sought to ease.

After Callum, with a little practice, they'd discovered that these two males weren't dreams at all, not conjuring of imagination, but real people. Callum's ability let her find them, watch them live their lives, learn details about them as if she were right there beside them. But they weren't the only ones she watched.

With Callum's ability, she watched people as if they were actors on a stage. A lady with grey hair and age-gnarled hands, watching her grandchildren play. Not an adventurous sight to be sure, but it was the absolute peace and joy she saw in the wizened eyes, the scent of bread baking, and firewood smoke that filled her with warmth.

She'd watched a young man pacing in front of a modest house in the village below. His hands were gesturing, his mouth moving, but he was alone. She watched with open curiosity to see what it was that made the young man nervous. Finally, he'd closed his eyes, drew in a great breath that lifted his shoulders and knocked on the door to the house. A lovely girl with hair the color of wheatgrass, freckles, and brown eyes answered.

She'd watched their romance bloom over the course of weeks. His visits to her home where they both blushed with every glance at the other, their first time being alone when the boy worked up the courage to take her hand. It was beautiful, sweet, and it filled Camilla with a longing that cast a dimness of envy over the couple when she watched. They didn't know, couldn't feel the dark cloud of her loneliness rolling into their lives, but she could and it stripped the scene of the purity and happiness that had drawn her back to them in the beginning.

It was nearing eight months since Callum appeared. It had taken days for either of them to believe the other was real and more time still before they believed he was dead. Until they learned to work together, manipulating her energies, she giving and he taking, the servants couldn't see him. He waved in their faces and yelled next to them, yet they saw nothing. Camilla, however, could see him clearly. The realization—that she could see him, touch him, interact with him when others couldn't—gave them their first clue as to who was responsible for him being in Westwood Castle as a ghost.

She hadn't killed him, of course not, but it was her fault he was stuck. They'd probed further into their connection. Camilla controlled Callum's ability. She could summon him to her from anywhere in the castle despite the wards, she could also send him away from her, although no matter what words she spoke she couldn't send him to his afterlife.

Despite the part she played in holding him, they'd become friends for which she was grateful. She remembered well what it was like in these spacious chambers with no one. In all this time, he'd deflected every inquiry as to what he witnessed while roaming unseen in the halls of the castle. He offered only vague pleadings for her to behave in one way or another, mostly to lie or deny outright the ability that tied them, about Callum's existence, with no explanations. He'd begged her trust and silence and she'd given him both because she did trust Callum and she owed him much.

She'd attempted to watch for herself, just as she'd watched the grandmother and the couple, but she was met with a great wall of white light that blotted her vision long after she stopped looking at it. It was wardings, protections, set up by Grandfather.

Grandfather had spoken many times of the Westwood strength and those who envied what they had enough to try and seize it as their own. Envy was an emotion with which Camilla was fiercely knowledgeable. As she'd spied on others, she'd envied until her fingers ached to have a sliver of what they had, to reach into the images and pluck it away for herself. What better way to quell aching and envious fingers than to prevent them from seeing the bounty within?

Callum had answers and she was no longer satisfied with sitting idle. The deaths that came howling toward her as if she were to blame were occurring with alarming frequency and she had to know the truth of it. Was it simply that the affinity for the dead was expanding to cover greater distance or was the surge in number happening within Westwood walls?

Eirnen Westwood, her grandfather, would certainly kill and do so without mercy if his family were under threat. If they were being attacked, she had to know of it. She might even be able to help somehow. If anyone could teach her how to turn this ability into something to be used to defend rather than the vile, leeching thing it felt like, it was Grandfather.

"He can help me, Callum. Tell me why you want me to keep this secret or release me from my vow to keep it."

The look on his face was apologetic, mournful and it tightened her stomach. "I'm sorry," he said, then tore her perceptions of her world apart.

There was nothing to do now but wait. Eirnen hated waiting, forced idleness, the feeling was helplessness. He'd never been a patient man. Some saw his inability to tolerate postponement of plans, even necessary ones such as this, as a flaw. He did not. It kept his mind working, plotting alternatives as a means to temper himself. The exercise reaped success on more occasions than he could recount. Conversely, the widespread knowledge of his impatience and the consequences of leaving him in such a state ensured his requests were honored as timely as possible.

Eirnen watched the hillsides and the village below. Shaughnessy was tucked away somewhere in Calame, he just knew it. It had been years, nearly two decades, since he'd had that niggling, intuitive feeling that came when this particular enemy was near. Why he returned now, Eirnen didn't know but the vampire would come to regret his decision. They'd battled many times, both lost much to the other. A smile played at Eirnen's lips as he pictured the Master Shaughnessy in a position of servitude.

One warrior was hardly enough to steal a victory from Abel, but if it were successful they would have an answer to how strong the host needed to be. It would be difficult to locate vampires equal to Shaughnessy in power, but not impossible. If Shaughnessy belonged to Eirnen, he'd serve as a compass to find others. He'd have no choice if his king commanded it of him. Eirnen clasped his hands behind his back and paced as he imagined the possibilities.

His steps quickened as he thought it out. Yes, the host had to be strong, resilient, but the essences he placed in it needn't be. Shaughnessy would master over them and Eirnen would be the master of Shaughnessy. All he'd have to do was assert his dominance over Shaughnessy, a simple binding, and the rest would follow. He could have an army of unstoppable warriors. If that happened, he'd rule over far more than just Calame.

I must have Shaughnessy.

"This is a room in which I am still permitted on occasion, my lord?" Marceline came a few more steps into his chamber and gave an immaculate curtsy made even more intriguing by the chiffon shift that gave glimpses of the body beneath.

She held the position as he circled her, waiting for him to acknowledge her before she would stand. He left her half-knelt, arms and thighs trembling with the effort required to not fall, and assessed her. Long dark hair fell around her face, nearly sweeping the floor. Olive skin made darker still by the hunter shade of the shift, heavy breasts and ample hips, all she used to her advantage. She was beautiful, there was no illusion of that in his mind or hers.

He clasped her chin and lifted her face, dark brown eyes snapped with amusement and defiance. She'd stay in that position until her limbs failed to hold her any longer before she'd ask permission to rise. It was probably that same wry disposition and the unwillingness to be broken that kept him from casting her from his home though she tested his patience at every turn. Delia had been sweet, timid, and meek in all things. Marceline possessed none of these qualities. Did he love her? No. Did she amuse him? Daily.

"He's with her again," Marceline said, a payment in exchange for permission to rise. His jaw tightened to the point of pain as he clenched his teeth. A male, alone with his Camilla. The pilfering fiend had to be an experienced caster, nothing other than that could take down the wards and leave no evidence of the disengagement. One of the guard, perhaps? "Wait," she said before he'd taken two steps toward the door. "Patience, Eirnen."

He stopped, but only because his attempts to catch the male before had failed. She was always alone when he or one of the servants went into her quarters. He'd toyed with the idea that her illusions had grown, that she'd conjured a companion of sorts to pass the time alone in her chambers, but he'd seen no evidence of it in their lessons. Which lent further credence to the theory she had a very real companion. A powerful one. Powerful enough to breach wards he himself had set, powerful enough to be coupled with Shaughnessy.

"Let me be her confidant," Marceline pressed.

"I should be her only confidant," he said.

"Don't be jealous of this male," Marceline said with amusement. "You are her grandfather and a man. She needs a female to speak with, to advise her and guide her. Especially in matters of the opposite sex. You've sheltered her too long, Eirnen. Did you expect her to remain a child with the needs and wants of a child forever?"

He...did. He saw her for lessons at least twice a month and it never failed to shock him that it was a young woman entering his quarters and not a squealing tot demanding the dragon story. Children did not play host to unknown men in their bed chambers. Winston Cleary, her promised and Eirnen's most powerful ally against Abel, grew impatient for his bride. If rumors of this male visiting her chambers reached Winston at Gladen, he would be incensed. Possibly enough so to sway him against Eirnen.

"I'll consider your recommendation," he said and yanked Marceline to her feet, turning her until her back pressed against his chest. "What did you overhear, Marceline?" He asked close to her ear, "You know I'm going to punish you for making me ask, don't you?"

His hands drifted down to rest on her trim waist. She wriggled her hips against him and made a sound close to a purr when she found him wanting. With one hand he skimmed up the front of her body, between her breasts, and stopped at her neck where his fingers tightened until she stilled. Though the feel of her softness rubbing against the rigidness between his legs was exquisite, he wouldn't give her the upper hand just yet.

"Laughter," she whispered. He loosened his fingers. "And cages." Her hands went to his thighs. She groaned and dug her nails into his skin. He caught her wrists, gathering them both in one hand hard enough to bruise.

"What else?" He nipped along her shoulder, up to her neck where he clamped his teeth tight when she didn't answer.

She shuddered, writhing on him once again. "Love. A warning to not allow expectations of men to exceed their abilities. Ah, gods, Eirnen," she cried. "No more, I heard no more."

She had to beg for him, want him more than he wanted her. This was the game they played. A game they delighted in. Marceline enjoyed being dominated almost as much as he relished breaking her. He had to earn the right to dominance, she would submit no other way. He released her wrists and fisted the silky material at her thigh, bunching it, letting it glide and tease higher and higher until she was bared. She groaned and began rolling her hips until the hardest part of him lay in the crease of her ass. He tightened his fingers around her neck, squeezing until her face reddened.

"You came to me uninvited, therefore your concern must have

been for my pleasure and not your own." He loosened his grip to clasp her jaw and wrench her head around.

She laughed and reached back to stroke him. "Your pleasure is my pleasure, sire," she said and dipped her head to take his thumb in her hot mouth to suck. She leaned forward, still sucking him, grazing over the pad with her teeth. Her palms flat on the dressing table, she spread her legs wide and arched her back in invitation, then bit down on his finger. Yes, she amused him greatly.

CHAPTER 2

TORTURE, MURDER, LIES and all manner of degradation happening in her very home, committed by her family. Not to defend against attack, not to protect themselves, but for gain.

"I have to see them, these gardens. I have to see for myself," Camilla said and lifted her skirts to get off the bed without tripping. "Take me. You know the way, I know you do."

"No, Camilla, trust me, that place is not for you."

"Then I must speak with Grandfather," she said and marched toward the door. Callum was there, blocking the way with both hands raised. "Let me by, Callum."

"Wait, just wait," he said. "If you believe any part of what I've told you, then you must stop and think." His brow dipped and then his features relaxed as if he figured out a new tact. "I've never told you how I died."

She stopped moving, stopped breathing, and stared unblinking at Callum. His words coupled with what she'd just learned about her family...An answer fell into place and she didn't want to believe it. He reached out and ran his fingers down her cheek. "They killed you," she whispered around a tight throat. "I need, I…" he took her arm and guided her to the armchair by the fire. "Callum?"

"I'm here, love," he said and knelt in front of her with both her hands in his. "I feel no pain. No thirst or hunger, not even the cold can touch me now. Please, don't cry," he said and caught the tears streaking her face. "I'm sorry, Camilla. I thought you would realize and you'd understand why I want you to protect yourself from them. They can't hurt me anymore, but you're still vulnerable and far too inexperienced to match them. Secrets are your best weapon. Keep them."

Camilla kept a tight hold on Callum's hand and watched the fire. Of course he'd died, but she'd imagined it as some tragic accident. Not this. She felt stupid and naïve, the child Callum and everyone else treated her as. No wonder. She sat in this room and daydreamed about princes and true love, childish notions.

"Why you?" she finally asked. "How?"

"Eirnen is trying to make warriors, creating them with a binding cast of sorts to make them not only powerful but subservient to him. He attempted to merge my essence and a vampire's into a werewolf. He failed, but we were fortunate enough to be among the first of his experiments. We died instead of living on as one of the creatures in his garden. It was my ability he wanted. I wasn't a willing participant. His solution was to instill that ability into something he commanded. Now, as if in mockery of his failure, it is you who holds ownership of the power he killed me to steal."

"And you're afraid of what would happen should I also prove to be an unwilling participant?" she asked.

"Of what would happen if you did." He sat on the floor by the fire and draped his arms over his knees. "Eirnen, in his way, loves you. I cannot deny it, although how a man such as he is capable escapes my understanding. However, he will make you a weapon if he can. Trusting girl that you are, you'd do so with a few well-spoken words without any thought as to where he was aiming you."

Indignation burned her tongue, even popped her mouth open to deny what he said, but just as quickly she cooled. Before the revelations of tonight, she'd have done anything Grandfather asked of her without questioning his motives, because she'd thought she didn't have to. She didn't believe the grandfather she'd known since birth was fabricated. How he was with her was real. But so was Callum's version of Eirnen Westwood.

"Perhaps I can speak to him, show him the pain he's caused," she said. He's not all bad, he couldn't be because she had seen him show kindness and love. She felt both from him.

"I've done as you asked despite my reservations. Now you do something for me," he said rather than respond. "Try to unravel your wards."

"I have tried," she said. "I haven't the strength."

"You would if you took more of my energy into yourself," he said. She was shaking her head before he finished the sentence. "I can feel you, your energy, it's the reason I can touch you, appear whole and alive near you. If I can take from you, then you can take from me."

"I already do," she reminded him.

"Just enough to use my vision as a toy," he said and she flinched. "I'm sorry, I shouldn't have said it that way. I miss using it and now that I cannot, jealousy makes me snappish." She nodded acceptance and that devilish grin she loved curled his lips. "I used it as a toy myself. A cherished, well-practiced, voyeuristic toy."

"Callum," she admonished, but her guilt was eased as he intended.

His smile remained, but his eyes changed. They held the sadness she'd seen before when he was lost in his thoughts but would say "nothing, love" when she asked what troubled him.

"When I was a young little lad, no taller than my father's hip, I was a bit of a rascal. I sent my poor mother into a fit of mouth-wagging outrage more than once. But, worry not, for I had two other young lads to share in my fondness for lizards in housecoat pockets and such. They were brothers and we fancied ourselves outlaws. We had great fun. Epic adventures the likes of which the world had never seen, by our estimation.

"One afternoon, when my chores were finished and my mother released me into the wild once more, it was to my friends' house that I ran as fast as my legs could carry me. I'd been banned from them for nigh a week, you see. Their father, Augustin, was a good man, a second father to me in many ways. That day he was laid out in the grass in front of his house, his wife, Grania, clutching at him and screaming for him to return. Never had I seen heartbreak of the sort.

"I crept to her side. She grabbed at me, dragged me down to my knees by my shirt. Her voice was shrill, but I scarcely heard a word. It was Augustin's face—bloated, purple and blue, the whites of his eyes red as new blood—that held me captive. Like a coward, I tore out of Grania's clawing hands and ran away. I ran home."

"And your friends," Camilla whispered.

"It was more than two days before my father returned with news. I'd not slept, part from fear and part from my shame in running. I was awake in my bed when I heard him come inside to my mother's greeting. 'They took them, Cess. They took them both and murdered Augustin,' he'd said. I didn't know who'd done the taking, but I knew, my gut knew, it was my friends who were taken.

"Of course, as I aged, I heard rumors of Eirnen Westwood. Things both great and terrible, people spoke of him in awe or fear, sometimes both. The Westwoods, their power so great they held within them abilities of telekinesis and could conjure flames the same blue as their eyes and yet were not burned by them. On top of that, each had an ability unique to them. To we normal casters in the villages, one ability was common, sometimes two, none had the base of innate abilities the Westwood line had."

Camilla glanced down at her fingers twisting in her lap and had the urge to apologize. "It is true we take these abilities for granted."

"There's no reason to feel shame or embarrassment about how powerful you are, Camilla. But, knowing what you are does mean caution is necessary until people get to see you as I have, to know your heart is good. Personally, until I learned a very hard lesson, I felt all the fear was nonsense.

"I grew up with my mother and father warning me to not reveal my ability to anyone. They seemed to suggest to those they associated with that I was a latent with no ability at all. I was not. I was strong, powerful. I proved it. For weeks nothing came of the display. I did it again. Nothing. Then one morning last autumn I was awoken by my mother. I'd been summoned to the castle by Eirnen Westwood himself. His infamous guards waited outside our home as my mother and father hissed and argued ways to prevent them from taking me with them. Augustin's face, which haunted me still, filled my mind and decided me. I would not see my own father in such a state because I refused an audience.

"I must confess, I was awed when I entered these walls. Though filled with dread at why I'd been summoned, I gaped at the power I could feel as a wind against my skin. It was a kinship. After years of being labeled latent, then feeling the need to prove myself, this place was a haven to me. Eirnen, the king himself, greeted me in the great room. I couldn't take my eyes from the golden throne on the high dais.

"'Welcome, welcome, young Callum. I have heard a number of intriguing things about you. If half are true, we are to become great friends,' he'd said and my chest filled with pride. 'If you would so honor me with a demonstration.' He'd actually lowered his head *to me*.

"I was eager, Camilla. You don't know how eager I was. A mirror was carried into the great room and I smiled at my own reflection approaching me as I gathered my power. I'd give Eirnen Westwood such a demonstration he'd know I was an equal. An upper-level caster of the highest caliber. I asked what he wished to see. He circled his hand in the air as if he had to think about it, as if he wasn't prepared. As if he might believe the rumors of me being latent he'd no doubt heard as well.

"This angered me. Determined me. As a young man of sixteen, goading me was not such a difficult feat. I also knew from whispers in the village that Eirnen's closest rival was Abel Lockley. I smiled at my own brilliance and conjured the image in the mirror.

"I was trying to incite Eirnen as he'd incited me. And incite him I did, a smile of delight crossed his face as he watched Abel on horseback chasing a beauty of a woman through the woods around Anselone. He patted me on the back and told me I'd done a fine job. He ordered one of his servants to ready his horse and tell the guards to prepare to leave for Anselone. Then he had another servant come in with the sole job of tending my every need.

"I was a king. I had a hot bath. A feast complete with all the sweet wine I could guzzle. A room that was more than twice the size of our home. I reveled in luxury for a full night, imagining how mother and father would react when I brought them here to live with their talented son. But when morning came and I decided to walk the corridors of this legendary place, which was now my home as far as I was concerned, I saw the brothers. My friends who'd been taken long ago. They were alive, though badly scarred and vacant of eye."

"Rowan and Riley," she gasped and clapped her hand over her mouth. Grandfather's most favored and trusted guards.

"Yes. They asked of their mother and father, to which I told them the truth. They urged me to leave at once, not just the castle, but Calame, speaking to me of the bindings placed on them to ensure their service and their fears I would see the same fate. I was a fool, I thought I could bargain for their freedom.

"Eirnen returned with the prize he'd stolen from Abel. Marceline. I demanded he release Rowan and Riley in exchange for me staying to serve him of my own free will. I vowed it. I would not run like a coward again. He laughed and locked me in the dungeons below to think about it. I'd serve him and he'd keep his guards. He tried force to get me to use my ability, I stayed resolute. Our bargain would stand. He never broke me, but you know the result. I am this now. A ghost. And my friends are still bound to the man who murdered their father to possess them."

She didn't know what to say or where to start. No place, no one question or utterance of sympathy seemed the right thing. She'd gone from ignorant to overwhelmed with information over the span of hours. She was sure he watched over Rowan and Riley still. Perhaps, there is an opportunity in that. If Callum trusts them, she could reveal a bit of herself to give him his friends back, surely.

"To what end did you tell me this story, to further chronicle Grandfather's treachery? If so, it was not necessary. You didn't have to recall such a horrible thing."

"It was but part of the story. You are upper level, Camilla. Stifled, yes, but it is there. I can feel it when I take from you to gain substance. If you were to do as a proper caster and fuel yourself with energies rather than skimming mine to see places and people outside these walls, there is no telling what you might accomplish." She opened her mouth to argue, but he held up his hand. "At the very least, you could get out of this room and see things for yourself."

Aside from having no way to know how it would affect either one of them for her to take Callum's energy, it would be the equivalent of feeding this power she wished would go back to the depths from which it had come. But now she knew she'd come by this darkness honestly.

Her brother, Ian, would be more suited to this type of ability. He trained to use his casts with strategy and skill, to someday rule. Camilla's education consisted of warnings of the ways of a world she'd never seen and trivial facts meant to amuse a future husband should he wish to converse with her. She could spin casts adequate to prove she wasn't latent—that was all she needed as far as anyone but her was concerned.

"Callum, I can't," she said.

"You can—"

A click against the shutters had them both looking to the window, another and they stood. "Let me," Callum said and then vanished.

The shutters were flung open as if hit by a strong wind and smacked against the walls. Marceline had power over the elements and in times of anger, she could rattle the very walls with rolls of thunder. Camilla looked to the sky for streaks of lightning and wondered what Grandfather had done to his wife as she crept closer.

There was no more evidence of a brewing storm, no thunderous clouds in the sky, just the last blazes of orange and pink on the horizon as night approached. Something flew through the opening and pinged on the floor until it came to a stop at her feet. A pebble. She picked it up, turning it in her fingers.

"*Give it back*," a teasing voice whispered through her head. She stiffened. A telepath? An incredibly powerful one if she had the ability to project words into another's consciousness. "*It's not a proper game if you keep all the pieces.*"

All the pieces? A telepath—if that's what she was—of this level could be very dangerous, but the voice hadn't sounded threatening. In fact, it was playful. Camilla inched closer to the window and eased her hand toward the opening. No resistance. The wards were disengaged. How? Camilla had to stand on her toes and lean halfway out the window before she saw a girl looking back up at her from the grounds below. She was too far away to make out many details besides dark hair. The girl twisted back and forth, making her dress billow out around her legs. She was also surrounded by pebbles like the one Camilla held in her fist.

If she was master enough to speak directly into Camilla's mind and tear down wards set in place by Grandfather, it was possible she could hear Camilla's thoughts as well. Fascinating. She'd never known anyone outside of Westwood Castle except carefully selected tutors and Grandfather saw to it they were gone before any sort of friendly relationship could be established. "They are here to instruct, to educate, anything more is a derelict of duty," he'd said. "Confide in no one outside of this family."

Camilla's curiosity was at full attention.

"I've seen her on the grounds before," Callum said as he appeared beside her.

"Who is she?" Camilla asked, watching as the girl dotted the sky with her finger as if she were counting stars.

"I don't know. She's always just wandering around, talking to herself. The guards are going to catch her if she's not careful."

"She wants me to give back the pebble, like we're playing a game." Perhaps the poor thing was lonely. But why come here to find company?

"Careful, Camilla," Callum said and urged her back. "She didn't just come here and show herself to play a game with you."

Camilla eased her hand out the window, marveling again at the lack of resistance, and let the pebble drop. The girl's hand snapped out and caught it before it could hit her in the face. She made a show of putting the pebble in a pocket on the front of her gown as if it were treasured. *"Oh, a present."* She sounded surprised to receive the pebble she'd asked for in the first place. *"Now one for you."*

Camilla stood straight and backed up a step to keep from being hit with the next thrown game piece. Instead, an image flickered through her mind too fast to catch. Colors swirled, black and grey splashed through with red, gold, and white. When they stopped, she was looking over a field of ash and ruin. Bodies and severed limbs were strewn around, blood cut rivulets of red through the dirt. She saw herself sitting on Eirnen's golden throne in the middle of it all. She wore a white gown that cut low down her chest and was untouched by the filth that surrounded her. She stared over the utter devastation with a cold detachment. Three massive warriors stood behind her, each smudged with soot and blood.

The colors swirled again then faded until she was looking at a solid panel of white. At her side, Callum called her name, but she couldn't answer him. Another picture was forming. A tree. It had no leaves but was heavy with branches that forked and twined, crossing in places before separating and sprouting new, smaller branches.

"Stop," she breathed and clutched at her head.

The tree shrank, drifting into the background. A bright blue sky surrounded its top, leaves burst into a cascade of green that shaded a small pool under the branches. Roses of the deepest red and moss of jade clung to a rock wall behind the tree. The image was framed, her fingers pressed into the cool wood of a wall, she was inside looking out. Her dress, though scant, spoke of wealth. Wide bracelets of silver that moved as water circled halfway up her forearms. A rounded, red-faced man of more than twice her age took her hands to kiss each of the bracelets and she cringed from him. Dark circles colored the skin under her eyes, her lips were red and cracked as if she'd been worrying them with her teeth, her skin pale.

Camilla stumbled backward to escape the image in her head and another took its place. This one was as full of life and growth as the others had been death and despair. She was walking barefoot through a garden, though it wasn't the one on the grounds of the castle. This one was smaller but no less beautiful in full bloom. At the sound of laughter, she turned to look back at a lovely manor. Her face glowed with a serene smile and a sense of pride. A little girl with copper hair ran squealing from the house, chased by a boy of the same age. Twins. They ran toward her and she gasped. They had eyes of Westwood blue. A pair of strong, sun-darkened arms wound around her and pulled her back until a masculine scent filled her nose and her eyes slid closed.

As fast as they'd come, the images were gone and she was sitting on the hard floor of her chamber, panting breaths. She looked around in confusion, ignoring Callum's worried words. She batted his hands away to leap to her feet. She ran to the window and saw the girl. *"On which branch will you choose to perch, little bird?"*

"Wait," she called, throwing her hand out only to have it come up against a barricade that was unseen but felt as a jolt that numbed her to the shoulder. "Don't go," she shouted, taking a step back before the wards gave her another warning zap. The girl blew her a kiss, then ran across the grounds and out of sight.

∽

Shaughnessy stood at the top of a hill in the center of a field, watching the greyness in the distance that was Westwood Castle. His enemy was within those walls, an enemy he had lost to many times. But not this time. Not with the aid of Marion. She had many claims about herself, some he believed, most he didn't. The ones he believed he'd seen with his own eyes.

Marion, a seeress with telepathic ability, claimed to not be a caster at all, but something more powerful. That part he did not believe. Every upper-level caster he'd ever encountered seemed to have an inflated image of themselves, as if they'd evolved into something special. Not to insinuate Marion wasn't powerful, the tiny lass raised his hackles every time she came near him. To set a master vampire such as himself on the instinct to defend against danger was impressive indeed, but nothing he hadn't seen before. Eirnen Westwood was one such caster, he was also the only one left alive who'd bested Shaughnessy.

It took ages for a vampire to get to a master level of power. With casters around, young vampires rarely made it to see past five years and most fewer than that. The haughty caster bastards treated all who were not upper-level casters as inferior beings, pets, or slaves. But for all their blustering about their superiority, they couldn't heal themselves. Oh, he'd heard how King Eirnen found himself a caster with a healing ability and turned him into one of the guards he kept close at all times, but most didn't have that luxury.

Hunters were sent to find vampires to drain of their curative blood. Unfortunately, the wolves hadn't the self-healing properties to share the burden of catering to the elite. At the order of the ruling casters, vampires were hunted until they were all but extinct so casters could be cured of every sniffle and limp. Casters were nothing if not capitalizing. As availability went down, demand went up. Eirnen captured a vampire it took his hunters weeks to find. Captured, not killed. They staked the poor bastard to a wall in the dungeons. Eirnen forced his captive to create new vampires of servants or villagers he wanted to punish or sent his hunters for humans.

New or old, the blood still healed injuries. Eirnen, loving to have those he ruled indebted to him, charged families to the point of poverty for one vial. Should they be unable to pay, he found another way for them to work off the debt. Some gave him their children to be servants, some he recruited to his guard, others he bided his time to see where they would be of use. He couldn't risk his captive vampire becoming powerful enough to escape. They were killed and replaced with one of their progenies before they reached a full year.

Worse than being judged inferior was being considered a potential threat. Creatures with any power were killed before they had the numbers to replace the casters at the top of the food chain. Some of the species survived, some didn't. As it was, Marion played guardian over a mismatched troupe of indigent absconders and had somehow managed to persuade the wolves to help her keep them undetected by Eirnen.

Finally. Marion emerged from the woods, her arms piled high with stones. He'd long ago learned that asking her questions generally wrought nothing but frustration, so he didn't bother. She didn't look at him, just folded her thin body onto the ground and started stacking the stones.

"Laying a foundation," Marion said as she arranged the stones she'd gathered into a square. "All manner of creatures do this, including you and I."

"And then they build upon it, yes, yes," he said and waited to see why they were out in the middle of the woods at such an hour.

"Some do. Some only ever get to see the potential." She began to draw symbols in the dirt inside the square she'd built. "Then another takes over and places their own design."

He crouched in front of her and lifted her face. Sadness touched her features, pouting her mouth, trembling her chin and making her eyes shimmer. "What will you have me do, Marion?"

"Do not destroy what I try to cultivate," she said. "So fragile." She lowered her face to watch her fingers wipe over the stones. "Tenuous."

She stood, dusted off her hands and just that fast, her moment of sadness ended. Her smile was wide, waiting as she stared up at him. It was an expression that gave him pause, because it was an expectant one, as if she was watching to see his reaction to something she already knew was about to happen.

"No," Shaughnessy said at the first hint of a scent he'd not encountered in many years. Vrykolakas. Marion nodded, smile fading, as the scent grew stronger. "Marion, did you have a hand in the creation of these things? Our allies unprotected in the village will suffer greater losses than our enemies behind guarded walls."

"I did not," she said. "Abel created. I am utilizing."

"We must leave here," he said. She stepped to the side as he grabbed for her arm. He could hear them now. They were close enough that even if they ran the creatures would likely catch them.

"If the doors and the wards that protect them were ripped away from Westwood Castle this night, if you were to witness such a breach, what choice would you make?"

"We are in the path of what sounds like dozens of vrykolakas and you want to speak hypotheticals with me?"

"Yes. I do. Choices, Shaughnessy. One's own design over the foundations I lay. Tell me yours."

He pictured it, the doors wide open, the guards distracted with fighting the vrykolakas, the possibility that Eirnen would be similarly engaged. "I'd not pass up such an opportunity," he said.

"The result of that choice," she said and showed him his own death.

The snarls of the vrykolakas tearing him to pieces, *eating him*, in the vision were soon joined with the snarls of those that approached the field. Try as he might, he couldn't shake off Marion's intrusion even as the beasts charged out of the trees, the closest less than six feet away from the two of them. He grabbed for Marion and found only air. He couldn't fight like this.

"I don't want you to fight," she said. "I want you to remember this lesson, Shaughnessy. I didn't ask you to meet me here because I required your protection. You are here because you don't trust me."

Her voice overlaid the vision, timed so that when she said he was here because he didn't trust her applied to both scenarios. Teeth clamped over his face, crushing bone even as the rest of his lifeless body was pulled and tugged in several directions by the powerful jaws of the vrykolakas feasting.

"Release me," he said at the sight of his intestines spilling and unraveling.

The vision was gone and he was on his knees in the field. Marion was now several feet from him, vrykolakas rushing past her on both sides but not seeming to pay either one of them any attention. As he rose to his feet, he watched one of them charge for her. She didn't move and even though he wanted to yank her out of the way, he didn't. Trust her, she said. Fine.

He could only stare openmouthed when the monster slid to a stop in front of her. The thing made her look like a doll, a toy, but rather than tear her apart, it cocked its head to the side as if curious. She reached into her pocket and pulled out a small grey rock she presented to the vrykolakas in her outstretched palm. It sniffed at the stone, ears twitching.

"Go on," she said and closed her fist around the stone, "serve your purpose." The vrykolakas's lips peeled back from its teeth as it bounded around her to catch up with the rest.

"Who did you set that thing loose on, Marion?"

"Camilla Westwood."

CHAPTER 3

C AMILLA CAME AWAKE to a thunderous crash. The room was empty and the only noise was the crackling of the fire, making her wonder if she hadn't dreamt the sounds. She'd fallen asleep in the chair where she and Callum had spent hours speculating after the girl's appearance.

It wasn't coincidental she chose to show herself and those contrasting images the same night Camila learned some hard truths about her family. There were no such things as coincidences such as these, Grandfather taught her that. If it wasn't a coincidence, then it was a calculated meeting. Why reveal the images in the visions? A warning? Why? What did she hope to gain? It was a manipulation, but to what end and to whose benefit? To show the images as if they were a life yet to come, she had to be a seeress, but a seeress with telepathic ability? Unheard of and would most certainly be much sought after by those of power. Why come out of hiding and risk revealing herself to a Westwood?

Telepath or seeress, neither was to be treated lightly. They could be dangerous, whispering like demons to steer circumstances to their benefit. Camilla's lessons had taught her that much. If she were a seeress, she'd given Camilla a glimpse of her future. They looked like opposite images, but according to her teaching regarding seers and their trickery, the images could be the same. One path to reach the others, in trying to avoid an outcome you took the steps that would lead you directly to it.

Distant screams from the village below drew her attention, then chaos erupted. It wasn't a dream. Her body shuddered and she twisted the blanket in her hands. People were dying. "What's happening? Callum!"

He appeared a moment later, wide-eyed and breathing hard though it was habit not necessity. "Vrykolakas," he said the word as if he didn't believe it. Vrykolakas were forbidden, everyone knew that, and no one would willingly create such a vicious beast. But someone had. These monsters were never an accident.

More screams, louder, closer, spurred her to run and pull the shutters open to look at the grounds below. Enormous beasts towered over all that surrounded them, more yet were running up the hill from the village toward the castle. The high fence surrounding the grounds didn't slow them. Their bodies were pale as death, almost glowing in the night, and muscled to the point of obscene. Too long arms tipped with a werewolf's claws lashed out, severing heads and cleaving torsos of guards that got close enough. Others sprang, shooting to unfathomable heights before dropping on their prey and tearing at them with teeth and claws.

Henrik stormed into the melee, more furious than scared and Camilla had to admit there was a certain amount of respect he was owed for it. She was locked away safe in her bed chamber, and she was terrified. He walked ahead, his power slicing the enemy in half as effectively as the vrykolakas' claws, leaving a trail of cleaved parts. The others in the guard weren't faring as well. For every one of the vrykolakas that fell, two of the guard did and there was nothing she could do to help.

Another crash shook the stone floor under her feet. *The main doors. They've breached the castle walls.*

The screams were coming from inside now. She prayed the servants made it to their quarters below and locked themselves behind the heavy doors. There were clashes of metal, someone shouting orders over wet snarls and animal howls.

Gods, I can hear their claws.

The scraping was too close, too clear to be contained in the galley. She held her breath and took Callum's hand. A shadow passed by the crack under the door, then stopped. There was a chuffing, it caught her scent. Her eyes slid closed in fear but sprang wide when it slammed against the door.

She backed to the farthest wall as the door was hit again and again. The thick wood bowed as if under the blows of a battering ram and she could go no farther. There was nowhere to run or hide in the room that the vrykolakas wouldn't scent her. She could do nothing but watch the abused door bow farther and farther inward and wait for it to finally give.

"You have no choice," Callum whispered as if the thing could hear him over the deafening booms. "I'm your only source." She started to assure him the wards would hold, it wasn't necessary. Before the words came, there was a harsh groan from the wood. "Do it, Camilla. Now."

Callum was made up of pure energy, finding it wasn't the problem. The problem was she didn't know if he'd be able to regenerate what she took or if she could stop once she started. Learning to pull energies without causing harm, especially from a single source, took time and practice. She'd had neither. They'd debated this before. His argument—that he used her energy to regain his physical body so why not anything she syphoned —made sense, but not enough for her to have risked it. Not for anything more than to satisfy curiosity. The battle still raged outside. People were dying and she was all but forgotten in their bids to stay alive.

She let down her guard and sucked in a deep breath. It wasn't a matter of pulling Callum's energy. She was flooded as it all but flung itself into her and was joined by that of the dead outside. Too much, too fast. Any intention of taking as little as possible to gauge Callum's tolerance was lost. His grip on her hand loosened, his image flickered. She'd kill him—or whatever the ghost equivalent was.

She slammed her guard back in place just as the door burst open and the vrykolakas landed inside on all fours. It shook its head, the muscles in its arms and shoulders as prominent as the black claws grating against the floor. It lifted a surprisingly human face that was twisted in rabid fury. The teeth were fanged top and bottom, ideal for the tearing she'd witnessed outside.

Behead it or burn it, those were the only ways to kill a vrykolakas. Blue fire licked up her arms. The creature didn't flinch away or show any fear. It roared and the low pitch vibrated through her chest and made her ears ring.

There was no reasoning with such a beast, no bargaining or threats that would hold any bearing. Despite the shaking in her hands, she hit it square in the face with a ball of flame. The howl of pain was pitiable, the smell of burning hair and flesh nauseating. It batted at the flames with its clawed hands, damaging itself further, but the fire was dying out—extinguished by its blood. It was blocking the exit and even if it wasn't, she could only hope it had destroyed the wards holding her in rather than just pushing through them. Something that should've been impossible.

As impossible as a seeress projecting her power inside. Either she'd been visited by two incredibly powerful beings, or the boundary was weak. Maybe she *could* get out. But where was there to run? Vrykolakas were fast. If it wanted her it would track her. Maybe kill others in its pursuit of her.

She didn't have Henrik's ability. If she did, she'd have beheaded it already without it getting any closer. "Distract it," Callum yelled. She threw up an illusion of the battle she'd watched on the grounds, hoping it would get confused by the choice of prey. It didn't. It lifted its mangled, burnt face to the air and sniffed, lips curling into what she might have said was a smile if it had been on anyone else.

"Tricksss," it hissed past its teeth and stalked forward. She hadn't known they could speak.

It swatted chairs and tables from its path instead of moving around them. Glass shattered, wood splintered. The smell of the oils and perfumes spilled on the floor was strong enough to taste. She hit it again and again with fire, but it ducked its face and on all fours, it didn't give her many targets. The skin she managed to hit blackened and peeled, but never caught flame. The puddles on the floor, however, caught with a whoosh.

"Camilla," Callum urged as if she couldn't see the thing getting closer. She had no weapon, even if she knew how to use a blade to sever its head. She moved, angling for the door out, and it shadowed her movements. She put the fire between it and her, but the flames died out as soon as their accelerant was burnt up. "Let your guard back down!"

She had to think. There had to be a way that didn't force her to choose her own life or taking what was left of Callum's. She threw her hand out, hitting the vrykolakas from the side with a force that would have sent most anything else flying until it was stopped by a wall. The creature only stumbled and growled through teeth clenched with effort. The vrykolakas was teeming with energies so bright they were near to cutting.

She was unpracticed at taking energies from others. Her teaching with regard to the subject consisted of the warning that she could kill someone weak enough to let her take it all. But she didn't care if she killed this creature by accident, she'd do it on purpose if she were capable. She knew Callum would never leave her willingly. She didn't have time to beg or debate that she wasn't sure what she was doing and may drain him as well. She turned to him with an apology in her expression.

"Camilla, you can't," he said as she commanded him to go. Just like that, she was alone with the vrykolakas.

～

Eirnen had to stop and watch for a moment to make sure he understood what was happening. His Camilla, his delicate angel, was draining the vrykolakas that had broken through the wards and was using its energy to push it back. She was weakening because she didn't know how to use what she stole to her best advantage. He could teach her. He grabbed the vrykolakas by the neck, choking the beast with a fist made entirely of his energy and flung it to the wall until it was pinned there under his power. She'd weakened it as well as herself.

Possibilities, possibilities. He looked at Camilla and the power strobing around her.

"Come here," he said and crooked a finger at her. Her legs wobbled as she made her way to him. Her hair hung loose from its pins and was soaked with sweat, her gown torn. Yes, she needed many lessons, but the aura of power surrounding her was undeniable. Where had she gotten the energies? It wasn't just the vrykolakas, there was too much, it was too potent. "What did you do wrong?"

The exhaustion on her face was joined with hurt and confusion at his question. The vrykolakas struggled, gouging holes in the stone wall under its claws. It roared its fury and Camilla flinched with a whimper. If he'd posed the question to Henrik at her age, he'd have let the creature go until he found the right answer. But he couldn't force himself to leave her at the vrykolakas's mercy. The look he gave her was harsh and she shrank from it, folding her shoulders in.

"Survived," she answered in a small voice. "I was just trying to survive."

"Exactly," he said and he thought she may cry. "Your failure wasn't in surviving, it's that it's the only thing you did. That is an enemy," he said and used her chin as a handle to force her face around to look at the spitting beast. "You don't simply survive an enemy. If you're strong enough to take their power despite them resisting you, then you own them."

"I don't understand," she confessed. "I did the best I could, Grandfather."

"Yes, but we are about to change your best so you may never use that excuse again."

Her lessons would continue tomorrow as scheduled and they would be more than a reason for him to spend time with his grand-daughter as they'd been in years past. He'd overlooked her potential, that was abundantly clear. Not anymore.

"First lesson," he said and started to draw the energies from the vrykolakas as she watched. "You were wasting what you gath-ered. The effect was minimal because you were throwing it out as quickly as you pulled it in. Save it, let it fill you. Then at the right moment—" the vrykolakas screamed under the pressure before its skull was crushed, collapsing in on itself like paper in a tight fist "—let it go."

Before this night, he'd shielded her from the very things now slipping in grey-red chunks down her wall and she reacted as he expected. She vomited. He sent her pale and shaking to the guest quarters, then sent what was left of the servants to scour her cham-ber. He'd have to strengthen and replace the wards, but that was little payment in exchange for the reward he'd gained. If the vryko-lakas was strong enough to break through, yet she'd been able to steal from it, she could've done it herself if she'd tried hard enough.

Rowan and Riley were waiting for him at the bottom of the stairs, both coated in blood. "How many did we lose?"

"More than fifty at last count," Rowan answered. "The remain-ing guard is yet in the village, the number of losses there is unknown until they return."

More than fifty trained guards. The number would be greater in the village. Godsdamn Abel! Vrykolakas. Abel was creating warriors of his own. Forbidden warriors. The vrykolakas were not controllable. These were the kind of creatures you kept caged, contained, until the moment you set them loose in an enemy's camp, as Abel had done tonight. Had Eirnen not kept his guard on the ready since the start of this war, the losses would've been devastating. Perhaps even beyond recovery. But he would recover this and he would retaliate.

Abel's castle in Anselone sat empty, save for servants to ensure squatters didn't take up residence in their master's absence, unlike Westwood, and that was a disadvantage. Abel knew exactly where to send his weapons, Eirnen had rumors and the half-truths of those captured and convinced in the dungeons. Not good enough. Clearly. Abel had a never moving, constant target, but Eirnen's never ceased moving. If this course continued, Abel would be victorious. A new tactic was needed, but when it came to his old foe there was but one sure advantage Eirnen had to play. More pieces had to be maneuvered into position first.

Camilla felt a flutter against the wards. Someone was coming in. Time for lessons with Grandfather. Normally, she looked forward to this time with him because she rarely saw him, but not after last night. She'd scarcely slept as she wondered away what was left of the night with worries of what these new lessons might entail.

"Missus," Tamara said in a small voice with her head bowed. "Your grandfather has summoned."

Tamara backed out into the hall before she turned. Camilla followed her down the corridor, then up the stairs. Camilla didn't try to talk to Tamara. She'd tried many times before and Tamara wouldn't speak unless answering a direct question. She wasn't much older than Camilla and at one time, she'd thought she could have a friend in Tamara. But if Callum were telling the truth, Ian was cruel to her in ways he wouldn't speak of and now she feared and hated all of them, even Camilla.

Callum was reluctant to tell her troubling things. She'd asked him questions and he answered, but she was certain there was more that he wasn't telling and she wasn't knowledgeable enough to ask. She only knew of Ian's cruelty because she'd asked—hoping to hear a flattering answer. All those years she spent as the docile princess locked in her tower where none of the depravity could touch her. She was foolish enough to believe the things Callum described didn't exist, certainly weren't condoned—let alone committed—by family of hers.

Unlike her chambers filled with baubles and delicate things, Grandfather and Marceline's was utilitarian. Two large fireplaces, a corner table with parchment and quill, and a sitting area. The rest was open and glowed with the morning light seeping through the shutters' cracks. Grandfather came into the room with a soft smile and Tamara curtsied before scampering away.

"My precious Camilla," he said and took her face in his hands, as he always did. "You look more and more like your grandmother with each passing year."

His hair was shot through with silver at the temples, but still black as a raven's wing where age didn't touch. His eyes were the same shade as hers, a blue he'd told her many times was unique to those of the Westwood lineage. They made her special, marked her as his blood family. No matter what coupling from outside the Westwood name, the blood still dominated and drowned out any variation in color. They were that strong. He'd also said that strength meant they had a responsibility to the lower casters and creatures of Calame. Before last night, she'd thought of him as a protector, a guardian of the weak. It was disappointing, almost unbearable, to think he may be the villain.

Her eyes flickered to the mahogany chair in front of the fireplace. She remembered curling up on his lap in front of the fire and listening while he told her fantastical tales, filled with beautiful princesses and heroic princes, that kept her enraptured for hours. The nighttime stories ended some time ago, but morning lessons had taken their place. Lessons that mostly consisted of tea and him listening to her tell her own stories of what she'd read in the books provided by one tutor or another. Today, that would change. She tried to not mourn the loss.

"I've given thought to what happened last night and the conclusion I've come to is I've crippled you. It was unintentional, but the result is the same. In my mind, you would be well protected in my keep until the time came that you had a husband capable of doing the same. My temerity could have meant your life. That changes, beginning today. Give me your hands," he said and held both of his out, palms up. She rested her hands on his callus-roughened ones that made hers look frail in comparison. "Find my energies. Close your eyes and focus on me as another caster, not your grandfather."

She did as he asked, but it was hard to forget he was someone she cared about no matter what she knew about him now. She wanted to pull away, but his bigger hands engulfed hers and held her in place. Death or irrevocable damage, that's what happened if she did this wrong. "I'm afraid I'll hurt you," she confessed, feeling shame in speaking it to a man who detested fear.

"Do you think me weak, Camilla?"

"No, Grandfather," she said, eyes flying open. "Of course not."

"Then this fear that you could harm me or that I would be unable to stop you from doing so is irrational." He loosened his grip until only their palms were touching once more. "Try again."

He had a point. Eirnen Westwood was the most powerful caster, even beyond Calame. His rival, Abel Lockley, was rumored to be next, but still below Eirnen. She couldn't hurt him if she tried. The acceptance of that was both a relief and disappointment. If he truly was this monster, she could do nothing to stop him. She closed her eyes again, but she didn't really need to.

His energies, so much stronger than her own, were like sharp zings and snaps across her skin. Lightening cracking. She let the guard drop and with such a bountiful source being offered, she couldn't stop her power from opening up and pulling it in great gulps after the first taste. It was life, power, more power than she'd ever been allowed to have. It filled her with heat and a desire to have more, as if she'd never get her fill.

A frustrated screech escaped before she knew it was forming when the power was abruptly cut off. It left her off balance, bereft. "How do you feel?" Grandfather asked with an edge to his tone that she didn't recognize. She opened her eyes to find that he was no longer in front of her, he was instead on the opposite side of his quarters. He was smiling and it only spread wider when her mouth popped open in surprise. "It's not such a great distance, but now you see you are capable. Let's see what a difference it makes, shall we?"

He opened the shutters and she recoiled from the sudden shaft of light that hit her eyes. Calame was beautiful—rolling hills the bright green of spring, the sun glinting off the river like jewels, and wildflowers growing in vibrant clumps even under the canopy of giant cedars. He closed the shutters and bid her to show him what she'd just seen. With the energy coursing through her, she felt giddy and flushed, barely stifling a giggle, her body languid with a feeling akin to floating in a warm bath.

It was as easy as breathing to turn to the open space and recon-struct everything she'd seen outside. In the span of a blink, the same cedars and wildflowers shot up around them in the corridor. The river snaked a path across the floor—

"Grandfather," she said with excitement as a heron she hadn't seen with the shutters open swooped close to the water.

She could feel the sun on her face, the breeze teasing through her hair, and the smell of evergreen and clean water filled her nose. It was as if she were standing in the field outside. The lulling warmth she'd had drained away. It was too real. It was Callum's ability. Her illusions were re-creations, reconstructions of people and places she'd seen, his were true visions of the present.

Did he remember Callum and his ability? Would he guess her secret? She held the image and her expression steady by force of will as he looked around them. Careless, she was careless.

"I can smell the pines," he said as if he couldn't believe it himself. He opened the shutters again to compare one countryside with the other. "Not a flaw," he said and kissed the top of her head. "You give me such pride, Camilla." He left the shutters open and went back to the sitting area. "Join me," he said. "I will have Tamara fetch us some tea."

She let the illusion fall away and went to sit as well. Her head churned with excuses, reasons for how this happened, things to tell him that wouldn't be the truth. She'd wanted his help before, she still did, but she'd not reveal Callum without his permission. She would never betray him that way. A lie it would have to be.

"Announce yourself well before you enter," he said to Tamara at the door before he came back inside. He sat down on the edge of the seat, his chin in his hand. "Will you try something for me?" he asked. "Would you try to watch Tamara making our tea?"

"I, I, don't think I can," she said and heat settled in her cheeks.

"Power grows, it expands and changes. Try, please," he said.

Camilla couldn't refuse to try, but she could fail to succeed. She'd never actually been to the kitchens and Grandfather knew it so she couldn't use the image of it, she pictured Tamara instead. She held her hand out in front of her and circled it as if she were cleaning the smudges from a mirror, as was her ritual for creating illusions, and Tamara was there. It wasn't the kitchens behind her but the hall outside Camilla's chambers. When nothing changed, Grandfather began coaching in gentle tones that didn't match the coiled way he perched on the seat.

"I'm sorry," she said when Tamara called her arrival outside the door. The apology wasn't only for the failure but the lie. She had never lied to him before. By omission, by not telling about this ability, yes, but never a blatant lie. It turned her stomach.

"This was only the first attempt. I would have been shocked, pleasantly so, but amazed all the same if you'd succeeded this quickly." He collected the cups from Tamara at the door and gave one to Camilla. It was hot and bitter, but soothing.

"Will Mother and Father or Ian be joining us?" she asked to change the subject, but also because she did want to see them. She hadn't seen her mother since just before Grandfather told her of the pregnancy. Now, she was to have a baby brother or sister in a matter of weeks and hadn't the opportunity to express her excitement with her mother over the arrival. Had mother chosen names? Did she believe she carried a boy or a girl?

"I'm afraid not. Henrik is attending to a matter for me and Belinda is still feeling poorly. Nothing to be worried about. She just needs rest. I believe Ian has taken his mare out this morning." He must have caught the rush of resentment that flooded over her because his expression went from sympathetic to reproachful. "Ian is eighteen and a man. Your defensive casts are far from adequate and you would be much more valuable leverage. There are things that can happen to a young woman that are less likely with a male."

Yes, yes, she wanted to say. The loss of purity for a future husband she probably didn't want, bastard pregnancy, she'd heard it all countless times before. It used to terrify her until she didn't want to leave the castle.

"I know you worry for me, but I feel so restless. Like I've outgrown my cage." He watched her and she didn't dare move. He hadn't said no, he was assessing her, thinking it over. Try as she might, she couldn't stop the swell of hope.

"I suppose that's only natural," he said and stood. "Come," she followed after him farther into the chamber. Marceline was sitting at her dressing table, looking regal and every bit the woman.

"My lord, Lady Camilla," she greeted with a bow of her head. "Accompany Camilla onto the grounds. You may take her to the stables to see the horses, but no farther." He turned his attention to Camilla and kissed her cheek. "Enjoy yourself, my dear."

He left the two of them alone and Camilla felt awkward. She'd never really spoken to Marceline since she and Grandfather married. She'd seen her, envied her, but hadn't the opportunity for more than a polite greeting. To Camilla, Marceline was an exotic creature who had not only achieved womanhood but excelled in it.

Thanks to Callum, she now knew Marceline once fled from Abel Lockley. Grandfather had saved her and now was wed to her. She was another he treated with kindness. Maybe Marceline would help Camilla in trying to get him to show the same kindness to others?

"Hello, little bird," she said with a smile that wasn't really one. It wasn't hostile or threatening, but it was as if it meant something besides happiness. "Shall we," she said and rose from the chair with a grace that was to be admired.

They walked side-by-side down the corridors. The servants were just ahead of them, opening the draperies as if lighting their path. Marceline seemed to glide. Camilla couldn't figure out what to do with her hands. Camilla's discomfort was soon replaced with the urge to run to get out into the sun faster. She wouldn't, of course. Marceline made her feel immature in appearance. No need to add mentality.

Rowan and Riley were at the doors and opened them wide as they came near. She met their eyes in turn, something she'd not had the courage to do before, as she thanked them. A warm wind blew through the opening and brought with it all the fresh scents of clean air. She inhaled deeply and lifted her face to the sun as the heavy doors closed behind them. Rowan and Riley hadn't followed.

"Magnificent."

"It is time for you to learn, you are not a prisoner," Marceline said. Camilla cracked her eyes open enough to see her expression was scolding. "You act as one, fresh out of chains."

"Father and Grandfather worry for my safety, that's all," she protested, despite knowing Marceline was right. She walked slowly to absorb it all before it ended. "I'm surprised he allowed me outside with only another female as escort. Even mother and I have guards when we leave the castle."

"Yes, but I am not as delicate as other females and Eirnen knows this well. I don't believe you to be as delicate or innocent as you have been tempered to behave, either."

"What do you mean?"

"You are a young woman with experience no more than a child. They treat you as a doll with your chamber as your cupboard. You've not been pressed or tested, given room to flourish, and you allow it. Continue to do so and you will be a doll to your husband as well, tucked away until he chooses to take you out of the cupboard to play with you."

An image of that red-faced man pawing at her as she longed to escape flashed through her mind. She had to swallow the hard knot in her throat to speak.

"Am I to take that to mean you were not treated this way before you married Grandfather?"

"Oh, no. I was raised by my mother, my aunt, and my grandmother, women who knew well of the cruelty and indulgences of men. They wanted me to be strong, to have my own mind and never be a plaything."

No mention of Abel, but she couldn't expect Marceline to purge her every secret just because Camilla was now brimming with the desire to know them. Marceline gave Camilla a sideways glance and another expressive quirk of lips then kicked off her boots and bid Camilla to do the same, luring her with descriptions of the lusciousness and warmth of the grass.

Marceline grabbed her wrist and ran, leading her barefoot across the courtyard and through the gardens. Camilla cast her eyes around for any signs of the creatures Callum described but saw nothing but hundreds of blossoms in every color she could think of.

"This way," Marceline laughed, her French accent getting thicker with excitement. An endearing trait that made her seem more real. A sharp turn to the left and they were off across the expansive lawns. Guards and servants alike stopped to watch them, which made them laugh harder. "I want you to meet someone," Marceline said and slid open the stable doors.

Eirnen smiled at the sounds of laughter as they ran hand-in-hand across the lawns. Marceline and Camilla looked to be the best of friends and hadn't yet been alone for more than twenty minutes. He'd expected nothing less. Marceline was skilled in manipulation and Camilla— his innocent Camilla—was so sweet, so guileless she failed to see it in others. He was hit with an unexpected pang of guilt. Had he not kept her isolated as he had, she might not have been so easily lured by one with ulterior motives.

It was for her safety. And her naivety is of benefit to me now, is it not?

Eirnen watched Camilla and Marceline trot across the lawns on the two giant beasts Marceline insisted on calling horses. At first, he was going to go put an end to it, but then he caught the look of exaltation on Camilla's face. He'd seen her smile, but he'd never seen her lit up the way she was on the back of that stallion. He wanted her happy, always, but her contentment was important now more than ever. Marceline, with her games and seduction, believed herself to have some power over him, but she didn't. Camilla, however, was undeniably a weakness. The only one he had.

Let her have her freedom. Marceline knew best how to handle such matters and he suspected she was also using this excursion as a means to entertain herself by taunting Abel. He'd know she was distancing herself from the confines of Westwood, but he'd never reach her before she returned herein to Eirnen. *Wicked female.*

He turned from the window and quickened his steps on the way to the study. Henrik was there, searching the pages for more clues as to why their creatures were still failing—outside the need for a more resilient host. Not only did Eirnen's impatience lead him to think of alternatives, he expected Henrik to do the same.

When Eirnen came in, Henrik leapt to his feet fast enough to send the stool crashing to the floor. White-blonde hair stuck out at odd angles, a testament to how many times frustration came before the excitement that made his eyes glitter now. His clothes were still torn and misted with rusty specks from the night before. He'd been there all night.

"Father, I've been waiting for you," he said and shook the bit of parchment in his hand. "Gigantes," he said. Eirnen waited, hoping there would be cause for him to share in Henrik's excitement. "The host. Why not gigantes? They're not matched in size and strength. Not even a vampire can stand and fight with one of them and they're damn hard to kill. Pain does little more than provoke them. They are relentless and ruthless."

"And slow, and lumbering, and loyal only to the other gigantes in their clan. Logistically, the closest clan is a full week's hard ride from here. They number close to a hundred at last count and are on constant guard. There's nothing but mountains and deep ravines prone to slides that are the only accessible pass to the valley. They'd trigger a slide to crush all aggressors before we were in sight of the clan. I've seen them do it. It's not worth the able-bodied fighters and energy sources we would lose only to capture one or two. The entire clan would have to be wiped out to do that and we wouldn't have enough men left."

"I'll go," he pressed. "And if I take the pack our numbers would overwhelm despite their superior strength. The wolves are strong, too, and the coordination with the way they attack won't be something the gigantes can contend with. They don't work as a unit, they don't think a fight through. They depend on brute strength and the defenses they have in place atop the ravines. The wolves could take out the watchers above that trigger the slides and then we pass with ease."

"Let's entertain the idea that you and the pack manage to make it to the valley intact, which is unlikely considering Abel's scouts. How many do you propose you return with and how will you transport them for the long ride back? They aren't going to submit just because you managed to subdue them once."

"I say ten, at least, and I can bind them with a cast. They have no defenses against it. If that doesn't work, I'll syphon enough of their energies to weaken them into docility."

"Then there's the question of how exactly you expect them to fight on our side after we've slaughtered their clan. Shaughnessy I can force control with a binding. In turn, he would be the more powerful of the vampires and maintain control over them, control he already has as a master vampire. With the gigantes, there is no force of control. It must be relinquished. They must be willing. To do as you suggest—invade and attack them—ensures their refusal. One, maybe my binding could be forced upon. But ten? Never."

Henrik thought it over, pacing, but gave no other argument. He wouldn't let this go, though, not now that he'd tasted blood. "Lilly is pregnant," he said and started sifting through the papers again. "She'll be moving here tomorrow and staying until the baby's independent of her. I can't risk another vrykolakas attack."

"And after?" Eirnen asked and raised an eyebrow.

"I have a wife."

"Your daughter is another matter," Eirnen said and Henrik looked up from the desk. "I believe it may be to our benefit to continue to delay her union to Winston Cleary. In addition to being able to forcibly draw from a vrykolakas, this morning she displayed an exponential increase in her power once I forced her to draw my energies. More than I expected. I fear that perhaps we have been too cautious with her. I want either you or myself to work with her every day on expanding her illusions and learning to draw energies from more than one source."

"To what end?" he asked as if he wanted to be pointed in a direction.

"I believe her illusions have grown into a true sight. It will take rigorous training since we've focused our attention on Ian. It's now safe to say he would be more useful in other areas. Winston Cleary has petitioned for Camilla and his line is adequate in power. But as long as he's tied somehow to the Westwood name, he'll be satisfied for now. He has a daughter. Elaine. I've granted permission for a marriage between her and Ian."

"And Winston?"

"If I'm right about Camilla, she's more of an asset than we anticipated. Imagine if we could watch Abel's every move as he makes it. Or any other enemy for that matter. We can't sacrifice the possibility of such an advantage. Winston will hold with the marriage of Ian and Elaine until after I've either been proven wrong about Camilla or she's reached her full potential. You will have to speak with Ian. Elaine is young, but she bleeds, capable of bearing children."

"We must speak about Marceline as well," Henrik said with foreboding.

"Thank you, Marceline," Camilla said as she brushed Abastor's jet mane. Her legs were aching and burning, she smelled like a horse—not an unpleasant smell at all, just better suited to the horse it came from—and her backside was numb. She'd never had more fun.

"I enjoyed our time together. Would you like to do it again tomorrow? Abastor has certainly taken a liking to you."

The offender lipped Camilla's hair and gave it a tug. "Tomorrow," she said, drawing her head back to free her hair.

The clip of hooves made her look at the entryway. She smiled when she saw Ian leading his mare. It had been too long since she'd seen him. She felt she barely knew him aside from what Callum told her and that was all vile. Looking at him now, the gentle hand he used with the horse, it was hard to imagine him as violent against someone as fragile as Tamara. He was taller than she remembered and still beautiful, angelic. His hair golden—as opposed to her near white—made him look healthier, giving his skin the appearance of being more deeply tanned than it was.

"Ian," she called and he flashed a wide smile.

"They finally decided to let you out, I see," he said and hugged her to him. His skin was warm after spending the morning in the sun and he smelled of horses just as she did. *Please let Callum be mistaken.* His body stiffened and his hold grew tighter. "Marceline."

"How have you been? Do you ride often? Do you think perhaps Father would allow me to come with you sometime?"

He chuckled at the excited questions and pushed her back but kept her hands. She looked up at him expectantly. It would be wonderful if she could go riding with him. She could get to know him better, as a sister should know her brother, and she'd ask him about what Callum said and prove he was wrong. "If you agreed to be my escort, they couldn't refuse."

"They could, but I might be able to convince them I'm responsible enough to keep you alive for one afternoon." His Westwood blue eyes were like looking at her own. Father's and Grandfather's were the same shade, but there was something older and harder about them Camilla couldn't relate to. It wasn't the same with Ian. "I am surprised that not only would Grandfather allow his wife out unescorted, he'd make her the only escort for you."

"Ian," Camilla admonished his suspicious tone. "I spoke to Grandfather, appealed to his sense of reason, and he conceded that I was due some freedom. Marceline was kind enough to indulge me."

"Really," he said, eyes narrowed at Marceline. "Why? What would a woman of your…experience have in common with my little sister?"

"It happens that females do enjoy the company of other females and the absence of men. That's what we have in common," Marceline said. "If you will excuse us, we must finish tending the horses."

"You could help us and then we'll speak with Father together," Camilla urged, gripping his hand. She wasn't ready to let go of him yet. They had so much to talk about, to catch up on. "Please, Ian."

"Capitalize on your freedom," he said, glaring at Marceline until she turned away. "It will go smoother with Father if I speak to him alone. And he's expecting me anyway." Ian hugged her hard again. "Be wary of the lessons you learn from her. You hear me, Mila?"

She nodded against his shoulder and he straightened. He hadn't called her Mila since they were little and the reminder of how much time they lost didn't make watching him walk away any easier.

Camilla brushed Abastor and built her courage. His black coat was shining and slick by the time she figured out how to word the question without sounding accusatory. "I couldn't help but notice there was some animosity between you and Ian. Has he given you offense?"

A soft smile curled Marceline's lips as she braided Abax's tail. "Ian is young and handsome. He believes these things will win him any woman he desires. His pretty face and daring speech were not enough to spread my legs before I wed Eirnen and he's bitter."

Camilla didn't think she'd ever get used to the bluntness with which Marceline spoke. It was rougher than the other women Camilla knew. Granted it was a number limited to servants, her mother, and tutors, but it put her in a place of awkwardness that made her feel disadvantaged somehow.

"Marceline, why did you call me little bird?" she asked to change the subject. "It's not that I disapprove or don't like it. I'm curious."

"Go on now," she said and gave her white stallion, Abrax, a pat on his hindquarters to usher him into the pen. "We are both in cages, you and I. Yours gilded and mine infinite but cages all the same."

Camilla stiffened. The exact words Callum said to her and now she recalled where she'd heard the nickname first. *Which branch will you perch on, little bird?* The words were spoken only in Camilla's head. Marceline hadn't the capability to hear thoughts, which meant the girl must be a seeress and had seen this day. Had she been trying to warn Camilla that Marceline overheard or just giving Camilla more reason to believe what she'd been shown?

"I happened to be passing by your chambers at the right moment," Marceline said.

"I," she started but didn't know how to continue. They knew this could happen. They'd become careless. The blessing was that Marceline hadn't told Grandfather or the lessons this morning would have gone a lot differently.

"I will keep your secret, Camilla," Marceline said. "You and I are alone here. We must be able to trust one another. I told you I knew not to frighten you. I want you to see that you can trust me. In the future, use more caution."

"If you've heard, then the servants," she said and held on to the wooden partition to keep her legs under her. She couldn't explain Callum to anyone, especially Grandfather. He would find a way to use Callum and he'd been used enough. She had to protect him.

"None of the servants want to be the one to tell their master his beloved granddaughter has a male suitor in her chambers."

"He's not a suitor. He's my friend and I won't have him back again," she lied.

"Very well," she said. They started the walk back to the castle at a much slower pace than when they left. "How did he manage the wards to come inside your chamber?"

"He has a knack for puzzles," she answered as an explanation. In truth, the wards had no effect on Callum coming or going from her chambers at all. "Are you really not going to tell?" She couldn't help but ask again and wrapped her arms around her middle.

"I will not," Marceline said and stopped. She stepped in front of Camilla and pushed her arms down and away from her body. "Stand straight, shoulders back, chin raised." Marceline demonstrated what she expected and Camilla copied her. "You are Camilla Westwood, granddaughter of the great Eirnen Westwood. Never appear vulnerable or shamed, not in front of anyone. Understood?"

"Yes," she said, though she didn't feel it. Marceline kept her eyes on Camilla's, lifted her chin another fraction, then arched her brow. Camilla concentrated on her features, working to display none of the doubt she felt.

"Very good," Marceline said and moved back to Camilla's side. She looped her arm through Camilla's as they began to walk again. "So, this friend, he is handsome?"

"I suppose," Camilla said.

"A vague answer perfect for politicking. Not so for curious females. He has a lovely voice, what I could hear of it through the door, that is. What's his name?"

"It doesn't matter. As I said, I'll not have him back."

Once she was in her chambers, Camilla collapsed on the bed. Her body and spirit were both exhausted, but she'd already asked Frances and Tamara to help her with a bath. Plus, she was waiting to hear footsteps coming toward her door. Grandfather must have seen them on the horses, and he would not approve. She'd known that before she climbed on Abastor's back, but she'd done it anyway. She'd take chastisement. It was worth it, but there might not be a tomorrow like she and Marceline had planned.

When the footsteps did come, it was Frances and Tamara with buckets of heated water. They'd recruited Cora to help as well. The water was hot, almost too hot, and pinked the skin of her legs the moment they were submerged. The women would be back with more in a while, even after her insistence this was plenty. There were a lot of stairs to climb from the kitchens to her quarters and the buckets had to be heavy, but Frances wouldn't hear of it. She was the oldest and by far the most intimidating woman Camilla had ever met.

The soaps smelled sweet, a gift from mother. As much as she needed to talk to Callum, the hot water felt too good on her sore muscles to rush out of it. Who knew riding a horse was this much work for the rider? She certainly hadn't.

The second and final round of water was beginning to cool by the time she got out and dressed in nightclothes though the sun had yet to set. All the day's events had left her worn and tired. She was unaccustomed to that level of physical activity. She also suspected that the sudden and substantial rise in power this morning had drained her further as it waned. She crawled onto the bed and all but collapsed with the resolution to only close her eyes for a moment while she waited for Callum.

"Missus," a stern voice jerked Camilla from sleep. She looked around in confusion before she figured out it was Frances and it was morning. "Ye father is waitin'," she said and put her fists to her hips. "Be of haste! Are ye trying to get us all whipped?"

"No, no," she said and groaned when she bounced too quickly to her feet and every muscle in her legs contracted to hard knots. Frances was there, all but tearing the dressing gown over Camilla's head. "Did you say my father?"

"Yes, so we must move quickly. It's not like you, Lady Camilla, sleepin' all day." Camilla stopped trying to help and became pliable for Frances. It was less painful that way. The pat Frances gave Camilla's backside as she shooed her out of the chamber reminded her of the way Marceline had patted Abrax.

The soreness loosened as she moved, but not enough for her to keep up with Frances's pace. She did the best she could with Frances giving her pleading looks over her shoulder. Frances didn't curtsy when they burst into the room where Henrik waited, but she bowed at the waist. Cora and Tamara were standing together by the far wall, looking as confused about being there as Camilla was to see them.

"That is all, Frances. Go," Henrik bit out and she left with one final glance at the other two girls. Camilla was used to the rough tenor her father used. He wasn't as patient as Grandfather and she rather disliked it when he hosted lessons. "Seek my energies, Camilla."

No preamble, not a greeting though she hadn't spoken to him in more than three months. He stood with his arms crossed and watched her with an expectant expression that promised he wouldn't wait long. She realized then, as her heart thrummed against her ribs, that she was as frightened of him as Frances had been. "I feel them," she said and swallowed hard.

"Find Tamara's and Cora's as well, then draw on all three."

She expanded outward and found Tamara, but not Cora. She shook herself and tried again, then once more before she could finally touch all three. She drew just enough to know Father would feel she was doing as instructed then let it slide back to them.

"More." She squared her shoulders and started again. Pulling, absorbing, holding, as Grandfather had said. He'd been right—she could feel power building, pressurizing. "More," he commanded again before she tried to stop.

Tamara's eyes hooded. She weaved on her feet, then began to sag. Cora caught her. Camilla immediately sent the energy back to them and took a step toward Tamara. "I'm sorry."

"Camilla," Henrik shouted the rebuke and she jumped at his tone. "Again. And you do not stop until I tell you to stop. Do you understand?" She nodded, her eyes on Tamara. "Do you, understand?"

"Yes, Father," she said.

She delayed, but eventually she started again. She tried to work with it, manipulate it until she was pulling more from Henrik and Cora, the more powerful of the three. But it didn't matter how slowly or how much, Cora and Tamara both began to collapse. They held onto one another for strength, knees buckling until they leaned against the wall. They looked ill, pale, sheened with sweat.

Henrik, however, didn't appear distressed at all. She pulled away from Cora and Tamara completely to draw solely from Henrik.

"Camilla," Henrik warned. She looked at him and saw Callum.

"No," she said and squeezed her fists at her sides. Never before had she defied him or anyone else. Saying no felt like a release. She turned to Tamara and Cora and forced all the energies she'd stolen, even those that had belonged to Henrik, into the two girls. "I'm sorry, to both of you. Now, please, go."

Henrik didn't try to stop them, not that the girls waited to see if he would. They ran from the room, Tamara with her head up so she met Camilla's eyes.

"Are you proud of yourself for your defiance?"

"No, Father."

"You are. I can see it in your face and in the way you dismissed the servants as if you are master here. Well, Your Majesty, tell me—how many of your subjects were victims of the vrykolakas? How many were guards and how many in the village? Children?" He stared at her with his chin resting on his fist. "Answer me, Camilla."

"I don't know," she said.

"Allow me," he said. "Sixty-three guards and a total of seventy-eight villagers. Even as you and Marceline were galloping off on the horses, they were still scraping body parts from the roads. Your grandfather believes you may be of value, instrumental even, in preventing losses of that number again. However, you aren't sufficiently trained and we haven't the time to go about it gently. Not only do we need to put you where you should be but expand it further if you are to be of use. Your squeamishness and petulance could kill them all. Including Cora and Tamara." He walked closer and lifted her chin. "Now your pride is gone. Go to your chambers, Camilla."

They both spun toward the door as a scream echoed through the castle.

CHAPTER 4

E IRNEN TOOK THE stairs two at a time. Echoes of the shrill scream pulsed throughout the corridors. From the last landing, before the lowest level, he saw the guards running as well, weapons drawn. Ian's quarters. *He's finally killed Tamara.* Eirnen knew Ian would be difficult to manage with regard to his betrothal to Elaine, but he hadn't believed Ian would kill the servant girl.

Eirnen slowed as he neared the open chamber door. All but Rowan and Riley moved aside to allow him to pass. That the rest of the guard remained at attention in the hall rather than entering should have been the first clue. Laughter bubbled from the room, hysterical and feminine. Eirnen shoved ahead and locked eyes with Tamara.

"It was done by the time we arrived, Sire," one of the guard reported. Ian, not Tamara lay on the bed. "We leave her to you, Your Highness."

"I am my own now," Tamara snarled. Blood dripped from the kitchen knife in her bony fist, trails of it trickled down her face. She smiled, victorious and delighted, as she lifted the blade and drew it across her throat.

Ian lay shirtless, on his stomach, with his face turned toward the door and eyes and mouth open. The blankets were bunched under slack hands as if he'd been clawing at them. From shoulders to knees, he wore a cape of red, some of the wounds in his back still oozing. Riley leapt over Tamara's dying body and searched Ian for any glimmer of life.

"Ian!" Rowan caught Camilla around the waist before she entered Ian's chambers, but that mattered little. None of what Ian had suffered escaped her sight. She was spared no detail. "Let me go! That's my brother! Ian! Stay, please stay!"

Eirnen looked to Riley with little hope, they all recognized death when they saw it. In answer, Riley took a tapestry from the wall to cover the body. The action didn't stop Camilla's struggles against Rowan or her pleas for Ian to stay. Henrik went to his knees in the chamber doorway, his face paled and horrorstruck. "Rowan, take Camilla to her chambers."

Eirnen closed his eyes as she was forcibly taken away, begging Ian, Eirnen, and Rowan. It was heartbreaking, her grief. Likewise, Henrik began to inch forward on his knees, hand outstretched to the bed where his firstborn child lay. Eirnen was struck with grief as well, Ian was his grandson. However, with his death came problems in need of solutions, duties.

"Prepare Ian for the pyre," he said to the guard and turned on his heel to leave and tend to those duties.

"Sire, what of the girl?"

"Throw her carcass in my gardens," he said through his teeth. "Henrik, bring Frances and Cora to me at once."

The hard set of Henrik's jaw and the thinning of his lips as he herded the two women into the room told Eirnen much. He knew his son's face to the finest detail and every expression in his cache. There was something weighing on him that he didn't want to reveal, but he would.

"Frances," Eirnen said and Henrik shoved the woman forward.

"Sire," she gave the bow that had become customary for her rather than the more feminine greeting of the curtsy.

"What do you know of this?"

"Nothing, my lord. Cora and I were on our way to the laundry when we heard the screams."

"And Tamara?"

Frances didn't answer, but Cora stepped forward. "Kitchen duties, Your Majesty," she said, ending with a curtsy.

"Did either of you know of her plans to assassinate Prince Ian?" Both denied it and Eirnen believed them, more so because it was becoming increasingly obvious that Henrik placed blame elsewhere. "Your former associate has created a great deal of work for you. Go do it."

Once the women were gone, he turned his attention to Henrik, who was too still and staring at nothing with his fists tight at his sides. "Speak," Eirnen barked and set loose the dam.

"Your *precious granddaughter* aided that whore in murdering my son. My *only* son." Henrik's anger was boiling over, his body shook with it. His hands opened and closed, tears streamed down his face and strained his voice until it rasped. "She was angered during her lessons and in retaliation gave Tamara an abundance of power. My power! The spiteful bitch used *my* power to kill *my* son."

"Henrik, you must get control of yourself. This solves nothing."

For the first time in all his years, Henrik glared at Eirnen with hatred. "Belinda may very well die and take the infant with her any day. Lilly is months from delivery and not my wife."

"The child will still be a Westwood," Eirnen said. "That alone undermines any claims of illegitimacy."

"Tell me, Father, what if it had been Camilla you saw killed in such a barbaric manner? Would I then be within my right to demand you control yourself?"

"Yes. I would be as you are now, but I would see the purpose of your words. You are a young man, still capable of making more children. But today, this day, the wolves come. Lilly arrives and we must notify Winston of Ian's death. He may demand Camilla's hand as payment to ally himself with us and we cannot allow it. Especially now."

"Give her to the old bastard. It will serve her well to learn a female's place of obedience." Henrik left without being of any help to the issues that could be dealt with now. Disappointing.

Eirnen pounded the side of his fist on the chair arm. Ian was dead and so was his killer. Nothing to do about either. It couldn't be fixed and it couldn't be changed. Henrik should be pragmatic enough to know that and do what needed to be done. That's how Eirnen raised him, but this was the first true test. To kill a firstborn son was to rip open a father's chest to expose his still beating heart. Eirnen's own father had lived through such a tragedy and carried on with his secondborn. Perhaps if Henrik had another son, his thinking would be more reasonable.

Henrik had said Camilla gave Tamara his power. He knew how difficult that was and she'd not been taught how to master such a thing. If he were thinking without bias, he would see the same possibilities Eirnen could. Energies wanted to return to their source, their true owner, to be a part of the whole. For her to have done such a thing was tantamount to what Eirnen did trying to make his warriors. It was something Henrik couldn't do, which meant his pride was now involved as well. Camilla couldn't be lost. Not yet.

Eirnen made his way down the dimly lit corridor, choosing his words with care. He knocked lightly at Belinda's door and felt the weakness of the room before he was invited inside. She lay on the bed, stomach rounded and swollen. The rest of her body was pale skin stretched over bone. Her face gleamed with sweat and though she was covered with heavy furs, shivers racked her body. Indeed, she was close to death.

"How are you, Belinda?" he asked and moved the dampened hair that clung to her face.

"Is it true? Is my Ian dead?"

"I am afraid it is the truth," he said and tears rolled down her temples to be swallowed up by the furs. "I have come to offer my condolence for your loss and to speak to you about Camilla's fate."

"I can't feel her anymore," Belinda said. It wasn't until she lifted her hand to caress her stomach that Eirnen realized she wasn't talking about Camilla.

"Belinda," he said and took her hand from her stomach. "Your son is dead. The child in your womb is as well. The smell of death hangs heavy in this room." She shook her head and let out a sob. "Yes, Belinda, you must listen to me. Ian was to be married to a young lady. Now that it is not possible, her father wants your only living child as his own. He wants to make her a wife and a mother to tie his line with our power. Just as your father did when he betrothed you to Henrik."

"Is he a nice man?" she asked and traced her fingers over her stomach, making cooing sounds and smiling softly. Delirium or denial, he wasn't sure which, but she'd forgotten the pain of loss.

"No, Belinda, he is not," he said harshly enough to make her look at him. "But he is too powerful to not appease." He softened his features and caressed her face. "You can help her. No one else, only you. You are lying in this bed, waiting to join your son and infant." His hand drifted downward until he met the furs and folded them back. He began to unbutton the dressing gown until her bare skin was exposed. He laid his hand on her chest, just above her left breast. "Your life is finished. All that remains for you is suffering until your last breath whether that be a day from now or a week. Either amount of time is a lifetime to Camilla. Allow me to help you. Allow me to end your suffering and save your daughter with one action."

He met her eyes and waited. She closed them, then gave a single nod.

"I'll not be able to keep quiet," she said. He moved his other hand to cover her mouth.

Her body bowed off the bed, her eyes bulging as one hard line of raw power drilled into her heart. She'd been wrong. There was no muffled sound under his hand, just one great sucking of breath that rattled her chest as her body went limp. He removed his hand from a slack mouth, closed her eyes, then buttoned her gown before pulling the furs back up to her neck. He watched her chest for any sign there was still life persisting in her battered body. There was none.

Everyone was still occupied with Ian, so no one saw him leave Belinda's chamber. It was just as well. Henrik would assume she passed naturally. He would be upset, but the last thing any of them needed right now was for him to be uncooperative with Eirnen's plans. Winston would be more than satisfied with this alternative. His daughter Elaine, wife to the next king. It might even be enough for him to agree to retract his petition for Camilla. If not, there needed to be a contingent plan.

All this maneuvering to appease Winston chafed Eirnen. He was king, Winston a subject under his rule. Winston ought to do as commanded because it was commanded of him and no other reason. Any other boon offered, such as a marriage, was just that, a boon. A kind gesture from a benevolent master.

He summoned Rowan and Marceline to his study where he would wait for someone to discover Belinda's body. Then, Henrik would come to him.

～

"Cry all you like, Princess. I'm here. Me. Not him. And I am free," Tamara sang and spun like she was dancing.

"You are not free," Callum said.

Camilla stayed curled on her bed with her knees drawn up, the way she'd been for what felt like days rather than hours. Since she saw Ian and Tamara. The puddles and sprays of red, the smell of blood and bowel so strong it was dizzying. Her throat worked as she tried to not vomit again.

Tamara had been waiting with Callum, rejoicing the murder rather than mourning her own death. Ian was gone beyond where Camilla could sense him. She'd felt it, the rush of power that followed his death, her own brother used as fuel. She had begged and willed Ian to stay, even if it was wrong to try to trap him here, she'd put all the power and intention she had into the commands and pleas. Tamara hadn't been a thought at the time, but she got to stay. How? Why?

It had taken a moment to realize who the slight, twirling girl was. Tamara alive had dirty hair that hung in clumps she used to hide her face. She was thin, small-boned, and skittish. This Tamara had light brown hair, grey eyes, and a constant wide smile. Her skin was supple and golden, she looked more alive now that she was dead.

"Henrik killed my daughter, his granddaughter, and now he knows how I felt. And Ian? He didn't care. Wasn't broken as I was, didn't seek to avenge his own child, he was relieved. He was grateful Henrik had done something he lacked the courage to do himself."

"A child? You had a child with Ian?" Camilla sat up and looked to Callum, who seemed as confused as Camilla was. "I didn't know."

"Of course, you didn't. She hadn't the chance to take her first breath. Henrik poisoned her even as I believed her safe within my body. You sit up here in your room, nice and protected. Your virtue guarded as if it were the answer to life's mysteries while your brother, your *father*, ruined me." Tamara's hands dropped to cradle a flat belly, "they took her from me. She was a little girl, I just knew it, I felt it. I couldn't wait to tell Ian so he could love her too."

"And did you? Tell Ian, I mean?" Camilla asked as gently as she could. Tamara caressed her stomach before lifting her head. Camilla recoiled from the hatred she saw there.

"They thought her death was a great gift. Greater still, I could conceive no more children because of the damage Henrik's poison did to my womb. No chance of a bastard pregnancy with the low-level caster servant. It meant he could have me as often as he wanted and—"

"Enough," Callum shouted.

"Words. Words not actions, and the precious Camilla can't even be subjected to that? She should know. She should have to hear every single detail. She should know her name was Iva. How I could feel, *feel*, Ian's relief as his daughter died inside me. That even after the very sight of Ian repulsed me, he thought he still had a right to me like I was property. He grew to hate me. He punished me for daring to become pregnant, blamed me for a child that shared his blood being destroyed because it also shared mine, the blood of a servant who would set the Westwood line back in power."

"Stop it," Camilla said, wiping the tears from her cheeks. "What happened to you was horrible. You have every right to be angry, but I didn't do these things to you. You know as well as I do, I can't even leave this room of my own free will."

"How fucking awful for you," Tamara screeched and shot across the bed at Camilla.

She hit Camilla in the chest like a boulder, ending up on top of her, straddling her while she screamed and clawed at any bit of skin she could find. Camilla's hands went up to shield her eyes and face. Callum was yelling. Tamara's body rocked as he tried to pull her off, but Tamara clamped her knees into Camilla's sides and filled both fists with Camilla's hair.

Camilla did the only thing she knew to do— she dropped her guard and started stripping away the energy Tamara borrowed to make herself solid. Tamara's hold began to loosen. Camilla pulled harder, letting it fill her body and noted that Tamara had more power dead than she did alive. The hands and body on her became insubstantial, a light pressure and a moment later she could see the rest of the room through her. Tamara was still screeching, her hands curled into claws that she brought down at Camilla's face, but they never touched her. She was mist, spectral, and then she was gone.

Camilla clasped Callum's forearms as he lifted her by the shoulders until she was sitting up. Tendrils of hair dangled in front of her face where they'd been torn loose from the pins. She assured Callum she was fine, just scratches, every time he asked until he gave up and sat down looking bewildered.

"Is she gone? I mean, not ghost gone, but gone?"

"No. I can feel her here and she's still very angry." They both searched every corner of the room as if they were expecting her to be hovering somewhere, waiting for the opportune time to attack again. She was nowhere in sight, but rage came at Camilla in heated waves. "I'm sorry, Tamara," Camilla said.

She sat, accepting the hatred that poured over and around her, draping her like a blanket. She'd never, not once done anything to help Tamara or anyone else. She'd like to think, had she known the treatment others were suffering, she'd have intervened. But she'd been told about the things happening here days ago and had done not one thing by word or deed to stop it.

Her stomach knotted, cramping and churning with nausea. There was nothing to do, nowhere to go, nothing to say or beg. Her course was set. It was done. There was no escape. There was no prince to take her in his arms and declare her worthy. She was worthless, had always been and would always be. It didn't matter how many times he whispered his love for her in her ear while he lay on top of her. It was all lies and she'd fallen for it. Stupid.

"Oh, gods," she said. "Tamara." She stretched her hand out, searching where she felt the beating of emotion the strongest. Tamara's ability was to feel the emotions in others, but Camilla hadn't known to what degree. The shame grew stronger. Fear and anger mingled with it as Tamara realized Camilla could feel Tamara's perception of herself.

Reconstructing and tightening her guard against Tamara was easy, a simple matter of will. She couldn't think with Tamara's voice of self-hatred battering around in her head. Camilla didn't understand how Tamara suffered her own thoughts without going mad. They were relentless. The emotions in the room dimmed to a faint notion rather than an intrusion. It was still there, she could tell Callum was eager, but worried. Something troubled him.

"What, Callum? Say it, whatever it is."

Callum pursed his lips and slid closer. "Not to sound insensitive, but you say she's still here?" Camilla nodded. "We need to test this, Camilla. Practice."

"We don't know if Tamara will come back to form or stay as she is now. I won't chance doing that to you." To lose Callum, to not see his face ever again but feel him so close like she did Tamara now. Devastating.

"Then don't drain me completely," he said. "Take a little at a time and I swear I will tell you to stop if I feel in danger."

"I don't want this, Callum. You don't understand what this feels like. Yes, there have been aspects that are wondrous, but what's left over is hollow nothingness. There's no color, no light, no life, only a hunger for death and pain that seems as if it can never be satisfied." It was the first image that the seeress showed her. "You ask me to feed it and I can't."

"Camilla, listen to me." Callum stood, brushing his hair from his face as he paced.

"There's something more. Callum, tell me."

He let out a long breath and looked at her for several tense seconds before he finally sat on the bed with her. "It seems all I've done is apologize to you these last days. Henrik is seething. He blames you for Ian's death. But it was not your fault," he said and cupped her face. "Understand? Tamara did what she did because of Ian's actions, not yours. That doesn't mean Henrik isn't looking to take his loss out on someone. You have to be able to protect yourself. I'm afraid secrets can no longer be your only defense."

Father blames me? Why? The pieces slid together. The only reason Tamara hadn't killed Ian sooner was she hadn't the power to do so. Today, this very morning, Camilla had given the power to her. Her eyes burned and she began to shake. *I helped Tamara murder my brother.*

"Camilla, please don't." She shook her head and pulled away when he tried to hug her to him.

"Go, Callum. Please, leave me alone." She barely squeezed the words past her tightened throat. He did as she asked and the moment he was gone, sobs racked her body.

She didn't know how long she lay there—not long enough to feel any less guilt—when there was a knock at the door. Before she answered, Marceline was in the doorway waiting for a proper invitation. Her expression was one of sympathy, her emotions were blank.

"Please, come in."

"Eirnen and Henrik are dealing with other matters and asked me to come speak with you."

"Tell them I am well," Camilla said, wiping her face. "Thank you, for looking in on me."

"I fear I have come with more distressing news. Belinda was unable to bear the death of her son and succumbed to her illness."

"Mother? The child?" she asked without hope. Her plea for a miracle was short-lived as Marceline shook her head. Tears scalded Camilla's cheeks, she put a hand on her neck to concentrate on breathing, pulling air in past the constriction in her throat. *Mother, Ian, and the baby. The baby with no name.* A sob hiccupped from her.

"Camilla," Marceline said and sat on the bed. "You have suffered great losses today, but there are other matters that concern you that I believe you have the right to know. The timing, my timing, is wretched, I know, but it cannot be helped." Her tone now was the no-nonsense one Camilla was used to. "You must swear to me you won't speak of my betrayal to your father or grandfather, for it would mean my life."

"Betrayal?" The world was off balance, nothing in it made sense and it was spinning too fast. "I, what?"

"Camilla," Marceline took her by the upper arms, grip firm. "I know you grieve, but I need you to listen. I need your promise and I need you to hear me."

Camilla closed her eyes and pulled in a deep breath. She would behave in a manner befitting her station. She was needed and she wasn't the only one who suffered these losses. She wiped the tears from her face and drew her shoulders back.

"Of course, Marceline, I promise," she said. "Please, tell me what it is that troubles you." Camilla reached forward, placing her hand on Marceline's.

"My troubles are many, but yours are more. It's for you that I take this risk." Marceline pulled her hand from Camilla's and clasped them together on her lap as she straightened her back. "Your grandfather's ally, Winston Cleary, wishes to take you for his wife. Eirnen appeased him by allowing the marriage of Ian and Elaine, but that's no longer possible. I overheard Eirnen speaking to your father. He is now to take Ian's place as Elaine's husband."

"But mother's body is not yet cold, no funeral rites have been performed, and already they wish to replace her?"

"It must be done if you are to remain here at Westwood. Eirnen aspires to make you an asset, an advantage in battle. His hope is that you could be used as a spy against Abel and you'd not have to leave Westwood Castle to do it."

"The heron," Camilla said and saw Marceline's confusion. "One flew through a scene I recreated with Grandfather, although there wasn't one when I was looking out the window."

"That explains Eirnen's actions. He'd not be this adamant and go to these lengths to keep you his property alone had he not seen the power he hopes for demonstrated. You must gain control over this power, Camilla. You have to be more powerful to him on your own than you would be as wife to an ally."

A sour taste crept over her tongue. Elaine was even younger than Camilla and Father accepted this proposal. Less than a week and her perception of her father had been completely upended. Although the same judgments should also apply to Eirnen, she found herself trying to excuse and justify his actions. Henrik was her mother's husband and Ian's father. He should refuse this union and not permit Eirnen to use his surviving child as a pawn. She stood up to her father, why could Henrik not do the same?

That defiance led to the death of my brother.

"Winston is sated, for now. But he still expects to have you as his own. Eirnen wishes to delay him until it's certain this ability will develop into something of use. This is an advantage for you. There are two things Eirnen loves: you and power. Even now he is making certain Winston accepts this delay.

"If you were to offer more power by the time the delay has lapsed, than Winston is capable of delivering, it would mean more power for this family as well as yet another reason to keep his precious granddaughter close. You are upper level Camilla, I can feel it. More to the point, Eirnen can too, despite your novice, and is salivating with the prospect of what that may bring him."

As if there weren't enough to think about, Marceline kept delivering news and revealing secrets. Father's pregnant mistress, Lilly, was somewhere in the castle as they spoke and would take Tamara's place until her condition no longer allowed it. Lilly's station was unexpected and not met with gratitude. She believed she would move into the life of a pampered princess, not a chambermaid. That, along with the preparations for Mother's and Ian's funeral and the arrival of close to a dozen wolves tonight was what kept Grandfather and Father too occupied to speak with Camilla themselves regarding her mother's death.

Marceline was also left to tell Camilla she was not permitted to attend the farewell to her family. Eirnen would not chance her out of her chambers when it may coincide with the wolves' arrival as well as his fear "there are enemies among the faux mourners. For her protection," Marceline had quoted.

71

Marceline had one last parting bit of information that sent a thrill of anticipation through Camilla's stomach. She wouldn't be replacing the wards as she left. She thought it appalling that Camilla was being denied the opportunity to bid her mother farewell and now she could watch from a window at the end of the corridor that overlooked the grounds, at least. In payment she requested Camilla be inconspicuous, to not allow anyone to see her out, lest Grandfather discover what Marceline had done.

But, with Father and Grandfather distracted now with preparation and later more so with the arrival of the wolves, it was a fair chance they wouldn't happen by her quarters to notice the wards that kept her locked inside were disengaged. Camilla could be free for the night and she already had a destination in mind. She needed to see the gardens for herself.

CHAPTER 5

I T WAS JUST after dusk, and the pyres were still burning high
and bright. Eirnen would keep the fires going until the bodies
were reduced to so much ash. A substantial number of the res-
idents of Calame were gathered to witness and offer condolence.
As they were expected to be. It was a heart-wrenching sight, many
of the women wept openly at the scene before the pyres were lit. A
mother holding her son tight to her body as they went together into
the afterlife. It was the symbolism more than the actual individuals
that caused the outbursts. Most didn't know Belinda personally and
despised Ian. But it was easy to forget that in the face of their deaths
and allowed the mothers to put themselves in Belinda's position,
cradling their own dead child. Marceline had moments of brilliance.

Henrik and Eirnen were greeted with sympathy and words that
spoke to their compassion. How could men who created such a
beautiful scene to bid farewell to loved ones be callous monsters
as they had been portrayed? Years of discord and mistrust wiped
away with a single act. Marceline was in her place now, beside
Eirnen and clutching Henrik's hand. She was the picture of grief,
which earned her more than one request for permission to pull her

into a consoling embrace. She accepted each with tear-filled eyes and graciousness.

"This is quite a show, Marceline," Henrik said low from where he stood next to her. "But it will not save you from your treachery."

She stared forward as if she'd not heard him. Henrik had discovered through one of the servants that Marceline was taking an elixir to prevent pregnancy. Her actions were treasonous and Henrik sought to see to it she answered for them with her life. What Henrik did not realize, though he should have, was Eirnen had condoned, even encouraged, Marceline to render herself infertile.

Wife or not, she had use beyond breeding. Eirnen had stolen Marceline from Abel, which was the final act that pushed Abel to war. Abel branded Marceline with power during her time with him so she shone to him like a beacon if the distance between them grew beyond the confines of his castle in Anselone. He'd used that tracker cast to retrieve her every time she attempted to escape, until, one night, she happened upon a different king.

Tonight, he'd use the advantage she offered. Better still, she was eager to be used.

Eirnen felt the tingle of power that meant the wolves had arrived. They stayed in the tree line far from the gathering, but some of the guests turned to look in the direction where they waited. Odds were, at least a few of the guests knew of Shaughnessy's whereabouts, were possibly even aiding him. The hunters were still in pursuit of Shaughnessy and it was a struggle for Eirnen not to take a few choice suspects into the castle to force his whereabouts from them. This was the priority. For now. If he were to disgrace this ceremony in front of the witnesses, it would destroy the loyalty he'd bought by doing nothing at all.

It felt like hours since the fires died before people began to dissipate. They'd lingered, socializing on the lawns as if Westwood Castle were a safe gathering place. It was amazing what one display, one act could accomplish.

"Your presence is no longer needed or desired, Marceline," Henrik said through clenched teeth once they entered the great hall. She turned her back to Henrik in a show of disrespect but curtsied low enough she could've kissed Eirnen's feet before she took her leave. Appreciative, he liked that. "Father," Henrik said, glaring at her back.

"Not now, Henrik," Eirnen said, taking the throne. "We have more pressing matters than female designs."

It wasn't surprising to see both Thomas and Grayson among the ten the pack chose as their best. He was wagering it would be one of the two that survived this night to become the new alpha. Thomas was unpredictable, impulsive, but Grayson was the dangerous one. He played the game, thought his actions and their consequences through as opposed to reacting. He wasn't any less vicious because of it. Eirnen could sense Grayson's anger like a razor edge to his energy that Thomas didn't possess. Neither appreciated Eirnen's interference in pack politics. Grayson stepped forward to present himself as spokesman even as Thomas was centered among the rest as if to keep him under control.

"Grayson," Eirnen acknowledged.

"Your Majesty," he dipped his head, unable to offer the full bow in front of the rest. It was a fine line; he must show respect to Eirnen without displaying weakness to the wolves at his back. "We have gathered our ten, as requested."

"Traditionally, it's the strongest fighter among the wolves that ascends to alpha, but history has proven it takes more than physical strength to rule. To this end, I have a task. There is another pack whose numbers match your own. These wolves are under Abel's command. I have it on authority the alpha is working closely with Abel in strategizing another attack against me and by extension all of you. You will hunt them and bring me the alpha of that pack. Should one of you be fortunate enough to relieve Abel of his head and present it to me, he will be handsomely rewarded."

They erupted into a fury of snarls and shouts too tangled around one another to comprehend more than a word or two. Grayson and a few others remained silent, even holding back those brazen enough to try and rush Eirnen where he sat on his throne. Henrik stood to Eirnen's right, vibrating with the power he was gathering if he needed to defend himself. Rowan and Riley looked to Eirnen, who gave a barely perceptible shake of his head. It would be to no benefit if he lost half the wolves before they even left Westwood Castle.

"Enough," Grayson shouted from the head of the group still determined to push forward. There were two others at his side that stood between seven angry wolves and Eirnen. Once they were quieted, resigned but in no way calmed, Grayson turned his attention back to Eirnen. "What you ask of us is an impossibility. We will all die."

"Improbable, but not impossible. It will require thinking, cunning, rather than brute force. This task will demonstrate your ability to strategize while also delivering a blow to our enemy. I require that the alpha be brought back to me alive. Those of you who survive can then choose among yourselves in the tradition of the wolves."

"Your Majesty," Grayson said just as Eirnen was rising to leave. The blade of Rowan's glaive glinted as he held it on the ready and, again, Eirnen stopped him. "I apologize," Grayson said, realizing his mistake.

"Am I to assume you have a request?"

"Yes. If we return with your prize, will you grant us a favor in return?"

Eirnen considered the question. "State your terms now and we'll see if we reach an accord."

"Allow us to give our alpha, Blacke, a merciful death. We know he lives on in some form. We can feel him calling to us for help. If I may, Your Majesty, we are aware that it would be a loss for you to destroy our pack. I don't believe you would hinder yourself in this fashion despite any anger you may feel for us. But you hold incentive for us to complete this task. I fear without this kindness as reward, some of those who stand before you tonight may succumb to the enticement of joining the other pack against you."

"I do hope you survive, Grayson Quinn, for I believe we will make powerful allies. Your favor is granted."

❧

Camilla's heart thundered in her ears as she peered around the corner and down the stairs. She jerked back and flattened against the wall as Frances walked across the lower level. Through the window at the far end of the corridor, she could see the tips of the flames that seemed to be reaching the sky as her mother and brother burned.

She licked her lips and chanced another look to see it was clear, for now. Even as she bounded down the stairs as quietly as she could, thoughts assaulted her with the certainty of failure. Someone was behind her or about to round the corner and catch her even as she found another wall to conceal herself behind. Callum was at her side and uncharacteristically quiet. He'd assured her he knew every corridor and room. He scouted ahead and reported that Frances and Cora were giving Lilly her duties in the kitchens, and Father, Grandfather, and Marceline were outside. This was the best chance they had.

Still, as she listened to Frances's biting tone echo up the hall, she wanted to run back to her chamber and hide. Poor Lilly. Camilla had yet to see the girl but already felt sorry for her as Frances outlined all the ways she was useless. Frances likely felt the same about Camilla. After all, she didn't know how to do any of the tasks Lilly was apparently unequipped to accomplish. Callum gave her a long, questioning look and let his eyes flicker back toward the stairs. Thinking about running was one thing, but to know it was so easy for someone to see her cowardice was enough to force resolution to rise. She shook her head and gestured for him to lead the way.

She held her skirts lifted high enough to keep them from scraping the stones and giving them away. Callum took quick steps and used the same care as if he would be caught as well. Before fear caught up in full force once again, Callum directed her through a door that left her standing in blue twilight.

This wasn't the gardens and that's where she'd told him she wanted to go. The gardens were in front where, according to Callum, the majority of the village was gathered along with her father and grandfather. "Are we to hide here then, until the pyre is dark?"

"No," he said, his expression growing weary. "This way, into the wood."

She didn't understand but followed anyway. There was a dirt-worn footpath, though she still had to push branches back to walk it. It was an effort to keep up with Callum and she was breathing harder by the time he stopped with his back to her. She put her hand out to rest against a tree trunk near the path and caught the first faint smell of rotting meat.

"I want you to reconsider. I know you feel you must witness this with your own eyes, but to hear of this is a different matter altogether from seeing it. There will be no more illusions as to what your patronage is capable of, no more lies or justifications you can make to give peace to your mind. And it will strike you like a blow to the gut when you realize the obvious in that the same blood runs through your veins. If you insist on going further, resolve that within yourself now."

Of course she knew what blood ran through her veins, but she understood what he meant. There was great shame in knowing they shared blood when she heard of their deeds. The affinity for death continued to grow and spoke to the possibility that if she were to gain full power, she could be an evil to rival them. She'd seen that truth as payment for a pebble.

She could go back to her room. She could turn around now, go sit in front of her vanity as she had countless evenings before this one and obey. No one would be the wiser. Tomorrow there would be lessons at dawn, breakfast served to her that someone else prepared, perhaps she and Marceline could take out the stallions again. Her life could be effortless. Father and Grandfather would lay out the path for her future and all she had to do was walk it, just as she'd always done. Marceline was wrong in that she had no training. She might be a novice caster, but in obedience and blind devotion, she'd become proficient.

"I can't go back".

Callum didn't try to sway her again. He led the way down the narrow path, the scent of rot getting stronger with each step. He was so certain she wouldn't change her mind that he didn't pause or give any further warning, but he did spin around to slap a hand across her mouth when the first sound of a scream broke from her. Worse, she couldn't stop. He moved around until he was behind her, one arm around her waist the other clamped tight over her mouth. The sounds were muffled, but forceful enough to make her face and head throb.

Creatures, things, monsters, she didn't know what to call the disfigured beings stooped over, feeding. Some had hands, some claws, but all were coated in blood and thicker things as they dipped again and again inside the body that lay in the long trough they surrounded. It was Tamara. Tamara's body they were ripping pieces from and lifting to their mouths.

They spared her only the slightest of glances, a few with growls of warning before turning the focus back to the meal. The sounds were horrible, the grunting, slurping, and smacking almost as sickening as the sight itself. Callum was bent over her, fitting himself to her back to hold her upright and he was saying things with a cadence she was sure he meant as soothing. Whether it was his dogged determination or the fact that she'd screamed her throat raw, she wasn't sure, but she did stop screaming. She straightened and Callum took his hand from her mouth inches at a time, until he was sure she wasn't about the start again.

"They're dead," she croaked.

That spark, the aura around all living things, was fractured to the point of missing all but a slice or two that shot around them like wandering stars. There was a sadness in watching the tiny bit of light searching in frantic, jerking motions for that which had been taken. In true death it dissipated, moved on to be where it was meant to stay as a whole being of its own. An imprint of the person that once was. That's what made up Callum, the aura and energy that had surrounded his living body. It was whole and intact, he was a thinking being with autonomy and will. These pitiful creatures had just enough orphaned energy to tether their bodies to this earth though they were but shells, driven by need and instinct.

There were similarities to them, yet they were different. She gave the arm still around her waist a pat to let him know she was fine to stand on her own. He let her go and didn't try to stop her as she took a small, shaky step forward. She wasn't foolish or brave enough to try and get close to them, especially not while they were eating.

She forced her eyes from the creatures and looked around the clearing. There were two more troughs, one had what looked like a mixture of rotting fruit, vegetables, and animal carcasses. The other was full of murky water not suited to animals. There was even a stone bench set on the farthest edge by the trees closest to the path they'd walked, as if someone spent time out here with them.

She inched sideways and lowered onto the bench. Callum sat next to her, but neither spoke as they watched. She was at war with herself, caught between being outraged into chasing them away from what was left of Tamara and leaving them be. Stopping them wouldn't bring Tamara back, it wouldn't save her. She was beyond feeling physical pain now. Still, she was glad Tamara wasn't here to see this.

She looked back over her shoulder and closed her eyes. She could see parts of Westwood Castle through the dense trees. This atrocity had been this close for who knows how long and she'd been blind and deaf to it.

"Did I just not want to know?" she asked Callum. "How can a person live their entire life with people capable of this and not suspect, not see this depth of evil unless they willfully refused to see it?"

"I've been here long enough. I see things and hear things people don't want seen and heard. This, your ignorance, was willful. They keep you in that room for weeks at a time. There are wards on the doors and windows that they always told you were for your protection, but in truth it was for theirs. 'Camilla's too tender-hearted to understand the difference between necessity and malice.' Those were Eirnen's exact words."

Camilla looked at the creatures, the *people,* Grandfather no doubt thought were necessity and saw nothing but malice. There was no justification for this. None. "These are the result of his experimentations, like with you. He's still doing it, knowing the consequences."

"Yes. Even now his hunters are out seeking Master Shaughnessy. Eirnen holds the belief Shaughnessy may be strong enough to withstand the conversion. Once he's caught, Eirnen will send his hunters again for a caster and a werewolf."

"And if it doesn't work, he'll hide them here. His garden."

She could see the scenario played out in front of her in the dozen or so hunched figures. They all had humanoid features, some more than others. There were two with distinct elongated snouts full of sharp teeth. Four more were as white as snow with webs of blue veins standing out in stark contrast against the exposed skin. One of those had hissed at her earlier, showing two pointed canines. There were dark circles under their eyes, their backs were bent and misshapen.

One of them looked back at her and Callum. The blood that covered the lower half of his face dripped from his chin. He raised on his hind legs to pivot around before going back to all fours. He crept closer, lifting his face to sniff the air but there was something deformed about his nose. His chest was bare, but his trousers were still in place and in markedly better shape than most of the others'. Callum stood and moved in front of her before the creature could get closer.

"Callum," she said with a hand on his arm. "It's alright." She looked around Callum at the creature that was assessing them both. There wasn't aggression. Curiosity and fear, but no hostility. "Do you know his name?"

"Blacke," Callum said, and the creature cocked its head to the side.

"Blacke," she repeated. He shook his head as if to deny it or dispel the name. There was a yap of pain and then deep growls that took her attention back to the trough. The fresh food was running out and they were still hungry enough to fight over what was left. Blacke looked as well, but then his head came back around. One moment Camilla's eyes were locked on Blacke's and the next he had her by the arms.

She tensed under the hard grip. His claws dug into her flesh. Her knees were pressed into his abdomen from the seated position, but he seemed to pay little attention. Callum was shouting for him to let her go, but she and Blacke were still staring each other in the eyes. He was trying desperately to convey something to her, but what it was she couldn't understand. He leaned in and snarled close to her face, his teeth gleamed wet and red with Tamara's blood, and then he shoved her backward so hard she hit the ground behind the bench. Callum helped her untangle the branches that snagged her hair on the way down, then lifted her to her feet only to have Blacke lunge at them.

He looked once more at the trough, then at her before another vicious snarl ripped from his mouth and his teeth came together with an audible snap. "Thank you, Blacke," she said and bowed her head to him as she backed down the trail. "I won't leave you like this, I swear."

She turned and took quick steps down the path with Callum close behind. The sound of a fight broke out and Callum gave her a hard shove between the shoulder blades. It was enough. She ran as fast as she could, ignoring the branches scraping her arms and face. She felt it when Callum relinquished his energy enough to be unseen and knew that meant they were close to the end. There weren't any sounds that made her think they were being chased, but there were still the deep snarls and howls of pain as they fought. She stopped while she was still partially concealed by the trees before she stepped out into the open.

She half expected to see the guards out with torches in hand, searching the dark for her, but they weren't. There was, however, a lone, hooded figure slinking out the door from the servant's quarters. Camilla recognized the fearful expression on Marceline's face, she'd felt it on her own as she snuck from the castle. But from what Camilla could see, no one was pursuing Marceline either.

Camilla stood tall and refused to hide as Marceline came closer, but Marceline was looking everywhere except at the path that would lead to the creatures. "She knows of this. Do not trust her," Callum said, trying to urge her back.

"All the more reason for me to show her I see her for what she is now," Camilla said and stepped directly into Marceline's zig-zagging path.

Marceline's eyes widened and her mouth gaped open before she started to sputter. Camilla said nothing, regarding her with a steely expression. "Camilla, please," Marceline said all while continuing to look behind her.

"Please what? Please allow you time to form an excuse for that," she asked and pointed behind her. "Or perhaps you'll say you didn't know, lie to me with the confidence I'll believe whatever you lead me by the hand to believe."

"No, of course not," she said and moved around until she could watch both Camilla and the castle. "I know of them, but what would you have me do? Challenge Eirnen and Henrik? I make sure that they are at least cared for as well as the livestock rather than leave them to starve or prowl the village for food."

"Is that your reason for skulking in the dark, fleeing the castle like a thief? Did you have it in your mind to watch them enjoy their meal of a girl driven to desperation enough to take her own life?"

"Camilla, I can see you feel betrayed, as you should, and perhaps I should have tried to find a way to tell you. But can you not see my position? Eirnen has barely allowed us contact and up until this moment I believed you to be completely loyal to him. If he were to find out that I was the one to enlighten you, it would have meant my life. I've never betrayed you, I've not spoken a word of your young man and I've told you things that would get me whipped. I left your wardings down tonight! Oh, gods, Camilla, you mustn't be seen returning to your chambers. He'll know!"

"What do you want from me, Marceline?"

"The same as I have given you: silence. Tell no one you saw me this night, I beg you."

"You're running away?" She had a moment of wanting to plead with Marceline to reconsider. "If you're caught, Grandfather will punish you."

"I have no choice. Henrik will see me dead because I refuse to be bred like chattel. This way I have a chance." Echoing shouts had them both looking for the source with Marceline gripping Camilla's hand hard enough to be painful. "The wolves," she said with panic marking her features. "You must get inside, now. The granddaughter of the king would make fine leverage indeed. Hurry, Camilla," Marceline said and drug her across the wet grass. "Run," she hissed with a final shove before she spun and darted off in the opposite direction.

CHAPTER 6

I T WAS WELL past noon and the wolves had yet to return. The idea of capturing a valuable member of Abel's forces had already taken root. If they failed to bring him the alpha, Eirnen would find another way. The details of Abel's strategy could be invaluable as well as providing the wolf when Shaughnessy's evasions finally ran out. And they would.

This very morning, one of the casters assisting Shaughnessy in cloaking himself from the hunters was caught. In fact, after a few hours of Eirnen's tender ministrations, she wasn't worth much to anyone anymore. So fragile these lower beings tended to be.

"There is death here," she rasped, the eyes reeling around in her skull flashing more white than brown. Her ashen skin glistened with the sweat that pasted her hair to her face.

"Aye, Marion Garvin, much," he said and watched her struggle to keep her legs under her. The warded restraints at her wrists wouldn't allow her to fall if she wanted to. "Are you ready to end your suffering? All you must do is tell me where to find Shaughnessy."

"It lives and breathes here," she continued as if he'd not spoken.

He got her by the chin, noting the coolness of her moist skin, and tsked.

"Have I broken you already?" he asked and let her head drop back to her chest. "Shaughnessy, Marion," he said and threw power at her. She bucked, arching away from the stones of the wall as if they were the source of the flames licking up her body. "You will burn but not die," he shouted over her screams. "Is one vampire, a being that treats our kind as refuse, worth this pain?"

Her screams formed words and he drew the heat away from her body but not so far as to let her forget it was awaiting her with ravenous hunger. "Its heart beats in this castle," she panted. With a twist of his fingers, the eager flames took her once more. There were no screams, but laughter, joyous as it boiled from her mouth. "Just as you revel in victory, all will be lost. Westwood will fall by your hand!"

With a muttered curse, Eirnen ascended the stairs that would take him away from the stench of the dungeons and the sound of Marion's laughter. He didn't bother to douse the flames. After all, they wouldn't kill her and he suspected she could sink no deeper into madness. She'd been sitting in the grass by the flower gardens, plucking flowers as if she were waiting for him, not twenty minutes after he'd sent Rowan to collect her from the village. He'd burn the sense back into the harlot. She'd not protect Shaughnessy as she was if it were simply an agreement of coin. She cared for him. He'd seduced himself allies, typical of what Eirnen knew of Shaughnessy, more than Marion if Eirnen's suspicions were correct. But he was king for a reason.

His study lay within the heart of the castle, a tower with casting essence ground into the very stone. His father, grandfather, brother, and countless enemies lent their bones in the building of this bastion of power that amplified his. With him atop it like a lightning rod, nothing or no one in Calame could escape his attention. The wind was fierce, blowing around him until his hair lashed his cheeks like a whip. He wondered if it was an indication that Marceline was entertaining him with her skill. Another gust hit him and was accompanied by thunder that made the very earth tremble. He smiled. Perhaps punishing was more accurate than entertaining. He deserved it, he was sure, but he now knew she still lived. She'd fail in her ultimate goal for this venture unless she was terribly lucky or Abel was foolish, but Eirnen hoped she would return with something of value. If not, if Abel kept or killed her? He was surprised to realize the prospect left an ache in his chest. He truly would miss her.

Lightning creased the greyed sky and rain began to pour, soaking him. He was up here for a reason and that reason was not to ponder the loss of Marceline. He'd sacrifice everything for this, even her. He took a deep breath, spread his arms and let his head fall back.

A searching energy poured from him and spread throughout Westwood Castle. It touched every darkened corner and galley all the way to the dungeons where it brushed on Marion's pain and threatened to buckle his legs under him. He could feel Henrik very near Camilla, who was burning much brighter than he dared hope, every servant and stablemaster that roamed the grounds. He sought them out and let the fingers of power curl in their energies before dragging it back to him.

He gathered it, those of lesser power weakening as he bloated. He opened his eyes and scanned the countryside and the village below from his vantage point. All who aided Shaughnessy would face repercussions and this day he would know each of them.

⁊

Camilla was finding it difficult not to lash out at Henrik while he doled out these so-called lessons. More like excuses to strike her. She prodded her lower lip with the tip of her tongue and tasted blood.

"Again," he shouted and she shrank when he drew his foot back as if to kick her. His posture loosened and his boot-clad foot settled on the floor instead of her midsection. "Again, Camilla."

Her teeth locked as she pushed herself to crouch before making her legs lift her to stand. She would not cry out, not one whimper for him. "You should not strike me, Henrik." She smiled down at the red that smeared the back of her hand even as her vision tunneled and pulsed. Her challenge earned a hearty laugh, more galling still was that his amusement of her warning was one of the very few times she'd seen a smile on his face because of her.

"Camilla," Callum warned. It was still amazing that Henrik was oblivious to his presence, but Camilla could see and hear him with crystalline clearness even when he was hiding from everyone else. Oh, how she wanted to rub this in Henrik's face. She could do something he couldn't. "Use your head, girl," he continued when she started gathering energy from everywhere, including Callum.

One moment a rising furious power was coursing through her and the next it was ripped away. Her eyes widened and she held her breath, searching with the same panic that touched Callum's features. Had Father sensed the aggressive power and taken it? He gave her no clues, only continuing to stare at her with an expectant and impatient expression. She'd lost her temper, let anger get the better of her. Thoughtless.

She cleared her throat and started again. How quickly she'd lost the viciousness that rose to the surface. One moment of uncertainty and fear was enough to send her cowering in humility, humbled and obedient. Since her discovery of the creatures and secret of Marceline's defection, the guilt of the knowledge left her waiting for someone to point an accusing finger.

"Someone has collected our energies," Henrik said. "Find and expose them." From the smug expression, he already knew who it was. Of course, she felt her power stripped and would have recognized it for what it was if not for her conscience screaming she'd been caught. Reason told her it was Grandfather who'd done it. What he wanted was for her to show Grandfather to him.

"Remember, just enough to keep him wanting, Camilla," Callum said.

It was easy enough to follow the path her seeping energies drew, all she had to do was close her eyes and let it lead her. It was hers, part of her, and wanted to stay whole with her. Just as that spark on the creatures sought out the missing pieces, this was the same on a much smaller scale. If Grandfather wanted and she wasn't strong enough to fend him off, he could do the same to her if he took too much. Right now she didn't want to fight him for it. She needed to use the signature of her energies to find him.

She straightened her arm in front of her and made small circles. The air against her palm stirred and a blurred image filled the room. Grandfather was naught more than a smudge of color, but he was atop the tower in the center of Westwood Castle. She could see it much clearer in her mind and could solidify it here in Grandfather's quarters, but she wouldn't.

"You're holding back," Henrik snarled. "More, Camilla."

She scarcely heard him. She was watching as if she were standing in the rain with Grandfather. Could he feel her there, watching with him? What would happen if he did? Brilliant green lights blazed up in the village below. There were at least six of them and another surge of power was jerked from Camilla hard enough to make her lurch forward. The six green lights held steady, but another flickered in the distance before it burnt bright and white as the moon.

Shaughnessy.

A sharp sting lit her cheek and she lost it all with a gasp. The image fell like dust as she clutched her face. Her eye started to throb. The lashes felt as if they were trying to tangle with every blink. Henrik was speaking, his mouth was moving, but the words were lost in the squealing in her ears. She opened her mouth, trying to force the ringing to stop.

Eirnen appeared as if out of nowhere and caught Henrik up by the collar. He threw him back until he landed on the floor in a heap. Camilla flinched when he reached to pull her hand from her face, but she let him. He turned her head with a finger under her jaw, his features tightening. To Camilla's eyes, he looked drawn, tired. Whatever he'd done to locate Shaughnessy had gotten him what he wanted, but it cost him as well.

"Henrik," he said without looking from Camilla's face. "If you weren't needed this day, you'd not have the bones left to stand."

"Father," Henrik said, the grunt of pain as he rose to his feet gave Camilla a wicked sense of satisfaction. "She is capable of more. She is holding back out of spite."

"I don't care the reason," Grandfather said and kissed her forehead before turning to Henrik. "You are never to hit her again. Never."

"Winston won't mind the bruises," Henrik said staring Camilla in the eyes. Before Ian's death, Father barely looked at her and when he did it was with an air of indifference. Now, hatred poured from him thick enough to whither the mightiest oaks in Calame. She started to whither under that glare, too, but caught herself and straightened her shoulders, which made him take a seething step forward. "Prideful whelp," he snarled. Grandfather gave him a dose of his own treatment.

Henrik recovered from the backhand across the face faster than Camilla had, but it still rocked him back on his heels. "If you're finished engaging in a battle of wills with a child…" Grandfather shamed him into submission where the strike hadn't. "Now, tell me of the progress."

"A barely discernible image of you on the tower," Henrik dismissed.

"Truly?" Camilla hated that her chest warmed when he looked upon her with pride. He was a monster. She'd seen it for herself. She must remember that. "Commendable, considering I was drawing energy from all of you and still my lovely granddaughter managed to leap forward in her power growth. An intentional image of me, even a hazy one, is far beyond an accidental conjuring while at full power. Impressive, wouldn't you agree, Henrik?"

"It would seem so," Henrik finally conceded, further shamed.

"Good. Now that we've established who has excelled this day and who has failed, mayhap you will get an opportunity to elevate your standing, son. Camilla, for now, lessons are over."

A dismissal. She didn't hesitate to take it. The corridor had no windows and was dim with candlelight. She could still hear the storm outside. There were no servants waiting to escort her, no need to keep on the mask of calm. She ran for the stairs that would take her to the second level and her quarters. There was too much happening too fast and she wasn't close to ready.

She had to work faster. They'd been practicing, but not enough. At first Tamara had refused to help. Camilla hadn't tried to force her, but she'd joined in because Camilla and Callum were "idiots who hadn't a raindrop's chance in hell without her." Tamara had unraveled the wards many times before in her role as servant and had much to offer.

They were making progress. Tamara wasn't at all happy about being unable to do it herself now, but she'd walked Camilla through the process. Tamara was happy, though, that she'd lost the ability to feel emotions. She'd been lower level and untrained, very little control meant she was feeling everything all the time. She wasn't nearly powerful enough to be a true empath, but the inability to shut anyone out had to be maddening. Camilla had asked if Tamara would be so kind as to offer advice in using this ability, but Tamara thought that was asking too much.

"He's found him," she blurted once she closed the door. "Grandfather knows where Shaughnessy is. He'll have him soon." She sat in the vanity chair to look over the bruises on her face. She was relieved to see that what felt like a trench in her lip to the tip of her tongue was but a thin line of red.

"He's a vampire. Let Eirnen have him," Tamara said with a flick of her fingers. "Does anyone but me think it odd that Eirnen hasn't raised an alarm over his missing queen?"

"Tamara," Callum said and narrowed his eyes. "Your tone insinuates you've more to say on the matter."

"Perhaps, should the right enticement be proposed," Tamara purred as she reached for Callum.

There was a knock at the door and Camilla was glad for the interruption. A girl she'd never seen before came inside, a small but pronounced pooch to her belly. Her hair hung free to her waist and was a warm chestnut color that would look dazzling in the sunlight.

"You must be Lilly," Camilla said and rose to meet her. She was petite, thin-boned and her eyes were the loveliest shade of violet. Odd, but lovely all the same. "I'm sure you know, but it feels rude to not introduce myself formally. I'm Camilla."

"I know who you are," she said with acid behind the words. "You have been summoned to the commons. I have been ordered to bid you dress in full Westwood finery." She curtsied and left the room to wait in the corridor.

Tamara whispered, "Eirnen knows exactly where his queen is."

Camilla twisted in her seat and stared wide-eyed at Tamara.

§

Come to me, Marion had written. Shaughnessy had done as she directed, as usual, and yet she was not in the cottage. There were no other messages waiting, no indication where she'd gone, so how did she expect him to follow? He was a vampire not a hunting hound. Tonight, however, distasteful as it was, he'd attempt to play the part of one to find her. Then he was going to choke her until she told him the way of getting to the girl other than allowing himself to become another of Eirnen's prisoners as she'd suggested. Absurd.

He'd been Eirnen's prisoner before, briefly. It wasn't something he was willing to repeat. It had taught him the foolishness of allowing himself to be caught as a way to inject himself into Eirnen's inner sanctum. He blamed the oversight on grief, not an overestimation of his strength and cunning. Cassandra had been beheaded mere days before. He was desperate to deliver revenge. He'd forced himself to leave the place where she died and walked straight into the fortress that would become Westwood Castle.

Eirnen's father, Malachi, had no interest in royal titles. He'd been a brute of a man who delighted in war and women and not much else. Lands he invaded, he conquered. He was a warlord without equal who preferred to don his armor and slice enemies through with his sword and his army behind him. Unlike Eirnen, who sent others to do his fighting while he twittered away in his castle spinning casts. When Eirnen had been but sixteen years of age, he'd stabbed his warrior father in the back, killing him. The dishonorable act of a coward.

Shaughnessy hadn't gotten within twenty feet of Eirnen before he'd been taken to the ground under the same army that had been trained by and served with Malachi. Shaughnessy had been right, Eirnen did go the way of the coward once more when faced with an enemy. He'd waited until Shaughnessy was weakened and restrained in the dungeons by Malachi's men before he showed himself. From there it had been weeks of Eirnen using Shaughnessy to practice perfecting the art of torture and servants collecting the blood that filled pail after pail under his feet for the army to use as a healing tonic.

True, he hadn't helped his situation at all by laughing at the boy, reminding him of his inferiority to his warlord father. Shaughnessy hadn't broken. Not once. There was never a plea for mercy or relief to pass his lips. Never did he allow himself to even entertain the idea of begging for the pain to stop as Eirnen demanded as his price. "I'll take your head, end this, if only you'd ask."

"Never," had been his reply and the torment continued until one evening a servant girl got too close to the beast while tending her duties.

Eirnen was still a coward. Malachi's army, once fierce and unde-feated, was long gone. There was no one with the same level of skill to train those Eirnen commanded now. Eirnen hadn't the capa-bility to do so himself. His pride as a younger man hadn't allowed him to ask the battle-honed men that once belonged to his father to teach him. Eirnen depended on his ability to cast, which was formidable for certain, but it meant that he was reliant upon the power of others. Without them to draw energies to fuel his abilities, he'd weaken quickly. This, Shaughnessy believed, was why Eirnen was attempting to use his talent as a caster to create warriors. He could hide behind them, send them out to wage his wars for him.

"Here." The voice came from outside and Shaughnessy stilled. Before the hope they would pass him by could take form, there was a crash that meant they'd broken through the door.

The sound of boots followed. He cocked his head and listened through the wall. A thump as they dropped something heavy, feet shuffling as they assessed for immediate threats. "Check every room." "Split up. Six upstairs, the rest stay down here with me," a male voice directed over the sound of flapping material. There was another crash and his nose filled with the scent of fresh air.

He followed the sounds of the heavy footsteps above where he hid from the sun. The continued pattern of material tearing and wood breaking told him they meant to flood the whole of the first floor with light. Lucky for him, he hadn't caged himself. The men demolishing the old cottage house provided cover enough to work his way through the passages between the walls unheard. Six upstairs, six down not including the male issuing commands. Thirteen casters. Did Eirnen think so little of him?

He wound his way up the narrow, spiral staircase, silent as a shadow. This house at one time was owned by a former lover. She'd long since moved on, married a nice respectable male and left to join his family. But before she'd become a proper lady in a caster house, Shaughnessy had gotten to know this one well. He stopped at the doorway and waited until he heard the six break off into smaller pairings to search the rooms.

More crashes. Stay behind the cover of the walls and hope they didn't discover one of the passages or attack? They'd come specifically to this house. They knew he was here somewhere and they wouldn't have the ballocks to go back to Eirnen with a failure. He eased the latches that kept the doorway in place and slid the panel to the side just enough to see how much light he'd have to contend with. The room was lit, the shutters torn free.

Since he couldn't go to them…he waited, crouched. Closer… closer…then pushed the wall panel to the side with one hand and grabbed the male in front with the other. Though it took but a second, his arm burnt and blistered before he yanked his catch into the dark with him. The other shouted a warning, but rather than fleeing, his steps were closing in on the panel. He thought to save his companion. Shaughnessy twisted his neck.

More pounding steps, but they'd be too late. The male on the outside beat against the panel, Shaughnessy had him in his grasp with his fangs buried in his neck before help arrived. He drank deep and hard, healing the burns, before he broke this one as he had the first. He sat them up against the panel, a flesh and bone barricade, then dropped over the railing down through the spiral.

At the bottom, he felt the tug that meant they were trying to syphon energy from him. Weaken him. He snarled. *They call me a leech.* He resisted the pull and none were powerful enough to take from him by force.

"Enough," the leader shouted and footsteps once more descended the stairs as they regrouped. "Burn it."

They were quiet but close. Their hearts were forever giving them away. Harsh thuds of heavy boots, purposeful, bringing them ever closer. Knees bent to spring, a long metal pole punched through the wall and into his chest. He grasped it, but before he could rip it free he was run through with another, then another. To the right and left of him, axes tore away the wall until the sun framed him.

He was struggling to free himself from the poles holding him fast, that was the only excuse he had for not seeing the loop of metal cable coming at him. Before he knew what was happening, it was around his neck and tightening. They meant to lead him by the neck, like an animal.

They want me, they can have me.

There was no way to win this, not with the sun fighting with them, but he wouldn't be the only one losing blood. Rather than fight to go back or up, he rushed forward. The remnants of the wall hiding him from the sun crumbled. Two men were knocked to the ground, but those holding the poles and the tie around his neck stayed standing. There in the middle of the floor, sat what was meant to be his conveyance to Westwood dungeon.

A box. A coffin. Shaughnessy growled and bucked, flinging one of the guards off his arm. The male rolled across the floor as the others converged. Cold metal slid into his flank, between his shoulder blades, his belly, his chest. He hissed pain, twisting to get away from it but found no relief. The sun seared his eyes, blinding him, his skin peeled under his captors' hands as they continued to pull and jerk and push, beating and stabbing him toward the box.

He couldn't see, the only scent his own blood, their hands slipped and slid over his skin as they lifted him. Once he was released, he began to fight again. Laughter filled his ears. "My son looks just that way when he's lying on the floor, kicking and screaming in a fit of tantrum."

Your son is dead! He shouted in his head, but no sound left him.

"Where is Marceline?" Henrik hissed. "She should be present as your queen."

Eirnen waved him off. "Sulking about your discovery. Let her be."

Rowan announced Winston Cleary and his daughter, Elaine, from the doorway then gave Eirnen a tight nod. Perfect. Frances scurried about, pouring wine from Winston's vineyard. Gods knew there was plenty of the bitter swill rotting away in the cellar. Henrik at last showed his upbringing by taking Elaine's hand and bowing over it to place a kiss on the knuckles. The girl looked to her father before dipping low and murmuring, "Your Majesty," in a small voice.

Winston followed suit, offering a bow before unbuttoning his waistcoat to accommodate the girth as he sat. "Your messengers indicated this is to be a quiet affair."

"We feel it would be insensitive to parade such a celebration this soon after the passing of Belinda and Ian as well Henrik's unborn. Be of ease that come spring, there will be a grand gala in your honor, dear Elaine." Elaine flushed and shifted in her seat, pleased by the idea, but her father was not so easily swayed.

"Are we to be the only to bear witness, then? What assurance do I have that my daughter's place as future queen will be secure once I have helped win this war for you?"

"Are you suggesting I would cast her out and deny any union between her and my son?" Eirnen challenged. From the way Winston's shoulders pulled back and his lips thinned, that was exactly his expectation. "What is it you require to assuage your doubt?"

"Camilla returns with me today to Gladen," he said and sipped his wine. "Lovely."

"No. She is needed here for a time," Eirnen said. "Rowan and Riley will gather witnesses for you, which will be sufficient." The guards nodded from the door and went about to do as they were told. If only everyone were like those two.

"And if I refuse?"

"If you refuse, you may take your daughter and any future hope of the throne and return to Gladen." Winston looked as shocked as Henrik.

"This is a rather uncompromising negotiation, Eirnen. I would think someone in your position would have more flexibility with someone in mine. I have much to offer the right king."

"I would make the same observation to you, old friend." Eirnen leaned back in his chair and took a drink of the wine. "Rancid," he spit and tossed the goblet into the fire. "I have had one person use that same argument with me, though not as eloquently veiled. And unfortunately for you, it happened recently so my patience is nil. But seeing as we have known one another for many years, I will offer a compromise." He glanced up and smiled. Winston followed his gaze and sprung from his chair, his face reddening with anger.

"What is this?" he spluttered.

"That is a glaive and believe me when I tell you Rowan is quite skilled with it." Winston's son Barrett, who Winston believed still guarded at Gladen, was near on his toes with the glaive under his chin. "Rowan is exceptionally fast, one of many talents. I assure you Barrett will spurt before you lift a hand against me."

Elaine appeared faint, Henrik confused and angry because he'd not been included in these endeavors. He'd find himself in that position more often until he once again behaved as a ruler should. The instability in him, his focus always on his loss or his retribution since Ian's death had rendered him untrustworthy and not predictable as he once was.

"Sit," Eirnen commanded of Winston as well as Henrik, who moved to stand. Henrik eased back down into his chair, his mouth a tight line and his eyes hard fixed on Eirnen. "Winston, sit. We still have our compromise to discuss."

Winston stumbled into his chair without taking his eyes from the glaive point. "Eirnen will not have power enough to spare you," he said to Rowan.

"Pay attention," Eirnen said. "I will allow your daughter to be wed to my son, the *Prince* of Calame, and in return, I have your vow of loyalty against Abel. Barrett will play witness, just as you required, and he will remain here with his sister until she becomes acclimated to Westwood Castle. After all, I want my new daughter to feel comfortable in her new home."

"You mean to ransom my son."

"Compromise. Truly, I'm being very generous. If that blade were to slip and you were to fall dead from sorrow, that would leave little Elaine here mistress of Gladen. As wife to Henrik, what is hers is his. You, Winston, are becoming redundant. That being said, it would take time I don't have and I'd no doubt be forced to make an example of a few of your followers, of which I need all I can acquire, to make Gladen mine. It would be inconvenient to remove you. And I concede your ability is of value as well. So, do we have an accord?"

"I see this for what it is, Eirnen. I agree or you murder me and my son then use my own daughter to steal what is mine. You filching bastard!" Winston's hesitation to answer made Barrett groan as the blade tip pierced his skin. "We do, we have an accord!"

"Splendid," Eirnen said with a clap. "Rowan, Riley, if you could show Barrett to his quarters to clean up for the ceremony."

Winston watched the guards lead the boy from the room, pushing up onto his arms to follow to the end of the corridor. It was humbling, the position Winston was in, to come here with the certainty that he had the upper hand only to find he'd never had it at all. Eirnen waited, watching with interest as the colors of Winston's shaking jowls changed. Elaine was looking rather pale herself, but she would recover just as her father was.

"I can object to the union," he said, settling into his seat once more. "It's my right to do so."

"Do you really wish to play this game of threats with me, Winston? If you go to the door you came through to enter my home, you will find your guards are dead. You, your daughter, and your son are in my home. If the whole of you were to perish, there is nothing stopping me from claiming Gladen. Beatrice's disgrace with a vampire has left you a son-in-law who is near powerless, hardly capable of defending Gladen." Winston opened his mouth to speak, but Eirnen cut him off with a finger. "Choose your next words wisely."

"Does this mean you intend to sever the agreement with regards to Camilla?"

"No," Henrik said, speaking for the first time and looking pleased with himself. Untrustworthy. Eirnen had indeed intended to rescind the betrothal as Henrik probably guessed. "She is still in need of a husband who will provide her with children that will grow the Westwood line in power."

"As I said before, she will remain here for a time. Though I must ask, what of your son? Barrett is in his fifteenth year? Perhaps he would be a more suitable match."

"No. He is promised. Camilla is to be mine," Winston said. "Will she be joining us then?"

"I have already sent for her," Henrik said before Eirnen could answer.

This irrational anger directed at Camilla was the only reason Henrik meant to present her today. She knew naught of Winston being her intended and the sight of him coupled with the announcement would distress her greatly. Henrik knew this, counted on it and relished the idea. Eirnen remained seated though he wanted to warn Camilla to show no emotion, take Henrik's joy in this moment, but he would not. Henrik would guess his motives and be more satisfied with the knowledge he'd distressed them both.

If all went to plan, Henrik would be very busy soon. Too busy for these childish plots. And, perhaps, a prideful victory would restore the heir Eirnen spent years molding, make him remember their goals.

Eirnen's features remained fixed in stoicism as Camilla was presented. She did better than expected when Henrik made his announcement. There was very little reaction from her, she offered her hand and a shy smile while quickly explaining away the injuries as a fall from a horse. Henrik wasn't pleased, but Winston was. Very much so. He had a penchant for lovely young ladies and Camilla was a beauty. Before Eirnen relinquished her to this man, Winston would know well the consequences should she meet the same fate as his last lovely young bride.

All through dinner, Eirnen watched her. It was difficult since she was seated next to him but be damned if he'd watch Winston fondle her at the table. Already he looked like a starving dog slobbering over the last steak. There was something different in her, a shift. He felt it when he pulled in her energies this morning and it spurred him to take more to try and identify it, but he couldn't.

As he watched her, she watched Barrett. He could see the allure. Barrett was handsome enough, he supposed, but next to the prospect of his father he must appear much more palatable. Another reason to keep a wary eye. Winston would not have her if she were spoiled. Lasses failed to appeal to him once they'd garnered some experience. Of course, should she be spoiled, Eirnen could insist as her liege that Barrett wed her for it. She could secure Gladen for him with such a union. Winston truly was proving to be unnecessary and bothersome.

His mood lifted significantly when one of the hunters sent for Shaughnessy appeared in the corridor just long enough to give a nod. Days. He was days away. Maybe less. With Marion and Shaughnessy both in the dungeons, all he was lacking was the wolf and there should be a few healthy prospects available soon. The surety of success and planning got him through the rest of dinner and well into the ceremony preparation.

Winston and Henrik whispered in the corner as they awaited Elaine to begin. More plotting, Eirnen had no doubt. Camilla knew it too, judging by the frequent glances at the two men. Barrett worked to hold her attention, but her eyes wandered, her body remained stiff and little snaps of power fired off at frequent intervals with her stress. Raising her caster hackles, as it were. Yet another area he needed to work with her. He should see nothing, but those sparks were warnings and tells that gave away her position.

He caught her eye and waved her to him. She excused herself from Barrett, but her demeanor didn't relax as she made her way toward the dais. Her expression was wary, guilty. Why?

"What troubles you, child?" She looked at her hands before raising her eyes for another glance at Winston and Henrik. "It is just you and I. They are paying us no attention."

"I am not feeling well," she said. "I would like to return to my chambers to lie down."

"What else? There is more yet you need to reveal, Camilla. I have known you since the moment of your birth. I was the first to hold you, squirming and pink, in my arms. You have never learned to school your expressions. I know when you are lying and when you are hiding something from me. Never doubt that, Granddaughter."

Her face paled more, her throat worked as she swallowed hard. She was going to lie or tell half-truths yet again. "I, just," she cut her eyes to the side and licked her lips.

"Look at me, Camilla," he said.

"That man"—she said—"he frightens me." Eirnen felt a softening in him that only ever happened with her. "Do you really mean for me to wed him, Grandfather?"

Camilla waited for the answer—though she already knew he did—unless, of course, she better mastered using Callum's ability. Looking at that man made her want nothing more than to go practice until she'd perfected the skill. She recognized him. He was the man from the second vision where she wore the bracelets. The girl had been warning her of this very thing, this proposed union, and if she'd been given a warning, the other two visions showed her there may be a way to prevent it.

Camilla didn't know what the seeress's motives were for interfering, but it likely had little to do with Camilla herself. After all she'd learned, she was but a means to strike at Eirnen. Had to be. Camilla had been a threat to no one, had never harmed anyone. Eirnen, however, had given many reasons for retaliation. Did the seeress know one of the creatures in the garden or had Grandfather done something else to the girl? But if so, why help Camilla? If what she was doing was helping at all.

While they were practicing in her chambers, she'd tried to use Callum's sight to find the girl, watch her, but was met with the wall of white. Coming up against that familiar blinding light she couldn't see through or around meant only one thing: the girl was somewhere in the castle. Callum found her in the dungeons, chained, tortured, and unconscious.

Camilla was close to dismantling the wards, but still couldn't get them down herself, not from inside her chambers. It was like working a complicated puzzle while watching yourself do it in the mirror. She would, though. She had to. She couldn't let Grandfather make that girl into another creature he discarded with the others.

"I've little choice," Eirnen said and it took her a moment to remember what she'd asked. Winston. Yes. He drew her down by the hand and kissed her cheek. "Barrett is waiting for you. Worry not. Enjoy this evening. It will be a long while before you are taken to Gladen, much can happen in that time."

Winston watched her, nodding at whatever Henrik was saying next to him. Even without the foretelling glimpse, she'd not have liked Winston Cleary. He was red-faced and sweaty while standing still. His eyes, set back deep into his face, assessed her as if she were something he considered purchasing. And he was always dabbing the corner of his mouth with his tongue. He made her want to cover herself though she was wearing a modest gown and a shawl over her shoulders.

She was steps from being in front of Barrett when a crack of thunder shook the stones beneath her feet. She jumped. Barrett laughed and met her, hands outstretched, to take hers. She instead occupied her own hands, tightening the shawl around herself. "Do storms frighten you, Lady Camilla?"

Barrett was kind enough, she supposed, but she knew every time his father's eyes were on her. She could feel it and it raised the hair on her neck. She would not be wed to that man.

"No. It just surprised me. Please, call me Camilla." From the corner of her eye, she saw Grandfather's lips twitch as if fighting a smile.

"I love them. The lightning, the rain, cleansing and invigo-rating." She nodded agreement, stealing glances at Grandfather. He called Riley and Rowan to him, their heads bent low as they discussed something that made Grandfather's jaws clench. "I'm sure it's nothing to concern yourself with," Barrett said and touched his fingertips to her elbow.

She wished she'd not asked Callum to stay away. He could tell her every word they said, but these casters and their abilities were unknown to her. It was too dangerous, too much risk, which is why calling him to her now was out of the question. Rowan approached Henrik, drawing him away from Winston, as Riley came toward Camilla and Barrett.

"There is a matter of some urgency," Riley said. "I will be escorting you and your father to your quarters."

"If there is danger, you should see Lady Camilla to safety first," Barrett protested and stepped to the side.

"Barrett." They turned to see Winston approaching with Henrik at his side. "Our hosts have a family matter to attend to and we must inform Elaine of the delay in her nuptials." Barrett gave one stiff nod and moved to his father's side. "We can see ourselves to our night quarters, Henrik. Lady Camilla," he said and took her hand. His was tacky with sweat as he raised hers to his lips to press a kiss on her knuckles that lingered longer than propriety dictated.

"Goodnight, Mr. Cleary," she said, easing her hand back. "Barrett."

Grandfather waved them away when they paused to speak with him. His jaw was set, his eyes hard as flint. He knew about Marceline, more, Camilla would wager the hit of thunder was hers and she'd been caught. That's why he'd sent their guests away, so they couldn't witness his wife's betrayal. Tamara was mistaken or Grandfather was a very good actor.

"Camilla—" The sound of the main doors being flung open echoed through the great hall before he could finish his sentence.

Grandfather cursed and shoved her behind him just as four men came into view. They were strangers to her and scantily clothed. They were wild-looking with their bare chests stained with dirt and blood, hair hanging to the middle of their backs tangled and plaited. One of the men, the biggest and angriest of the four, wasn't at Westwood of his own free will. He was dangled by the arms between two men and a third bent at the knees to use his fists against their captive's ribs when he thrashed.

"Grayson," Grandfather said and stepped forward with blue fire snapping at his curled fingertips. "You charge into Westwood Castle?"

"We do as we like now," the man in front said. The other two tossed the captive onto the floor hard enough to bounce his face on the stones.

"Truly? This is not the male I asked you to retrieve."

The male in question managed to raise onto his hands and knees with great effort and pain, if his contorted features were to be believed. Grandfather knocked him back down with power hard enough that Camilla heard the sickening snap of his spine. He lay motionless. She swallowed reflexively, taking small retreating steps backward, just stifling a scream when her arm was caught.

Rowan, with his brother at his side. Almost in unison, they shook their heads. Rowan looked angry, as usual, but Riley touched a finger to his lips and winked. Rowan leaned down without taking his eyes from the strangers still arguing with grandfather. "If I tell you to run, do it."

"He was unavailable," the lead male, this Grayson, said. "As was a great majority of the pack. This is the second in command." Camilla jerked straight when she realized these men weren't men at all, they were animals. Werewolves. "He didn't give us a name, I'm afraid. Perhaps you'll have better success."

"Second is not alpha," Grandfather shouted. "Our arrangement is void. Blacke remains mine." Camilla stiffened again. The twins noticed her reaction because they were instantly closer on both sides. An admission. Not just seeing what was done to the creatures and hearing it was him. He admitted it.

"I think not." Camilla waited for the smug expression on this Grayson's face to get him killed. "We will have our alpha so we may grant him mercy and then *we* will choose the next on our own terms." He put his fingers to his mouth and let out a sharp whistle. More footsteps and then two more men came with Marceline between them. "Found something of yours. Give me what I demand, and not only will I give her back, but I'll tell you where we found her. Trust me, you will be interested."

Marceline struggled and made furious sounds behind the filthy gag between her teeth. Not just caught but caught by creatures outside of this household. Camilla's heart was beating so hard and fast she was sure it would call attention to her spying any moment.

"Traitorous whore," Henrik said and slapped Marceline hard across the face. To strike her was bad enough, but for him to do it while she was bound, gagged, and held by two men was abysmal. "Your head," he said and spat at her.

"Of course, we could always take her back with us," Grayson said and lifted her hair to his nose. "She's a fetching lass. The pack will be consoled, I'd wager."

"Rowan, Riley," Grandfather snapped and turned heated eyes that narrowed further when he saw Camilla standing between them. "See Camilla to her chambers," he said like a threat. "And then come retrieve your queen."

∼

"Take your eyes from my granddaughter or lose them, wolf."

"Thomas," Grayson admonished and the wolf finally removed his salacious gaze from Camilla. "Your queen and the second in command for our alpha and the right to run our own pack." Grayson took Marceline from the other two and hauled her within reach. "And no member of our pack is to be made one of your creatures again."

Marceline wasn't crying or looking upon him for help, she was pure and unadulterated hatred under all that filth. He returned her glare until her chin lifted. To anyone watching it was a show of defiance, but to Eirnen it was a nod. Amusing and useful, his wife.

"Do we have a bargain?" Grayson said and pulled her back a few inches.

"Keep the bitch," Henrik said.

"We have a bargain," Eirnen said and Marceline was flung into him. If he hadn't steadied her, she'd have knocked them both to the floor. She stunk of wolves and the mildewed earth that clung to her hair and tattered gown.

"Where?" Henrik demanded.

"In Abel's bed," Thomas said with a wide, satisfied smile.

"Watch them," Eirnen said to Henrik and drug Marceline through the great hall. She fought. He tightened his hold and dragged her all the faster.

Once they were out of sight, he slung her around into the

servant's stairwell. Her back hit the wall and he pinned her there with his lower body. Mumbled protests came from behind the gag. "I think I like this," he said and ran his fingers over the material. More cursing and he tried to not chuckle at her. He had to admit, he'd missed her. "Quiet," he reminded her and untied the knot behind her head.

"Revolting." She worked her jaws, her face scrunched up in distaste. "I want those wolves dead, Eirnen. They dragged me around like a toy. I have scratches and bruises. They had no respect and were too stupid to understand that I could strike them down. We've no need for that kind of ignorance."

"Who won our wager?" he asked.

"You already know you did, you arrogant bastard. He was ready for me, didn't believe my plea for asylum. Which also means, he'll move his camp once he's finished with the gigantes."

Marceline thought to kill Abel herself, and Eirnen had granted her permission to do so *after* he raided the gigantes for Eirnen. He'd known she hadn't the ability. If she had, she'd have done it while she'd been in his capture all those years before coming here. It was unfortunate that Abel hadn't bought her act, however. Now he had no leads as to where Abel might regroup his camp. But it did make the wolves' opportunity to "capture" her and return her from Abel's clutches as leverage easier. Too easy. Eirnen cocked his head to assess her expression. She swallowed hard, the lift of her chin prideful.

"Tell me, sweet Marceline, how was it the wolves managed to pry you from Abel's grasp? After all, my stealing you from him was the final catalyst to set him in a warring mood. I'd think he'd keep a tighter hold on something so treasured."

"Firstly, do not ever call me that again. Secondly, you did not steal me. I am not an object nor am I your possession. I chose you."

His smile widened. "His rejection was humiliating, I see. Tell me, let me soothe your sting, tell me what he said."

"Never."

"He left you as a treat for the pack, didn't he? That's how my wolves got you but not Abel. He left you to go to the gigantes camp." She bared her teeth at him. He was right. "I can't say your return to me isn't pleasurable."

He moved a lock of dark hair that found its way into her mouth, ignoring her threatening looks. The wolves brought him the second, Marceline was returned, Abel was out making himself a new enemy and, hopefully, Eirnen new allies. Not a total loss.

"Open your mouth," he said and put the gag back to her lips. "My prize of victory demands it," he said.

"Wait," she said and turned away from the gag. "Camilla has been to the gardens. I saw her the night I left here."

"Open your mouth," he said between his teeth. "I have Shaughnessy and his ally Marion in the dungeons," he explained while he tied a knot behind her head. "You're going to enjoy the same accommodations for a day or two and listen to their every word for something that may be of use to me."

Her eyes widened then narrowed. Knowing his wife, she'd had dreams of a hot bath after her time with first Abel and then the wolves. Footsteps approached and he needed her angry, livid with him if Shaughnessy was to believe them in discord. Plus, it was her bad luck that she'd been the messenger of Camilla's withholding. She'd left the castle, seen the creatures, and had witnessed Marceline's departure yet had spoken of none of it.

"Tell me, sweet Marceline, did Abel have you? Let you beg him for asylum with your body as payment before he revealed he'd no longer have you?" She bucked against him, snarling behind the gag. He took her arm and steered her back into the hall. Rowan and Riley appeared a moment later and he shoved her at them. "Put her in the dungeon."

The wolves were waiting when he returned to the great room. "I will take you to your alpha," he said to Grayson.

"You take him nowhere without me," Thomas said and came to stand before Eirnen, looking the picture of defiance.

"Very well," Eirnen said. The look on Thomas's face once they were in the gardens should be priceless.

It wasn't a long trek through the back gates and Eirnen knew the path well. He was also used to the sounds, the yips and snarls of fighting. His acquaintances were not. They bristled at every snap of a twig. Thomas kept his claws unsheathed as if an attack was imminent. Eirnen couldn't promise anything. The servants may not have fed the flowers today. They broke into the clearing where the feeding troughs were set as well as a bench. Marceline did have an uncanny fascination with the beasts and enjoyed watching them. He thought it was good for her to see what he was capable of, to remind her to stay loyal.

Grayson and Thomas rushed past him, their keen eyes scanning the clearing and the woods beyond where movement surrounded them. They lifted their faces, trying to scent Blacke. Unsurprisingly, Grayson was the first to locate him. He ran between two tall cedars with Thomas on his heels. There was a low growl followed by a cry of pain. Did he forget to tell them the pets bite?

"Blacke, stop. Please," Grayson said.

"Sara?" Oops. "You son of a bitch," Thomas bellowed a moment before he lunged into the clearing all canines and claws. Eirnen threw a ball of blue fire that sent him flying back. The wolf was furious and now injured, doubly so. He sprung from the ground and came again. This time Eirnen stretched a hand and closed his fingers as if the wolf's neck were already between them. Thomas stopped, eyes widening, then tore at his own throat in an attempt to relieve the pressure there.

"Not the smartest of creatures, are you?" Eirnen tightened his fingers in the air another fraction. Blood vessels burst in the exposed whites of Thomas's eyes, his claws continued to rake his skin, but the motions were slowing. "You never relinquish your leverage until the time you have what you want and are in a position to leave with your lives."

"I do have one more bit of information," Grayson said as he stepped out of the trees, his hands red and dripping. "Drop Thomas. My other wolves are already gone, far out of the reach of your assassins. I'd imagine your twin killers are rather bored."

"You surprise me, wolf," Eirnen admitted. Then again, he expected little so it took little for them to do so. He brought his power back to himself, dropping Thomas to the ground to figure out how to breathe. "What is it you want for this information?"

"Your word that Thomas and I leave here and there will be no retaliation because of your wounded pride at being bested."

"Bested?" Eirnen laughed. "You have bested no one. Whatever bit of gossip you possess is also known by my sweet wife. I entertain this because I'm intrigued by your tenacity, nothing more. If safe passage is all you require, it is granted. As I have said, you and I would make a formidable pair. I do hope you win alpha."

"Sara," Thomas croaked and struggled to get to his feet. It took several tries, but he managed with a firm hold on Grayson's proffered forearm.

"If you wish to give mercy to your bitch as well, you may. I have no use for her any longer. Leave the carcasses, the others need to eat." Grayson did well in hiding his disgust. Thomas didn't even try. "Tell me this information so we can be done with this. I have other matters to attend."

"First, tell me how you came to have Sara. The truth."

"Offered by your former alpha freely," he said. "Blacke was as eager to win this war as I, though for his own reasons of course. What was her name?" Eirnen asked and tapped his chin. "Oh, yes, Cynthia. The mate who left him for the alpha of Abel's pack."

"What do you know of Cynthia?" Grayson's closed fists shook as he took a step forward.

"Very good, wolf. I was beginning to suspect there was no fire in you at all. Bravo." Eirnen sat on the bench and crossed his legs at the knee. "The truth, as you requested, is that Blacke came to me. Apparently, his young mate fled from him to be with her lover. The alpha I requested you bring me."

"What happened to her?" His tone was more subdued. He didn't know Blacke had been withholding from his wolves.

"Tit for tat, Grayson."

"The other wolves, the alpha and most of Abel's pack, were traveling to the valley where the gigantes live, led by Abel himself. Your female told Abel you wanted the gigantes, to somehow turn them into a tool to defeat him. He means to see that doesn't happen. Now tell me what you know of Cynthia."

"I see," Eirnen said with a wide smile. "Your Blacke came to me, sniveling and crying with her blood still on his hands. It seems Loke, the other alpha, didn't take to the idea of having someone that had already turned traitor against her mated male as a member of his pack. He let his wolves use her until there wasn't much left and then brought her home where her mate also rejected her and showed his displeasure by tearing out her heart."

"Lies," Grayson said without conviction.

"Your kind can smell a falsehood as if it were a bleeding wound. You know I speak the truth. Blacke wanted his revenge for what they did to her and he wanted it no matter the cost. Sara was not the first of his wolves he offered, though she was the first to live. Blacke offered himself because he believed he was powerful enough to withstand the conversion and would have the ability afterward to rip Loke's pack apart."

"The other wolves will follow our scent here," Grayson said as he turned to go into the woods, presumably to find Thomas. "They will come for their second."

Eirnen supposed that was a bonus for answering questions he must have had long before tonight. It wasn't lies that cause the most pain, it was the truth. The thought brought his mind around to Camilla and what she'd heard. He went back down the path, leaving the pups to find their way home. He replayed the conversations from the start to seeing her standing there with that lost expression. She'd heard plenty.

He stopped at his crossroads for the night. Did he go to speak with Camilla, ease her, maybe offer an explanation, or did he go to Marceline and Shaughnessy? Camilla needed time, he decided, and took the hall that would lead to the stairwell to the dungeon. She would understand why he did the things he did. She must. He would give her this time and then he would speak to her as an adult rather than continue to shelter her as a child. Gods knew she'd seen enough depravity these weeks to corrupt the innocence he'd fought so hard to protect.

There was power in Camilla, buried but potent. He'd find a way to bring it out of her. He wouldn't strike her as Henrik had. She'd serve him out of love and the desire to please him. He would explain and she would understand. After all, what did she hear? A few harsh words? Males in a quarrel forgetting the presence of a lady, nothing more. The creatures? Would take some thought.

The familiar sounds of rage behind a gag made him quicken his steps. He suspected Henrik was feeding his sadistic nature with Marceline and worked to control his temper. What if he'd gone to Camilla instead? How far would Henrik have gone with Marceline? He'd have killed her, or very nearly so, and called it justice delivered to a traitor because he didn't know she was an accomplice.

The dungeon now had enemies inside, no good would come of showing contention between Eirnen and his son. He came to the door and took a moment to solidify control. Shaughnessy would scent emotions in one breath and use them as a weapon. He was an old master and not one to be toyed with. Eirnen understood this perfectly. Henrik did as well, but the stress of the last weeks was threatening to break his heir.

Marceline was bound, dangling by the wrists and pulled high

enough that her toes barely touched the floor. Henrik jerked back from her in guilt when he heard Eirnen come inside, but it was too late. Eirnen had already seen his son's hands on his wife. Red lines ringed her arms like branding bands from Henrik's use of his power. He could have decapitated her with it had he wished. As suspected, Shaughnessy grinned like a madman where he was staked to the opposite wall.

"Oh, my memory," Eirnen said and took slow steps to the still form bound not six feet from where Marceline hung. He grabbed the hair on the back of Marion's head and brought her face up. She was alive, but only just. The breath sawing in and out of her was harsh, noisy, and her eyes didn't open. "I completely forgot I left this little thing burning." He dropped her head and wiped his hand on his slacks in disgust.

Shaughnessy bared his considerable fangs and fought the stakes that riddled his body until dark blood poured down his bare stomach. "Father," Henrik said, voice both guilty and apologetic. Eirnen wanted to thrash him.

"No need, son," Eirnen said and waved him away from Marceline to take his place in front of her. She was nude, not one shred of clothing to conceal her form from Henrik, Shaughnessy, or the yet-to-be-named wolf who appeared to be unconscious. It was a humiliation that she would not bow to, no matter what Henrik thought. Marceline was very prideful of her body. She was exquisite and she knew it.

"Eirnen," she whispered, but before he could wonder if Henrik had tamed her already, her eyes opened. They were dark pits of hatred and fire and no doubt had her binds not also contained her power she'd have burnt him where he stood. "Your boy has strong hands," she purred.

"Father, she may this moment be with Abel's bastard," Henrik said and opened a line across the perfect, golden skin of her abdomen.

"No, she is not. There are yet three days before the herbs she took to prevent pregnancy are out of her system. My wolves found her in time, didn't they, wife? Any babe in her belly will be mine."

"I will tear it from my womb with my bare hands," she screeched.

"Enough of this. That matter is resolved. Now, how is it you came to know of Henrik's desire to use gigantes?" Henrik spluttered and Marceline cackled laughter. "Oh, yes, my son. At this moment Abel's forces are laying waste to the gigantes clan."

"Father, you must let me go see if even one can be spared. Please. This may be our last chance if Shaughnessy is not strong enough."

"He will be," Eirnen said with certainty.

"Or I'll be the prettiest flower in your garden," Shaughnessy said from behind them. "Tick tock, little Westwood," he taunted. Of course Henrik was fool enough to dive after the bait.

Eirnen placed a restraining hand on his son's shoulder and met his eyes, conveying his displeasure with his lack of self-control. Henrik closed his eyes and tension left his body under Eirnen's hand on an exhale.

Henrik bit his lower lip and began to pace as he thought of a different angle. "Even if they're not needed for the conversion, they could still be of use if any survived. They will want revenge on Abel now as well and will fight on our side. Their strength could aid us against Abel's wolves."

"You say 'they', yet you aren't certain that even one still lives. One would hardly be an asset, nor would five or six when wagered against the risk of retrieving them."

"We must try." Henrik's jaw set and Eirnen recognized the expression for what it was. On this, he would not relent. There were times when Henrik disagreed and no arguments could sway him. In truth, Eirnen felt pride in those moments. It was a relief to see a glimmer of the son he'd raised. This would work.

"Very well. I fear it is a fool's errand, but if this is what you feel you must do, then go with my blessing."

"Thank you, Father," he said and bowed at the waist. "I'll gather the guard and leave at once."

"You may take fifty of my guard with the exception of Rowan and Riley. If these gigantes will be as thirsty for Abel's blood as you suspect, it shouldn't come to a fight to bring them to our side."

Henrik bowed again and bounded up the stairs with the joy of a child with a new bauble.

"Does he know he just fought for the right to do exactly as you wanted him to do in the first place? And the woman—your spy—gallant effort."

Eirnen turned his smile to Shaughnessy then released Marceline.

CHAPTER 7

R ATHER THAN BEING exhausted as she should be, Camilla was energized. They'd practiced all night. Not only had she unraveled the wards, but she'd been able to whittle a hole in the wall of white to see things within the castle walls. She was on a kind of high like she'd never felt before, as if lightning were snapping through her insides. So much energy, power. Everything was simple. Replacing the wards: simple. Seeing every twist, knot, loop, and false turn placed as a trap was as obvious as if the pathway were numbered.

Before Father returned to interfere, she'd make her own bargain with Eirnen. She was ready.

"Rowan's coming," Callum warned as he appeared next to her dressing table. "Riley isn't with him."

"There's something wrong with that?" she whispered and pinned her hair high on the crown of her head.

"Yes. Especially since he's coming to your private quarters. Has he ever done that before?"

"Well, no, but the servants are all busy tending our guests this morning. That's probably why."

The gold necklace with the drop of rare tanzanite that dangled low on her chest went around her neck. The deep blue color of the precious stone was the same as the eyes of a Westwood. Each member of the Westwood family had a piece of jewelry with this stone given to them. It was a symbol of family. Her mother had given her hers on her tenth birthday. Those who married into the family were given gifts with precious stones, but none were permitted to wear tanzanite.

"I think I should tell Rowan and Riley about you. I think you should speak with them."

"If what I suspect is true, we might not have a choice." Before she could ask what he meant, Rowan opened the door without knocking. He looked around the room as if expecting someone to be inside. Marceline had told her secret.

"Rowan," she said and stood. "To what do I owe the pleasure of this *abrupt* visit?"

"Forgive me, Lady Camilla," he said. If she didn't know any better she'd swear a blush stained his cheeks. "Your Grandfather has granted young Master Cleary's request for an escorted tour of the grounds. I am to accompany you."

"Challenge him," Callum whispered. "Tell him you know the other reasons he's here. Not about me or Tamara, not yet. See how he reacts first."

"Is escort the only reason you've come here?" she said and turned to select a perfume to collect her nerve. "Not to try and catch me with a male in my chambers?" She could see his reflection in her mirror, his brow furrowed. "Or, is it because Grandfather wanted to see if perhaps your talents may be of use in telling him about my ability?"

"Good, Camilla," Callum said. "Now give him a minute."

She faced him and waited while he stared at her with narrowed eyes. She'd sworn no more ignorance. She needed to know about the guards that were a near constant at Grandfather's side and

Callum had told her. Rowan dealt in strength. He could sense it, or the lack of it, in others and use it in a physical way like she drew on energies to fuel her casting power. It made him faster than most, stronger of body.

"How do you know of my ability?" he asked and she grinned at him. That wasn't something Eirnen wanted known because the enemy might find a way to counter it.

"Why should I divulge anything?" she asked. "You offer nothing in return and I know all I need about you and Riley."

"Easy, Camilla," Callum warned. "Don't even insinuate a threat to Riley."

"Why don't I put it another way," she hastened as his face drew down into a scowl. "How do I know if I tell you anything that you won't betray me to Eirnen?" She gathered her shawl and went for the door. "Perhaps we both need time to consider our positions."

⁓

Eirnen wiped the sweat from his brow with the back of his hand before he thought better of it. He laid his hand out flat, the silver-spiked knuckle cover heavy on his fingers, and saw he'd smeared blood on his face. He balled his fist and struck the wolf once again for bleeding on him.

"Abel—" the wolf coughed and then grimaced as the motion grated broken ribs "—he's right. You are a coward."

"You will not goad me into releasing you to fight. I don't want to fight," he said and connected another blow to the wolf's mangled side. The skin there gave way too easily. The bones hadn't time to tie themselves back together and now the pieces were spread farther from one another. The wolf drew in a great whooping breath and held it as if afraid to breathe. "I want your misery," he said.

"Kill me," the wolf panted. "I will tell you nothing."

"You are too valuable to kill," he said and punched the soft skin of his groin. That got a scream. He stood back, watching the blood drain from the wolf's face. The instant pain turned to fury. He hit him again.

"Please, stop," Marion whimpered from her place on the wall.

"Then you tell me," Eirnen cooed. "Tell me how this war is to be won and I'll not strike him again."

"Marion," Shaughnessy warned and Eirnen felt his lips curl at the edges.

"Death," Marion whispered and Shaughnessy snarled. Eirnen turned and cut him off, coiling power around his neck. "This war will be a Westwood victory won by death. It will rise up and swallow all in its path. It will lead an army of damned. The night will weep with their screams of anguish when as one they fall."

Eirnen loosened Shaughnessy enough to hear him growl. Of course there would be deaths, many, and in her precious emission Marion had said he'd be victorious. She spoke of death as if it were a person or persons. Army of the damned? He turned his attention to Shaughnessy.

"Your kind are known as the damned, are they not?" he asked and the vampire's teeth came together with an audible snap.

Some believed them to be death animated, although anyone who'd met a pure necromancer would adjust their thinking. Eirnen recalled tales told to him by his grandfather of hundreds of corpses rising from the ground, in various stages of rot, and walking the earth at their master's command. They descended upon the land like locusts, destroying anything in their path. His grandfather's armies cut them down, and yet the pieces continued to crawl and wriggle to do the bidding of the one who controlled them.

They discovered the way to kill the walking dead was fire and lots of it. Some of the men had sworn even the ash shifted toward them. The only sure way to destroy the dead was to destroy their master. There was one necromancer left in this world tucked away so tightly she may yet be useless, but Eirnen couldn't bring himself to extinguish such power. Not until he found a way to harness it, command and control it.

Had someone managed to locate and loose her? Was that the Death Marion spoke of? No. Impossible. None alive, save for him, knew where her prison was hidden. He'd feel it if the tie to her cell were broken, which meant she was as yet secure and would not be winning this war for him. His grandfather said he barely managed to imprison the necromancer the first time and he was not a humble man. To admit such a thing, it must have been a harrowing feat. If she had been freed, or was to be freed, this war would most certainly not end in a Westwood victory as Marion said. Therefore, it had to be Shaughnessy. He'd have a vampire army.

The catalyst for the change from human to vampire was death. Vampirism reanimated the body. Therefore, Shaughnessy and those like him were death animated.

Eirnen clasped his hands before him and laughed. "You are to be my success," he said wiping the wolf's blood across Shaughnessy's lips. "I need you strong."

He left the guards with instructions on the vampire's feedings and how he was to be dealt with should he become uncooperative. He then sent his hunters out to find humans, lots of humans, an army's worth. Vampires had long been hunted until they left the area or were killed. He hadn't time to track them over the continent, therefore he would use Shaughnessy to create more. With those powerless creatures multiplying and spreading like a plague, finding humans wasn't going to be difficult.

Eirnen needed to go to his chambers to make himself presentable. He had to speak with Rowan to learn what he'd discovered before he went to speak to Camilla. In truth, part of him thought it despicable to resort to trickery against Camilla. The larger, more vocal and strategic part of him thought it despicable that she'd forced him to this level. She was hiding something more from him and that meant he'd lost some of the trust he had for her.

She didn't understand, her mind unable to fathom the number of beings who had tried to hold their secrets from him. He knew the eyes of the guilty, the body language all the way to the set of a mouth determined to stay closed. The very energy around them told a tale and Camilla's had been boiling with turmoil as her secrets ate at her. Many far more adept at deception had broken in the dungeons, but that was a length he wouldn't take with her. He didn't need it.

He wished she'd not seen the creatures. Now that she had, she was confused, maybe even a little afraid of him. That saddened him greatly. He didn't want her to fear him, but if the damage was already done there could be an advantage to be found.

He looked out the window over the grounds. Her dress was the palest blue and glimmered like ice in the sun. Barrett was, by all appearances, completely enraptured by her. His eyes didn't leave her. He found small ways to touch her. His Camilla was truly a treasure. She was sweet, gentle. No wonder she'd been frightened into silence. This was his doing and he would find a way to repair it.

Callum was doing a great job of helping Camilla learn to school her expressions, as Grandfather called it. While Barrett described the beauty of Gladen, Callum poked fun at him. Neither Barrett nor Rowan could see or sense Callum, or at least she didn't think so. Rowan's brows dipped and rose as if he were having a conversation with himself in his head. She wondered what he was talking about. If he could sense power, as Callum said, perhaps he was sensing something of Callum here now. But it wasn't as if she could ask.

They'd walked the paths in the flower garden on the front lawns. This was where Barrett revealed that he was a cultivist and demonstrated by hovering his hand over the turned soil until a rose the exact shade of blue as her eyes sprouted from the ground. He'd presented it to her with a bow. Callum snorted all the while.

"He has no intention of having you as a stepmother," Callum commented. She had to agree though that's what Barrett had said when she inquired as to the invitation for an outing. He wanted to get to know her better since she was soon to join his household, he'd said.

Slowly, too slowly, they were making their way back toward the castle. It wasn't that she didn't like Barrett, but she had no intention of going to Gladen as his stepmother or wife or even as a visitor, for that matter. His flirtations made it clear enough even to her that his affections weren't that of a potential son. The prospect was strange enough, Barrett was only a year her junior.

"Barrett." They looked up and saw Elaine waving from the doorway. They quickened their steps and as soon as they were close, Elaine gasped at the rose Camilla still held. "Oh, it's beautiful. I was going to ask Barrett for white and pink ones for the ceremony, but may I please have some in this shade? I am to be a Westwood, too, now. I think it would be a lovely sentiment."

"I agree and by all means," Camilla said. Elaine hugged Camilla, thanking her, before taking Barrett inside, still talking about the flowers she wanted.

Camilla watched them, Elaine talking and clasping her hands in excitement while Barrett nodded, until they were no longer in sight.

"She seems happy enough," Camilla commented in the silence.

"She doesn't know any better," Rowan answered, surprising her.

Rowan, though he seemed much older than her, really wasn't. She remembered seeing him and his brother once or twice when the three of them were all children, she'd thought they were the sons of one of the servants. They hadn't had the scars then, the ones she'd been studying as much as she could without being obvious today. She now knew where they came from. They weren't battle wounds, not all of them. Riley, she recalled, had a spiral on his face. Rowan's face was clear of scars, but his arms were covered in delicate Xs and bands that circled around to connect on the other side.

"Henrik gave you those, didn't he?" she asked and nodded toward his arm.

"To tell us apart," Rowan answered.

She worried her bottom lip. She wanted to tell him about Callum. They'd been friends. The brothers had to know he'd been killed, maybe even how, and she knew Callum wanted to talk with them again. But, being as close to her as he was now, Callum could reveal himself if that's what he wanted. He wasn't doing so and it wasn't her place to decide for him.

"Rowan," a male voice called once they were at the top of the stairs, nearing her quarters. "Riley has been injured sparring."

"Go," she said when he looked torn. "See to Riley," she said and started for the door to her quarters. He waited anyway until she was in front of her door before he ran down the stairs and to his brother.

"I think we can trust them, but it's not me who's in jeopardy if I'm wrong," Callum said once they were alone.

"Is that why you haven't revealed yourself to them, because of me?"

There was a knock, then the door opened before she could speak. Winston Cleary was on the other side. "That is a unique flower, Lady Camilla," he said. "Did Barrett grace you with a showing on your outing together?"

"Mr. Cleary, it is improper for you to be at my chamber door."

"I've come only to request your company on a tour of my own. You are my fiancé, my betrothed, mine by right."

"Not yet," she said. "And as this is improper, I bid you to take your leave now."

"Camilla"—Callum said, his tone a mixture of anger and nerves—"shout for Rowan." He'd never hear her and all three of them knew it.

"When I've only just now managed to get you all to myself?" He took a few steps inside, turned and closed the door. She came up against the table behind her and began groping its top for a weapon of some kind. "You can't imagine how pleased I am to finally witness the beauty I've only heard about before. Do me the honor of a private walk," he hooked his elbow around hers.

"You would do well to not take such liberties, Mr. Cleary," she said and jerked her arm away. He grabbed it back, just above the elbow, and tucked it between them.

"It's rude to deny the simple requests of esteemed guests and since I *am* your fiancé, I must insist that we have privacy to discuss our impending nuptials." He stroked her inner arm with his finger and leaned in closer. "A ceremony in the famed rose gardens of Gladen, where there's a pool as blue as your eyes."

"Stop," she said and planted her feet when he started tugging her toward the bed. "Mr. Cleary," she said and slapped his face with her free hand as hard as she could.

"Henrik has told me of your stubbornness, but I will break you of it." She wrenched her arm from him again and turned to leave. His hands closed around her upper arms. is Fingers pinched. She was tired of being bruised by men.

"You will break me of nothing. Enjoy this feeling of your hands on me, because you will get no other."

He leaned in close, inhaling deep at her neck. "Soon, I will. You will wriggle and squeal beneath me and Eirnen will not be there to stop me from having every corner of your tender body." Something wet probed at her ear and he groaned, pushing his hips against her. "Can you feel me, lass," he said as she fought to free her arms.

Camilla's mouth went dry as his hands began to wander, pushing past any barriers her constricting clothing formed. "Please, stop," she gasped as her vision pulsed. Her plea made him all the more eager.

Winston was still talking, still moving against her, but her world tunneled and he was on the outside of it. His voice took on the same warped quality as the voices of the victims of Westwood as the tunnel walls pulsed. Callum was in this tunnel with her and, surprisingly, so was Tamara. She was already pulling them to her in smoky ribbons with no thought as to what to do with the energies once she had them. Save it, Grandfather had said so that's what she did.

Their energies intertwined, adding to her own yet still distinct. She could feel Callum's, warm but also angry. Tamara's was a scalding fury. Camilla couldn't feel him against her anymore, not through the barriers of this glorious tunnel. All she could feel was the power swirling into a howling storm, a ripping, tearing funnel cloud of destructive power with her at the helm. All she had to do was let it go, just as Grandfather had said.

Her head fell back and her eyes closed. The wind screamed. In her head, she saw the tree at Gladen from the vision and she laughed while branches twisted and snapped under the assault. Power flowed out from her chest, whipping her hair around her body like a cocoon. Her fingers spread wide. If she closed them the life she held there would be crushed. She could feel it fluttering against her palm, the pace quickened until it was more like fast-beating wings than a heart.

Camilla's body jerked forward and she hit a wall. It was warm and hard under her hands. She struck out again with this newfound strength. A groan of pain came to her, then hands caught her by the shoulders, shaking her hard enough to snap her head back and forth. She growled and twisted the limbs again until they broke.

"Camilla"—a low voice said as if to get her attention—"you must stop."

All the strength left her in a flood. She was caught around the waist before her knees connected with the floor and was up against a muscled chest that she followed up to an equally hard face. Rowan. He'd weakened her to protect himself.

"I…" he met her eyes and gave the smallest shake of his head. She clamped her lips tight on what she thought might have been an apology or perhaps an admission of guilt. "Thank you."

He had her folded against his side with one arm, the other made a line paralleled by the wooden staff of the glaive that was always with him. It continued past where his fist gripped it hard enough to make his knuckles white and ended with the sharp point against Winston's neck. Winston was still alive, but his arms and legs were twisted in unnatural positions that made bile rise in her throat.

His pale skin sheened in sweat, lips drawn to a thin line, and spasms he couldn't seem to stop caused his breath to come in short, shaking bursts. She'd done that to him, to another person. She'd been unable to stop herself, didn't think to find the will to do so. She'd laughed while he screamed his agony. She'd never felt the tie to the Westwood blood in her veins as potently as she did at this moment.

If Rowan hadn't stopped her, she would have continued on the path of breaking each part of Winston Cleary, saving the killing injury for last to drink in his suffering. And it was his suffering she drew power and strength from, not just the death as she'd thought. The death was merely the grand finale of a glorious symphony. She rebelled hard against the desire to finish it despite no longer having the coward's image of a tree and only the man, the enemy, that deserved to be broken, at her feet.

"Don't kill him," she begged of Rowan. The monster inside her gave a scream. "I'll be lost," she whispered when the tension continued to roil from him without hesitation.

Rowan's chest heaved under her face and then his glaive arm lost some of the tight cording as he relaxed it with the decision. "I should kill you," he said to Winston with the blade still at his neck. "When you're questioned about how this happened, you're to say that I broke your bones for touching Lady Camilla without consent."

Winston opened his mouth and the blade pressed tight again. Blood welled to fall on the stones under him in fat drops.

"You will speak of Lady Camilla's involvement to no one or what you have suffered this day will be nothing once I put Barrett under my blade again. How many strips of flesh will you see shaved from your son before you beg me for your turn? It won't save him and I won't spare him, but I think you will plead with first blood."

Rowan and Winston continued to stare at each other, measure one another, even as the sounds of shuffling feet echoed toward them. Winston was the first to relent, letting his eyes flicker back at the door and whoever was approaching. Camilla dared not breathe for fear of drawing Winston's attention. If he thought Rowan was bluffing, he was a fool. To her surprise and horror, Winston barked laughter that was as pain-filled as it was dark.

"I will possess her and all that she is in the end," he gasped through a pained grimace. "You make it easier to pry her from Eirnen's grasp with this coerced lie."

"Look away," Rowan said and let go of her. She ducked her head but didn't do as he asked. He flipped the glaive and drove one hard jab into Winston's temple. His head lolled, his mouth opened, but his chest moved with breathing. "Riley wasn't injured. That was Winston's lie to get me to leave you before I replaced your wards. I apologize, Lady Camilla."

"Please, don't apologize to me, Rowan. I can't take it. Not now."

"Very well," he said. "I must get Riley to tend his injuries."

"Camilla?" Eirnen came rushing to her side and drew her away from Rowan. He looked down at Winston's body and then at Camilla's face. "Explain," he said to Rowan and hugged Camilla tighter against his side.

Rowan didn't answer immediately, he was giving her the chance to do so, to go along with the lie he'd bullied out of Winston. They were spared a few more seconds when Riley came into the room, but Grandfather was getting more and more tense.

"Mister Cleary took liberties not afforded him," Camilla said as fast as she could. "Rowan saved me." All truth, less a detail or two.

"Rowan, how was it Winston was able to take such liberties if she were in your care?"

"Mr. Cleary persuaded one of the guard to deliver a lie of my brother being injured. I waited until Lady Camilla was behind her door but did not replace the wards. Once I knew of the lie, I suspected and returned. Mr. Cleary was treating Lady Camilla indecently. She requested he stop. He did not. Now he is incapable of molesting her in such a fashion."

"Is this true?" he asked and she nodded without taking her eyes from Rowan's face. "You should not have left her unprotected!"

"No, Grandfather, please. It wasn't his fault," she said and pushed out of his embrace to stand between him and Rowan. "I told him to go. The blame is with Mr. Cleary and myself, no one else."

Eirnen didn't pay her any attention. His furious gaze stayed on Rowan. "You and Riley take Winston to his quarters and heal him. Do not allow Barrett or Elaine to see him broken and then I will speak with you alone, Rowan."

The sound of bone grating on bone as they lifted Winston from the floor was awful enough it somehow made her teeth ache. Once they were gone, Grandfather closed the door.

"Are you alright?" he asked and sat in the chair that matched her vanity.

"Yes, I am," she said with as much dignity as one could feign while straightening a bodice displaced by assault. "Thanks to Rowan."

He nodded then dropped his head and pressed his palms together between his knees. "We have much to discuss, I think." He raised his face to look at her. "If you're well enough."

"I am," she said after checking again that her dress was in its proper place.

"You were never meant to witness the exchange with the wolves. The speech and actions were harsh, you must have been frightened. I am sorry you were forced to witness the uncivilized behaviors of myself and our unexpected guests. That man the wolves brought to me is another wolf and an informant for my enemy. I know you have heard the name of Abel and I can only guess what you know of this war, but I think it's time to give you the truth of it. You're a woman now whether I want to see it or not."

"Did you kill him?" she asked.

"No, I have not. I won't lie. I have taken lives when it was necessary, when someone threatened me or my family. In that, I am uncompromising, and some would say brutal. This has earned a reputation that is, for the most part, unwarranted. Anyone of those who sits in judgment of me would use everything at their disposal to protect theirs just as I have with mine. Abel wants to take it all—Westwood Castle, Calame. He wishes to enslave or kill those loyal to me. I fear the fate you will suffer should he be victorious will leave you wanting for death. You are a beautiful young woman and my granddaughter, neither will be of benefit to you in his hands."

She wasn't sure what to say. He sounded sincere, but those creatures, his experiments, what had they done that forced him to defense? What had Callum done? He had the caster girl, who Callum said was named Marion, Shaughnessy, and a wolf in the dungeons now to do it again. When? Tonight? Tomorrow? Today after he punished Rowan?

"I can't help but notice you asked of a wolf, but not Marceline. I thought the two of you had grown close."

"I know she told you of a male voice in my room after she swore she would not. I also find curiosity in that you haven't mentioned it. It makes me wonder if you didn't mean to use her to see what other secrets I may give away."

"How did you come about this information?" Eirnen asked.

"Is it true? Did you intend to continue allowing me to believe I had a friend in Marceline?"

"I don't deny I tried to give you a confidant, a woman you could speak with about what it is to be a woman. I also don't deny that I asked her to seek answers for what was occupying your mind you felt you couldn't come to me with. Nothing is ever one-sided, Camilla. A wise person gets all sides possible before striking a blow that may prove to be ill-aimed."

"I give you the same recommendation, Grandfather," she said and moved to the open center of the room. "Here is my side. It was not a suitor," she said. "Practice. I want to talk to you, but not as your granddaughter."

"Well, that will be difficult," he said and fought an indulgent smile. "But I will try."

"I wish to enter into a negotiation with you. I don't want to do it this way. I'd rather my choices in the matter be honored, but you and Henrik are forcing me to desperate measures with regards to Winston Cleary."

She was nervous, shaking, as she delivered her preamble. Interesting. "Are you going to tell me what these desperate measures you speak of might entail?"

"Not tell," she said and shook her head. "Show." He watched with narrowed eyes as she drew in a deep breath and let it out as if to center herself. Her hand came up and made the circles that were her ritual for constructing a scene. "Abel," she said and he stopped breathing.

Trees shot up around them, not just the flimsy images she usually built when not drawing energies, but as if they were standing in a grove of firs. Her power had indeed grown an astronomical amount if she were doing this on her own steam. She had to be, she wasn't drawing from him at all, though, for this, he'd give all he could stand to lose. He could smell the resin clinging to the trees and feel the breeze on his skin. A battle-worn Abel Lockley on horseback rode toward them at a fast gallop with a pack of wolves chasing behind in a wave. The number was worse than he'd feared.

"Camilla," his voice sounded choked to his ears. The image fell away and he was overcome with joy. "You have mastered this then?"

"I have," she said.

"Do it again. Show him to me again," he said and stared out at the empty room as he waited for it to fill.

"No." It wasn't until he heard the tone that he looked at her. Her shoulders were back and her head was high, her usually innocent expression hardened into a mask of neutrality. "This is of value to you. I want to know what you will pay."

"I see," he said and crossed his arms over his chest as he positioned himself to face her. "I am disappointed. The safety and lives of your family should be payment enough, yet you want to bargain. So, name your terms."

"Rowan is not to be punished," she said.

"What else?"

"Your answer first."

"Fine, Rowan will not be punished although he was derelict and it could've meant your suffering."

"No more wards on my chambers," she said.

"Those are for your protection," he answered. "They keep people out as well as keeping you in. Should Westwood fall, those wards may be your only savior. Today should've proven to you how valuable they are."

"They are my imprisonment and will be no longer."

His insides quivered with the possibilities of what she could show him, the advantage she could provide. With her and his warriors, there would be no stopping him. No waiting for an attack. He could simply send his assassins to Abel's hiding place with Camilla navigating them. Anselone would be his and next he would take Sera. He was aware that she was scrutinizing his every action and it was an effort like none he'd ever undertaken to conceal his excitement.

"Very well," he said.

"I will not be wed to Winston Cleary."

"Camilla, you do not understand what you ask."

"I do and it is nonnegotiable."

"Do you know what Winston's ability is?" She shook her head. Of course she didn't. "At his will, he could shake the very earth beneath us until Westwood Castle was reduced to dust and rubble. He is practiced, he has waged wars to keep Gladen his alone, and time again he has won with ease. I cannot forsake that power in trade for an unstable one. You've only just done this today. What is my guarantee you can sustain it?"

"I can," she said and swiped a hand through the air. No circles, no words, by thought alone Abel was before them again. His camp. She revealed his camp. Eirnen struggled to pick out any detail that would mark the location before she jerked the image away again, leaving him with nothing.

"Where was that?"

He watched her shrink back from him but in the moment was too crazed to care he'd frightened her. He had been searching for months with no hint of where Abel made his encampments, but she showed it with ease. The few places he'd appeared to have cropped up were traps where Eirnen lost many men. Even where Marceline had been taken was a temporary settlement that was long gone.

"Where?" he thundered and took her by the shoulders.

She gasped and tried to pull away, but he wouldn't loosen his grip. "You're hurting me," she said with the voice of a child on the edge of tears.

"As you hurt me," he said. "You will tell me, Camilla."

"No," she said and cried out as his fingers dug deeper. There was a surge of power around her. It was oppressing and dark, her expression changed to match it. Her face darkened as if a shadow had been cast across it. It gave her cheeks a hollowed appearance. Her long hair churned around her. Her anger may yet reveal something more.

"You mean to attack me, Granddaughter?" She blinked and that lovely face was all berries and cream once more as if he'd imagined it. "I wish I could grant what you ask," he said and released her shoulders.

"You can. You must," she said and seized his forearms. "Don't you see, as Winston's wife I will be duty-bound to serve my husband? To forsake all others and that includes you. He is a greedy man. What is to stop him from using my ability to his advantage against you?"

Stunned. That was the only excuse for why Eirnen allowed a burst of laughter to break through during these careful negotiations. "You are my granddaughter," he said and drew her against him for a hug. After a minute she softened against him as she'd always done so easily before. It pained him that she'd felt so stiff and guarded when he first reached for her, but he'd earned it. "I must apologize," he said. "You were behaving as a worthy adversary and I lost myself for a moment. I agree to your terms."

"Thank you," she said and sagged with relief.

"But tell no one. Not yet. We must take care now, Camilla, as our positions are growing more precarious."

What she demanded was steep. It was also a surprise to see her rise in strength and stubborn resolve. It was inconvenient, but it gave him pride. Three weeks ago, she'd been incapable of standing up for herself and would have crumpled under his anger. As for Winston, there was no reason to rush in either direction. As of now, Camilla had what she wanted, Winston had what he wanted and most importantly, Eirnen had what he needed.

CHAPTER 8

I T WAS ON the edge of sleep that the first of the whispers came. Camilla woke, her chambers were empty. She'd not slept properly in days, so it was within moments that she was being lulled under once more.

"Listen." the word was but a breath across her face, but Camilla recognized the speaker at once. Marion.

"There." Marion's voice breathed through Shaughnessy's head. The smile on her battered face was serene, as if a great worry had been lifted.

Shaughnessy?

"What has happened?" he asked so only Marion could hear. They'd gotten quite good at communicating in this fashion despite his aversion to it. But, necessity.

Sleeping no longer, Camilla sat up in bed and hoped the connection was not lost. She was hearing a silent conversation between Marion and Shaughnessy. Marion was sharing this with her. But why? She tucked her hair behind her ear and drew her knees to her chest, her entire focus on Marion. Another voice, this one Shaughnessy's, or rather his thoughts as Marion was hearing them.

So strange, but so intriguing. His voice was deeper than Callum's and the accent much thicker, but Camilla heard him as if she were in the room and he were speaking aloud. Marion was powerful indeed, which begged the question—why had she allowed herself to be caught? Camilla listened, waiting to hear answers.

ॐ

Marion didn't answer. She leaned against the wall and watched the ceiling like she could see through it to the floors above. Maybe she could. He was definitely in the position of disadvantage in their friendship, if you could call it that. She knew his every thought, saw his actions before he made them and the result they'd have several years into the future. Maybe to the end of time. He didn't know and she wouldn't tell him. Yet, he knew little about her with any certainty.

She claimed immortality. True immortality. In the next sentence, however, she said her death neared and there was much to be done.

One such as he had claimed immortality as well, but he could be killed. Not as easily as some but killed all the same. According to Marion, this denounces true immortality such as she possessed. He'd asked, how, if she were superior to him in her immortality, her death neared? She had answered that she'd give away pieces to be put whole again. It was at times like that he believed her to be touched with insanity. He didn't doubt how powerful she was, despite his beliefs in her mental state. He'd seen too much to deny.

Soft laughter chimed through his head. It was weak, tired, but it was music.

"I am infinite and finite all in one breath. I can feel it coming, sense it as if pieces of my soul are tugging in opposite directions until, finally, they break free. When I first came upon this plane, I felt my time of expiring coming near, though I did not know what it was. In coming here, I was given a bit of mortality. An end. Those pieces of me *scattered, I could feel myself in them, each of them simultaneously, even while soaring miles apart from one another. Some pieces were larger than others, some but specks no bigger than dust motes. It was frightful.*

"I entered wombs where a piece of me was absorbed into the growing babe and forgotten for a time. The result is the wagon psychics, the humans who are empathetic to a degree considered outside of the natural. The larger, more conscious parts, settled into the closest warmth they could find, damning them to asylums or solitude against my screaming for them to release me as if they were my jailors. I can feel them still, Shaughnessy. I love and hate them in equal measure, because they are a part of me, as if they are my children, but also the parts of me that are now theirs, are lost to me."

He listened, enraptured, but also with growing dread. She didn't tell him her secrets now for no reason. She meant to die here—or scatter the pieces, as she called it.

Camilla swallowed around a lump in her throat, sharing Shaughnessy's sadness.

"My end will come. It is unavoidable, but I have learned to hold a degree of control over where and how deeply these fragments are splintered. This cycle I have become enthralled with the Westwood legacy, with the gigantes, and with you. As harsh as it sounds, you are all a means to an end, but that does not mean I cannot help those I use.

"I was not banished here alone. I had a sister, Edythe. I cannot find her, can't sense her even though since birth we have been connected, bound. She is the other half of me and Eirnen is a direct descendant of the man who imprisoned her. She believed herself in love with him, trusted him enough to tell him what we were. That was a mistake. He imprisoned her, forced her to bear his children then stole those children from her breast to be raised as Westwood casters. He discovered we were as powerful as the sorcerers and sorceresses of old he so worshipped and used her to grow his family line in power. I must find her. Camilla is the key.

"In the end, there are simply too many choices. Too many directions

the branches of life can grow for me or anyone else to possibly see them all to their finale. I am but tying a bit of string around the vine to guide it in the direction I wish it to take. Once I am gone, for a time, the vine will go where it may. I've tied all the strings I can tie. Now, we must see if they follow the branches I've tied them to, or veer off onto other branches."

That tree. The damned tree. She was always talking about it. He stared over at her with new eyes. He was looking at the closest thing he, or anyone else he'd guess, had ever come to seeing a true goddess.

"Not a goddess," she corrected. *"Just another being, a caster as we are dubbed here, only I'm not of here."*

"How long?" he asked, sensing a loneliness in her thoughts that even he didn't yet possess although he'd lived long enough for two human lifetimes.

"Many, many, of my lifetimes, which are considerably longer than yours," she said in her cryptic way that meant he'd not get a number. *"Now, I must focus. Tonight, Shaughnessy, you leave me."*

"The girl? You're going to ask me to not kill her, aren't you? If she is the key, you were never going to let me kill her."

"As I said, tonight, you leave me. What you do after, is your choice. As what I do is mine. Take solace in knowing that though not all will end happily, it will end."

Balls.

"Camilla," Marion said and Shaughnessy's voice and thoughts faded to the background. *"You must come to me tonight. Please. Please, help me."*

⌇

She leapt from the bed and saw it was still dark outside. Good. Cover of darkness would help—assuming she could get to the dungeon undetected, release Marion from mystically reinforced bonds and then get the both of them through the castle and outside without seeing anyone. Considering the guards were on constant patrol and the night servants would be performing their duties all around the castle, she needed an advantage. Thankfully, she had one.

"Callum," she whispered once she was dressed.

"What's wrong? Why are you dressed? It's the middle of the night."

"I'm freeing Marion and I need your help," she said, grabbing her brush to pin up her hair. "Do not look at me that way, Callum. I must. I promised."

"Do you know what will happen if you're caught? Have you any inkling of what you provoke?"

"He'll be angry, yes, but he needs me. He is absolutely covetous of what we can do. He won't do anything to make me angry enough to deny him."

"I wish I were as confident about that as you are," he said.

"But I don't intend to get caught, especially if you help me."

It was a small pleasure to not feel the wards. Eirnen kept that part of their bargain even if he didn't intend to hold to the other. She'd always thought him a man of his word, but she was learning Eirnen was tricky. He had a loophole, some trick in wording he'd use when it became necessary because she was no longer more useful than Winston.

Callum's energy swirled within her. She used it to glimpse the path to the dungeons. He stayed close behind and closer still once they were descending the stairs. It was cold and damp. Water dripped somewhere at the bottom and echoed up to meet her. She stopped, giving her eyes time to adjust to the dark. It was an ominous place, full of residual pain that tore at her psyche. Howling, screaming, and begging whispered all around even though the people who'd made the sounds were dead and gone.

"Come to my web, little fly," a voice said as she took a step. Was he free? She swallowed hard and peered around the corner to meet the eyes of the man that had been drug in by the werewolves. He lunged at her, gnashing his teeth, but was propelled back by chains at his wrists and a collar around his neck. "Don't fear, lass," the voice said again. "We are quite contained, I assure you. Come closer."

She barely managed to swallow the scream building in her throat. What she'd seen was true but paled in comparison when coupled with the awful stench of sweat, blood, and bowel. They were all beaten and bloodied. Tortured, just as she'd seen. Except, of course, for Marceline who was once again in shackles, though Camilla didn't know why. The others here had seen her free, knew she wasn't a real prisoner. Perhaps another game understood only by her and Grandfather.

"Marion." She went to the girl bound to the wall. The dress she wore looked more like shredded paper than cloth. When she lifted her face to Camilla, she smiled through blood-stained teeth and split lips.

"Two to choose, one to keep. Both will rejoice and both will weep," she said and rested her head on her shoulder like a pillow. Camilla stood on her toes to reach the metal circling Marion's wrists. They wouldn't budge and there was power running through them. "I am not who you came for," she said and met Camilla's eyes again.

"You are," Camilla protested, still trying to bend metal and magic to her will. "Tell me how to open them, I know you can."

"Your legacy, as you wished. Life or death. Blood or wine. They are both delicious, are they not?" Camilla's fingers paused on the metal. "You'll be much happier with the one I chose, though you will curse me later. Yours is beautiful, an enticement not easily resisted. All branches lead to destruction. Sorry."

Two to choose... "James and Dorin," Camilla said no louder than a breath, but the girl nodded. "They weren't dreams at all, were they? It was you. Why?"

"Because it was in my power to give life to a dying path, of course." It made no sense, but she had no more time to question the caster and went back to the binds. "I will meet Dorin before you do, but, please, no jealousy. He is not my male. Three. That's a good number, two in one," the caster continued to babble even as Camilla groaned with frustration.

"Camilla," Marceline's tired voice called. "It is no use. You can't break them."

"I can," the man who must be Shaughnessy said from behind her. "Free me and I'll do what you cannot."

"No, Camilla," Marceline said. "It will be a betrayal Eirnen would not ignore. You will be punished and in the end, your sacrifice will mean nothing. He will gather more, he will not relent on this, not until he has his warriors. You must leave here now."

"You know what they plan to do with me and our snappy-jawed friend over there, Camilla."

"Don't listen to him. He lies. He's a vampire, it's his nature."

"You know. And if you do nothing to stop it, our deaths are yours just as Eirnen's," Shaughnessy urged. "It wouldn't be such a hard thing. A little tug and pull, as it were." The way he said it and the expression on his face made her think it was meant to be lascivious, but she was too overwhelmed to feel embarrassed. "Let me go, Camilla," he said with more force.

"Free him and he will drain you. He will kill you, Camilla. I know you feel sorry for him, but you mustn't. Please, trust me on this."

"Trust you," Camilla growled. "I see you, Marceline."

"He means to do this thing to us tonight and dawn nears," Shaughnessy said to accentuate the urgency. "You don't have to believe me. Get your little pet there to pop in and listen for himself." Shaughnessy nodded to Callum and they both froze. He could see him. Shaughnessy could see Callum. "Ah," he said. "Now we have a bit to wager with, don't we lass?"

Shaughnessy was staked to a wall and yet he seemed to slump

with smugness. Camilla, who was free, stood stiff and tense enough to knot the muscles across her shoulders. Should she beg him to keep quiet? It was too late to feign ignorance. A threat? But with what? To leave him on the wall where he could tell anyone he pleased? Would Grandfather believe him?

"Who's he talking about, Camilla?" Marceline asked, equally urgent. "You have to tell me. Camilla!"

Shaughnessy put his head back as much as the stakes and the wall behind him would allow and howled laughter. "Secrets, secrets. Set me loose or who knows what may spill forth from my lips. We vampires are a chatty lot, especially when we're hungry. And, lass, I'm starving."

"Camilla," Marceline said and rattled her chains. But Camilla couldn't force her eyes from Shaughnessy's. His mocking smile melted until he wore an expression that made her feel like a child. "No," Marceline, shouted. "Eirnen!"

"You must hurry, pet. She's called the cavalry." Camilla had no idea where to start or what to do to free him. The metal spikes impaling his body were flush with the wall, built into it. No latches. No release lever. How had they managed to get him on them in the first place? The ends that protruded inches from his skin were blunt and squared. "Take my hand," he said, wiggling the fingers on his left. "And yank back as hard as you can."

"Swear you won't kill me," she insisted, stepping close to him. "Your word. I will know if you are lying."

"I swear," he said between his teeth at the same time Marceline screamed, "He lies."

The metal was driven through his palm. Even if she managed to free his hand, there were other stakes in his wrist, his elbow, his shoulder, the center of his chest and all down the other side. Not to mention the ones in his thighs. She did as he asked, with the sound of Marceline's relentless screaming for Eirnen in the background.

"I can't," she said when he groaned and his hand barely moved despite her best effort.

"Camilla, don't try to use physical strength you don't have," Callum advised.

She stepped back from Shaughnessy to gather her wits, then began to pull energy from Marceline and the wolf. As much as he was fighting, he could spare them. She sent out what she'd collected to test the stakes for weakness, more power was needed. Just a little. *Tamara.* She appeared as she'd been summoned and going by the frown on her face, she wasn't happy about it. But Camilla didn't have time to play nice, not with Marceline yelling. She added Tamara's energies and felt them come together with a click like a puzzle in her head.

Both hands lifted to hover inches from Shaughnessy's upper arms, she surrounded him with power, cradled his body with it, then jerked it back to her, bringing him with it. He dropped to the floor on his knees in front of her. He was at the wall in front of the werewolf before she could draw in a breath. His back was scored with holes, but blood barely trickled from them when she'd expect much more.

"Try and attack me or the wee lass and your heart will still be beating when I pull it from your chest," he warned and clasped the cuffs. There was a groan of metal and a snap, then the wolf was free.

The wolf bared his teeth as he passed, and Camilla shrank back. He went to Marceline and struck her hard across the face without pausing to give it thought. Marceline slumped in her chains, quiet now. Camilla's attention was brought back to Shaughnessy with another snap of metal.

"Marion, open your eyes," he said. "I'm taking you from here, love."

Camilla watched the vampire cradle the caster's face in his hands. The caring gesture was in direct contradiction to everything she'd always known to be true about the species. They didn't regard any but their own with anything but disdain. The highest level another creature could rise to in their estimation was a pet. *You must hurry, pet.* That's what he'd said.

"No," Marion whispered with her eyes glittering.

"You know what Eirnen means to do with you. You can't survive it, he doesn't intend for you to, and he will find a new wolf and vampire." He brushed sweat-drenched hair back from her face and bent his knees until he was level with the much smaller girl. "I can't leave you to that. Don't ask me to."

Marion leaned in and embraced Shaughnessy with a strength Camilla didn't think she had left. There was also a finality to the gesture that pained Camilla's heart. Marion was near dead on her feet and, unfortunately, Camilla now knew this with frightening certainty. What should have been a brilliant, glimmering green aura surrounding her was murky and sluggish like tar oozing around her body. It was little more than tenacity that kept her alive now.

As she said, "I want to be the one to tell him how Westwood will fall," Camilla saw a spark of sizzling energy flash through the dimmed aura like a comet. "I told you, I will not die. Not really. And it's time."

"Shaughnessy," Camilla said. Her voice was meek and scared to her ears and seemed to incite the wolf in some way. He strode toward her, fingers curled until Shaughnessy halted him with a look. Marion's eyes met hers and instead of seeing hatred for what she'd suffered, Camilla saw a plea. "You have to go. Please. Before they catch you."

The snarl Shaughnessy gave her over his shoulder didn't match the gentleness he still held Marion with, but now she knew why the wolf had stopped. Marion covered his hands with hers and she once again had his full attention. She rose to her knees to whisper in his ear. Camilla ducked her head from the private moment. What it must be like to say goodbye in a place such as this, knowing the fate of the one you leave behind. Tears rolled down her cheeks and she wanted to demand he take her from here no matter what Marion wanted.

"I'll wait no longer, vampire," the wolf said, shattering the moment. "I suspect if I am seen, they'll not be long in checking on their other prize."

"You must go now," Marion said, moving out of Shaughnessy's arms. "Top, left, straight, stop, wait to seven, left once more. Visit the mountains, I do so love the lake." With that bit of direction, Marion's legs gave out and Shaughnessy eased her to lie on the floor. She met his eyes and slapped his hands away. "Three, two, one…"

Before the countdown was completed, Shaughnessy had Camilla in his arms and made the twenty wide stairs to the top in one swift leap. She scrambled to hang on to his shoulders even as she called for him to release her. "You're coming with me, lass. It's your choice whether you stay conscious for the journey."

Yes, all gentleness was gone from him now. They were motionless and by the time she realized they were stopped for the seven as Marion said, they were moving again. They slithered right behind Frances and Cora. Without those seconds, they would have collided with one another. Shaughnessy's hand clamped tight as iron across her mouth and was nearly as cold. Everything was happening so fast. She was so overwhelmed, the idea of screaming hadn't occurred to her until he moved to silence her.

"It's terribly rude of me, I know, but necessary if we are to successfully abduct you."

She struggled as if she hadn't known what he was doing before he said it, but it didn't do any good. His arm was locked around her and he didn't seem to notice she was fighting with all the strength she had as they moved through the castle. The last left took them outside, but he didn't slow. The air was cold and damp, colder still because of the speed with which Shaughnessy moved.

Dawn couldn't be more than a couple of hours away. Someone would discover her missing, but it was still enough time, at this pace, for him to have her miles and miles from the castle. He ran, never seeming to tire, until the cover of the trees ended. He stopped and his muscles twitched with the need to be moving again, to get as far from Westwood as possible. She couldn't blame him.

"You've gotten far enough you won't be discovered," she said and tried to get her feet on the ground, but he squeezed her tighter. "You don't need me anymore."

"I do. As I said, I'm hungry," he pulled his lips back and bared his fangs at her. She shrank away as far as she could and he smirked. "As I suspected."

"Leave her here, vampire," the werewolf said. Until then, Camilla had forgotten about him. He paced a tight circle with his hands fisted. "They will hunt her to their death. I've heard of this one. Eirnen's precious jewel. He'll not rest until she's back and will kill any he encounters on the way."

"No one said you had to come. None invited you to stay, either."

"Get yourself killed," he said and took to the east across the field.

"Put me down," she said and wiggled in his hold. "I won't try to run, I swear."

"But we need to run and be faster about it than your little caster legs can manage." He looked down at her with eyes the color of honey and full of mischief. "Besides, if you really wanted free of me, you'd have given a fair effort. Not one cast, nigh even an attempt of one against me. I suspect you're as glad to be free of Westwood Castle as I am."

She turned her face away and felt the chuckle in his chest. It was an odd sensation that reminded her she was skin-to-skin in places with a male, a *vampire* male. Heat crept up her face. It hadn't occurred to her to try casting against him. Still compliant as first instinct. She exasperated herself.

He ran, faster than she imagined anything could, but she feared it wouldn't be enough. Eirnen had likely discovered his wolf and vampire missing. As soon as Marceline came around, he'd know Camilla was gone as well and the role she played in releasing the others. That werewolf had been right. Eirnen wouldn't stop searching her out, not now that she'd given him a weapon to use.

Her heart felt like a caged thing that stopped its frantic beating every time he jumped over a fall of rocks where she couldn't see the bottom. He loosened his hold. She felt herself slipping out of his arms and scrambled to hold on to him, clinging to his shoulders with all her strength. She was terrified. A wicked smile curled his lips.

He'd sworn he wouldn't kill her. She believed he meant it at the time, but it didn't mean he couldn't change his mind. Perhaps he decided if she died of fright it was her weakness that was the death of her and no fault of his. She looked around when the trees grew thick again, squinting against the stings of her hair whipping her face. It was too dark for her to see much more than vague outlines, but he was having no difficulty. He bounded over stones and fallen trees without so much as a stumble.

If he didn't scare her as much as he did, she might have been in awe of him. She'd never seen a creature move as he did, with both strength and grace. His breathing was even, steady, though they'd been running long enough for orange to tint the horizon. She could feel the muscles in his arms and chest as he moved and see a faint luminescence to his eyes.

"Admire me all you like, lass," he said and jumped without looking from her face. He perched on a high stone ledge and cast his eyes around. "Not much farther," he said and cut a twisting path upward. *Visit the mountains*, she'd heard Marion say. He was taking her advice once again.

There was an undeniable sense of excitement to all this, an adventure. She wanted to ask if this was the famed Chesslain Woods where the amarok were rumored to be confined. But she doubted he would answer as if she were taking a tour with him as a guide.

She'd never seen the amarok in person, only sketches. In a way, it was as romantic as it was tragic the way these monsters were made. From what she'd learned, it was most often the heartbreak of losing a true mate which caused the man to retreat into the beast to escape the pain. These beasts were truly animals with no trace of their former humanity.

It was said they were bigger than the wolves that continued to hold human form and even they would die in the jaws of the amarok. Surely Shaughnessy wouldn't hide with them? If they came upon one, what would he do? What would she do? They would attack in defense of their territory. Could he beat them? Could she?

She eyed Shaughnessy's face once more. He was set, resolute in his destination. Was he as set on her fate? She took a breath and closed her eyes. She could feel him, his energies. With dawn nearing ever closer, she hoped he wouldn't waste time fighting to keep her rather than seeking shelter from the coming sun. Perhaps he'd drop her here in the middle of unfamiliar woods where any manner of creature may dwell. Cowardice. Compliant. A Westwood caster should not fear the what-if situations that resulted in escaping an enemy.

With all the skin-to-skin contact, this should be easy as dropping her guard. To keep from prematurely alerting him, she lowered her guard a fraction, enough to but sip at the power he offered. He looked down at her, leaning his face close to hers so she could watch his fangs run out to their full length, and snarled—"Mine,"—then slammed the door on her.

She could fight him for it. She could feel it in his guard. There were fissures her energies wanted to pry apart, dismantle bit by bit. Should she do it now, attack him? Could she tear his guard apart before he ripped her to pieces? Probably not. "Do you expect me to just allow you to kill me, to not even attempt to save myself?"

"You should have come upon your survival instinct sooner," he said, then everything vanished.

Darkness outside is not darkness. She blinked fast, trying to get some semblance of what surrounded her as her skin prickled with awareness. Shaughnessy's pace slowed and there were the echoed sounds of water dripping. It must be a cave. There was a sense of tightness, narrowed walls, the scent of dampness and earth.

"Shaughnessy." Though she whispered, the endless echo made it sound too loud in the space. With every step deeper into the cave, the awareness intensified. Not her imagination. "You have to go back. There's someone here. Someone powerful."

He acted as if she hadn't spoken and continued forward. The sensation grew stronger, until she let go of his shoulders to scrub hard on the skin of her arms. It seemed to make the biting itch worse, but it felt so good while she was doing it. She was moments away from saying modesty be damned and lifting the skirts to rake nails across her legs.

"You've made yourself bleed, lass," he said, his voice rougher. It stilled her mid-motion with her nails sunk into her forearm.

She didn't know what to say to that. What did someone say? She refused to beg. After a moment of stillness, she could take it no longer and with a growl resumed clawing at her skin. He'd been all but drained dry thanks to those spikes. He had to be starved. At the moment, she didn't care if he bit her as long as she didn't have to stop chasing this sting.

"Isn't this driving you mad?"

"I feel nothing." He was enjoying this and why shouldn't he? It was her family that tormented him, her family that was in all probability doing unspeakable things to Marion at this moment to force information from her. He had every right to take pleasure as she mentally deteriorated because of the crawling sting that saturated her skin. She had to admit though, going out this way was not how she'd imagined. A Westwood, defeated by an itch.

"You might want to close your eyes," he said even as his body coiled tight under her. On instinct, she wrapped both arms around his neck to hold on.

She could see nothing except the lack of earth beneath them and a sense of swallowing nothingness. She screamed, not out of fear amazingly enough, but to hold on to him meant the incessant itching and burning was gaining ground.

"You did that on purpose," she accused when she was jostled. They'd landed on solid ground. Her tongue was as sand in her mouth and burned as she spoke, her lips felt too full.

Her hands and feet plumped, swelling until there was no space between fingers or toes. It was biting and unforgiving as it burrowed deeper into her body the farther into the cave they went. She bowed in his arms, nails digging into her palms until the swollen skin popped like ripe fruit. All sense of pride and stubbornness to not beg him fell away. She'd do anything, *anything*, for a moment's relief.

"Do you hate me this much?" she cried. "This is unbearable, please!"

The words came out garbled, but she hoped he understood. The itch was no longer an itch but the burn of acid in her veins that raced its way to attack organs. Her insides felt too full, bloated, the cinch at her waist a pressure that kept her from a full breath. She was glad for the moment that she couldn't see because she knew her skin was bubbling up in blisters. She could feel them growing, testing boundaries until the skin could stretch no farther and rip open in a hot gush.

"Fuck," Shaughnessy said and started to run as he had outside. "You do not get to die yet," he yelled like she had a choice in the timeline.

The clamped teeth and whimpers gave way to ear-splitting screeches she couldn't draw in air fast enough to sustain. The blisters broke and oozed only to form new ones on the raw meat where skin used to be. It was eating her alive a little at a time. She mentally begged for him to help, to make it stop and vowed to pay any price, but the words wouldn't form around the screams. Hot, putrid liquid poured down her throat, replacing the screams with an awful bubbling and yet she tried to gasp in more air. She coughed and choked until he turned her in his arms and the fluid erupted from her open mouth as she dragged in wheezing breaths.

A too-bright light seared her eyes. She couldn't see anything but blurred light and her eyes felt wrong in their sockets, too full. Each blink was a torture to match the teeth gnawing at her insides. She gasped as she was enveloped in cold, blissful relief. For a precious second, she felt nothing but overwhelming pleasure as her body was submerged in icy water. Her face broke free and immediately she was thrown back into the fire. That was it, her breaking point. It must be, she didn't know how it would be possible to take anymore.

Her gown was torn from her body, allowing more water access to her skin and releasing the pressure around her stomach. Another taste of relief. She wouldn't waste it. "Kill me."

His hard hand clenched her jaw to turn her head. Her skin slipped and slid under his hand. She wouldn't fight him if she could. She sighed and let go when his fangs pierced her neck. It's over. He's giving mercy.

CHAPTER 9

"SHOW YOURSELF," EIRNEN thundered at the ceiling. A ghost, a lost spirit, it was the only explanation for what Marceline had witnessed. Seen by the vampire and no one else, except his precious, deceitful, granddaughter. She'd not told him, not a word regarding this development. How long? How long had she been keeping secrets and lying?

The bellowing was of no use—which he was aware of before he even started—but he was down to his last options. He'd summoned the wolves to track them only to have them return empty-handed. They'd trailed them to Basslyn Wood where the wolf had broken away from Camilla and Shaughnessy to head east. After the clearing, they could get nothing. No scent at all, which was an impossibility for a nose as keen as a werewolf's. The only answer was concealment. A cloaking of such a massive scale it would have taken more than ten casters pooling their energies to place.

That raised questions with but a few possible answers and none of them reassuring. If Shaughnessy had access to such a place, where he could be hidden so thoroughly, why did he venture from it when he knew he was being hunted? He wanted to be caught because the master vampire was anything but careless. But why? For the sole purpose of abducting Camilla? But why? To kill her to make a strike at him? At first, it seemed likely he was attempting to free his caster lover and Camilla's abduction had been opportunistic. But the caster had delivered herself to the door of the castle and he'd left her behind. None of it made sense.

Perhaps not an abduction at all, the suspicious part of his nature spurned. Camilla knew of the gardens and the creatures as well as how they were created. It was this sense of guilt and righteousness which bred the sympathy that moved her to free Shaughnessy to spare him the same fate. But there was no need! Did she not have faith in him at all? Shaughnessy could withstand the conversion should Henrik fail. And if Henrik succeeded, it was Shaughnessy's essence he wanted for his warriors.

"Marion is lost, I fear," Marceline said and licked blood from her knuckles. No wonder. For the last three days—since Camilla had been gone—Marceline had been working on the caster with a skill few possess. She was an artist with a vicious imagination that could break the strongest of men. "Riley can heal her body, but her mind will not return. Nothing but babble and silly rhymes."

"There could be some lucidity hidden amongst the rambling. Keep listening," he said. She shrugged and raised on her toes to kiss him swiftly. It wasn't enough at the moment. His arm snaked out, curling her waist to draw her back to him for a proper kiss. He poured all his fury into the motion at her mouth, biting at her lips, and she devoured it, moaning into him. "Did you moan like this for Abel, wife?"

"With thoughts of you," she said and nipped at his lower lip. "Promise me, Eirnen."

"I have given my word, is that not enough?"

"I need to hear it once more," she said and fisted his hair in her hands. "Please, once more."

"Abel is yours to kill, Marceline." She closed her eyes as if picturing it. "I swear it."

He let her go to put her considerable skill to use as only she could. She resented him for being right about her failing to kill Abel on her little trek, but she was grateful she hadn't at the same time. To have killed him in his bed would have been singular, unsatisfying. She craved to have him here amongst all the toys at her disposal. With Riley's help, Marceline could bring Abel to the brink of death again and again. He'd even heard her muse about forcing a vampire's curse on the male so even old age would not free him from her. Abel deserved everything she could dream up to do to him.

He'd murdered not only the betrothed she loved, but her mother, grandmother, young siblings, even her aunts. Every person she could use to comfort herself, to take her mind from what he did with her, anyone she had hope of running to, he stole. And he'd done it all in front of her. If she'd been capable of defeating him, she'd have done it then or when she was a prisoner. She was an unmatched beauty, which she saw as her curse. It led to Abel's obsession and had driven him to not only possess her but punish her for denying him.

Eirnen had been all too eager to release Abel's captive, to listen as she told the secrets of the invisible. Abel never thought she'd escape, never believed she'd get aid. He spoke freely in front of her as if she were a piece of furniture. And she'd run to Eirnen. Yes, she was beautiful, but her physical beauty was not what he coveted most. She knew that, was grateful to be used for more than a release. Age would steal even the most perfect face and body, but age would grace the power. He had to thank Abel for one aspect of his bride—the ruthlessness born in the time she was in his possession. His treatment of her had sparked a bit of insanity in a beautiful, useful way.

Camilla had shown him where Abel was, but it was a nondescript landscape that looked like a thousand others. If only she could show him once more. He'd learned little from those few scenes she'd conjured. Victory chants, cheers, and too much drink. He'd watched nothing more than the celebration of Abel destroying the gigantes clan. If Camilla were here, he could see if the festivities had turned to strategizing. He could see if any of the gigantes survived. How quickly he'd begun to rely on what she showed. He felt blinded and that was unacceptable.

"Rowan," he barked and the dutiful guard appeared. "What of Winston's seeker?" He loathed that Winston knew of what happened, worse that he was aware his help was required. Barrett was loyal to his father, but he should have remembered he was not in his father's house. Once Camilla was returned, he would be reminded.

"Will arrive at sunrise," he said. "The wolves tracked Abel's second as far as they could but lost him at the Hile River. They couldn't pick up his scent again. We must assume the direction was Abel's camp. The scouts are still searching but on naught but faith and luck."

"Abel's camp will be as well shielded as Shaughnessy's." Placed by the same casters for all he knew. Shaughnessy could be Abel's and if that were the case, Camilla was with the enemy. Eirnen raked a hand through his hair hard enough that he came back with strands wound between his fingers. Was Abel using Camilla to watch Eirnen right that moment? She could get through the protections, the blinds he placed to keep out prying eyes. She was strong enough to bore through them. "What of Henrik?"

"Nothing." Of course not.

He'd been so confident that he'd have Camilla's ability to use at will, he'd not taken the time from Abel to look for Henrik. He should have. That was abundantly clear now. For all he knew, Abel left some of his forces to deal with any stragglers and Henrik happened upon them. Henrik was strong and vicious in his own right. He'd be back. Whether it was with a bounty of potential warriors was another story.

He'd used his one shot with Marceline. The scouts had failed on every occasion. Finding Camilla was the only option. Winston's seeker was the way to accomplish the task, loathe as he was to find anything associated with Winston of any use.

His lips curled at the distinct sound of a feminine whimper. Marcus came through, herding several girls from the village. Not just any girls—casters, the ones connected to Shaughnessy. "Ladies," he greeted, "which of you is the least tolerant of pain?"

⁓

This, *this,* is to be the end of Eirnen Westwood? Shaughnessy stared down at the scrap of nothing lying on his bed and admitted to himself he couldn't see it. He knew better, or at least he should— casters didn't have to be physically large to be powerful. But this waif was pathetic. Not even before she'd gone through the aversion spell that caused her skin to bubble and dissolve had she looked the part of a proper caster villain. Blood healed the wounds. Blood he couldn't believe he'd spilled for a fucking Westwood.

He'd thought to cause pain and disfigurement with the aversion spell—something to make her as ugly and diseased on the outside as she was on the inside—but she'd tried to die. That more than anything told him she was no lower-level caster. Those who set the boundary spell made sure strength of ability wouldn't allow those who hunted him to push through. Just the opposite. The lower the power level, the less affected they were by the aversion spell. Some misdirected human who wandered into the cavern may have walked away with nothing more distressing than intestinal troubles or perhaps a bothersome rash. This caster was melting in his hands, boiling and putrefying from the inside out, as he carried her deeper inside. That was proof enough. She was powerful indeed. No matter how weak she looked.

Hair more white than golden reminded him of her father, Henrik. Another tiresome Westwood shit. Perhaps worse than Eirnen, for Henrik was, at his core, a coward. Eirnen was greedy. He was cruel when making a point. Henrik was cruel for the fun of it, especially to those less powerful than himself. Eirnen exerted his superiority over the man so thoroughly when he was a boy, Henrik soothed his wounds by putting others under his feet. Tormenting for sport because he was stronger and daddy made him feel weak. Stomp a foot in his direction, he'd piss himself.

Eirnen, though, was another story. Shaughnessy first met him when Calame was nothing more than a mud hole and Eirnen himself was but a boney black-haired child who looked the part of a weakling next to his warlord father and brother. Eirnen's father, Malachi, had been a master swordsman. He used his blade as an extension of his power. Shaughnessy doubted Eirnen had picked up a weapon since he'd come into his own. Then again, he didn't need to. He could turn a creature's energies, their aura of power, against them. Taking a part of them and weaponizing it, there was no escaping themselves. His ability to manipulate energies was legendary. Once, Shaughnessy had hoped it was exaggerated. He'd learned Eirnen wasn't just a hollow braggart. He could do as he claimed.

He looked down at the girl again. Her lips were purple and she was shivering. She still wasn't waking. The longer she was out, the more he believed Marion's story about the girl being stronger than Eirnen. 'Kill her now or lose your chance later. Eirnen will lose everything and she will be the cause. But should she take his path rather than one of her own, you will never stop her.'

If there was a chance, if he could truly play a part in taking everything from Eirnen Westwood, he couldn't pass up such a luscious opportunity. Marion said he had to have patience, let her see beyond the lessons of Westwood walls. She's ready, Marion said, she can see now. He'd listen to Marion, for now. He had time before

Camilla came into full power. Killing her, taking her from him would be simple but there'd be no real payoff. For Eirnen to know his end came to him at the hand of his cherished granddaughter? Delicious.

A rattled breath interrupted his blissful daydream. She was trying to die again. Damn.

❧

Camilla coughed and shook her head. Someone, something, was leaning over her. She pushed out with her hands and dug her heels into the ground to scramble backward. Shaughnessy. He sat on his haunches, watching her remember where she was and what happened. She winced at the remembered pain and brought her hands up to look for what should be layers of skin missing until bone shone through.

"Good as new," he said and ran his tongue across his wrist.

She touched her fingers to her lips and stared in horror at the red staining the tips. "Have you...am I to be...?"

"Vampire? No," he said and moved to sit with his arms draped over his knees. She remembered something else as she looked at him. "Although, the thought of doing just that to spite Eirnen has crossed my mind. He'd be positively disgusted. Enough so to kill you himself."

"You bit me," she said and her face flamed.

"I told you I was hungry."

The moment his fangs broke skin she'd been awash with heat, but not the acidic burn. That was chased away by something else. Something headier. She'd fallen against him, ran her hands over his shoulders and moaned for him, begged to have him. With the memory came an awareness of her body and the lack of covering.

"Where's my gown?" she asked, trying to force the shirt she wore—the shirt he'd dressed her in—to cover her legs. "Avert your eyes," she said as she shifted to pull the blanket from under her.

"Your gown was rancid and there wasn't much left." He'd ripped it from her in the water. Her eyes narrowed and he did as she asked until she was looking at him in profile, but she could see the smile he was trying to tamp down. "Shy are you, lass? I recall you being exquisite with abandon despite the condition of your skin."

She managed to pry the blanket from under her, then brought it up to her chin. One pallet. One bed of stacked blankets and straw. Had he… they? She remembered nothing after that embarrassing, shameful behavior. Brought on by a vampire's bite no less. If Henrik and Eirnen could see her now, they might very well banish her. Because by pure caster standards such as those held by the Westwood lineage, she was now and forever sullied by the bite alone. Contaminated beyond repair as was all offspring grown within her womb.

It made no sense that this was the belief for female casters, but not males. Male casters had been bitten on battlefields for centuries, but the bite was nothing more than another scar, another testament to their strength and how hard won the battle had been. They also gave the blood of a vampire to both the males and females, yet the bite was a sullying of women. Ridiculous.

He reclined on his hands, the muscles of his bare chest and shoulders bunching in the most interesting way. She'd seen men, of course, but never like this. Never alone. The wolves that stormed into the castle were shirtless, but she'd been too frightened to appreciate them. Was that what she was doing, appreciating him? More like studying, she decided. He was a vampire. A master, if what she'd overheard was to be believed. It was the rare vampire that aged to any real power level. Most were captured for their blood by casters for healing properties. They'd be drained, discarded, and the blood sold to weaker casters who hadn't the ability to capture a vampire for themselves.

The blood of a vampire was said to have the power to bring beings back from the edge of death, as long as the heart beat.

One as old as Shaughnessy would likely be passed over by those who hunted and harvested the vampires. Too much risk. Within the castle, there were hunters whose job it was to do this, to hunt vampires for their blood. She knew the same as she knew there were cooks in the kitchens and seamstresses making finery.

Everyone had a job to do and she'd regarded the hunters as she had the tutors and the stable hands—just people doing their job. Now, here she sat, having been saved by vampire blood, given to her by a master vampire who'd been locked in dungeons and tormented. Did he know? Was he aware that she'd been given vampire blood as a child each time she'd gotten a scrape to keep her skin flawless? She'd accepted that living beings were being slaughtered so she'd have a better chance enticing a powerful husband and accepted it as one more thing in the day, like breakfast.

"Eirnen will find you and kill you for this," she said, looking over the dark water that had soothed the burn.

"Am I mistaken, or do I perceive the tiniest speck of sadness for my plight?" She laid her cheek on her bent knees and memorized the ceiling of the cave reflected in the water rather than explaining it was shame she heard in her voice. "Eirnen has tried and failed more than once to take my life."

"I don't know him at all, do I?" She switched to the other cheek to see his face. "Shaughnessy, why did you take me?"

"Because Marion told me you would be of benefit to me," he said. "She said you would save my life."

"And you put that much faith in her visions, to risk this much? Eirnen will send everything he has after me because of what I can do for him. The irony is, it's not even my power he'll kill to find and keep. It belongs to someone still in the castle with him at this very moment."

"Your specter," he said.

"If I'm supposed to save your life, does that mean you won't take mine?"

"I've expended a lot of blood and energy these last four days to prevent your death. It would seem wasteful to kill you now."

"Four days?" she asked and found it wasn't as distressing as it should be. Before now, she'd not spent one night outside Westwood walls. She turned her head to look at him and saw him again against the wall in the dungeon and the things she'd witnessed done to him. "I'm sorry."

His eyes narrowed as he scrutinized her, but she hadn't the energy or care to be frightened. "You cannot leave here without me. Keep that in mind. Whatever your game is, you will not be successful, Westwood."

"I fear those in my home, who call themselves my family, are more an enemy to me than you. Therefore, there is no game. I'll not cast against you unless you force me into defense."

Again, he regarded her with suspicion. "You speak truth," he said as if it baffled him.

"The people I've trusted my whole life turned out to be some of the cruelest I could imagine. Maybe it's time to listen to those I've been warned against by those same people. I know Eirnen sent Marceline to get Abel to slaughter the gigantes in hopes a few would survive. 'They will come to me and beg for what I can give them.' That's what he said."

"If enough gigantes survived Abel's attack, it will prove to have been a brilliant play. I've encountered the gigantes. If one of them gets hands on you, you're dead. They're willful to a fault, impossible to control, but if they were to come to him seeking vengeance and he gives it to them, he will have their loyalty."

"And if none survived, he'd have had an entire innocent clan wiped out for nothing. He was willing to chance it because he believes you are strong enough to accept the conversion, too."

"I'm not," he said without pretense. "Marion saw that much."

"I'm sorry about what happened to her," she said and met his eyes. They flared bright, more amber than honey, but the fire died out. "Did you love her?"

"Not in the way you imagine. You are young, yet a girl in most ways. You still hold on to the idealistic notion of fated love and soul mates. I'm old and cynical enough to know better."

"Not that idealistic," she said. "I believe it's possible for someone to love more than one person. There are all kinds of love. It stands to reason you can find two people you love equally, but differently."

"Your James and Dorin," he said and smiled as her mouth popped open. "Aye, Marion spared few details with regards to you, young Westwood. I demanded nothing less of her if she were to have my aid."

Two to choose, one to keep... She stood, legs weak and shaking, and stumbled over her own feet to all but fall to her knees at the edge of the water. She looked up and found the moon was the source of diffuse light filtering into the cave through a narrow opening. *Please work.* She passed her hand over the still surface, her every thought of Callum as if she could call his power to her even here.

"Show Dorin to me," she said. Nothing. Marion had also said she'd meet Dorin first. But did that mean she was going to escape or that he'd be a prisoner with her?

"I'm afraid your ghost's ability is long gone. Your energies have been drained and replenished time and again in these last days. The aversion ward did quite a number on you."

"I remember," she said, thinking aversion too mild a word for what she experienced. "I also remember it didn't affect you at all, which means it was cast for you specifically. If you have this place, how did you allow Eirnen to catch you?"

"As I said, Eirnen and I have a long history. He has taken much from me," he said and his jaw clenched. He was angry and the timid part of her said to not push him, don't anger him further. Obey, be compliant, agreeable.

"He took from you. You were going to take from him. Did you always plan to take me or were you going to kill me?"

"Kill you and arrange your body parts into a lovely wreath to hang upon his door." She flinched, not only at the description but at the excitement lighting his face. Her reaction caused his lips to curl upward, smile or snarl, whichever it was she shrank back further.

"But now you won't because of what Marion said?"

"She offered me something better." He turned to her on the tips of his fingers, eyes glowing, fangs exposed. He looked like the predator she'd always heard vampires to be. "The Westwood line ended, corrupted, and I get to play a part. Everything Eirnen Westwood holds dear will be torn from him a piece at a time and I'm going to watch it."

He leaned in to inhale at her neck. Chill bumps broke out over her skin. She shuddered as the primitive part of her that knew she was being hunted urged her to run or fight. He leaned back to look at her face, his own twisted in anger. She held his eyes and raised her shaking hands to coil her hair to one side then tilted her head, exposing her flesh to him. "Go ahead."

He stopped stalking her and blinked fast. "You offer it freely?"

"I do." His features softened though his fangs were still long and sharp.

"Are you certain you are a Westwood?" He moved slowly, wrapping his arm around her waist. His hand followed her spine upward where it settled between her shoulder blades. "Tell me now and I will find a meal elsewhere," he said with his mouth hovering above her neck. In answer, she laid her hand on the back of his head and gave the lightest of pressure, urging him forward.

He didn't hesitate again, though she was surprised he did in the first place. He struck. He held her tighter as she stiffened and put her hands on his shoulders to brace herself. It felt just as she would imagine having two spikes driven into her skin would feel. Painful, frightening.

This wasn't at all what she remembered about the first time he bit her in the water, but she wouldn't try to get him to stop. He'd been feeding her his blood to heal her. That in itself said a lot about Shaughnessy. For him to give of himself something her kind had killed and imprisoned his to take, was honorable. She owed him a little back.

After a few seconds, even as determined to be cooperative as she was, the blood loss coupled with the feeling of it being pulled from her caused an anxious flutter in her chest. The flutter grew until her entire frame was shaking. Anxiety morphed into fright, which sped her heart, pumping the blood to him faster.

He growled. The sound shot a thrill of fear through her that raised goosepimples on her flesh. She felt the vibration in his chest under her hands. She realized it was a signal and not him losing control when all the pain drained away and was replaced with what her limited experience told her was lust. A flush crept over her skin, sensitizing parts of her that drug a moan past her lips. Closer, she had to get closer. Her body moved of its own accord until she straddled his hips and molded herself to him. The hard muscles in his back writhed under his skin as he worked at her neck. Her fingers dug in, testing them before she scored him with her nails. This. This is what she remembered his bite to be.

At this moment, she knew without a doubt she'd deny him nothing. Her hips rolled and her chest brushed his with the motion, drawing attention to the thinness of the shirt she wore. Somewhere, a dark corner of her mind maybe, a rushed whisper told her this wasn't real, she didn't want this with him. It was easily cast out as mistaken. She was on the precipice of something that tightened her belly and made her ache in a way she knew he could satisfy. It was a feeling she'd only had during her fevered dreams of Dorin. His kiss was consuming, his body on hers overpowering, and he could manipulate her in ways she didn't believe possible.

Real or Marion's visions? She didn't know now. She'd watched him with Callum's ability many times. Every night after, she'd dream of them together. The same had happened with James. Could they have been possible futures, things she might experience firsthand? Alone in her chambers, she'd been satisfied with them being dreams, had treasured them to the point that she'd sought to force sleep to be in them. Now, however, with the idea of them being bits of a future to come, the dreams weren't enough.

All too soon the skin on hers cooled, the scent in her nose changed, the eyes were honeyed and not the odd green she'd spent hours analyzing. Shaughnessy. He'd taken the pain of his bite and exchanged it for pleasure. Of course, he had. Of course.

"I'm sorry," she said, untangling her legs from his waist to move away. She waited, preparing herself for whatever scandalous or humiliating remark he was going to make about her behavior. She'd wanted him. There was no denying it.

"Come," he said and pulled her up from the cold ground. She let him lead her to the pallet where he pulled the covers over her. She gripped them tightly as if they could take it all back. "It was the bite, lass," he said and wiped a tear from her face.

"I have no idea why I'm crying," she sniffed. "You didn't hurt me, well, not after a few minutes, and not bad even before."

He slid in behind her and she was comforted by the closeness. "You've never been had before, have you?" She shook her head, embarrassed again. "What happened, what you felt, it was all false. Those feelings you had for me were your body reacting to a toxin, a poison of sorts. There is no denying it and no fighting. I should have realized."

"You're oddly gentle and understanding for a blood-crazed beast." He laughed lightly with her and then he was gone. The movement was too hurried, too swift to be him just offering space. She sat up, on immediate alert. "What is it?" she whispered.

"Stay here," he said and ran faster than she could track through a dark crevasse in the far wall.

She strained to hear anything of what alerted him, but there was nothing except the trickle of water that fed the pool. Who would it be coming through the way Shaughnessy left? It could be the guards, maybe even Rowan and Riley, or Eirnen himself. If they came for her, would she fight to stay or leave? She hadn't thought about that question, there were too many more to address. Henrik was on his way to see if any gigantes had survived Abel's and Eirnen's savagery. Surely he had not returned yet. Out of all of them, he was the last one she wanted to come for her. Not that she expected Eirnen to be any less cruel than his son at this point.

There was a howl. It sounded miserable but was unmistakable as one of the werewolves, and Shaughnessy was alone. She tossed the blankets back and ran to the crevasse. *Light, light, I need light.* She grinned in the darkness and focused her power to her hands until they crackled with blue fire, just like Eirnen. It wasn't a lot, but it was enough to light the ground a few feet ahead. She barely remembered the trip down the tunnel, but the massive opening was vivid in her mind. There was no way she could jump it, but she'd deal with that if she came to it.

There was another animalistic sound of pain followed by a very human one, or vampire one, as it were. She doubled her efforts and prayed she saw any holes before it was too late. She caught a flash of movement ahead and then a loud crash that rained rock and debris. She raised her hands to get a look at what was in there with them, but there were only brief glimpses of pale skin. More vampires? She moved fast, but cautiously, to get closer. If Shaughnessy was having this much trouble with his considerable strength, Camilla stood no chance.

"Camilla, go back." Shaughnessy appeared a few feet ahead on the path. A pale, sleek figure sprung out of the darkness and tackled him. They rolled out of sight and she watched in horror as three more similar shapes ran to join the fight.

"Shaughnessy," she yelled. The furious snarls stopped.

A pale head poked out from behind a stalagmite. Eirnen's creature. It lifted its face and sniffed at the air. This one was more wolf than human, its claws dug into the dirt as it crept toward her. Shaughnessy came up from the ground with another by the neck. This one looked as human as the creatures could. It twisted in his hands and snapped fangs to rival Shaughnessy's inches from his face.

"Shaughnessy, wait," she said. "Don't hurt it yet."

The half-wolf in front of her cocked its head to the side as it assessed her. It was eerie, but at least it wasn't lunging an attack. In the clearing, the grotesque bent body with its claws like talons and reddened eyes had scared her. Now, she looked deeper, beyond the outward exterior. If she'd done this with her family, maybe she wouldn't have made so many mistakes and believed the masks they wore for her. Its eyes cut away, showing so much white Camilla interpreted it as a display of submission. It lowered to the ground in front of her feet.

"What's going on?" Shaughnessy asked.

"Not sure, but let it go. Let it come to me." She held the back of her hand out to the other wolf. It sniffed at her skin, then turned a circle before curling on the ground like a big dog. "I think they followed me here," she said, her words coated with disbelief. But one-by-one they came to her. The smallest female wrapped herself around Camilla's legs and whimpered.

"How is this possible?" Shaughnessy asked, his expression as stunned as hers must be. "Eirnen would have sent wolves to hunt you and if they didn't find you, these things shouldn't have been capable."

"And there's the matter of the aversion spell," she pointed out. They weren't affected and by all rights the skin should be melting from their bodies. "There were more," she said, looking around.

"I killed four," he said without apology. There were four at her feet. Two more, at least, were missing. Maybe the other wolves had taken Blacke after all or they'd killed each other.

They followed close behind her back to the cavern. Her gasp was loud in the space as she took in Shaughnessy's bare back. It was bleeding, marred with deep scratches and bites. When he turned to see what startled her, she saw the front hadn't fared much better.

"You're hurt," she said, pointing out the obvious when he stared at her with a blank expression.

"You've seen me with worse." She whirled around as she realized he was undoing his trousers. "I've seen you bare, love. I have no shame in admitting I lacked your self-control. I'd take no offense if you wanted to even things out a bit."

"No, thank you," she said over the splash of water.

"Your innocent eyes are safe now," he said, but she went to the pallet to sit before she risked turning around.

The creatures gathered close, all but one. A male smaller than the rest settled against a wall, with stone at his back, and regarded everything with wary eyes. There weren't any claws visible on him. His hands looked human. He had the same ice-white skin and blue veins as the others, but there was something familiar about him. Could he be one of the surviving casters? Maybe. She'd seen no evidence he'd retained the ability to cast and she couldn't bring herself to test his defense capability. He'd been experimented on enough for one lifetime.

When she turned back, Shaughnessy was watching her watch the creatures. He said nothing, his expression showed nothing, but she began to feel awkward, scrutinized, and guilty. "You're looking at me as if you want me to explain, but I swear to you, I cannot."

"If they didn't scent you, and I don't believe they did or else Eirnen's wolves would be baying at the entrance, there was something else they followed. I think it's connected to your power. It's rare, very rare, for a caster to be able to interact with ghosts. Rarer still for them to absorb the ability of the spirit they encounter. Tell me, how long have you known your poltergeist friend?"

"Nearing a year," she said, not seeing the harm in answering.

"And the other?" He cocked an eyebrow at her. "Listen, Camilla, I know you're hiding something. I can scent the deceit and fear in you now with my questions. There's power in you. I know it and so does Eirnen, although I get the impression he believes it to be the seeing ability that belongs to your ghost because that's what you led him to believe. I know better."

"Why do you want to know? Do you think to manipulate me to use it for you? You took me from my home. I didn't ask you to do that. I saved you from the dungeon. I paid you back in blood. I owe you nothing."

The creatures stirred, lifting their heads to bare teeth at Shaughnessy. She reached out to stroke the head of the half-wolf closest to her in an effort to calm him. Sparse, wiry fur poked at her fingers, but he seemed to like it. He made a contented chuffing sound and curled his face into her thigh.

"I am not Eirnen," Shaughnessy said. "I don't need to know your power to manipulate you. If you knew anything at all, bothered to learn more about what we are beyond what you've been fed with your silver-plated spoon, you'd know it, too." He ran a hand over his face to clear the water that clung to him.

"As for taking you, you were desperate to escape even if for a little while. You love that I gave you no choice. Now, when you go back out of duty or discovery, you can tell them the evil vampire plucked you away. You weren't responsible. You didn't actually have to muster the courage to do something on your own more daring than travelling to your backyard."

"You wanted to get caught and so did she," Camilla accused right back. "Marion is a seeress. You can't tell me she wouldn't have seen Eirnen coming for her and you left this cave. Did she tell you I'd free you at her urging? Did she get you out in the open by telling you you'd get your chance to rip me to pieces that way? It must have been disappointing when she told you that you couldn't kill me after all. But you got to have a slice of the pleasure she stole in watching my pain at the aversion spell. I bet you were delighted when I begged you. You ask me to tell you my secrets, but you're nothing more than another person who decided to use me to your own ends. You're right, you're not Eirnen. Even he never took joy in watching me suffer."

"She didn't tell me I couldn't kill you," he said with menace. "She showed you what you are to become or what you could. Either one will bring an end to the Westwoods. I forfeit that end if I kill you, but she left the choice to me. Although, I find it hard to believe now that I see you in all your cowardice that you will one day be worse than Eirnen Westwood."

"A coward wouldn't have come to the dungeons to save you," she said.

"Truly, Camilla, what did you risk in releasing me? Nothing. Eirnen may have been furious, at first, but you and I both know that he would've patted you on the head. His silly little naïve girl had been overcome with sympathy. He'd continue his quest for warriors all while having his prized spy under his hand."

"You didn't take me and then decide on the way to let me live. You and her—Marion—the two of you have been using me, are still using me to meet your own ends. Thanks to her, I'm not sure of truth and lie of my memories. I did not ask to play the part of pawn."

"But you do it so well," he said and she had no argument. She hadn't fought him in any tangible way when he took her from her home. She'd made no attempt to stop Henrik or Eirnen, not even a chastisement after seeing the gardens. She'd accepted Marceline's so-called help with gratitude.

"You said there was very little Marion didn't tell you about me," she said and lifted her chin. "You made a comment about me one day being worse than Eirnen. She showed that to me. What she didn't show me was how to reach or avoid each outcome. But, she did shove the two of us together. Why?"

"She did tell me something of you and your paths, but I think I've revealed enough secrets to a Westwood who refuses to share hers."

"Tell me this one thing and then I'll answer," she said. Following a wild hunch offered by Callum, Camilla asked, "Did Marion give the vrykolakas my scent the night they attacked?"

"I watched her walk up to that beast and speak to it as you do these creatures when she presented it with a grey pebble."

"It's true then. She did this. I wouldn't be here. Grandfather would never have taken such interest in my ability had he not witnessed me with the vrykolakas that night."

"Before you lose that temper of yours, caster, may I also point out that had Eirnen not been presented with the possibility of your power you'd be wed to Winston Cleary, perhaps even now. I believe Marion also gave you a glimpse of your life of wedded bliss."

"Shaughnessy, please. Please tell me how I keep from becoming worse than Eirnen. I know you know."

"We had a bargain. I answered what you asked. I'll give no more with nothing in return."

"I don't know what it is," she said, exasperated. "The only one who knows the whole truth is as clueless as I am as to how to control it or what I'm capable of. He doesn't think it's wise to share what little we know. And incidentally, neither does the guard who saw me break a man's arms and legs and laugh about it."

That last bit got his attention. It wasn't something he expected from her, that much was clear. And that was the problem. It wasn't something she'd expected of her either. "Who else knows? The whole of it or only pieces," he clarified. "Close your eyes. I'm getting out."

"Callum, Tamara—she's the other ghost—a guard, and Winston Cleary." He muttered something that sounded like *bloody wanker*, but she couldn't be sure. "Callum knows the most, I think. Rowan can get a sense of the abilities in others, but I don't know how much."

"That's a hardy list," he said over the brush of fabric. "You can open your eyes now. Shoo those things off the bed." They looked so content she felt guilty, but she did as he asked and they immediately obeyed. He nodded like that answered a question for him. He sat beside her, wrinkling his nose.

"Your cuts. They're gone," she said and resisted the urge to touch him to make sure her eyes weren't playing tricks. "One of those things I should bother to know?"

"We heal fast, as long as we're well fed. So do the wolves. And our sense of smell can be our worst enemy at times," he said with his face twisted in disgust. "As for manipulating, I could compel you to tell me everything I want to know. Your natural defenses as a caster would be enough to keep the younger, weaker ones out of your mind, but I'm not young or weak."

"So why don't you? If you wanted to know badly enough, I probably couldn't stop you."

"Because, wee lass, I also am not stupid. Lesson one in staying alive is to know who to fuck with and who to leave alone. And you are best left alone. You look and act innocent with your easy blushes and sensitive nature, but there's a turbulence under the surface that sparks my survival instinct."

She closed her eyes. "You can see it. It scares me. I see Henrik and Eirnen. Their greed for power drives them to acts of cruelty and I can understand it. I understand why they do the things they do. A good person is not supposed to find understanding in evil. It should be inconceivable. When I used this power on Winston, I loved it. It was freedom. I rejoiced in being strong and powerful for once instead of weak and unassuming."

"It will continue to scare you until you've mastered it. Once you have, it's your choice how you use it. But, Camilla, with the evidence around this power, people will begin to draw their own conclusions, which is sometimes more dangerous than the truth. In the short time I've known you, I have my own."

She was tired. Mentally weary and worn and though it might be foolish, again, she trusted Shaughnessy. It was clear she couldn't trust anyone in her own family and right now, she needed to trust someone. Especially someone who might be able to tell her what to expect of this ability and knew the answers to Marion's riddles. She wasn't lying when she said it scared her. Each time it arose, it had been as a result of anger and gave her the power to be as malicious as she wanted, seemed to want to be. It felt like a release.

"My best friend, my only friend, is a ghost I condemned to be one. I didn't do it on purpose. I don't even know how it happened exactly. Just one night I came awake, gasping for air as if I'd been drowning. I felt myself sliding away and I screamed. I was dying, I knew it. Then it stopped and Callum was in my chambers and as confused as I was.

"I feel every death at Westwood Castle. A few weeks ago, I gave an abused servant power because I'd taken enough of hers, she nearly lost consciousness. She used that power to kill my brother before slicing her own throat. My brother is gone. I don't know where, just gone. Even though I begged him to stay, I couldn't will it so. The girl, Tamara, is still in the castle. In the dungeons, I could feel the pain there. I could hear whispers of the things that had been done and screams of agony as if the pain had been so great it was imprinted in the walls. These poor creatures. They're dead save for one small spark that hovers around them as if it were lost. Are you seeing a pattern here?"

"Your ghosts, can you command them as you do the creatures?" he asked, ignoring the snarky question.

"I don't unless it's necessary. They have their own thoughts and feelings. I won't make them my slaves. Most things I don't know I can do until it happens. I could feel Winston Cleary's heart beating in my hand as if I were holding it in his chest. I knew I could kill him if I closed my fist, but not until I felt it."

"Vampires are said to be dead but animated. This power of

yours deals in death and could make a lot of my kind very nervous. It's not reaching to assume you could make us your puppets as thoroughly as you have these things."

She smiled at him. "Silly Shaughnessy, you should bother yourself to learn more about your kind. You're not dead. Your energies burn bright and white as the moon."

"I was right about you. You are a terrifying lass, though you are wee."

CHAPTER 10

EIRNEN SAT IN his study, drumming his fingers on the desk. The creatures were gone. Camilla was gone. Both untraceable. Winston's seeker had been trying since daybreak to find even a whiff of the direction they'd gone but failed at every turn. None of the caster females had knowledge of Shaughnessy's lair, fueling the suspicion that Abel had Shaughnessy and Camilla and it had been casters in Abel's employ shielding them now.

The topper to this day was the announcement that Winston would stay for the duration. Pompous bastard. Eirnen wasn't sure which was worse, Winston's smug disposition or Marceline's certainty of victory. She deemed the casters Abel brought as lower-level peasants and therefore could be discounted.

He couldn't fathom why Abel waited to strike, unless he was using caution in anticipation of resources Eirnen didn't have. The scouts that weren't discovered and killed had seen vampires, which meant Abel would attack at night. Abel's wolves already outnumbered Eirnen's own. If he could find Abel's main base instead of small clusters of his followers, he could force his hand. Taking the fight to him during the day would cut off a substantial backing.

"What," he said to the knock at the door. May the gods show mercy if the person on the other side was there to deliver more bad news because Eirnen would show none.

"Henrik approaches," Rowan said, as always getting to the point quickly. "He's brought them."

Eirnen's boots slapped the wood as he dropped his feet from their prop. "Take as many men as you need. Find Jeremiah and his mate and bring them to me. We haven't time to wait for Shaughnessy to be found."

Rowan said *them*, which suggested more than one. But how many? How many warriors had his son brought? He made his way to the great hall as fast as he could without running. This must be presented as a gift, a favor to them born of sympathy for what Abel had done. They must relinquish control by swearing loyalty to him. He'd have to hide the elation that shook his hands before they were in front of him. That little seeress said he would have his victory and for the first time, he could see it unfolding before him.

He climbed the wide steps that would take him to his throne. He held tight to the golden arms to keep his hands from betraying him. By the time the doors opened, he'd fixed his features. When they rounded the corner and he caught sight of Henrik, he gave a curt nod. Henrik's clothes were torn and coated with a thick layer of road dust, as was any exposed skin. He'd been in a scrape, judging from the bruises and swelling to his face.

"Father," he said once he was at the base of the stairs. "I am saddened to report we arrived too late to prevent the destruction of the Fagaras Clan, but we did retrieve the survivors, though one is gravely injured."

He bowed in the customary fashion, then sidestepped as if to present the men he described. Eirnen rose from his seat as they approached. He couldn't stop himself. They were magnificent. Two held a mauled man between them. There was no other way to describe it. The skin of his chest was mangled. He was flayed open across his gut where he held his arm as if it were the only thing keeping his insides on the inside. The two holding him looked unblemished other than grit and the blood of the man they held. The one in back was marked with lines made with surgical precision. Either Abel had a caster with an ability in the same family as Henrik or someone took a fine blade to him with a steady, practiced hand.

He had to measure. He had no choice. Every step closer left them taller and wider. They were smaller than the gigantes described to him in tales in his youth, bred down as their bloodlines became diluted, but they were still exceptional. Four of them. He'd hoped for more, but expected fewer, if any. The real prize, his son. Henrik stood tall, full of pride and confidence.

"Henrik, please help me see these men to the infirmary. We will aid you in any way we can," he said to them.

"We were ambushed on the road here. We lost ten of our guard before the aggressors fell," Henrik said.

"Your son fought well," the one with the straight-line cuts said in a rumbling bass voice.

"As did you and your brothers, Gabriel," Henrik said and quirked an eyebrow at Eirnen. Brothers? This was better than anticipated.

The injured man overflowed the table to the point Eirnen feared he may fall from the side. His legs dangled off the edge from the knees and there was no room for his arms on the table that was hidden entirely beneath his wide body. His brothers formed a cage around him. Without his arms to cover his abdomen, it was clear his wounds were fatal. The smell of bowel was heavy in the air. The mound of ruined skin that used to be his chest wasn't bleeding any longer. Eirnen suspected, given his pallor, there wasn't much blood left.

Riley was already there, explaining every move before he made it. Riley always had an easy manner with the sick and injured, but the extra care was a product of the protective postures that promised violence with any misstep. It was impressive. Riley was also a man not easily intimidated. He and his twin were the two best guards in Eirnen's army, but he understood these four. He would be the same if it were Rowan on that table.

"His wounds are deep and there are many," Riley announced without taking his hands or his eyes off his patient. "I need more."

"Henrik and I have plenty to spare. Please, do as you must to save this male," Eirnen said. He let down his carefully constructed guard and allowed Riley to pull his energies to heal the gigantes. One of his warriors. As his was leeched from him, he sought more throughout the castle to fuel Riley's efforts. "He lives, Riley," Eirnen said, knowing Riley had been around long enough to hear the rest. People often gave everything they were capable of giving if their lives were at stake as well.

"If you would permit me"— Riley said, looking up at Gabriel — "to give him vampire blood. I fear my ability alone may not save him without the blood to supplement."

"Yes," the brothers answered in unison. Eirnen called for it to be brought to them as quickly as possible.

Eirnen and Henrik both felt the drain by the time the skin was knit together, using all the remaining vampire blood they had in the castle stores. When they'd turned the gigantes to his stomach, his back was crisscrossed with deep cuts that looked like they'd been made by claws. If it weren't for the vampire blood, this male would have indeed been lost. Riley was gifted and powerful, but he had his limits. It was astounding the gigantes survived the attack let alone the journey and was even more proof of the species' resilience. This would work. He could feel it, picture it as if a premonition.

Riley collapsed in one of the chairs, his arms and legs sprawling. "He will sleep to finish it," he said with his own eyes closed. Eirnen had seen Riley like this many times. He would be out of commission for several hours.

"Thank you," Gabriel said and extended a hand that swallowed

Eirnen's when he accepted. "There is much to discuss once our brother wakes." His accent was a thick mixture of what Eirnen suspected was a cross between Dacian and the lost Greek the gigantes once spoke. "We will wait here until he does."

"Very well," he said. "I'll have the servants prepare quarters and food. You must be tired and hungry after your ordeal." Gabriel's wounds were still open and raw. "Until Riley has regained his strength, allow me to have someone tend you."

"I am fine as I am."

"When will Nox wake?" Eirnen turned to face the one who looked to be the youngest. "I am Nikolai. This is Dorin," he said and tilted his head to the man at his right.

"Riley will be out for a few hours, but once he's regained strength, he'll assess Nox for pain or missed injury. If he finds none, he'll draw him from sleep." They nodded and went back to staring down at their brother whose face was lax in the way that comes with deep sleep. "I have matters which require my attention, but someone will be outside your door. Her name is Frances. All you need do is request whatever you require and she'll see you get it as soon as possible."

Henrik followed him out into the corridor and they went straight to the kitchens where Frances was most likely to be. Of all the servants, she was who he trusted most with this task. He hurriedly described exactly what was expected. In addition to making sure the gigantes got everything they asked for, no one was to enter the infirmary. Cora and Lilly were sent to ready quarters before preparing a suitable meal. The next person to see was Winston.

Winston and Barrett's hushed whispers carried out into the corridor, but the words were indecipherable. This was another area where Camilla would have been of use. Barrett had become rather taken with his would-be future stepmother in the short time he'd been there. A young man could be distracted by a lovely young woman, driven to prove himself a man even if it meant defying the father he'd shown unfaltering loyalty.

True, Camilla didn't possess the skills of women like Marceline when it came to capitalizing on her wiles. In this case, wiles would not be needed. The boy had made it his ritual to ask of any word of her each morning. Physical restraint was required to keep him from riding off in search of her himself. Now that Winston was here and Camilla was not, he had the boy's full devotion once more.

"Winston, Barrett," he said at the doorway and they fell silent. "I don't know what the two of you are whispering about and I don't care. It's time for you to earn your alliance." Barrett immediately came to his feet like a soldier. Perhaps he wasn't out of reach just yet.

"The boy, what is his ability? Winston has never revealed it, but now it's time we know."

"My silence was not a deception, nor was it intentional, I assure you." Lie. "I'm told my seeker has yet to locate Lady Camilla, but he will continue to the best of his ability."

"Yes, I'm sure," Eirnen interrupted. "Stop stalling. Is the boy useful or am I to assume your tight lips are concealing that he is latent?" The taunt brought Barrett closer and creased a frown across his face. Of course, he wasn't latent and Eirnen felt sorely underestimated if the boy believed he didn't know the power he allowed in his home.

"I'm not latent," Barrett said. "I'm also no boy." His eyes flickered to Winston. Interesting. "I'm a cultivist."

Henrik barked laughter, but Barrett's expression remained impassive. Eirnen was sure he'd had plenty of practice perfecting it. "Fine, fine. We'll show you to the kitchens. You can help the women with a fetching centerpiece for our guests."

Foolish boy.

The shutters burst open and Henrik's chortling died in his throat. Two jade vines hovered outside the window like cobras ready to strike, and strike they did. Eirnen stepped to the side to let Henrik learn his lessons as the vines coiled his wrists and pinned him to the wall. He fought like a trapped animal, so hard in fact that he didn't see the third that slithered in and dangled at his windpipe. The vine swayed in front of his face as if to get his attention and his eyes invariably found the long thorns that wrapped it.

"As I was saying, I am a cultivist. And this"— he said— "is a variation on the catbriar." He came closer to Henrik, who couldn't let his eyes leave the vine that occasionally reached out as if tasting his skin. "I believe I can be of use to you, King Eirnen." To prove his point, the thorns shot out to double their length and Henrik shuddered against the wall. As he should. "And if it wouldn't offend, I have some ideas to propose."

"Well, Barrett, there is no denying you have my attention." Instead of beaming with fatherly pride, Winston was furious. Perfect. "Henrik, if Barrett is gracious enough to free you, there is to be no retaliation. You earned this. Own it."

The vines at his wrists began to loosen, but Eirnen gave a shake of his head and they tightened once more. "I swear it," Henrik spat and Barrett dropped him to the floor.

"Now, Henrik, if you would accompany Winston? I want a wall of earth around the perimeter of Westwood Castle. The grounds are not to be visible to anyone on the outside even from the knolls." His warriors were to be a complete surprise, hidden from any onlookers. Plus, the time-consuming task would ensure Winston stayed occupied. "Barrett and I are in need of a lengthy discussion."

"It's not working, Shaughnessy," Camilla said, rubbing her forehead in frustration. Hours before, the atmosphere had been hopeful. But now he was doing himself harm and making no progress to heal the creature he said he knew. "You're weakening. I can see it."

"Rissa was proud. I cannot, will not, leave her like this." The words were forced out as he grappled with the female creature. Rissa, he thought. "If I can't fix it, I will put her out of her misery."

Camilla woke that morning to find him kneeling over her, eyes locked on the small female that had curled against Camilla while she slept. He'd been horrified not only to see her like this, but that he hadn't recognized her. He'd described a red-haired, tenacious beauty who loved to laugh and fight. No wonder he hadn't recognized her. There was no sense of the former personality he described. There wasn't a shred of recognition when she looked at him. Shaughnessy was on the paler side, but there was a liveliness to his skin, a radiance. Rissa was the color of thick ice, the blue veins covering her from face to feet paled her further. As for the long fiery locks, there were none.

Camilla was getting worried about him, but he'd rejected her offer to allow him to drink from her—with the stipulation that he didn't do the lust bit. It was nice. Who was she kidding? It was fantastic, but also embarrassing and unsatisfying. She'd also rejected his offer to relieve the tension caused by the arousal. She thought her face would catch fire when he suggested it, which made him laugh like a fool. Still, he scored his wrists and force fed blood to Rissa again and again. He'd bitten her but couldn't drink the blood because he said it was bad whatever that meant. His bite and mind manipulations had no effect other than causing her to be hostile.

He was hungry and so was Camilla. He'd brought berries and nuts in from outside, but after having them the last few days, she didn't want to see any more. She exhaled and tossed a berry in her mouth, pretending it was venison. The creatures had little trouble finding food. They hunted in the morning. Shaughnessy was not amused when they'd dragged their kill back to the cavern.

"You manipulate death," he said. "You told me they were dead save one spark. Even her blood tastes dead. You can help her."

"This isn't about death, Shaughnessy. It's about life and energy. Hers has been fractured and I don't know how to find it to give it back to her. I don't know if it's even possible." She put her fingers to her throbbing temples and rubbed in deep circles. Gods she wished she could fix this, give them back what was taken. Give it back. She'd done that with Tamara, hadn't she? She'd given her back her energies, true, but had also strengthened her with Henrik's. She gave Tamara Henrik's energy. She stared at first Rissa and then Shaughnessy.

"You've thought of something," he said and moved to tower over her. She was still watching Rissa and that single, dancing spark. "Camilla," he said, kneeling to take her hands from her face. "Tell me."

"I need another vampire. Two if you don't know one as powerful as you are. I have an idea, but you have to swear you will stop this if it doesn't work. You're tormenting her and yourself."

"Nothing I'm doing is working anyway, so if you give it everything you can and are unsuccessful, it stops. I swear." He stood and glanced over his shoulder at Rissa. "Give me two hours and I'll have them here."

"Wait," she said, jumping to her feet. She hadn't thought this through. "The second you leave the boundary, Eirnen will know it. He could catch you again."

"If they catch me, then come get me, lass," he said and winked.

"Don't doubt it," she vowed and there was no playfulness or smiles. If Eirnen put him back in that dungeon, she'd find a way to level Westwood Castle if it was necessary to free him.

She watched him leave with a sinking feeling in her gut. She'd always been told that beings other than casters were dangerous, vicious. The vampires were master manipulators who took pleasure in toying with people until they were driven to insanity. Shaughnessy explained the bloodlust was true, but only in the very young or the starved. According to all her lessons, it was the nature of the vampire to be in a constant state of bloodlust. She'd had tutors, scholars, she spoke and read several languages and yet, she knew nothing.

Shaughnessy had proven himself to be honorable and to Rissa, he'd shown loyalty and compassion. He hadn't hurt Camilla. In the beginning, she knew he wanted to, in retaliation against Eirnen. But he hadn't. He'd challenged her, told her the truth of what he thought of her, both good and bad. He risked his life now on nothing more than the idea of an unmastered caster who he should despise and mistrust. He was playful and unscrupulous when it came to teasing her, but not malicious. He'd shared parts of his life with her while they talked well into the day before they fell asleep. She knew more about him than she had her own brother. Yes, she'd go get him.

Now that she was alone, she decided it was time to get in the water and wash as best she could. His comment about their sense of smell left her self-conscious and sympathetic to him since he slept next to her— a person who hadn't had a proper bath in over a week and had very recently shed skin like a serpent. Rancid. He'd said her gowns were rancid. He'd left to give her privacy to do this a couple of days ago, but it was a rushed process. She'd stayed on edge and watched the crevasse for him to come in to embarrass her. She was in and out in minutes.

The water was freezing. Her teeth chattered and the two wolves watched her with curious expressions. They were male, but until now she hadn't given being naked in front of them any more thought than she would have a housecat. It was wrong of her to think that way, but that was the truth of it. She'd think better from now on. The caster was also male, but more skittish than the rest. He kept to himself for the most part but occasionally came to lie close to her. Unlike the others, he didn't like to be touched and she respected his wishes. It must be hard to be as they were and him without the fangs and claws of his competition for food.

She'd watched for any sign of his ability to show itself, but there was none. There wasn't enough of his energies left for it, was her guess. The wolves weren't shifting form either. It was as if they were frozen in one state. The largest male had more human features than the other, power level at the time of attempted conversion must have been a factor. Blacke had been almost all human save for claws and teeth.

She was huddled under the blankets, attempting to get warmth to return to her body, when she heard voices. She held her breath and waited for one of them to be Shaughnessy's. A relieved smile stretched her face when she knew for sure it was him. It faded when he came in with two others following behind that didn't look pleased to be there.

The man was taller than Shaughnessy by a few inches, with a shock of dark hair and a severe expression, but he didn't even glance in her direction. The woman, though, was glowering with green eyes lit and fangs lengthened. Camilla wasn't sure the proper thing to do in this situation to not irritate the woman further, but it turned out she didn't have to do a thing.

The vampire's mouth dropped open and her brows shot up when she spotted Rissa. The snarl that ripped through her chest and the sound of her teeth gnashing echoed through the cavern. Shaughnessy put himself in front of her, cutting off her view of Camilla.

"I told you what you would see here, Micha."

"I didn't want to believe it. Not from you, Shaughnessy. A fucking Westwood did this and there one sits in your bed like a lover. Is that what she is, Shaughnessy? Please tell me she is a means to pain Eirnen and Henrik Westwood."

"As I told you before you agreed to this, she's going to try to reverse what was done to Rissa. You are not to harm her, no matter the outcome."

"I won't promise you that."

His hand was around her neck and her feet dangled before Camilla could take a breath. "I am master here. She is to be unharmed for no other reason than that is what I command."

"You would threaten one of ours for her?" the man said, his hushed tone more frightening than the female's snarls.

"For the disrespect, I will kill one of ours," Shaughnessy corrected. "Let me ask: How many beings did you see for me to feed from on the way here? And how do you suppose I'm satiated, yet she is not fearful of me? She gave to me freely for no other reason than I needed it. Yes, she is a Westwood. She has been told we are vicious killers her entire life and you are set on proving them right. You help Eirnen and Henrik now when you could help us by showing her differently."

"Did you have a hand in this?" the man asked, finally looking at Camilla, who was very busy trying to keep calm.

"I did not. I didn't know of them until recently."

"Devlin?"

"Aye, there was no deceit in her." Shaughnessy turned his eyes back to Micha, who nodded though she looked reluctant to do it.

He sat her on her feet and there wasn't a hair out of place, not a mark on her neck. She ran and dropped to her knees beside Rissa, which put her within striking distance of Camilla. She reached out to touch Rissa and was almost bitten. Rissa growled and backed up, pressing tighter to Camilla.

"Why? Why would you do anything to help us?" Micha stood, hurt at Rissa's rejection plain in her expression. "What do you hope to gain? Answers for your king?"

"What Eirnen did was wrong. I want to try and fix it. That's all."

"Truth," Micha said, looking more and more confused. "But, why? Why would you go against Eirnen? Do you believe yourself powerful enough to defeat him? Is it your intention to usurp Calame? Is that why she's here, Shaughnessy, to align with us against him?"

"No. I mean, yes, I went against him to free Shaughnessy, but no I do not wish to rule Calame." Was that what Grandfather thought? Did he believe even now she conspired against him with his enemy? She had certainly made a friend of his enemy.

"Camilla." The way Shaughnessy said her name made her think it wasn't the first time. "You've gone pale, love." He knelt in front of her. "All the thoughts I can see running through your expression are not problems for this day."

She nodded and drew her shoulders back, lifting her chin. "You're right. Of course, you're right."

To regain focus, Camilla looked over the new arrivals. Shaughnessy was the only vampire she'd seen, but now that there were two more for comparison, she knew for sure not all vampires were created equal. There were levels to them, just like with casters. Shaughnessy burned brightest, his essence almost pulsating around him. Devlin was next and Micha was nearly cream next to them. She wanted to ask questions, see if she could learn to determine a vampire's approximate age this way, but didn't think it wise.

"Alright, Camilla," Shaughnessy said, "do as you will."

She hesitated before pulling the blankets back, more aware than ever that she was dressed in one of his shirts that barely covered her knees. She'd have not been able to force herself to do it a week ago, but apparently Shaughnessy's teasing was also desensitizing. She pulled herself upright in preparation for more shouting about lovers once she was revealed as indecent, but neither of them reacted at all.

"I've never drawn energies from a vampire before. I don't know what will happen so bear with me." Devlin gave a short nod and Micha crossed her arms over her chest. "You have to do what I say, when I say it. No questions." Shaughnessy narrowed his eyes in suspicion, but she ignored him.

She started with Micha, partly because she was weakest and would have the least effect if this went wrong, and partly because she wanted to put the vampire in her place. Micha's arms dropped to her sides and her head fell back. She looked like a statue. Camilla hadn't intended to put her that far in place and she'd barely started pulling.

"Micha, look at me," she said and the female's head came forward. She stared, unblinking at Camilla and she was reminded of what Shaughnessy said about puppets. He was too by the way his brows dipped. As cold as it sounded, it was better with Micha this way so she wouldn't argue later.

Perhaps Shaughnessy had been right. Could she control the vampires, make them do as she commanded? Were they nothing more than animated dead? Now was not the time to ponder this, but later, oh yes, this was worth investigating.

Power was already swirling in her. It was a tingle under her skin and a metallic taste on her tongue that made her think of blood, though she tried hard not to. No more practice. She reached out and pulled from all three at once. Devlin's eyes glazed like Micha's then cleared, then glazed again until they were almost flashing. Shaughnessy's eyes stayed clear, his fists clenched at his sides. Camilla's eyes fluttered and her head fell back. So much power.

Keep it, a part of her whispered. *Imagine what you could do—anything, you could do anything.*

It was seductive. She was ashamed to admit it was a struggle to relinquish so much power and possibility, but she shook her head to clear it and stretched her hand out toward Rissa. She was an instrument, a filter for the energies that flowed from the palm of her hand to Rissa. She'd done something similar with Tamara, which was what gave her the idea, but this was a bit more complicated.

Rissa writhed on the ground and shrieked, the energies tore into and then through her to get back to where they were taken. She was too altered. Too much death surrounded her. The white was fused with green as Camilla gave up some of her own energies to bind the power to the vampire that wasn't one anymore.

When it stayed with Rissa, it started to build, swirling around her like a tornado and she began to pant. This was an unexpected side effect of the ability she'd feared. It wasn't just death, it meant life for Rissa and maybe even the other creatures if she succeeded. It didn't have to be all darkness.

"Drain her," Camilla said in a voice bordering on a snarl. Micha didn't hesitate, she bent over Rissa's curled body and used her fingernails to slice open Rissa's throat. Black blood poured from the wound, spilling over the edge to float on the water like oil. Rissa's movements slowed and so did the flow of blood. "Now, feed her. All of you."

Micha stumbled and dropped to one knee before righting herself. Camilla eased off to take more from Devlin. They took turns letting Rissa tear at their wrists while Camilla kept a steady stream of power flowing into her. The flow faltered when Camilla saw her outstretched arm had a subtle luminescence and was considerably paler than normal. But she felt fine, better than fine, and pulled herself together. Micha wasn't faring as well. She swayed on her feet, then fell to the ground and Devlin had gone puppet. Shaughnessy had Rissa at his wrist. From the looks of it, she'd been savage with her bite, but he didn't flinch.

Rissa sat up with her eyes closed and her chest heaving, but her back was straight—something Camilla hadn't seen from her. She was still pale, but didn't look as ashen and sickly. The blue veins were gone. She was improving. It renewed the need to fix what had been done and the resolve helped to steel her nerve.

"Shaughnessy," she said and he looked at her with eyes full of awareness. "Bite my wrist and try to keep her from taking my hand off." She raised the arm not directed at Rissa in front of his face.

"This is a big cast, Camilla. You can't lose blood, too."

"Please, Shaughnessy. She's so close but she needs nourishment that you can't give her. She has to feed."

He set his jaw into stubbornness. "Fine." She whipped her arm back. "Devlin," Shaughnessy cursed and grabbed her forearm. He bit and she ground her teeth. It was more painful than the neck by miles.

She knelt in front of Rissa and put the wound to her lips. Rissa inhaled then latched on, jerking Camilla down by the arm and wrapping around it as if it would be taken away. Camilla stopped pulling from Devlin and felt faint. When she stopped taking from Shaughnessy too, she could be in big trouble. Arms wrapped around her from behind and lowered her the rest of the way to the ground with exaggerated slowness to keep from startling Rissa.

Camilla reclined against Shaughnessy's chest, relying on him to keep her upright as Rissa's pulls grew stronger. "That's enough," he said. The words no more than came out of his mouth before Rissa's eyes snapped open. They were the color of warm cinnamon and clear.

Camilla's lids threatened to close but Rissa fixed it by tearing into the wrist at her mouth. Camilla screamed and arched back, losing the connection with Shaughnessy and instantly dropped into darkness.

What could have brought Shaughnessy from his hiding place? Eirnen wondered as he stared down at the map. More important than the motive for now, they had a search area. Winston's seeker had been keeping a constant vigil for Shaughnessy and it paid off. He marked a spot on the map where the vampire came into focus and then lost it in the same area about an hour and a half later. It was the boundary of the concealment ward and it was nowhere close to the territories Abel had been occupying.

Shaughnessy had taken Camilla for his own purposes. Whether it be to use her as leverage, revenge, or he sought to wield her as a weapon, Eirnen wasn't sure. If it were him, and a young, impressionable girl with wavering loyalty to her family fell into his lap, he would do everything possible to turn her completely to his side. The leverage would always be on hand and the treachery of betrayal would be revenge, plus the added power to the ranks.

The hunters were being led by the seeker to retrieve her with orders to dispose of Shaughnessy. He had another vampire and Shaughnessy was proving tiresome. Whatever plans he may have had for Camilla were moot because the leech was soon to be dead. If she was still alive, she'd be back at Westwood Castle where she belonged and the wards were never coming from her chambers again. Both times she'd been given freedom of them, she'd strayed.

She'd found the creatures when Eirnen had been certain she wouldn't leave the castle. Castle? He'd been certain she wouldn't leave the corridor outside her chambers. He believed she would seize the opportunity to watch her mother and brother's rites and scamper back, scared out of her wits of being found. But no, she'd not only left but found the gardens. That poltergeist of hers was the only one who would have shown her the way. It had to be the ghost of one of the dead in the castle, but which was difficult to say. It was male, he knew that much from what Marceline had gathered, but that narrowed the options marginally.

He could only imagine the conversations and deeds the thing had witnessed and carried back to her. It was possible she knew everything, but he would wager it was only recently she was enlightened. Could her confidant be the wolf shown his place with the tip of Rowan's glaive the night they came here demanding their alpha? One of the servants who'd expired less than a month ago after an unfortunate accident on the stairs while tending Marceline was also male.

Now that he had time to reflect and enough doubt for her to do it honestly, her behavior had been different for weeks. She used to fly into his arms with a joyous smile when she saw him. As of late, he had to approach her with affections and those smiles were hard-won and not a result of any action of his. When had she acquired this ability to speak with the dead? Why had she not told him? Her power was growing by leaps and bounds with nothing more than a little training. How powerful would she be at her apex?

A true Westwood. Despite his annoyance with her rebellions, he smiled with pride.

He went to the window to see if the sun was sinking lower, though he knew it wasn't. Tonight, he would make his warriors. The gigantes not only agreed, but demanded he give them this power. They were hungry for revenge and would have it regardless of Eirnen's "gift" or not. They swore blood fealty to him, which was supposedly unbreakable by gigantes law, but was also the surrender he needed to bind them. They'd come to regret the oath eventually, but he was going to see to it they remained bound to him in case gigantes law proved to have flexibility. He'd worked too hard and too long, paid too much, to lose them.

"It's done," Barrett said. Eirnen frowned at the sun once more, then plastered a pleased smile on his face.

"Splendid," he said and clapped the boy on the shoulder.

"There are whispers that Lady Camilla's return is imminent," he said.

"Indeed. I have my best man going for her now. She could be returned to us by tomorrow night."

"Tomorrow night? She has been in the clutches of that vampire far too long already."

"It's a long trek to the place where we know to even begin searching, and it's unknown how far the concealment net was cast. We will find her, don't worry."

"Your Majesty," he said and stopped their slow stroll to turn and square his shoulders. "I will have you know that if Father will no longer have her, I would. I place my claim now, if it would not offend."

"Honorable," Eirnen barely managed to choke out in a civil tone.

There was only one reason Winston would rescind his claim. It would fit Shaughnessy's nature to attempt seduction, but Camilla would never sully herself—He cut the thought. There had been too many of his beliefs of her that began with *Camilla would never...* that had proven false. He clasped his wrist behind his back and tightened until his fingers tingled.

"I was informed of your betrothal to another when I suggested you may be better suited for my granddaughter. What of that?"

"I was promised by Father's choice, not mine. I made no claim, nor agreed. As a man and the heir to Gladen, it's within my right to decline an offer of betrothal."

"My blessings are yours," he said. "I enjoy the prospect of this match. You are young and strong and have proven yourself capable of defending her if need be. I'm pleased and I'm sure Camilla will be as well. Rest easy that she will be told of your dedication to her rescue as well as the efforts you have made for her family."

His face lit with pride and Eirnen could see the claim he already had in his mind and it had no bearing on whether his father still wanted her. This day, all the pieces were falling into place.

For the second time in two weeks, Camilla woke choking on blood. Her head throbbed hard enough to drown out whatever Shaughnessy was saying, but she got the idea when he shoved his bleeding wrist back in her mouth. She didn't argue. She'd drink sludge if it would ease the headache. To her relief, Shaughnessy's blood didn't taste like sludge and it didn't taste much like blood either. It was tart and sweet, but with enough of a metallic tang to remind her of what she was drinking.

After two swallows, the pain ebbed to a tolerable level. She withdrew but he shook his head. "More."

"Enough, Shaughnessy. I'm well and you need it." He drew his arm back, though the way he was watching her had her waiting for him to insist on more. He didn't. He licked the punctures and fell next to her. "Rissa?"

"Improved," he said. "Devlin and Micha have taken her to

feed more. She's not yet the same, but soon will be. When they departed, she was lucid enough to curse me for breaking her jaw to get her off your vein. It's a good sign."

"Will they bring her back here?" Camilla wanted to see for herself, but Shaughnessy shook his head.

"What you did, the way you took total control of them, spooked them badly. Each of us has had energies syphoned, but that was never a side effect."

"I didn't know," she said. "They must really want me dead now."

"Aye, but they have given their word and they feel indebted for what you've done for Rissa. They will not harm you nor will they speak of this to others. I implore you, as a favor to me, do not tell Eirnen of the effect you have."

"Of course, I won't. You were the same all the way to the end, even when I stopped taking from the others but was still taking from you to stay conscious. You are very powerful. No wonder Eirnen wants you as his or dead." She was learning Eirnen wanted to be surrounded by the most powerful beings he could possess as long as they don't surpass him. "Are you spooked by me now, as well?"

"It would be a lie if I said I wasn't at all wary, but I can say with complete honesty that I don't believe you'd use this power unprovoked." He wrapped an arm around her shoulders and pulled her to his side. "It would also be a lie if I said I would never again provoke you, so at least try not to kill me."

"Deal," she said. "What about the others? I think I can do the same thing with enough werewolves to fix the two males, and a few casters for the boy."

"It's too dangerous for more reasons than we're being hunted. You were depleted, your heart nearly stopped before I pried Rissa from you. If you were to try something like that without me there to heal you, it could very well kill you."

"But if I can, I have to do it. You understand that don't you? I can't leave them like that now that there's a way they can be saved. I swore it to Blacke and neither the wolves nor the caster will require feeding on my blood. I will be fine."

"They'll hold a bit longer, love," he said. "Besides, there are other things to discuss. Have you given any thought to your plans or are you to continue this life of a rogue with me?"

"Eager to be rid of me now, I see. You kidnapped me, aren't you supposed to be the one with the plan?"

"I had one, but we've established I won't kill you. I'm too much of a scoundrel to devote my affections to just one lass. You don't act the type to tolerate dalliances and I so enjoy dalliances. Can't kill you, can't bed you, I have no other talents with women. I'm at a loss so the decision is yours."

"Oh, Shaughnessy, my heart is broken. I will pine for you." He gave her a playful shove and she laughed.

It felt nice to be both free, well semi-free, and laughing with someone she was sure wasn't just stuck with her. She loved Callum, treasured him, but she was his only option unless he wanted to be alone all the time. She knew he cared for her too, genuinely. She didn't doubt that, but there was always the wondering and the guilt that she'd trapped him there. If it were her in his position, she didn't know if she could be as forgiving.

Shaughnessy's comment about continuing the rogue life with him was his teasing way of saying she could stay if she chose. It was tempting, very tempting. No more warded doors, no betrothal, she could go wherever in the world she wanted and be the master of her own life. No one would have to know she was a Westwood if she travelled far enough that her eyes didn't mark her for who she was by those who knew.

"I have to go back," she said, though it tightened her chest.

He turned to her, his expression somber. "You can't stop Eirnen. He'll have his warriors, Marion was certain. The only thing up for manipulation by removing you was to ensure Marion didn't become another of your pet ghosts."

"Did she see herself trapped with me in the castle? That's why she had you take me." Shaughnessy nodded.

"It's too late now to stop this. You don't have to go back. I can take you to your James. Marion told me of him and I now see why. I am to be your way to him. You can have the future Marion showed you and be done with this."

"I can't. Not yet. Callum. Tamara. They'll be trapped there unless I find a way to free them. The creatures. You thought me a coward before, but I would feel that way about myself if I run away and leave them there."

He stood, holding out a hand to help her up. "She was right, again," he said. "I should force you," he said, then shook his head. "But I won't. 'She will hurt, but she will grow. It is necessary.' I'm sorry, Camilla. I didn't think I would be, not when it came to a Westwood, but I am."

Camilla swallowed hard and shivered. What had Marion seen?

CHAPTER 11

THE TRIP BACK out the tunnels was much more enjoyable. True, there wasn't anything to see since it was black as pitch, but there was also no searing pain, and this time Camilla trusted Shaughnessy to not drop her in a hole. As soon as they were outside, she pulled in deep breaths of the crisp, fresh air.

The moon was just rising. It would be full tonight. The chilled air tickled against her bare legs and she wished she had them covered. Anyone who took one look at her dressed this way and in the company of a man would make assumptions. She was to walk back into Westwood Castle where assumptions were guaranteed. But the only available covering was the trousers Shaughnessy was wearing and that would be worse.

A warbling sound caught her attention. While she looked for the source, a solid thud came from behind her accompanied by a groan of pain.

"I am sick and bloody tired of being staked to things," Shaughnessy growled. She recognized the weapon buried high on his chest near the shoulder the moment she saw it.

"Rowan." She ran to where Shaughnessy was working the blade

loose from the tree at his back. It had cut straight through him. "Hurry," she breathed and used her body to shield his. Rowan was out there in the dark somewhere and he was almost as fast as Shaughnessy. With any luck, he'd run ahead of the hunters to scout and was alone.

She glanced back to see Shaughnessy snap the staff over his knee. By the time she was facing forward, Rowan was there. "Move away from her, Shaughnessy."

"Rowan, wait," she said and grabbed hold of Shaughnessy's arm with both hands when he moved forward. "Shaughnessy, please, go. Leave now. I'll be safe with Rowan, but he will kill you."

"There is no leaving. The king has ordered you dead on sight." He pulled the two short swords that were his brother's preferred weapons from behind his back.

"We wouldn't want to disappoint the king," Shaughnessy said in a distorted voice that meant his fangs were at full length. His eyes glowed amber and he crouched forward. Blood coated one side of his chest, but the wound had stopped bleeding. She wasn't sure anymore that Rowan would win this fight.

"No, stop," she said, giving his arm a jerk. "There is no need to fight. Rowan, I'm coming with you. He won't try to stop us." Rowan was already shaking his head.

If Shaughnessy ran, there was a good chance Rowan could catch him and one of them would die. They were on edge now, each waiting to see what the other would try first. Rowan's expression tightened every time his eyes wandered down to the shirt and her legs. Assumptions.

"Then we have a problem," she said and dropped her hand from Shaughnessy's arm. "I won't let either one of you kill the other."

"Camilla, you know what Eirnen will do if I pass this opportunity. The vampire deserves to die for what he's done."

"He has done nothing," she hissed. "At least not what you're letting your filthy mind fixate on. It's only the three of us here.

Grandfather need not know you didn't find me wandering lost in the woods."

"Camilla, you don't know what you ask."

"I do and I'm not asking. You have two choices. We tell Eirnen you found me in the woods alone or you tell him you let Shaughnessy go free. Choose."

"We will have another day, vampire," Rowan said and loosened his stance.

"Thank you." She turned to Shaughnessy with a knot in her throat. This was goodbye. "He's right. They will hunt you always. You have to get far from here."

"Worry not, wee lass," he said and planted a kiss on her forehead before vanishing out of her hands.

"Put this on," Rowan said, holding a coat open behind her. She slid her arms through the sleeves and the heavy material weighed down on her shoulders. It wasn't much longer than the shirt, but it was warm. "Are you well? Have you been harmed in any way?"

"No, I haven't. You know I would've done the same for you if it were the other way around." He nodded and then narrowed his eyes on the cave entrance. The three remaining creatures crept out into the open.

"They followed you. Eirnen will be displeased that you know of his creations."

"I bet Eirnen is displeased about a lot of things right now." Rowan scooped up his broken glaive from the ground and she fell in beside him as they made their way back down the mountain. He was quiet, which wasn't out of character, but there was a discomfort to the silence. "What aren't you telling me?"

He let out a long breath and kept his eyes forward. "Eirnen is actually quite pleased. Henrik procured his gigantes and he tries this night to make them warriors."

Cold slithered down Camilla's spine. She reached out her hand to touch the wolf on the other side of her.

❧

"Father, I will beg this of you if I must. Two essences and no more. These four are our best hope. Let us not squander it."

"Riley must be present," Eirnen said as he bore down in the heavy crank that would open the roof of his tower. The gears clanked, turning slowly, but the series of clicks told him the hatch was sliding open.

He'd done all he knew to increase the odds of survival for the gigantes, but it was not enough that they survive. They must be unstoppable. This was what Henrik refused to understand. He had skilled guards. He needed warriors. The gigantes had been so restless in the day, ready to strike at anyone and anything. They even tried to leave when he explained they would have to wait until night for the conversion.

Nox was by far the most volatile. He'd exploded in rage and reduced the wall in their quarters to pebbles and dust. To save more of Westwood Castle from their violence and to prove a point, he'd shown them to the training room. They'd sparred with Riley, wielding long swords against Riley's twin short swords. Riley and his weapons looked like a child and his toys next to the gigantes, but they'd learned a painful lesson. Riley bested each of them, first with one-on-one combat and then the four of them at once.

They were slow compared to Riley, who looked like a dancer as he worked them, and Riley wasn't half as fast as his twin. Their physical strength was more than Eirnen had anticipated, but it was of no use if they couldn't catch their quarry. Their defenses against casts were even more disappointing. They were wide open. He could manipulate them into complete stillness with a flick of his hand. The vampires and even those primitive wolves had a natural shielding that made casts against them more difficult. The gigantes had none.

"Blacke could not withstand even one essence. The addition

of vampire made him a creature. Two, please, use the wolf and the caster. They already possess more strength than most vampires, and their healing—"

"Is not fast enough for a battlefield," Eirnen interrupted. "They heal at half the rate of the wolves. It doesn't matter how many blows they can withstand before they fall if in the end they will fall. Do you forget already that an entire clan was taken by a pack of wolves and a handful of casters? A clan of more than seventy and we have in our possession only four."

Henrik paced and worried his lower lip with his forefinger. He stopped moving and his brows dropped. He had an idea and was sorting out the details before speaking. Eirnen waited while he put his thoughts in order. "They are bonded. Brothers."

"Go on," Eirnen said and folded his arms over his chest.

Another quick bite at his lip and Henrik was speaking again. "I believe them to possess some level of telepathy. I noticed things on the journey here. They would look to one another before speaking. I'd see one nod as if in answer to an unspoken question."

"This is unconfirmed," Eirnen said, though he had suspected the same. As he'd pointed out, they were brothers. They could very well be answering to nothing more than a gesture or a facial expression as the twins did. "Even if true, it's likely to be lost in the conversion."

"Yes, but there's no need for the pack mentality regardless of that. You've witnessed how protective they are of one another, how synchronized they move. They already possess the most essential quality of the wolves we hoped to gain."

"Congratulations, son. You have earned a compromise." Henrik looked as full of pride as Eirnen had ever seen him. "We'll begin with two, but if it becomes evident that one more can be withstood, I will."

"Agreed," he said, knowing it was the best offer he'd get. He left to notify the rest they were ready to finish this.

In truth, it wasn't only whether the gigantes could withstand this. It was Eirnen as well. He would admit that to no one, not even his son. Each time before there had been one host and the energy he expelled had left him drained. Tonight there were four hosts. He looked up at the night sky and hoped the sacrifice to come would be enough.

Never before had there been so many witnesses. The caster Marion and a second caster, whose name Eirnen didn't know, huddled together in the corner as if they were hidden. Marion was still babbling incessantly, speaking to death as if it were a person. Now he knew it had been at one time and refused to leave. The ghost was no doubt gathering more testaments to Eirnen's monstrosity to convey to Camilla. A problem to deal with tomorrow.

Without Shaughnessy, it took two of his horde to come close to matching his power. Jeremiah remained proud and challenging, but his female was fighting her bonds like a wildcat. He'd had to go back on his deal with the wolves since Abel's second scurried away, but Thomas wasn't here to bear witness to what awaited him. He was in the corridor with the other provisions. Eirnen hoped he'd get to gentle the beast down a bit.

Winston knew naught of what was to transpire this night, but Barrett did. This was his final test. Eirnen had forbade him from speaking of this to his father. He would find out just how much Barrett was willing to do to keep himself in Eirnen's favor and closer to Camilla's hand. He wished Rowan were here but was at the same time grateful he was not. Rowan's ability to travel with a talent close to the now-extinct teleportation was a trait that tempted him for his warriors. A temptation perhaps too great to pass up if it were in front of him in the moment.

"I advise you to lie on the floor by your own will now. It will hurt less than when you are dropped there in a moment." The brothers exchanged one of those looks Henrik was speaking of then lowered themselves to the floor. "Keep your minds connected as long as you are capable," he said as instinct spoke to him.

If they could do this, the strongest two could help bring the other two over. The certainty with which he knew this to be true sped his heart. He couldn't stop his eyes from travelling to Marion. She spoke the truth he would have his warriors.

"Let's be done with this, warlock," Nox rumbled. Eirnen had thought Gabriel to be the largest of the four, but Nox had been stooped, guarding his abdomen. It was astounding how much difference a straight back made.

He'd given his orders to each of his men in the room. They all knew their parts to make this as seamless as possible. There was nothing else he could do but begin as Nox requested.

This will work, it must.

Jeremiah and his female resisted the pull, costing Eirnen more of his own energies as he fought them to take theirs. At this rate, he wouldn't have enough left to bind the warriors. That was not an option. With the ones before them, he'd endured weakening to savor the loss that meant he'd won, but there was never this much at stake.

He wouldn't use his own energies, waste them on these two, not when there was a bounty in the village below. He could harvest the energies and his would infect them until they were his own in time to bind the warriors. He had hoped Henrik would inherit this, but he had not and neither had Camilla. They could borrow, but it was like filling a pitcher with water. There was only so much the container would hold. Eirnen absorbed energies, made them his own, and only got stronger rather than spilling.

Eirnen's power was almost parasitic. He would never die by being drained of energy. His body would simply go on a sort of automatic survival strategy and rip power from the closest source without discrimination. He did it at will now, pulling from both the beings in the village as well as the vampires. The female fell first, but he didn't stop. Jeremiah dropped to his knees next to her, his face a mask of pain. Their skin dulled and greyed, their eyes shriveled in their sockets. Jeremiah's skin shrank tight to his bones, peeling his lips back to expose yellowed fangs that still tried to bite.

The brothers had their heads kicked back on the stones to watch. The movement of the vampires stopped once the tap was dry and the brothers turned back to Eirnen with ferocity. "You did not tell us of this," Gabriel said and they moved as one to stand.

"Now you know," Eirnen said and knocked them back down with the force of the vampire essence he threw at their hearts like a spear. They sprawled and fought to hold in the screams, but they would scream. They all did. "Now," he said to Riley as he continued to batter the bodies on the floor.

They bowed high, teeth clenched, yet they still didn't cry out. The energies of the gigantes were the color of fire and began to consume all he was putting into them. One lower vampire for each brother was brought in by the guards. They were needed for the blood that was part of a vampire turning as well as the healing it provided, not their power. Which was good since they were so lower level Eirnen doubted they'd been made more than a year. Henrik and Riley had to pry the gigantes' jaws open. In one clean slice, Henrik opened the vampires' throats. The dark blood poured into the gigantes until it overflowed and spilled from their mouths. It was either swallow or drown and this close to death, their survival instinct wouldn't allow them to take the route of drowning.

The energies were still battling and the fire was winning. It was remarkable. This wasn't just the energy of a vampire but the entire essence, the life force, and all the energies of the beings before failed to expel it. It had eaten away the essence of caster and wolf hosts alike until there wasn't anything left but a pathetic, mewling creature. He released some of his own into the gigantes and it acted as a glue, bridging the other two until, finally, they merged as one and bound them to him in one swoop.

The bothers' bodies slid flat, their expansive chests pumping hard and shimmering with sweat. Eirnen stumbled, catching himself on the edge of a table as his head spun. "Their hearts are slowing," Riley said with an astonished expression. He hadn't believed this would work.

"Father, this is success enough," Henrik said with urgency.

"No, no, no it's not," Marion sang and laughed. "Not for our greedy, greedy, gluttonous king." She swung her arms like a child and pirouetted around. "Children born and children die, some never make it to this side. Fate collects them in her womb, cradling them close in their tomb, she demands a price and the price is high, balance to be paid here and nigh."

She sang it like a nursery rhyme, giggling despite the ominous wording. Henrik gave a shudder that ran head-to-foot and his mouth hung open as he stared at Eirnen. "Father," he breathed as Marion began to sing the rhyme again and tried to elicit the other caster to dance with her by clasping her hands.

"Listen, listen and I will tell you." She spoke to the girl in front of her but his warrior Dorin's body jerked. She was trying to do something to stop this. His victory would not be lost. "Dance with me!"

His fists clenched as he watched the girl's delight and Dorin's body pull taut as a bowstring. Eirnen raised his hands and she spun to face him with her arms spread wide. He ripped the essence from her chest on a furious snarl. She let out a sigh as she crumpled to the floor.

"You must sleep," Rowan said again, but Camilla shook her head.

The sun was rising. They hadn't stopped walking all through the night despite Rowan's insistence or the other guards' grumbling. The seeker, Bosch, was the only one who agreed with Camilla that they keep moving, though for vastly different reasons. *He* needed to return Winston's betrothed as soon as possible.

Once they'd met with the rest of the people who'd come with Rowan to find her, it had been an instant fight. Some wanted to continue on to hunt Shaughnessy despite her lie that she hadn't seen him in days. All of them wanted to kill the three creatures. They looked at them with fear and disgust, which was apparently reason enough to kill them.

Bosch fought hardest since he could sense Shaughnessy was close but not with pinpoint accuracy. Camilla thought that meant he'd returned to the cavern. She wished she could warn him he wasn't concealed as well with Bosch this close, but she couldn't. She could only hope the aversion ward would keep everyone out until he did as she asked and left Calame.

Rowan was still mad at her, probably for more reasons than making him let Shaughnessy go, but he'd taken her side on both arguments. He wouldn't let any member of his guard kill the creatures and he said he wouldn't risk them against Shaughnessy without him. Since Rowan was staying with Camilla, none of the guards would accompany Bosch and he didn't argue for the right to go alone. She wished he had. Shaughnessy would rip him apart.

She wanted to get to Westwood Castle now more than ever. If Eirnen had tried the conversion last night, the gigantes could be doomed already. She couldn't fix them without more of their species to feed them energy, and the rest of their clan was dead. It was possible she was rushing back just to feel helpless. She hoped the conversion had been delayed. Eirnen would want to take extra precautions with this attempt and precautions took time. He might have made a choice that changed what Marion had seen. It was a small hope, but it was better than nothing. All the previous ones had been cast at night. If they were still alive she had until nightfall.

If she could get to them and convince them of the conse-quences, there was a chance she could steal them away as she had Shaughnessy. She'd have to convince them, show them the creatures, because there wasn't a chance if they fought her to get the revenge Eirnen promised.

"Stop," Rowan said and grabbed her arm. Everyone in front and behind froze mid-step. His brows dipped and he scanned the landscape. "There are casts here."

"Abel?" she asked and looked around too, though she could feel nothing out of the ordinary.

"Not right for Abel. This is too young, unstable, but powerful." He looked to the sky as if he'd find the answer there and then knelt to spread his fingers over the ground. "The cultivist. Barrett laid traps for Abel's scouts."

"Barrett?" Camilla asked and Rowan nodded. "What kind of traps?"

"The right ones," he answered. By his tone she understood triggering one wouldn't result in an eruption of daisies. "Please, permit me," he said then caught her behind the knees and back to scoop her feet off the ground. "The rest of you, do not move until I'm in the lead and then follow my steps precisely."

Rowan used great care to slip between the other men who didn't move to allow him to pass. Camilla kept quiet, holding her breath to keep from making even that bit of sound. He made it to the front and reminded her she would die just as surely if she didn't breathe. He cracked a smile. The seeker stayed no more than an arm's length behind Rowan and the rest fell into a straight line, some showing visible relief once they made it to the path. She worried over the creatures, but there wasn't much she could do besides hope they understood or could avoid the traps with their own path.

"Do not step on the stone," Rowan warned and made the short leap over the suspicious flat rock. "Over not around," he added and she found herself impressed by him and Barrett both. "They're getting thicker. We're close to Westwood Castle."

After another agonizing mile, Camilla decided her definition of close differed from Rowan's. The ground rumbled beneath their feet and Rowan cursed. He pivoted in a tight circle on his toes in time for them to see a great tree burst full-grown from the earth, its branches impaling three guards to carry them higher as it grew. They were screaming and fighting with the branches that jutted out of chests, abdomens, arms, and legs. She put out her hands to pull them free, but Rowan trapped her arms at her sides.

"I can help them," she protested.

"No, you can't. Don't move," he yelled as another of the guard had the same idea, but it was too late. The tree acted as if responding to an attack. A hooked branch came out of the back of the guard facing it. Blood and intestines spilled onto the ground with a sickening wet plop. "Don't vomit, girl," Rowan said and turned them away. "Follow," he called over his shoulder and they walked forward with the screams for help scraping in her ears.

Eventually the screams stopped, but she could still hear them, begging for the rest to not leave them to die. She suspected their agony would be with her for the rest of her life. She'd never heard a more nightmarish sound. Not the aggressive growl of the wolves nor the vicious gnashing of a vampire's fangs wanting to tear at her flesh affected her this deeply.

The sun was starting to set by the time a wall of stone and earth resembling a rocky mountainside rose in front of them. Westwood Castle was hidden behind it. Winston must be here. The failure to save the guards, hunger, and exhaustion left her feeling defeated. There was no way she could stop Eirnen. She couldn't best a tree. Rowan sat her on her feet once they were clear of Barrett's traps with the advice that she did not appear weak or injured enough to need carrying.

The creatures made it alive and went down the path that would lead to the clearing where she'd found them. It was just as well and she couldn't blame them for not wanting to go back into the castle after what happened to them in there. Rowan passed his hand in front of the wall and a thick slab of rock slid to the side to create a door. At least now everyone else was imprisoned, too. The remaining guards left them without a word, though Rowan and Bosch stayed close at her side.

She stood straight, shoulders back, head high, and forbid herself to be shamed by her appearance with the first echo of feet coming toward them. There were plenty of other things to fight without fighting her own prudish nature, as Shaughnessy called it. They rounded the corner that showed the whole of the great hall and gave her a look at the welcoming party. Perfect.

Winston's face changed to an ugly puce as he scrutinized her from head to bare feet. Barrett watched him, but his expression was getting more relaxed with every new shade of his father's face. Eirnen was the worst. He smiled and came at her with hurried steps to take both her hands in his. "My precious Camilla," he breathed. Behind him, she saw Henrik frown, then turn on his heel to stalk from the room.

"I set Shaughnessy free from the dungeons. Though, I'm sure Marceline has already made you aware." She pulled her hands from his and resisted the urge to wipe them clean on Rowan's coat.

"You're safe and you're home. Everything else is inconsequential."

"Inconsequential?" Winston's dam finally broke. He came toward them with his finger wagging in the air. "She released that demon and remained in his company for over a week. Now she appears in nothing but a coat and you dare say inconsequential."

"I have his shirt beneath," she said with a disinterested tone that shocked even her. Shaughnessy would be proud. His eyes locked onto the garment peeking out at her chest before his eyes came back to hers. His hand cracked across her face.

"How many times did you spread your legs for him, whore?" he shouted as he struggled against Riley and Rowan dragging him back. She kept her hands fisted at her sides to keep from letting him see her rub at the sting on her cheek. "I will not have the discarded seconds of a vampire."

Well, that was easier than expected.

"I will have you, Lady Camila," Barrett said.

"No, you will not." His face was enough to tell her he hadn't thought she'd say no. Especially now that all other honorable prospects were gone after being sullied by an affair with a vampire.

"There is much to discuss"—Eirnen interrupted before she could finish telling Barrett what she thought of his proposition— "at a later time. Camilla, you are in need of rest. I'll have Frances prepare a hot bath. Rowan will see you to your chambers."

"I recall the way perfectly," she said and left them staring after her.

She hadn't planned on being confrontational, only not shrinking, but she couldn't stand it. Eirnen's touch and false joy sickened her. At least Henrik had shown his true feelings. Once she was behind the door of her chambers, nerves assaulted her stomach. "Callum," she whispered.

She felt him close a moment before he engulfed her in a hug so tight it cut her air. "Oh, gods, Camilla. I'm both overjoyed and disappointed to see you. Why did you come back here? Why didn't you run when you had the chance?"

"I couldn't. You're here and if I ran knowing what I'm leaving to happen, I would never forgive myself." She wriggled from his hold and raced to the wardrobe for a gown. "You must tell me of the gigantes. Are they in the dungeons? Am I too late?"

"You are," he said. "The conversion is complete. They survived. Eirnen has his warriors. Four of them." He took her hand and tugged her down to sit. "I am sorry, Camilla. There was nothing I could do to stop it. I tried, I swear I did, but without you close I'm nothing. I can't touch anything or even speak, only watch."

"Callum, I believe you," she said and he shook his head. "It's not your fault, Callum."

"No, you must listen," he said and took her hands in his. "One of the warriors, his name is Dorin."

❦

"I want that demon caught," Winston shouted once again. He'd already chased Barrett from the room with his tantrum. He was as angry with his son as he was Shaughnessy, but Eirnen was pleased with the boy. He'd not only done as he said and placed his claim for Camilla, he also hadn't spoken of the gigantes to his father.

"As do I, Winston, and you will have him."

"That I will," he said. "Bosch, tell me everything that transpired."

"Rowan went ahead then came back with Lady Camilla. She claimed to have escaped him in the day while he slept and was lost, but I could sense him close. It was clouded still but being under the concealment blanket with him allowed him nowhere to hide. Lady Camilla was insistent that he was gone and Rowan would not permit any of the guards to risk a fight with Shaughnessy without him."

"I see, and why did you not hunt and kill him yourself?"

"Winston, use reason. Shaughnessy is a master. Bosch on his own would have been no more than a nuisance. Your bias against Shaughnessy taints your judgment. Rowan was right to stay with Camilla. It was his order to do so."

"Can you still sense him?"

"No, which means he is yet under the concealment and I can find it again."

"Go. Take Barrett with you for the snares and whatever guards we have left here. I want him staked to the wall in Gladen within the week."

"How will your son feel about leaving his betrothed so soon after her ordeal?"

"My *son* will seize the opportunity to avenge his bride." Winston rose to leave and Henrik moved as if to stop him.

"Let him go, Henrik."

Eirnen couldn't hold the smile as he watched Winston stalk

away. No, there would be no more begging for aid from Winston. It was follow, join, or fall under the blade of his warriors. They were even now training with Riley and Rowan. He yearned to see them again and let the draw of the connection he'd instilled within them lead him. They were his and more magnificent than he'd dared imagine.

Henrik rushed to try and talk to Winston, to soothe their ally, rather than admire Eirnen's creations. The caster's little rhymes still set Henrik ill at ease about them. She'd talked of death and balance and it had been met. He'd taken lives and had given new life, elevated life. The numbers didn't matter, it was the quality he created against those he destroyed. There was no comparison. He would sacrifice every being in Calame if the reward were more gigantes.

They moved with the nimble grace and speed of the vampire, matching Rowan with ease. Though their kind had been more likely to rip a small tree from the ground to use as a club rather than handle a real weapon. They'd taken a liking to the long swords. Rowan and Riley were instructing them on how to wield them with expert skill and they caught on quickly. Particularly Gabriel, Nikolai, and Dorin. Nox still held a penchant for the intimacy and savagery of a close kill.

They claimed to be brothers, the four of them, but Nox was an obvious oddity among them. He was dark hair and eyes from the start and more volatile than the rest. The others were all golds and greens when they'd arrived. After the conversion, they were uniform in the color of their eyes at least. Black. No whites or tints of color, just dark pits that promised hell. He couldn't wait to set them loose on Abel.

Riley broke away from the session to give yet another report. Eirnen wanted to know how they fared and progressed several times a day. Riley was the best to tell him if there was any sign of sickness in them. "Nothing, your highness," he said, breathing hard. "If anything, they grow stronger by the hour."

"Their skill has increased impressively with the addition of Rowan," he observed.

"Yes. He can move fast enough to give them a challenge, but they're faster." He stared at them, as in awe of them as Eirnen himself. "We'll be pitting them against one another after a few more lessons with the swords."

Eirnen nodded his approval. They wouldn't get better if they weren't challenged and once they'd learned all they could about swordplay, the twins wouldn't be enough. Gabriel knocked Rowan back and held the tip of the wide blade under his Adam's apple. If Rowan swallowed, he'd lose the ability to speak. "I think the need for a challenge has come to pass."

Riley chuckled, but Gabriel remained expressionless as he lowered his sword. They exceeded every test and expectation. They retained their telepathy but could only communicate with one another. The sun didn't burn them though they were sensitive to it. Wounds healed as quickly as they were made. Riley reported earlier that he believed they held some of Marion's foresight by the way they moved to block an attack. He'd conceded that it could be a product of the warrior's vampire-like ability to perceive the slightest change in expression or muscle movement. They'd know soon enough. Eirnen would be doing more training of his own later.

Rowan and Riley set them up, Nox against Gabriel and Dorin against Nikolai, then split the pairs to advise from the sidelines. At the first clang of metal on metal, Eirnen left them to it. There was no chance of the brothers delivering a killing blow to one another. Eirnen on the other hand, they'd like to. They felt deceived, but their grievance would pass once he gave them their revenge.

His thoughts turned to Camilla and what would be done about her. She'd betrayed him and admitted it openly in front of witnesses not of this household. There must be repercussions. There was no way around it and she was deserving. There was the problem of the convenience and advantage her ability offered. If he angered her now, it might be lost when it was needed most.

At one time, Winston's seeker may have been of use finding Abel, but now with Winston's mind turned to revenge, he'd do nothing else until he'd found Shaughnessy. Also, Eirnen's pride would not allow him to beg such a request of Winston. And after all the things he'd done to remind Winston he was but a subject under Eirnen's rule, the bastard would accept nothing less than begging.

Removing the wards around her chambers was like untying a knot, it wasn't difficult to unravel if you knew every loop as he did. She sat in the vanity chair, still unwashed and dressed in a man's shirt that had to be Shaughnessy's. She didn't turn to look at him, she kept her eyes on her reflection in the mirror. He could see what she saw and he had to admit, there were differences. The dark circles half-mooned under her eyes would be cured with the sleep she so obviously needed. But the weariness was deeper. There was a new wisdom to her that only came with harsh realities.

"There's blood on your shirt," he said but she did nothing other than blink. There was a rust-colored blot at the collar which made him think Shaughnessy had fed from her as if she were one of his blood whores. The other was a wide, tapered smear on the back at her shoulder blades. "Bosch says you escaped Shaughnessy in the day while he slept. It's unlike him to be so careless." She said nothing. "It's petulant and below you to employ the silent treatment. It equates to the actions of a toddler kicking on the floor for a treat."

She swiveled in the chair and looked at him with narrowed eyes. "You want to talk to me about toddlers and petulance? You lock me in this room like one. I had thought that I was in a prison, but now I know better. I've seen your prison and what you do with those in your capture. I have no more illusions about you, Eirnen."

"Eirnen? I see," he said. "You can call me by my given name if you like, but it doesn't change the fact that it is my blood, my power inside you. Distasteful as it is." Her eyes flickered from him and back. "It must have been upsetting to see the dungeons, but you condemn me without giving me the benefit or courtesy of defense."

She stood, grasping the spindly back of the chair to whip it across the floor. "Defense? You want me to allow you to defend what I saw? Then tell me, Grandfather, defend the torture of a caster female. Shaughnessy staked to a wall and a wolf in barbed chains. What justification will you give me that can restore my trust in you after the fifty-nine lives you took to create your warriors?"

"Your ghost is a chatty one isn't he," Eirnen said and wished he could get his hands on the little prig. The look of surprise lasted but a second before it was eaten away by anger. She wouldn't be distracted. "Marion was a traitor. She fed, housed, and hid Shaughnessy to aid him in carrying information back to Abel."

"I don't believe you and even if it were true, it still doesn't excuse what you've done."

"I never said anything about making excuses and that's not what you asked for. Tell me, Camilla, why do you think Shaughnessy took you? Do you believe he wanted to make a new friend of the granddaughter of the man who took everything from him? I know you're naïve and I am in part responsible for that, but think, Camilla."

"He told me he was going to rip me into pieces and leave me on your doorstep," she said, but it lacked fear.

"Ah, but then why are you still alive after almost two weeks in his company? Shaughnessy and I have a long history. I first met him when I was younger than you are now, when he readied to challenge my father but thought better of it and left Calame. He returned once my father died. He thought me weak, easy prey. He came for my family, not for me directly, those I loved. He and his horde did far worse to my younger sister than what was done to Marion. Shaughnessy had Cassandra for weeks, feeding her his blood to sustain her life and his amusement. I was minutes from having her back, or so I thought. I was young and prideful. He was waiting for me with her body.

"It was a painful lesson, but I learned to not underestimate or trust an enemy to be honorable. I'd won. I'd found him and defeated his army. I believed he would give her over. I was a foolish child. He fled like a coward. Cassandra's body lay broken in the dirt and he just left her there before me. Shaughnessy and I have had other battles and each he lost, but none as devastating to either of us as the first. I've learned, Camilla, but every lesson was bought with the violence and pain I sought to protect you from. You see your chambers as a prison, I saw it as a shelter. I have more enemies than Shaughnessy or even Abel. Any one of them would relish the opportunity to take you from me."

"I'm sorry," she said. "I hate it that those things happened to you and made you the monster you are now so others suffer the consequences. It saddens me that you're sincere, you truly believe you're doing what's necessary and that it includes using not only your children but your grandchildren. I know why you come to me now and why you're telling me these things to garner my sympathy. You want me to show you where Abel is hiding and nothing more."

"I am a monster, as I will continue to be until the time comes that I no longer need to be. You have been my one weakness, Camilla. I didn't love my sons and daughters as a father should. They were tools I used to the greatest benefit. Your aunts and uncles were married and bearing children by their fifteenth year. Their sons and daughters are doing the same or making preparations to do so, but you are in your sixteenth and unwed.

"From the practical sense, before this power of yours arose to give me further motive to hold on to you, you should now be round with child. Winston's child. He put a claim on you before you were in your second year and has been pressing for his right since your thirteenth. I've denied him and delayed him and now you've put him off you completely. No one could understand why

I didn't turn you over with the same ease as I had my daughters. The only explanation in the mind of my enemies is you were too powerful to relinquish or too cherished. Both made you a target as a means to weaken me."

"But if that were true, like you said, why aren't I dead? Shaughnessy could have killed me. No, he wouldn't have had to even expend that little effort. He could have let me die."

"He let you drink from him?" She nodded then raised her chin and crossed her arms over her chest. Eirnen smiled, but it wasn't pleasant. "He saved you from a killing injury that you wouldn't have gotten if not for him. Let me tell you what I know of Shaughnessy and then I'll leave it to you to make a decision with regard to his motives. He saved you, was gentle and kind with you, confided in you and did things that earned your trust. He gave you pleasure your inexperienced body wasn't prepared to defend against with the bite he didn't force on you. You offered, allowed it." He was right and she couldn't hide it from him that he was. He pushed his advantage to the tipping point. "Do you think he stole Cassandra from me? She went to him, a young girl in love."

"It's not true," she shouted with her fists balled at her sides. "This is true," she said and sliced her hand through the air.

An image appeared before Eirnen's face, close enough that he could believe he was in the dungeons with Marceline hanging and bound. "She is impressionable, too full of her own innocence to sense betrayal in others. With one outing and a couple of steeds she's as good as mine. I'll know her secrets, Eirnen, I swear it to you."

The image vanished as he ended Marceline's words with a deep kiss and another began. Marceline free of bonds, using her natural assets to tempt and torment Shaughnessy. She licked his lips and rubbed against him. She smiled wickedly at Eirnen as he came down the stairs and doubled her efforts with Shaughnessy.

"Difficult to resist when she's this enthusiastic, is it not?"

Eirnen heard himself ask the vampire who was trying to fight the obvious pleasure her strokes and licks were bringing his body. "You did well, wife," he said and fisted her hair in his hand to yank her head back from Shaughnessy. He leaned down and kissed her even as the rest of her was pressed tight and began to writhe against the vampire. "Camilla has shown me Abel with her power for little more than an unlocked door and an agreement to stay my hand with Rowan. She is yet my lamb even though she's trying to grow her claws."

"I told you," Marceline said and groaned as Eirnen moved to her neck. Her hand worked fervently against Shaughnessy who'd closed his eyes and leaned his head back. "A little rope. That's all it would take to make her gracious again. May I have him, my reward?"

Once the image cleared and they were again the only two in the room, Camilla said, "As you know, you told her yes." He had to admit, to have that displayed as it was, by her especially, should have been appalling. But the actual scenes were overshadowed by the fact that she could conjure those images as quickly and precisely as she had despite being exhausted.

"I don't deny that I've done things you may see as cruel." He went to the door and stopped. "I won't put the wards back. I made a deal with you and I broke it. I was hasty and I apologize. Winston is no longer on the grounds. Feel safe to do as you please. These trials, they've made you stronger. Your power has grown and it was hard won, just as mine was. Search yourself and you'll know you would commit acts now to protect those you care for you wouldn't have considered before."

Camilla went to the door and slammed it closed behind him. She was mad, mad and confused, and what she wanted to do was sit on the floor and cry out her frustrations. But she wouldn't. There was no resolution or productivity in it. She stripped the shirt off and threw it then stepped into the now cold bath.

Was it possible that she'd fallen for the tricks of yet another with greater skill to manipulate than she had to see through it? She didn't want to believe it, but thoughts she couldn't help whispered questions she couldn't answer. Eirnen's motives were known. Shaughnessy's weren't, not completely, which left it open to speculation. She was reminded again of what Shaughnessy said about evidence surrounding a situation. He was right. People do draw their own conclusions and he hadn't taken her just to give her respite from her life.

She dressed and decided to test the bounds of this new freedom. It was nearing morning and she should be sleeping. Her eyes burned and her limbs were heavy with exhaustion, but she couldn't rest. It wasn't out of kindness or trust that Eirnen left her free. She'd shown him she'd seen beyond his wards and he knew they could no longer hold her. He was trying to get her back on his side.

The people in the village were innocent. They had lives and futures he stole to fuel the energies he needed to make warriors because he couldn't beat Abel with his own power. He'd called Shaughnessy a coward, but she wondered if Eirnen could see as plainly as she did Shaughnessy wasn't the only one.

Dorin. Was it truly her Dorin or another? She intended to find out. For this, she had to go alone. The brothers were—at least in part—vampires, which might allow them to see Callum and Tamara. If it was her Dorin, no matter what he had been, he was Eirnen's now. She couldn't trust him to hold her secrets.

Loud crashes of metal and sounds of male exertion met her in the corridor. The training room, of course. Eirnen would want them as sharp as any other weapon he possessed. A few steps down the passageway, she paused, craning her neck to try and glimpse them before she went any farther. She gasped and stumbled back, throwing her hand out to steady herself and thanked the gods a wall was there to catch her. Impossible. She turned and let her feet carry her without any thought to where she was going. She just had to be away.

It was only a second, but it was enough. She knew him, knew every line and curve of his wide back and shoulders, how they felt beneath her hands. The way she felt beneath him. Feminine and protected, loved and safe. She'd memorized him down to each alternating sliver of green and blue that gave him eyes the teal color she'd spent hours staring into while she pulled his soft hair through her fingers. Now Dorin—her Dorin—not some other poor creature bearing the same name, was Eirnen's and Marion had known he would be. *I'll meet him first.*

He stood tall, his skin bronzed rather than cold and dying, but he was still a creature. How could something born of the evil committed against him be anything other than what it was designed to be? The deaths of all those people had been thrown into him, pounded in until they were part of his very soul.

She felt him before she looked up. The first tear dripped to her cheek when she saw the proof of her fears. His beautiful eyes were replaced with black marbles. There was no life to them, no sense of the man she'd wished was real a hundred times over though he was standing in front of her in the flesh.

"Why do you grieve, female?" Gods, his voice was the same.

"For the same reason anyone grieves. I've lost someone," she said and pushed past him. He followed and she quickened her steps to get away from him and what he'd become. "Dorin, please, let me go."

He caught her arm and moved her around without effort, the movement so fluid it was a dance. Her back brushed the wall and he caged her in with his hands planted on either side of her body.

"What do you know of my name?" His elbows bent and he curled his body until she could look nowhere but at him or some part of him. The black eyes glittered and his lips twisted until she could glimpse fangs. "Are you another lie, another deception to hold me and my brothers to this place?"

"I—I don't know what you mean," she stuttered and rolled her eyes to the side. Instead of finding help in the corridor, she saw only his shoulder. That shoulder bunched before he drew back and slapped his hand against the wall with a loud crack. She cringed and brought her eyes back around to his as he wanted. "I had nothing to do with this," she whispered. "I swear. I wanted to save you."

The sound that came from him could have been laughter if it weren't so full of outrage. "Devils proclaiming themselves saviors and even the Fates disguised them as angels. Mayhap my brothers and I are damned after all."

He shoved off the wall, giving her just enough space to run. She didn't stop until she was in her chambers. She bent with her hands on her knees to force air into her lungs and assured Callum that she was fine. What had he done? If she didn't know any better, she'd think Eirnen let her out to torment her with Dorin, to show her how much he could take. But that wasn't possible. He didn't know of her watching Dorin or James. He couldn't know how much pain it would cause to see one of them lost. Could he?

James.

She sat back to conjure up an image of James, something she'd done when she needed peace and balance. He was so gentle, kind, and yet protective. She'd watched him, shared his pain and fear when he first shifted form to that of a great black wolf. He hadn't known what he was, hadn't imagined he was a beast like those his adoptive father and brothers hunted. They feared them, hated them as unnatural and against their single god.

James hadn't hated them, even before he discovered his truth. He'd argued they were as natural as the humans that hunted them because of their ties to the earth and land around them. God had to have created them as well. No one listened to him. They laughed and poked fun at the gentle nature she so appreciated.

Now he'd taken the dangerous task of using his heightened senses to seek other wolves, to warn them and free the ones snared in metal traps. She feared he would be discovered and shot with the muskets his family enjoyed so much. Even now, he was sneaking away under the cover of night while Camilla watched from a room filling with warm sun.

James was fine. Untouched by Eirnen's cruelty.

"Camilla, you have to leave here. Go to him. Go to James. You saw the life you can have, the vision with the children has to be your future with James. Go, please."

"And then what? Eirnen sends Winston's seeker for me again. Only this time it puts James in jeopardy. I won't do that. Besides, I can't just leave you and Tamara here."

"Then take us, too," Tamara said. Camilla turned to explain she couldn't but stopped herself. Could she? "We're attached to you, right? So why can't we go wherever you go or wherever you command us to go?"

"I tried calling Callum to me in the caves. If it were that easy, it should have brought him to me."

"But the concealment spell may have blocked the way somehow," Callum said, excitement lighting his eyes. "We should test this. It could be a way for us to all leave this place."

Camilla agreed to start testing the limits of their bond. It would be wonderful if they could go with her, start a new life, especially Callum. For now, she was too tired to think, but so keyed up at the same time she wasn't sure she could sleep. Callum excused himself to let her change. Tamara stayed, wandering around the room, trailing her fingers over furniture and bottles.

"Is there something you wish to discuss, Tamara?"

Tamara sat in the vanity seat and watched her own reflection. "If we are attached to you and not just this place, do you intend to take me as well when you leave?"

Tamara did her best to look as if the answer wouldn't affect her one way or another, but Camilla knew it mattered a great deal. "I know you and I haven't gotten to know each other well, yet, but I will not leave you here alone."

"Thank you." Tamara's thin shoulders fell with relief.

"Tamara," Camilla said and reached out as if to take Tamara's hand, but stopped. "I am sorry for the life you've had here and part of me wants to hate you for what you did. You took my brother from me. There is nothing you can ever do to make up for that. I do understand that he may have been my brother, but he was your tormentor. I'm not saying we will be best friends, but I will not punish you for saving yourself."

"I loved him, you know. Before I hated him, I loved him." She looked up with a sad smile. "Good sleep, Camilla."

"Thank you," Camilla said to the empty room.

CHAPTER 12

FOR THE SECOND day, Eirnen watched Camilla on the grounds, walking farther and farther from the castle. Though she appeared to be alone, he could see her conversing with some unseen trespasser. She'd refused him each time he asked for her assistance, or her company. Today, she'd outright laughed in his face. It had taken everything in him to not lash out at her, although, at this point, a little punishment might be the only way to bring her back to heel.

"You know what you must do." Marceline slid her arms around his waist, pressing herself tight against his back. "She is no longer simply defiant, Eirnen. She is challenging you as king. Are we to have a queen of Calame now?"

"You go a step too far, Marceline." He pushed her away from him.

"Do I? Or do I speak truths you don't want to hear? She is too powerful to tolerate tantrums from her, Eirnen. You know this now. You've tried appeasing her and she released your oldest enemy. I know being harsh with her will be difficult, but you mustn't fight to regain the upper hand alone, My Lord."

Regain? As if he'd somehow lost the upper hand. Ridiculous. He turned back to the window and found Camilla sitting in the grass, laughing. He fought a smile, forgetting for a moment she was no longer just his treasure. She was a potential ally. Was it possible she could become an enemy? Would leaving her unchecked now result in him warring with her later, maybe killing her?

She lay back in the grass, arms spread wide, the sun playing in her hair. She looked like an angel. A tear slid down his cheek. "It must be done."

"I shall take care of everything," Marceline assured him. "Remember, my husband, bringing her back to her family is more for her good than ours. For how would a Westwood fare, alone in a world full of enemies?"

⌁

"I wager you'd unclamp your thighs for him, wouldn't you, princess?" Tamara dropped her knees to the side to flash Camilla and Callum for a second until her shift fell to cover her. She laced her hands behind her head and laid back on Camilla's bed with a wry smile. "Don't look scandalized, Callum. You've seen much more of me than this."

"You didn't," Camilla shot Callum a hard look and let the image of Dorin fall away. She still couldn't believe that not only was he here, but he was one of Eirnen's warriors. A killer. She'd watched him train with his brothers at a relentless pace all morning to do just that at Eirnen's bidding. "How could you, knowing what happened to her?"

"I didn't touch her," Callum said and Tamara laughed.

"Only because you couldn't. But Camilla is back," she said and slithered off the bed until she was hip-to-hip with him. "You can feel me now, can't you, Callum?" she purred and licked the side of his neck. "I saw the way you looked at me. You wanted to touch me."

He caught her upper arms and pushed her back. "Tamara," he closed his eyes and ground his teeth. She groaned and closed her eyes as if pleasured.

"Not in my room," Camilla said and was proud to note there wasn't a hint of heat in her face.

Take that Shaughnessy, she thought, but the sudden lightheartedness of the moment faded. She tried again to see him, but he was still veiled behind the concealment spell, lost to her. She missed him, missed his teasing, and their talks.

So far, Callum and Tamara could be with her anywhere on the grounds, but to really test it they needed to go farther. They'd been searching Winston's wall for openings, weaknesses or doorways. Callum and Tamara were watching the guards to see anyone who left. There was the doorway to the rear that led to the creatures. It was the only one she knew about. Surprise of all surprises, there was a guard posted there at all times. After what Eirnen had done, her taking a casual walk through the village without a guard was not wise.

To that end, Callum decided to speak with Rowan and Riley that afternoon, to show himself and explain what he was. They knew where the doorways were and Callum believed once he spoke with them, they would escort her away from Westwood Castle far enough to know if the grounds were a boundary. She hoped he was right. And if they could, if they could all leave here together, they were planning for that also. Granted, they hadn't gotten far given that none of them had ever left Calame, but there had to be a way. They would find it.

They wondered if they could find a vampire who could take her to Shaughnessy. Camilla thought she could find Rissa. There was something there, a slight tugging she believed may be her energies calling for her from inside the vampire. She didn't dare attempt to summon her. Firstly, it may not even be possible, the tie not strong enough to compel her to obey. If by chance Rissa couldn't resist the call to Camilla, Westwood Castle would equal her death.

Tamara and Callum were still laughing, but the teasing had lost the raunchiness. She shook her head and went to the wardrobe to change. For him to speak with Rowan and Riley, she had to be with Callum, and the surest place to find the brothers these days was in the training room with the warriors. She smiled and pulled out the dark wine-colored gown that Callum said looked best on her. It was most certainly not to catch Dorin's eye.

"Leave some of your hair free," Tamara advised. Callum nodded. She did, carefully plaiting and pinning sections in the front to keep it out of her face, but the rest she let hang to her waist.

She'd caught Dorin watching her while she was outside. Tamara pointed out his expression as one of admiration. Camilla had to admit his expression hadn't been hostile, it had been thoughtful, almost tender. As for Camilla, she'd been brazen, meeting his eyes and offering what she hoped was a flirtatious smile. Callum and Tamara had been with her. Either he couldn't see them or he could and hadn't divulged her secret. She wanted to trust him but knew it was the person he'd been she trusted and this version was an identical stranger. Maybe.

She'd been thinking about her visions of him. His clan had been so far away, how had she met him? Even if she solved that mystery, how had she continued sneaking back to see him when he was more than a week's ride away? She had no answer to these questions, which made her wonder if perhaps what she'd seen of the two of them together occurred after he'd been altered? After he was Eirnen's warrior? It made more sense. But his eyes?

She'd been replaying what he'd said, particularly the part about her being a deception to trap him and his brothers. She wanted to know what he meant. Maybe she could talk to him, convince him she wasn't the devil he accused her of being. He'd said devils disguised as angels, which made her hope he saw Henrik and Eirnen for what they were. She would make him see her, too.

A scream had her spinning around to find Callum and Tamara on the floor. "Camilla," Callum shouted, cradling Tamara in his lap. "I don't know what this is. Something's wrong."

"Eirnen," she growled.

It had to be him. He was doing something, retaliating for her refusal to show him Abel. She swiped her hand through the air to see Eirnen in the great hall and he wasn't alone. Henrik, Marceline, Rowan, Riley, and a man she didn't know stood with him. They were all staring up the stairs as if they'd heard Tamara's screams. The man was speaking, but she couldn't hear the words over Tamara's painful pleas and Callum's calls for her to do something.

Tamara's hands began to fade, even as she clutched Callum. Oh, gods, Callum. She stared, but this time it wasn't screaming that sent a shudder over her body, it was silence. Tamara was still there in Callum's lap, but she was insubstantial, tinted air. Her mouth opened and closed like she was trying to breathe.

Fear and confusion shifted to something dark when Callum doubled over, his teeth bared with a hiss of pain. Tamara was almost gone, and Callum was next.

She ran down the stairs, dragging energy to her from anywhere she could take it. "Stop him now or I will," she said and aimed at the man whose chants spoke of banishment.

"This is for the best, Camilla," Eirnen said.

"Lies," she said and threw enough power to slam the banisher's body against the wall. He slid to the floor, head at an odd angle, and silent. "I'm no longer so easily led by your flowery words, Eirnen."

"You are still easily led, Camilla, but don't fault yourself. You are outmatched," he said just as Callum said, "it's not over."

"Where's the other?" she demanded and he smiled.

"Hidden. How fare's your spy?" She cast another worried

glance behind her. "You can stop this, Camilla. Show me what I need to know to save this family and it'll stop."

"Camilla, don't," Callum said and flickered. "I'm already dead. I shouldn't be here anyway. Let me go. Don't give him this."

"One image, one look to tell me where Abel is hiding, that's all. It costs you nothing but buys you much." Until he wanted her to show him something else and then he'd threaten them again.

Camilla could feel Tamara. She was terrified and far enough gone that there were moments of nothing until she roared back through Camilla's awareness. She was fighting to stay and Callum was asking to go. "I can't let you go. Not like this. I'm sorry, Callum"

Eirnen held a hand out as if to stop someone coming into the room, but when Callum's body relaxed, she realized he'd stopped the banishment. "Show me, Camilla. Now."

The room opened up until the walls disappeared and were replaced by a heavily wooded landscape. She recognized it as the woods she'd gone through first with Shaughnessy and then with Rowan. There was something else playing in her mind, something she couldn't pull forward, and the image blurred as it tried to push through. A moment of a different place, a valley with a creek, flashed into view and then the trees thickened again. Callum was the only one who could fight her on this and he was exerting his authority over his ability.

"Basslyn Woods," Eirnen said. "He's that close. Get the guard together." The image dropped and Camilla shot a questioning look at Callum as everyone's attention was on other things. Henrik took Riley and Rowan from the room, presumably to fetch the warriors, which left Camilla with Eirnen and Marceline.

"He doesn't bargain, Camilla. Not really," Callum said. He looked at her as if he felt sorry for her as she crouched next to him. "I love you. None of this is your fault."

"Callum, what are you talking about?" She looked behind her to see Marceline and Eirnen watching her.

"Continue," Marceline said. "Did you think I would forget that you let that wolf maim me while I was helpless?"

Callum grabbed Camilla's face to pull her back to him. "I was never with you because I had to be," Callum said, his hands on her face getting more and more tentative. "I was there because I wanted to be. I'll help you as long as I can, but you have to leave here. Promise me, Camilla," he said and arched.

"Grandfather," she screamed. "Please. Please, do not do this!"

"Eirnen said the banishment would stop, he never agreed that it wouldn't resume." Marceline was alone now. Camilla searched for Eirnen. "He's still weak when it comes to you. He couldn't bear to watch his treasure suffer this loss."

"Then you will stop it," Camilla said and stood to face Marceline. Though tears streaked her cheeks, rage rose within her. Hatred, this is what hatred felt like.

"You do not want to play these games with me, little bird," she said. Marceline opened her mouth to say something else, but Camilla didn't want to hear it. She lifted her right hand and speared Marceline. Her back and head hit the wall with an echoed thud and Camilla held her there.

"All that spills from your mouth are lies," she hissed, twisting the power in Marceline's chest like a blade. "Everyone tells me I am no good at manipulations, seeing them or using them. I've decided they were right. I don't want to play your game, Marceline. You are going to play mine."

It was the same as the morning with Winston, but now she knew what was happening and welcomed it. Invited it in as she called Callum to her side. Tamara was gone and Camilla felt the hollowness of her not coming when summoned. Callum was trying to get her to stop, to not be lost, but lost sounded like release. Marceline betrayed her, lied, and manipulated. She helped Eirnen hurt Dorin and now she was trying to help him take Callum.

Camilla screamed her rage and plunged deeper into Marceline's chest, raking through until she held the source of that traitorous life in her palm. She squeezed, nothing more than a small flex of her fingers to make sure Marceline knew what was coming. Camilla fed on her fear and pain, drank it in as wine as her fingers closed by increments and shared the bounty with Callum.

Marceline's soul tried to tear itself free from the dying body. It struggled and reached until there was a hazy outline around Marceline, but Camilla didn't want her free yet. Callum said he felt no more pain now that he was spirit, at least not until today, and Marceline hadn't felt nearly enough. Marceline's spirit could taste freedom, Camilla could feel its desperate hope to escape the agony. She let it have a moment to believe relief was in reach before she plunged it back into torment. Now that she'd caught a glimpse, she could see it hovering just under the surface. It called to her, pleaded with her.

Camilla's body shuddered and Callum's voice begged her to stop before he killed her. He? Not Callum, she thought a moment before another shudder rocked her. She felt the unmistakable signature of Eirnen. In the face of someone she wanted more, she ripped the power from Marceline and hurled it down the line of energy that ended with Eirnen's body. It pierced him and she was as filled with disbelief as she was joy. She could stop this, stop him. No one else would suffer at his hands.

"Please, Camilla, they're killing you!" She knew that. She could feel him battering her with his power and the slices that opened her skin as Henrik came to his aid. They would all die here today. Callum sounded stronger, but she could feel he wasn't. The banisher was fighting her for him. "Dorin, help her," Callum begged on a strangled cry.

"Callum," she wailed as he was torn from her at the same time Eirnen slammed more power into her.

"I'm sorry to take this from you, female." Heat and darkness enveloped her. Death was warm, she mused.

❧

Eirnen sat with his back to the wall and wondered if Dorin held Camilla to his chest to save her or his master. He certainly hadn't put himself between Camilla and Marceline. His beautiful wife, his avenging siren, sat slumped to one side. He crawled to her, took her face in his hands and had to support all the weight of her head to meet closed eyes.

"Marceline," he said and stroked her cheek with his thumb. "Look at me, Marceline." Her eyes stayed closed. Her pulse was steady, her breaths even, but she didn't wake. The energy that surrounded her, once so strong and bright as a beacon, was now shrouded in the same darkness he'd watched Camilla command. "I'll find a way to make you whole again," he vowed and lifted her from the floor.

Camilla was limp as a doll across Dorin's arms. She was bleeding from the wounds Henrik made once she'd weakened enough for him to break through the barrier around her. She wasn't dead, which was good because his granddaughter had a lot of suffering to do. He carried Marceline, ignoring the pain in his body until he laid her in their soft bed. He lay next to her and curled with his hands clutched to his chest as if that would contain the stabs that burnt from the inside with each beat of his heart. Marceline whimpered and writhed next to him, feeling the same or worse.

Camilla built a cell and locked Marceline inside, far out of Eirnen's reach. He manipulated energies and hers had been buried deep enough that he couldn't sense them.

There is death here. It lives and breathes here. Its heart beats in this castle. Just as you revel in victory, all will be lost. Westwood will fall by your own hand.

Marion's words replayed again and again. He'd thought she'd been speaking of the spirits and Shaughnessy, but now he had a different thought. Camilla was the death that walked this castle.

He'd not have believed had he not witnessed with his own eyes. She'd pulled death into herself and wasn't consumed. The opposite, she was empowered by it, sustained and encapsulated as it followed her every movement, obeyed commands as if it were a living thing. For the first time in his life, Eirnen was fearful of another being. His precious granddaughter.

This war will be won by death. It will rise up and swallow all in its path. It will lead an army of damned. The night will weep with their screams of anguish when as one they fall. He now realized Marion had said the war would be won, but not by who. Camilla hated Eirnen now. It could be him that was swallowed by her wrath.

It infuriated him most that it was her, the one person he'd loved and cherished with a purity that was beneath him. Even if she'd been latent, he'd have felt the same. Her power had been secondary. She betrayed him. There was no other way to think of it. He knew better, had been taught this lesson well enough by his father, but he'd allowed himself to love Camilla. She was his, of his flesh and blood. He'd spent her lifetime molding and protecting her from anything that might turn her against him. And he'd failed.

He wept for her loss as if she were dead. What he'd seen in that room was not his light, his peace. She'd been darkness with no moon or stars, a void of black space. It fell over her face until she was in shadow as she spoke to Marceline. Her voice had not been her own but overlapped with echoes as if floating up from a deep pit. It didn't waver as she turned it on him.

"Your Majesty," Riley said from the doorway. "Henrik sent me."

"Marceline," he croaked and rolled to his back to give Riley room.

Riley's hand swept her body head-to-foot then back again to settle over her forehead. Sweat gathered on his brow. He could do nothing and feared speaking it. Eirnen lay motionless, waiting for Riley to gather the courage. "I see her with my eyes, but it's as if she's not here. There's nothing below my hands."

"Leave, Riley," Eirnen said.

"You're injured as well," he protested. "There are holes. If I can find a way to restore you, it may lead to Marceline's revival."

"Go. You are not to heal Camilla unless Henrik has cut her deeply enough to kill. See that she is restrained, her power bound until I decide what is to be done with her." Riley hesitated but bowed and left to do as he'd been tasked.

Camilla was lost now. She'd wielded her power with malice against another. Whether she knew it or not, she'd killed the banisher, crushed his skull. Eirnen would bet she knew and had used the death she caused to strengthen her more. When she came to, she would be altered irrevocably. Eirnen should know, he remembered the day he was lost with perfect clarity. It was the day he'd killed his father because of a girl he could barely remember the face of now.

He'd reminded himself of the dead man today. True, he hadn't seduced and bedded anyone, but he'd still used the weapon he knew would cut deepest. Just as his father had done. In time, Camilla would see this friend was not the most important aspect of life. She would learn that it took a firm hand. Sometimes things she now saw as cruel would become necessary, for not only her survival, but the survival of everything she held close. Until now, her view had been as limited as it was simple. This spirit was a friend, maybe the brother Ian hadn't been, and she could see nothing else. Just as he could see nothing beyond Isla.

Father had been relentless in his taunts. Eirnen was coveting what was between one woman's legs, legs he couldn't spread, when there was any number of ripe lasses that would gladly take the son of a warlord to their bed. But those other girls weren't Isla and couldn't quench his thirst for her no matter how many lay beneath him. He'd changed for her, begged for her with nothing more than a toss of her hair. But in the end, she preferred warlords to their sons. A lesson hard learned when he went to the stables, as he did every morning to care for his horse, to see his father pumping into her, hearing her moans and pleas for him to not stop.

The pitchfork was in his hand and through them both, connecting them for eternity at the chest before he'd decided how to kill them.

His father lived long enough for Eirnen to watch him smile with blood dripping from his chin. He'd been proud as he looked at Eirnen and said, *My life for a lesson.*

His father had seen on Eirnen's face what Eirnen felt. He'd seen himself in his son for the first time and smiled even though it had cost him his life for a brief glimpse before he died. Eirnen set the stables ablaze, leaving the bodies to burn, and then claimed Calame as his own. He held it ever since, by any means necessary. He wasn't his father, though. He wouldn't sacrifice himself to teach Camilla her lessons. Calame was still his and would stay that way as long as he was alive.

⤳

"It's done."

Camilla blinked, feeling oddly sore and cold. Her eyes tried to slide closed again but the lids were lifted. She pulled her head back from Riley, her chin went to her chest as soon as she was clear of his hands.

"Stay awake for me, Camilla."

"Move," Henrik growled. His fingers dug into her jaw until she was looking at his face through hooded lids. He squeezed harder, but there was no need, she was awake.

"Back away from her, Henrik," Rowan said with a nervous edge to his voice that made her giggle. Her head stayed up when he released her and she met the eyes of everyone in the room—Henrik, Eirnen, Rowan, Riley, and another prisoner to keep her company. Eirnen and Henrik brought guards, for protection from her. As they should. Callum was gone, they'd killed him. Well, banished him, which equated to the same thing in her mind.

"Where's Marceline?" she taunted, knowing exactly where Marceline was. She was stuck. Half here, half dead. Trapped.

"Abel was not in Basslyn Woods, as I'm sure you know," Henrik said. "The valley that bled into your conjuring, you will recreate it."

"Are we back to that again?" she said and let every bit of tiredness with the subject leak into her tone. "Come closer, Eirnen, and I'll tell you a secret."

He came just as she knew he would, no showing fear for Eirnen. She leaned forward as much as the bonds would allow.

"It's Callum's ability that you're desperate for, not mine. I borrowed it from him and now your new tactic to bend me to your will means you will never have what you want." She leveled her eyes on him and was pleased to no end to see the shock plain in his expression. "It was right here, with you this entire time. And the infallible King Eirnen, most powerful caster in all of history, couldn't seize it. And then you destroyed it. Fool."

She saw the valley in her head in detail. Callum had seen to it that she knew the way, but he didn't want them to have it. Maybe he hoped she'd turn on Eirnen completely and go to Abel, but she wouldn't do that either. It would be suicide and how could she know if he was any different than Eirnen or Henrik? His reasons didn't matter. She'd do as he wanted. His final wish, as it were. They would never know what was in her head. She laughed long and loud until it was closer to howls, which earned a snort of amusement from the real wolf tied to the other wall.

"But you saw it the same as the rest of us. You can recreate it and you will. Callum Dunn was a caster who died here a year ago. Your original power was in you well before his arrival."

"I feel like a butterfly," she said and looked around as if she could see them fluttering in the dungeon. "Riley, how long have you left me sleeping?"

"Your Majesty, she is not well. Give her food and water and allow me to heal her wounds. Anything she says now will be unreliable."

"Can you reverse what you've done to Marceline?" Eirnen asked. "The truth of it, Camilla, and I'll let Riley treat you."

"Yes, I can," she said and smiled at the dark corner where Marceline's fractured spirit hovered. Fractured in spirit just as the creatures had been fractured in essence and energy. They were trapped in a broken body while Marceline couldn't get back into her perfect one. Delightful. "But I won't."

He asked for the truth, but he wasn't happy with getting it. His hands curled to claws and she braced for whatever method he was going to employ in changing her mind. Instead, he grabbed the sides of his head and backed away. He was crazed with his rage, but for some reason he restrained himself. It wasn't fear of retaliation from her, Eirnen feared loss of control and little else. He gave his head a violent shake that had even Henrik staring in confusion.

Anger at her response was one thing. It was understandable and expected. But this was something else, something more. As she focused on his energies, she thought she knew why. There were dark spaces. Not many, but they roiled through his essence like storm clouds. She'd taken something from him and what she'd given in its place was eating at him.

He paced with his head in his hands. His lips moved, though she could only hear the hiss of whispers rather than words. His bellow echoed off the stones as his fist connected against a wall with a sickening crunch. He stilled, his back widening and falling in flares, in time with rapid breaths.

"If I turn to look at you, I will strike you down," he said.

"Go with him," Henrik said as they watched Eirnen stumble up the stairs. "But, Riley, come back as soon as he's settled."

For a long moment, Henrik did nothing but look at her, his expression neutral, almost calm. It was quite disconcerting, but she met his level eyes with defiance in hers. She was used to him shouting, even striking her, but this silence was menacing. He gave no clues as to what his intentions were. For all appearances, he was completely indifferent to the whole situation. She couldn't stand it any longer.

"How did it feel, Henrik, when you discovered Marceline and Eirnen used you as if you were nothing more than a utensil the same as everyone else? Proud Prince of Calame and yet they didn't have enough trust or confidence in you to include you in their plans." She smiled, remembering what she'd watched. "Even Shaughnessy knew and yet you had no idea that you were begging for permission to do exactly what Eirnen wanted you to do anyway. The gigantes had been your idea as hosts, had they not? So eager to earn daddy's affections, you wagged like a dog at his feet."

"Are you trying to incite me, Camilla? I am finished with your games and will engage in them no longer. Your treachery nearly turned my father against me. But he sees you now, just as I always have. He knows he was the one played for a fool."

He pulled two wide silver cuffs from where he'd concealed them at his back. Their surfaces shimmered and had roiling movement as fluid as mercury. She'd seen these before and knew where she was going.

"I didn't kill Ian," she said and anger flickered over the calm.

"You have injured our king—*that* you cannot dispute. Rule of Calame and everything in it is mine while he recovers. And since I see you as responsible for the death of my son, my opinion is the only one that matters."

"He's resting," Riley said, but neither of them acknowledged he was in the room. Henrik was finally going to have his revenge for Ian. He wouldn't be distracted from it.

"I've had time to envision this day. Lots of time. I've watched you die a hundred times, each gratifying in its way, but wholly unsatisfying. Why should I grant you the mercy of final release when I have no end to my suffering? It came to me as if a muse whispered my deepest desire into my head. I want you broken. I want you at my feet, begging me to allow you to demonstrate the obedience you lack the intelligence to give now."

"Once again you aspire to things you will never glimpse," she hissed. She thrashed as he pinned her body to the wall with his, but it didn't budge him. He stretched out, reaching up for the manacles around her wrists. They clicked and slipped away only to be replaced by the wider ones.

He stepped back and her hands fell to her sides, free of the chains that had held them high. Her fingers burned with the returning blood, but the heavy metal circling her wrists was freezing. Sharp stings bit into the skin under them. She clawed at the metal until her fingernails splintered. There was power in them, a lot of it. She couldn't loosen them or move them to get relief. They fit tight, as if molded from clay solely for her.

"Although I am enjoying this, your transport awaits." He smiled at her alarmed expression. "Riley."

CHAPTER 13

"*CHILDREN DIE, SOME never make it to this side.*" Eirnen growled and pounded his fists against his head until he beat Marion back. Of course the little bitch would be here now. She wouldn't miss it.

Lilly screamed the agony of childbirth though it was too soon for the babe to be born. Marion sang in his head, determined to finish the rhyme. But he was stronger. She was dead and he was alive, which proved it. Elaine crouched, pale as the birthing woman next to her and flashed fearful eyes to Eirnen. He had no comfort to give even if he cared enough to try.

"She's bleedin' out," Frances said with the cold tone of reality. She had tended countless births, midwifed many of the women in the village. The babe would not survive. She knew it as certainly as Eirnen. From the number of rags soaked in blood with yet more spreading, Lilly wouldn't either. "Riley, come where yer needed 'stead a gawkin'."

Eirnen could understand his discomfort and his reluctance. Riley couldn't save either one of them but did as he was asked. To leave Lilly with her life, he'd have to spare her the expulsion of the babe, which wasn't possible. Lilly would be healed only to start the entire process again. Riley did what he could to ease the woman's pain, but not even he could relieve it all. Eirnen, on the other hand, would not stay to bear witness. There was nothing more for him to do here.

"Henrik, please." Lilly's small voice told the tale of how near she drew to death.

"Elaine will stay," Henrik said and joined Eirnen. "Where are you going, Father?"

"Wherever I please. I am still king here, am I not?"

For days, each time he tried to leave his quarters, Henrik was there to remind him he was ill and insist he stay in bed. When that route failed to yield the result he wanted, Henrik resorted to manipulation. Eirnen knew he was being managed and he'd allowed it because Henrik was right—Marceline was calm with him close. Any time he left their bed, she whimpered and sawed her legs until he returned, but that changed this afternoon. She was still, so still and cool under his hands. If not for the rise and fall of her chest, he'd have thought her dead.

For the first few days of her condition, he'd waited for her body to whither. She took no nourishment, had no bodily functions save for her heart and lungs, but she remained untouched. He believed she was inside that skin-and-bone prison, just as he'd been at times since Camilla had touched him with death. Marion would begin to whisper, to sing and wrestle him down to a pit of blackness. He could hear and see all that was happening around him, but no matter how loud or long he screamed, no one heard him. His addled mind made no sense of it until he roused to sanity. He was left in the dark with Marion's songs until he clawed his way free.

He'd killed many, many casters, beings of all legend really, but it was she who tormented him. If it weren't so quaint, he'd begin to believe she'd laid a curse on him. She hadn't the power. Only the sorcerers and sorceresses of old had that ability. They were all dead and dust and would remake this world by fire if they could see the state of things now. Their greatness sullied, diluted, as casters who were closer to gods debased themselves with lower beings and allowed the offspring to grow to do the same. It was written that the Westwoods were descended of such a line and Eirnen was working to rebuild what had been lost.

Many were of the opinion that Eirnen merely wished to war and steal lands from their rightful owners. And while that was a small consignment, a minor appeasement meant to whittle away time, his true aspirations were not nearly so petty. The power he possessed was but a speck in a dust storm compared to the pure divinity in ages past. He'd devoted himself, his children, and their children to reclaiming even a fraction of that power. As Camilla had proven, Eirnen wasn't failing to cleanse his line.

He himself had created, made new life and species with his warriors. If that wasn't in sight of the gods, he didn't know what was. None before him but the gods themselves could perform such a feat. *"Now you think yourself a god!"* Marion cackled.

"Father?" Eirnen stopped and blinked up at the bright sun. He didn't remember coming outside, let alone why he'd done it. "What is this of gods?"

"As you should be, I am asking for safe passage to the afterlife for that concubine and your babe," he snapped and breathed a sigh of relief when he saw Marcus. He called the guard over to him as if that had been his intention all along. Henrik was already taking too many liberties with the ruling of Calame while Eirnen "rested." If he knew Eirnen's mind was being stripped from him a piece at a time, he would take the advantage and call it generosity. "Marcus, take the other guards and prepare a pyre in back where the fires will be unseen from the village."

"Yes, your highness," he bowed low, but when he rose his eyes settled on Henrik. "I will ask again that you reconsider sending a number of the guards to the perimeter now that the cultivist's snares are no more."

Henrik's lips thinned and his eyes narrowed. "Your king has given you orders." Marcus offered another bow before he departed.

"Mayhap this would be an opportune time to discuss what has transpired in my absence."

◈

"If your goal is to kill him, you are about to succeed," Camilla said through gritted teeth.

Winston smiled and another blade thumped into Shaughnessy's chest. "Master vampires are amazing creatures," he said from his chair where he was safe from her feet, teeth, and fists. Henrik may have bound her power with these cuffs, but they were heavy enough to raise a knot on a man's head. As Winston was now aware. "As long as the head and heart are not completely destroyed, they can heal most anything with a little blood. Bosch!"

Camilla swallowed back bile before the thing that used to be Bosch shuffled through the door. He was grotesque on his own, but she now knew what she'd have looked like had Shaughnessy not saved her from the aversion spell placed on his cave. The exposed skin she could see reminded her of melted wax that had been allowed to harden in place. His face was distorted until he was unrecognizable. Deep ridges were cut out in places, leaving the skin thinned and transparent, while there was excess in others. His mouth and left eye wouldn't close until both leaked clear, thick fluid that dripped from his disfigured jaw.

He clasped the handle of the first knife with obvious effort. His fingers had melted together until there was webbing between them—rather than spaces—that bled when he closed his fist. She turned her head as the first knife was ripped free. She'd seen this enough to know what it looked like and didn't care to see it again.

There would be eleven more knives before Bosch was finished

taking them from various places in Shaughnessy's body and surprisingly little blood. He was covered in slashes, some thinner as
they healed and others gaping like bloody mouths. One of Bosh's
legs dragged behind him as he made his way back to Winston with
all the knives in both hands. He bowed over them and laid them
on a small table at Winston's right hand as if they were priceless.
To him, they were. He stayed bowed until Winston waved him off
with a dismissive hand.

"He moved that time. You get no reward for failure," Winston said.

Bosh didn't argue. He went to the bureau and collected his
bowl. The rim was flaked with dried blood. Bosch took the knife
closest to him and put the tip to the soft flesh at the bend of his
elbow until blood overflowed his arm, then hastened to collect it
in his bowl.

Shaughnessy's eyes were hooded and wheeled in their sockets
as Bosch drew his head back with a handful of hair. His mouth
was lax and open, which made it easy for Bosch to pour in the
small amount of blood he'd collected. It was just enough to keep
him aware and conscious for more torture, but not enough to give
him back his strength. Camilla's current plan of escape hinged on
first getting close enough to Shaughnessy to feed him and second
keeping him from tearing her throat out.

Shaughnessy came awake on a growl that had Bosch moving
closer to his master. Shaughnessy's lips peeled back to show fangs at
full length and his eyes glowed amber as he homed in on Camilla.
He lunged against the rack, jaws snapping as if her flesh was already
between his teeth. There was no recognition from him, only a
hunger that demanded to be fed. He looked like a crazed animal
that if freed, wouldn't stop until everything in the room with a
heartbeat had no more to give.

"Bloodlust," Winston said and sipped his wine. "He'll come
back to himself in a moment."

Bloodlust. Shaughnessy told her it happened in the newly made, until they learned control, and the starved. Shaughnessy wasn't a newling, but one look at him when she woke here days ago told her he was starved. His skin was pale and had lost that bit of radiance, it pulled tight over his bones until there were hollow spaces between his ribs. His stomach was sunken, making the bones at his hips prominent. His face was nothing more than pale flesh stretched over bone. With his sunken cheeks and dark discoloration around his eyes, he appeared as death.

The snarls died down from that of an animal to the fury of a man. Camilla met his eyes. They were still lit with fire, but he saw her now. Winston had placed her on the bed with Shaughnessy bound on a rack at the foot, precisely because he wanted them to see one another. He wanted her to watch Shaughnessy's pain and see him lose himself until she was nothing but food to him. Winston was convinced that Camilla was in love with Shaughnessy since she'd given him her virginity. "It's female nature," he'd said. He meant to show her how little she meant to him. Or any other vampire should she be tempted in the future.

For Shaughnessy's part, he was made completely vulnerable. His body was wholly revealed and on display. Though he'd been brazen in the cave, this was different. It wasn't of his own will. It was meant to make him feel weak and helpless. The tendons in his arms and wrists bulged and he squeezed his fists so hard, but he wasn't fighting the bonds. Part of his torment was having her witness every defiling act committed against him, for her to see him overpowered by the likes of Winston Cleary. She kicked her chin up and stared at his eyes without wavering until there was a change in them, a hardness that replaced the shame.

"Can you not even stand to look upon him now?" Winston chuckled.

"Doesn't need to," Shaughnessy said with a ghost of that mischievous smirk tugging at his mouth. "The wee lass memorized me, felt me for days."

Winston surged to his feet, fisting one of the knives as he charged Shaughnessy. "Don't," Camilla yelled, knowing it would do no good but unable to remain silent. Winston buried the knife to the hilt low in Shaughnessy's stomach. When there was no more response than a groan of pain, he twisted and pushed as if trying to screw his body to the rack behind him.

Shaughnessy finally broke. A roar of pain tore from his chest. He yanked at the chains tying him and she prayed this time the links would snap so Shaughnessy could rip Winston to pieces. Bosch saw to it that wouldn't happen. He raised a hand toward Shaughnessy and closed his fist. Shaughnessy stilled. Bosch was a seeker, but as Winston had explained when she saw they'd managed to snare Shaughnessy, "What kind of seeker would one be if he lost the quarry the moment he found it?" Bosch not only found them but contained them as well.

Winston must have noticed how close he'd come to getting in range of Shaughnessy's fangs because he jerked back with a shocked expression. He was easy to anger to the point of thoughtless action—another trait that may play to their advantage.

"Well done," Winston said and offered the knife to Bosch. Bosch moved faster than Camilla thought him capable to fall on his knees under the dripping blade. He positioned until every drop fell into his open mouth. When the blood stopped dripping, Bosch's tongue rolled out and he inched closer to Winston on his knees. "Obedience. You will do well to take note," Winston said then wiped the congealed blood from the blade across Bosch's tongue.

Bosch groaned with pleasure and lowered to grovel at Winston's feet. "Bless you, master. Your generosity knows no bounds. Bless you."

"Look at him," Camilla said as she watched Bosch. "He isn't obedient, he's pathetic. You ransom what he needs to make himself whole in exchange for sniveling and to have someone lie to you about your magnificence."

"No," he said and wiped the blade clean on a rag while Bosch watched as if on the verge of tears. "He owes me recompense. As do you and Shaughnessy. I will drain every last drop of Barrett's blood from that demon. He killed him, Bosch allowed it, and you are the reason he went to hunt that creature. He'd not have gone if not to avenge his betrothed."

"I don't believe you," she said and dug her heel into the mattress to push herself up straighter. The bedding under her scraped every raw lash to her back with the movement. Sweat covered her face and saliva pooled in her mouth as her stomach rolled, but she didn't give him so much as a whimper. "I know you're lying. You're trying to claim Barrett went on his own when I know you sent him after Shaughnessy. You're the one who sent your son to die because he wanted me even after I'd made love to a vampire and took your opportunity to have me first."

"Shut your whoring mouth," he thundered and threw the knife. It clanked against the floor and slid to a stop. Bosch scrambled for it, then lifted it to run his tongue over the groove where the hilt and blade met in his desperation to get even one more drop. Winston pounced onto the bed and slung one leg over her waist until he was straddling her. "I will hear you scream!"

"Not if you are half as skilled as your son," she said and arched under him. He froze. All the color drained from his face before it flamed red.

"Barrett did not lay with you," he said without conviction.

"Why do you think he was so eager to have me all to himself?" She saw his arm draw back and then nothing.

❧

Eirnen paced in a furious line, too incensed to even begin to see a calm state. *Twelve days. Twelve days I was gone, not three. I remember three. It was only three, they lie.*

"Come dance with me, Eirnen."

"Quiet!" he commanded, and Marion giggled.

"You are so much more pleasant when we dance, please come back. Children born and children die..." He let go of a scream that drowned out that detestable child's voice and when he finished, he was alone in his head.

As predicted, Lilly was dead, as was the daughter she was carrying. Henrik blamed it on that insipid girl and her chants, but she was not due that amount of credit. Stillbirths and hemorrhages were common occurrences, 'twas coincidence. Henrik refused reason, citing his new wife's lack of conception as further proof. Trickery, that's all. Fallacy. A ploy to rein Eirnen to his side with Abel. Negotiation! He kicked one of the candelabras, sending lit candles across the great hall. One of them rolled perilously close to the tapestries before it extinguished, but he didn't care if it lit the whole of Westwood Castle on fire. He would destroy it all before he watched Henrik do it.

Assassination. Claim the throne. Send Camilla away. Camilla. Only means of recovering my mind. Wants me weak. Assassination. "Marcus! Marcus, come!" He spun in a circle until he found the guard. "Is it done? Where are Rowan and Riley? My warriors?"

"We are here, my lord," Riley said with Rowan next to him. *My life for a lesson. Westwood will fall...* He made another revolution, feeling closed in and surrounded. "Eirnen," Riley said sharply, drawing his attention. The guard was closer now. He hadn't seen him move, yet he was feet away.

"Careful, Riley," Rowan warned with a pointed look at Eirnen's hands. They were ablaze with blue fire that he didn't recall conjuring.

Riley took another small step and raised his hands in front of him. "I mean no threat," Riley said. "Let me help you."

He's Henrik's man now. This is his opportunity to seize on your weakness. A shanty, no more than a square with gaping boards. A woman on her knees, begging to keep her sons. Eirnen shoved her away with the side of his foot and picked up his two new finds by the scruff. He passed them to his guard. "Make them perfect," he commanded. Bright light came through the open door, blinding him until he was forced to block it with his forearm in front of his eyes. "Please, Your Majesty. I beg of you! I'll have nothing left," the woman cried.

The picture evaporated, swallowed up by the light. Voices that spoke of waking came to him and they were blessedly clear and familiar. Of course, Riley nor Rowan would attempt an assassination. They couldn't. The guards had made the two caster pups perfect with skill, but Eirnen had ensured they were incapable of harming him or standing idle as someone else did. Even if his mind told him lies now, that was a truth put in place long ago.

"You will speak of this to no one," he said and refused the hand Marcus offered to help him from the floor.

"Yes, Your Majesty," they said in unison. Yes, they were his, never Henrik's.

He straightened his tunic and ran a hand through his hair until he looked the part of a king. "As you may know, I have had a difference of opinion with my son. Have you secured him as I asked and is Thomas truly gone from the dungeons?"

"Yes, Your Majesty," Marcus said. "Henrik has been bound and is sealed behind the wards of his quarters as you requested. What do you wish me to do with regard to the wolf, my liege? It's been four days since his release. He is well back to his pack now."

"As you say, he's with his pack. There's nothing to be done. Abel's messenger is another issue altogether. Who has Henrik charged with meeting him and where?"

"Myself and one other guard of my choosing are to meet a man at the edge of Basslyn Woods three days from today. That's where we caught the trespasser a week ago and discovered the cultivist's boundaries no longer held."

Henrik was aware the protections failed, which meant he'd known Barrett was dead when he sent Camilla to Winston. He either truly hated his daughter or meant to keep Eirnen trapped in this cycle of mindlessness. Perhaps it was a touch of both. He'd said it was to break her as well as ridding this house of her power in hopes it would heal both Eirnen and Marceline. He spoke as if he thought what she had done to them was a cast she continually fed to sustain, but Eirnen knew better. So did Henrik. His backbone had softened under Eirnen's lashing and he said whatever he thought might save him. The final act that forced Eirnen to admit his successor was a coward. But, for the moment, he had no other.

Unless Camilla has been tamed but not broken.

"It's a two-day ride to Gladen, four if Henrik sent Camilla by carriage." Rowan nodded that he had. Seven days Winston's had Camilla in his possession. "She is to be returned to me as soon as possible. Marcus, fetch me my warriors," he said.

His head was clear now and there was much to repair. Henrik proposed a truce. A truce! Even revealed the warriors to that scout as motivation for Abel's acceptance. Eirnen meant to unleash them and watch Abel's face as he witnessed his absolute defeat. More amusing still were the opening terms of negotiation.

Father, he is second in power only to you, Henrik had flattered him. *Imagine if he were an ally rather than an enemy. He has sons and daughters. Amelia yet has two unwed daughters, Durbin four sons. The Westwood line would flourish with such unions.*

Of course, Abel would be salivating at the chance to merge the lines. Such bindings would strengthen the Lockley family exponentially. It would also give Abel a certain amount of control in the rearing of the offspring. Sharing control with Abel was not something Eirnen would abide, nor would Eirnen's queen who would be returned to him soon. He'd promised Marceline Abel's head and she would get it.

"Marcus, when Abel's man delivers the message of acceptance, tell him Henrik will be pleased and wishes to have a personal audience in a place of Abel's choosing. Don't speak of me except as if I were a thing of the past. As if I were already dead."

"Abel is cautious. He'll anticipate an attack at the meeting place regardless of the guise of truce," Rowan said. "He'll be ready for it."

"Oh, aye," Eirnen said. "But to deliver the message of truce, the scout must return directly to Abel. To the camp we have long sought. You will mark the scout so I may trace his movements."

The place he'd sacrificed Camilla's trust to see, forcing her to use a power that wasn't even hers. No, hers had a ruthlessness about it to rival Eirnen's, a sinister edge that brought torment and misery upon those she wished to punish. He cast his eyes to Rowan. The kind of power that could snap the limbs of a man who took liberties. Eirnen believed their lie because he couldn't imagine his genteel granddaughter was capable of such viciousness. Now he knew better. If it were true, then Rowan and Winston had conspired with her to keep this secret because Winston had laid blame at Rowan's feet.

"Rowan, I need a word."

It was a work of determination Camilla didn't know she possessed to show no reaction to Shaughnessy's screams. At least she wasn't being forced to watch Winston have his fun this time. In a way, this was worse. While the vile acts were being committed in front of her, she thought nothing could be worse than bearing witness, but to be separated from him, left to only guess what they were doing to his already battered body, was a torment all its own. She'd see the evidence that remained eventually and be horrified anew with the reality, but first she had to contend with the images already in her head. Gods knew she had plenty as example after her time at Gladen.

When she arrived, the grounds looked nothing like what had been described. She'd chalked it up to one of the lies meant to intrigue her to come here. That wasn't the case. According to the whisperings of the servants who passed the cell, Barrett had made this place an Eden with his ability. When he died, so did all the beauty he'd conjured. The emerald grass browned, the trees and flowers shriveled to compost. Winston had been less than satisfied that Riley pulled her from sleep, allowing her to see the state of his once grand home, but the early awakening had had a purpose and she'd forever be in Riley's debt for doing it.

Convince him you've bedded every male in Calame if you must, Riley had said with desperation. *He absolutely despises the haughtiness of the Westwood family. Use that as well. Treat him as if he is so far beneath you, he doesn't even merit your notice. You don't fear him. He's not worthy of it.*

He'd told her Winston took master's rights with every maiden in his charge who caught his attention. She didn't think she could do as he asked, but one look at the girls in the castle had her steeling her resolve. They were Tamara. Pathetic and skulking waifs who looked as if they did all possible to be less appealing to their master. As he'd demonstrated the night she arrived, it wasn't the appearance of a girl that enticed him, it was the fear, the struggles, and the screams.

She'd asked Riley why he would take such a risk. His answer brought tears to her eyes: "Callum Dunn."

She held her stomach and swayed in her cell. She failed. Callum was gone forever. Her best hadn't been good enough to keep them from taking him away. She'd taken Riley's advice, even if she didn't deserve it. As it turned out, it wasn't needed. Winston's hatred over Barrett's death far outweighed his twisted lusts. He wanted his pound of flesh, his revenge. And Henrik offered her up to him bound, unable to cast against him or even to escape. She was powerless, in the caster sense, but she'd learned she wasn't helpless.

The servants fetched her from her cage the morning after her arrival. They'd stripped and scrubbed her raw before dressing her in a shift thin as paper. She didn't fight or plead as they led her to him or when they shoved her into his chamber where he waited. She straightened her back, though she felt naked in the clothing, and did what every Westwood excelled at—she looked down on him. It didn't matter how they forced her to dress or that they'd bound her casting ability, she was still a Westwood, which meant Winston Cleary was beneath her in both bloodline and power structure. She made sure she put every ounce of that knowledge and judgment of his inferiority in her expression. It infuriated him.

That was also the night he'd taken her to Shaughnessy to show her what he'd done to *the demon who made you wanton, ruined*. She hadn't been ready or prepared for that. The resolve slipped until he got his scream from her and it cost Shaughnessy. No more.

She looked up, though she could see nothing but dark ceiling. Shaughnessy was in bloodlust again. She kept her eyes upward at the sound of whispers. The guard that stayed most often stepped away to hear the message, but the echoes meant if she was quiet enough, Camilla could hear them too. Her lips quirked up at the news that the creatures had once again evaded the hunters. She knew they would follow her here, just as they'd done at the cave, but neither Winston nor the hunters seemed to know where they'd come from or what they were.

In the moments she was left alone, she whispered for them to slaughter everything that moved.

She swayed as she lowered her face. Dizziness washed over her. She grabbed the bars to steady herself only to jerk back on a hiss as the barbs pierced her skin. This must be what imbibing felt like. Her head swam and her eyes refused to focus in their fight to slide closed. She couldn't close them. At least not until she learned how to sleep standing without falling or leaning back. That was the purpose of her cage seated in the corner of the farthest cell so it was under a constant veil of shadow. The edging darkness worked to lull her toward sleep, but the barbs lining every bar of the cage allowed her not even enough room to turn. She could do little more than move her head and even that was a risk.

After the first two nights and days, she thought it impossible to stay awake this long of her own free will. It took one time of succumbing to sleep for her to learn differently. She'd stumbled back and was hooked to the cage wall. The barbs pierced the skin of her back and no amount of lifting to her toes could free her body of their hold as they tore at her. They were sharp as rose thorns and curved just the same, not long enough to snare organs vital to life but more than enough to make her reconsider her earlier beliefs on sleep.

She finally convinced her warring body that even if she did as it wanted and closed her eyes, there wouldn't be relief, only more pain and humiliation. Winston had relished the sight of her caught and bleeding, unable to free herself. It had inspired him as well.

She shuddered at the darker memories of what he'd done to wrench screams from her. It wasn't in the way she'd thought he wanted, but it still excited him. Another lesson she'd learned—no matter how strong you fancied yourself, or how solid the resolve, you would scream eventually. What Winston had learned, she made him hurt her until she was unconscious and no longer capable of screaming.

He seemed to enjoy taunting her with the scars he'd given her. He'd vowed to raise them on every surface of skin. *Eirnen boasted with regards to the flawlessness of your skin, silken berries and cream, he said.* Her back bore most of the marks, but there was a long stripe across the top of her right thigh and a check mark that gave her left eyebrow a bit more arch.

He wanted a fight, wanted fear and forced submission, but it was as if he were afraid to commit that last act that would bring this to its finale. Camilla had begun to believe he feared her, that after what she'd done to him, the power she had wielded over him, made him hesitate despite the warded bracelets. After all, she was an unknown power, even to Eirnen Westwood who she'd lived in the same home with and to whom she'd also done the seemingly impossible. She'd beat him. No matter the reason, Camilla was grateful he seemed to have lost his taste for her.

The guard returned and was as nonplussed as ever. He was a perpetually bored-looking man, as if he'd seen everything and nothing could surprise him. For some reason, Camilla found this amusing and began to giggle until she let go and laughed fully when he didn't even raise a brow at her odd behavior.

"Deredon," Winston's voice was followed by the creaking of metal as he opened the main door to come inside. "Are you regaling our young guest with your wit?" The guard didn't answer and Camilla's laughter died at the sight of Winston's own wide smile.

He twisted a bit of red cloth in his hands that, once he was close enough, she realized was him cleaning blood from his fingers. He stopped, mid-motion, and looked at her face.

"That's a nasty bruise there, pet," he said and stopped just on the other side of the bars. "Here," he pushed his bloody hand close to her mouth. "Go on, give them a suck. Might be enough left to do you some good."

The barbs took bits of skin from the top of her hand and upper forearm, but it was worth it. The metal cuff thumped on Winston's wrist when she brought her arm down as fast and hard as she could before he pulled away. He cursed and cradled his arm close to his body while he paced a circle. He dropped the arm to his side and flexed his wrist back and forth. Not broken. Damn. He'd force fed her Shaughnessy's blood a few times when his enjoyment of her suffering went too far, but she'd been unconscious when he did it. No way would she take it willingly, no matter how injured she was, even if it didn't mean sucking it off his fingers to get it.

More maddening than the lack of food and sleep, was her power. The cuffs bound it, blocked it, but didn't erase it. It was still there, seething under the surface, but despite all her efforts it never broke through. What she wouldn't give to have it at this moment, with Winston looking so self-satisfied. One side of his mouth lifted as if he could read her thoughts. He passed his hand over the lock and the door swung open.

"I've had a thought," he said and jerked her out by the arm.

"A first for you, I'd wager," she said and lifted her head high. He hated it when she acted like a pompous Westwood brat so she did it as often as possible.

He steered her into the room she knew well, the one where they kept Shaughnessy. Her eyes refused to close, to even blink. Whole strips of flesh had been cut from his body until wet, white bones stood out in stark contrast to the loose meat and ligaments. She commanded herself to not turn to the slurping sound, but she wasn't in control of her body at present. Bosch squatted over a ceramic bowl full of wriggling muscle, greedily sucking blood from the tissue.

Winston kept her arm even while he danced back as the bile from her stomach emptied onto the floor. "Disgusting." He took a handkerchief from his breast pocket to dust at his jacket.

He whipped her forward until she sprawled across the bed. Still gagging, she crawled to the end, reaching for Shaughnessy. He wasn't breathing or moving. Her fingers touched the tacky moisture of his chest before she was hauled back, but still she reached. Winston's arms wrapped around her from behind and tightened as she fought.

"Oh, now, don't be ungrateful," he said with his face to her cheek. "That blood will make Bosch more tolerable to your sensibilities."

Winston's breath huffed out hot against her face as a stray elbow caught his soft belly. It wasn't as forceful as it could have been, had it been a measured and intentional hit, but it was enough to loosen his arms. She scrambled free of him, but he had her in the same position within seconds. He used her wrists, crossing her arms over her body, pinning them and using her own arms to pull her tighter until she reclined against him.

"Let me go," she thrashed until she was exhausted, but his hold didn't loosen. She stopped when she felt the evidence of the mistake she'd made against her back.

"Today is the day," he said and licked her neck in one long swipe. "Bosch!" The man stood from where he'd been on the floor at the foot of the bed. Some of the damage had been repaired. The blood on his face made it difficult to say how much, but given the way his eye still drooped, it wasn't enough.

Bosch knelt on the end of the bed. She pulled her legs back when he reached for her ankle. The movement put her tighter against Winston. Bosch kept coming, his hand skimming up her calf, streaking Shaughnessy's blood across her skin. He stopped to stare down at it as if mesmerized and then dipped his head. His tongue snaked out to collect it, the sight and feel of him had her retching again. His face was fuller, some of the ridges filled in, but the fluid from his eye dripped on her. She whimpered. It was the wrong thing to do, but couldn't stop it.

She forced herself to look at Shaughnessy's face. Bruised and swollen as it was, he was still beautiful, still him, still her friend. She willed his eyes to open, to look back at her so she wouldn't be alone with them. Hands and breath climbed higher up her body until she felt teeth at her stomach, nuzzling and licking through the thin material of her shift.

Shaughnessy. Look at Shaughnessy.

The weight of Bosch left her as he went to his knees to throw off his shirt, his now bared chest blocked her view. Winston tightened his hold when he felt her muscles coil, but it didn't help Bosch and only gave her leverage. They wanted her to scream, so she did. She screamed as she hit the mangled chest, that kept her from seeing her bit of peace, with both feet. Bosch tried to catch himself, arms flailing but finding only air. He hit the rack Shaughnessy was chained to and the thing fell over with a deafening crack as wood splintered.

Winston tossed her away from him, more concerned with the possibility of a freed master vampire than a powerless caster. Camilla sprang from the bed, her eyes on the knives lined up on the table. She spun when she closed her fist around the metal hilt, expecting to see one of them about the take it away, but they were both distracted by Shaughnessy. One of his arms was limp at his side, free of the chains. He still wasn't moving but the worry plain on Winston's and Bosch's faces told her they believed he was alive and dangerous.

She stayed on her toes and darted up behind Bosch where he leaned hard on Shaughnessy's chest with both hands. Even if Shaughnessy came to right now, Bosch was keeping him from fighting back. There was no hesitation—Bosch had to die. It was that simple. She jerked his head back by the hair and cut a deep line from one side of his neck to the other. It was harder cutting through him than she'd imagined, more force needed though the blades were sharp, but she did it. She took a step back to watch with interest as Bosch's hands tried desperately to hold the blood inside his body. It spurted out between his fingers, spattering across the floor and Shaughnessy.

"No, no, no," Winston staggered to his feet, his eyes wild with fear. Bosch fell forward. The blood pooled around him, inching toward Shaughnessy.

Winston eyed the door, escape plain in his features. It was still daylight. If he made it outside, he'd be safe until nightfall. He could get away, run to Eirnen for help. *I can't allow that. He dies here today.*

"He's going to make *you* scream," she said, blocking the door. "And I'm going to watch."

The fingers on Shaughnessy's free hand twitched. She smiled as Winston paled. Muscle so deep red it looked purple crept thick as earthworms down the bone of Shaughnessy's arm. The blood around him soaked into his skin and the muscles built faster, strengthening him until the pool was as a creek flowing toward him.

She welcomed the wash of death that shivered up and through her, bowing to it like a cat being stroked. If her ability wasn't bound, she'd have absorbed everything Bosch had been. All his energies, his power would have been hers as a trophy of battle.

"Guards," Winston shrieked and charged her. She lashed out with the knife, opening a line across his rotund middle. He put his hand to his stomach, then lifted it with a look of shock that she'd cut him.

"Please keep bellowing. He'll be hungry after everything you took from him." He made a lunge for the rest of the knives and she shadowed him, throwing the knife out in unpracticed swipes. She grazed him but didn't stop him from reaching his goal.

"Now, little girl," he said and flipped the knife until he held the hilt instead of the blade. She froze and watched him. She'd witnessed how precise he was with a throw. He could kill her without taking another step closer.

He looked over his shoulder at the sound of wood clattering against the floor and Camilla smiled, straightening. If she'd seen something like Shaughnessy in this state a few weeks ago, she'd have been paralyzed with terror. Just as Winston was now. He stood tall and glorious with his sabered fangs and glowing eyes. The skin on his arms was transparent, the muscles beneath thinned until they looked atrophied. Both legs were still in the process of reknitting skin to cover muscle, but they were well enough to allow him to stalk Winston in a low crouch.

Shaughnessy gnashed his teeth and snarled while his prey backed farther into the room. Winston made it to the window and ripped the covering away to flood the room with sunlight. Shaughnessy flinched but was too lost in bloodlust to care that he was burning. He caught Winston from behind and spun them until his back was to the wall and his front was shielded from the sun by Winston's body. Shaughnessy's arms were still burning, his newly grown skin flaking up and glowing like hot coals. He struck on a growl, tearing at Winston's neck until the blood ran in heavy rivulets down Winston's chest. Winston thrust the knife behind him as his face twisted in pain. The blade glanced off the stones, nicking Shaughnessy's waist on the pass.

Shaughnessy repositioned his hold, pinning Winston's arms, and then he squeezed until there was a series of snaps. Winston's howl lasted perhaps a second before it quieted to wet gurgles as blood and froth boiled from his mouth. Shaughnessy was still at his neck, but there was so much blood everywhere else Camilla didn't see how he would get enough in him to make him lucid. The guards hadn't come. Once Winston was dry, there would be no one left but Camilla. She moved into the brightest shaft of sunlight in the middle of the room and prayed it would be enough to keep him at bay. He'd come around eventually, he always did off of the small amount Bosch gave him, but if it would be before or after he attacked her was another question.

She jumped at the sound of Winston's heavy body hitting the floor. Shaughnessy crouched again and her mouth went dry. His lips peeled back, his teeth gleaming and red. His body filled out as she watched, but he was still skeletal compared to what he'd been before. It would take a lot more than Winston to restore him after what he'd been through.

"Shaughnessy," she said and put her hands up. "They're gone, you're safe." Nothing. He didn't recognize her yet. He had, however, come back to himself enough to not charge into the sun after his next meal. He kept to the wall, pacing like a caged tiger without taking his eyes from her. "You have to snap out of this. I need you," she said and her throat tightened. *No.* She would not cry. If she started, she wouldn't stop. "The guards will come and you can't kill them all no matter what you believe right now."

His snarl let her know how much stock he put in her words. If she ran, he'd catch her. The best chance she had was to wait him out in this sun sanctuary. She was exhausted, scared, hurt, and starving. Her whole body shook. She decided to sit down before she fell. Even with him like this, she still felt safer than she had twenty minutes ago.

Her lids were heavy. She let herself slide down to lie on her side. Shaughnessy was still watching her, but with more caution than hunt and the reason made her apologize and reassure him that she wouldn't hurt him. She was a caster, Winston and Bosch were casters, she'd been present for some of his torture. In his confused state, it was entirely possible he lumped her in with them.

Her eyes closed for a moment, or at least it felt like a second, but when she opened them, the whole room was dark and Shaughnessy knelt over her. "I'm sorry I couldn't help you."

"I know, lass," he said and picked her up from the floor. She studied his face and twisted in his arms, running her hands over him. "Don't fret," he said and carried her through Gladen Castle like he knew it.

The low light in the sconces flickered, but the fires always burning in the many fireplaces of Gladen were dark. It was cold and silent. Winston had a few of his own wolves, rogues mostly who didn't want to commit to either of the two larger packs, some shifters, and more guards. Where they were now, she didn't know. But unless they were here when Shaughnessy began his spree and fled, they'd be back.

"You're you. I mean, the old you," she stuttered and that's when she saw the first body. She wrenched her head around as they passed another dead guard, then another. The feet of a servant woman stuck out from around a corner. "You killed them?"

"Vampire," he said in answer.

"All of them?" He gave one small nod, his expression unreadable. They made it outside without anyone yelling about escape. He must have really done it. It was hard to process the idea of him doing this alone, but the proof was all around her. The carnage spilled out onto the grounds. Most of the bodies were guards. There were men dressed as stable hands, but few women.

"The wolves? Did you kill his wolves?"

"Gone when I woke. Shifters, too. Some of the servants ran."

"Stop." She clawed at the cuffs as if this time they'd snap open. "Shaughnessy, put me down."

"Why? Can't stand to be touched by me now that you see what I am?" He dropped her feet so suddenly she stumbled forward, just catching herself from falling. "This was nothing. *This* was entertaining," he said and waved his hand at the body-riddled ground behind him. "I am not weak, Camilla!"

"I know you're not weak. I have never, not once, thought you were." They shared another of those stares they'd become accustomed to using as a means to communicate more than words could convey. Finally, some of the hardness left his features. "I wanted to ask if you would please take off these cuffs? I cannot bear them a moment longer. Please, Shaughnessy."

She held her arms out to him, wrists up, then pushed them closer when he hesitated. She wasn't afraid of him, but his look of caution reminded her of when he was coming out of bloodlust. He didn't trust her. It hurt more than she'd have thought.

Without a word, he began tearing the first cuff free. It creaked and groaned in protest, the casts inside sparked and sizzled, burning her flesh and his but he wouldn't relent. With a final pop and hiss of magick, the cuff came free. The skin underneath drank in the cool air. Who knew wrists could feel so good? The second took less time, without hesitation or caution, he wrenched it from her arm.

He dropped the metal to the ground, but they still moved and shimmered. There were still casts in them. Could someone else use them, take the power of another the way Henrik had done to her? No. She gathered power and then squeezed her fist. The metal on the ground crumpled and crackled with the dying magicks until they were nothing more than silver dust.

"Thank you," she said, taking a few steps back toward Gladen Castle.

It looked even more sinister in the dark. The spires were like massive horns rising from the earth. She imagined the brown, dead vines draping the walls were brilliant green ivies before Barrett died. Everything around it, the grass, the trees, the flowers, were all wilted and dead. So much pain here, leaving it standing was not an option. Hatred and rage burned through her as she looked at it and she let free the power Henrik bound.

She reached out to Shaughnessy where he stood beside her and took his hand, twining her fingers with his. They watched as the castle was engulfed in flames. The heat of destruction and Shaughnessy's closeness were comforts. She hoped it was the same for him. Gods knew he needed some. She moved closer to him when she had a vivid memory of why.

"You feeling guilty because a wee thing like you couldn't save the likes of me is a kick in the ballocks, love," he said without taking his eyes from the fire. "You forget, I couldn't spare you, either, even though if I so desired I could take that castle apart a wall at a time. I had to watch, just as you did."

"He hunted you, trapped you, and tortured you because I let him believe you did something you didn't. It was selfish and cowardly and I'm sorry. If I would have stood up to Eirnen and Henrik and left you out of it, you wouldn't have been here."

He turned them away from the flames to start walking. "Ah, that bastard has been aching to get his hands on me for years. Me that close and him with a talented seeker, he wouldn't have let it pass no matter what I did or did not do with you." She cocked her head for more and that troublemaking smirk came full tilt. "You see, love, I really did bed his daughter."

"Shaughnessy," she admonished but laughed with him. "So does this fulfill Marion's prediction that I'd save your life?"

"Bloody hell no. You got me in that mess," he said and wrapped his arm over her shoulders to pull her in against his side.

∽

"They've recovered her," Gabriel said. Eirnen closed his eyes in relief. Two days he'd spent waiting to hear such news, two days he'd not allowed himself to sleep out of fear Marion would win the struggle he was even now fighting.

Thank the gods, this will be over soon. "And her condition?" He pinched his lower lip between his fingers.

"She's in need of healing, rest, food, and water."

"But did she try to keep them from bringing her home? Has she attempted to flee from them? What of Shaughnessy?"

Gabriel tipped his head to the side, asking the questions of his brother and hearing the answers. Spectacular. When he healed, Eirnen's warriors would conquer this land for him. Now, he had another potential weapon in Camilla. In her way, she was as marvelous as the brothers. The possibilities swirled in his mind. Marceline, his queen, his avenging siren, at one side and an avenging angel on the other.

"She hadn't the capability to do either. Exhausted and beaten beyond consciousness," Gabriel answered. "But the vampire, this Shaughnessy, would not release Lady Camilla. His death was unavoidable if she was to be retrieved."

"Shaughnessy fought to keep her? How romantic! And now you've killed him. She will never, never, ever help you now. Never, never, ever, lost, lost, all is lost..."

"Leave me, Gabriel," he bit out between his teeth.

Once again that common son of a whore may prove Eirnen's undoing. *Bastard!* The stones grated away the skin of his knuckles and the bones crunched, his blood smeared the wall. The sight and the pain infuriated him further, inciting him to strike again and again until sweat stung his eyes and his shoulders burned. As satisfying as it felt to hit something, the pain served the purpose of clearing his head. Marion's whisperings fell silent, allowing a moment of rare peace.

Eirnen paced, preparing for every possible reaction she could have and the perfect counter argument. She had to understand why he did everything she condemned him for. It was for her and her children, her grandchildren. He could secure them, make them powerful beyond imagining. But here, in this life, he did what he must to make their world safe until the day came there would be no need for acts like the ones he committed. There would be none to contend with what he cultivated now. Surely she'd see the end his efforts would give the generations after them, when both he and she were long gone.

But the blood thief, what of him? Perhaps it would satisfy her to see his murderers punished. He would hang the warriors Niko and Dorin by the wrists and whip the skin from their backs, until she felt their debt to her had been paid. He'd allow her to lash *him* if that would get him closer to sanity.

The echo of the doors opening had him drawing a deep, steadying breath and begging Marion to keep to the dark. *Just let me talk to her. Explain. Please,* he thought with his head bowed as if he were praying to the caster as a god. And then he prayed the gesture would appease her before raising his head to go face his salvation or his doom.

All calculating dissolved into genuine fear when he saw her body draped over the warrior Dorin's arms. She was pale, thinner. She'd always been slight, now she looked frail, breakable.

"Give her to me." He made a cradle of his arms and his heart broke at the sound of her pained whimper as she slid into them. "Shh, I've got you," he soothed. "If Winston Cleary is not dead, it's your lives," he said to the brothers.

"He's very much dead, I assure you," Niko answered.

Her lovely skin was marred with bruises and—gods help him—whip lashes. Angry lines raised to welts, some split to bleed, ringed her tiny wrists where the bones jutted up painfully against her skin. Henrik would pay for this as well. Eirnen fought to keep the order in his mouth when everything in him was screaming to send his warriors to show Henrik how Camilla must have felt with Winston.

"I went too far, my treasure," he said and smoothed her hair. "I allowed aspirations that began noble to become coldness and greed. But I did *not* do this thing to you, I didn't send you to him. I swear it, Camilla."

"Grandfather?" Her lashes fluttered against her cheek.

"Yes," he said and kissed her forehead. "Forgive me, Camilla," he begged. Tears rolled down her temples, caught by her hair, which was nearly black with dried blood and all manner of filth. "Please. I only ever wanted you to be safe."

Her eyes opened, no longer dulled with pain, but glittering in the light above her. "You took Callum from me," she accused and her anger seemed to strengthen her. "You imprisoned me, deceived me, intended to send me to Winston once you wrung all you could from me."

"If you're waiting for denial, I'll give you none. All you say is true. I have no words that will suffice. I will apologize now for every wrong I've committed against you. I can't apologize for all my actions you see as callous, but for all against you, I am sorry. You're my granddaughter. I tell myself all I do is for my family and yet here you are, like this. The moment I saw you, your pain, it struck me I've used you as surely as Winston did and deluded myself into truly believing it for the greater good. I believed you'd come to my side, understand my goal, with time. You confronted me, defied me, and I treated you as an enemy I had to best."

"I thought you loved me and would never hurt me, but you

did. You took from me someone precious to my heart. I demand of you the same price."

Marceline. "Camilla, please."

"Those are my terms. Your soul will be your own, but hers will remain mine." She swung her legs over the table, the dress gaping until he dismissed every other male from the room, but she appeared unaffected. "And you do not interfere when I speak to Henrik about my banishment," she said and for the briefest of seconds, he saw the foreboding shadow crawl across her face.

She held his eyes, unblinking. To accept her terms was to be free of Marion, his mind his own and clear. It was also condemning Marceline and Henrik.

"Will you agree to release them in time? Once you've had your due?"

"I'll make no such bargain. They will suffer. I promise you one day you will be tempted to give them the mercy of a dagger to the heart." She dropped to the floor and though she was several inches shorter than he, the power around her was a storm of catastrophic proportions. He recognized some of Marceline in the charge, she used her spirit even now. "When that time comes, be warned that to grant them release means you take their place. Choose, Eirnen. I could just as easily take the rest of you, as I have your wife, before I claim your son as well."

"Stay as I am now, this half man, or become a slave to you? Is this what you're offering, Camilla?" She gave one stubborn dip of her chin. "I will earn your trust back," he vowed. "I accept your terms."

"I knew if it meant you'd have to sacrifice yourself to save your child which you would choose," she said with disgust.

The power around her surged. She meant to cure him of this without delay. Her hair churned like seaweed caught in the tides around her face and body. He couldn't force his eyes from hers as they deepened, the blue of midnight rather than jewels. He winced, groaning as he doubled over with his arms clutched against his chest. It was as if she were splitting him wide, excising his breastbone to reach his heart. The pain was excruciating, but welcome. It was the same agony that made him this way, logic said it must be thus to draw out the blackness she infused within him. *Infused...* he hissed a chuckle. Camilla was the same as him.

The pain ebbed, though an ache persisted in his chest. He drew shallow breaths into his lungs as he straightened inches at a time. Camilla stood before him. It had given him a sense of pride to think she was like him a moment ago, but now that he saw how much, he thought it a tragedy. Gone was the sweetness, the inherent childishness in her features. She'd been stripped of such things and he'd had a hand in it. He reached for her, but she shrugged back with a look that dared him to try again.

"You'll find Henrik behind wards in his chambers." He leaned back against the table and rubbed at his sternum as suspicion flitted across her face. "I meant what I said. I will earn your trust back. You kept your end of our agreement and I'll keep mine."

She glided from the room, emanating hatred like poison while her fingers curled at her sides. A clap of thunder rolled through the castle, confirming his suspicion of Camilla's ownership of Marceline's ability. This day she'd command Henrik's as well. But as he searched his mind and found nothing beyond his own thoughts, there was no room for grief. Henrik and Marceline lived, Camilla's intention was not to kill them. Once her anger receded, he'd convince her to release them. He'd tell her how agonizing his torment had been, remind her it was but a fraction of what Marceline and Henrik felt as a result of her punishment. The soft-hearted Camilla he knew didn't simply vanish, she was buried deep at the moment, but she'd resurface and her guilt would drive her to free them. Likely with an apology.

He called Riley into the room and received the definitive diagnosis of recovery, though he'd had little doubt. He could feel it, or more to the point, the lack of barbed serpents coiling in his skull. The memory of the snares slithering in a wet tangle through his brain forced a shudder. The fullness, the constant ache and chatter was gone. Forever.

Niko and Dorin came as he bid them do with Gabriel and Nox flanking though the other two hadn't been summoned. No matter, it was best they would all hear what he had to say. Camilla hadn't mentioned Shaughnessy, which led Eirnen to believe she was as of yet unenlightened to his death.

"Shaughnessy fled and you allowed it under my order. Understand?" His voice was a croak, but the warriors did him the honor of preserving his dignity and showed no reaction.

"Aye," the two brothers answered in unison.

A scream of fury was joined by one of pain, an ominous reminder of what awaited him if Camilla could not be won. Fear closed his throat and chilled his bones. *Can't go back there.*

He cleared his throat twice, a resolution made as the storm raged on outside the walls. There were two ways he envisioned this going—Camilla as a formidable weapon or foe. Tears streaked his face and again his warriors spared him. As long as she lived, the threat of that demented pit loomed over his head. He warred with himself. If it were anyone else, his course would be clear. But this was Camilla, his light. All her life he'd needed nothing more than to be near her to ease his heart.

His earned reputation alone had staved off many a would-be challenger to the throne. But she'd still looked upon him as a saint, a noble protector she was proud to call grandfather. It was all he'd needed. She would never look at him thusly again. Even if he strived to be everything she'd thought he was, it was too late. She'd never forget, always be tainted against him.

"Be merciful with her," he pled and turned his back before he could watch them go to their task. He planted his feet and squeezed his fists, commanding his body to remain rooted until it was done.

He shook so hard he was all but bouncing when he heard her voice in the corridor. *Go to her, stop this, it is not too late.* While one part of him begged to spare her, the other held him in place. A brush of metal as a sword left its sheath, a gasp of fear and confusion. "Grandfather?"

"Camilla," he was running before he could stop himself again. He was in time to see Gabriel keep her body from falling as Nox withdrew his sword from her chest. "No," he fell to his knees and bellowed wordless pain. He went to his side and rolled into a ball with no care who witnessed the display. *I'll kill them all.*

A clapping sound filled his ears and he stiffened at the ethereal giggle. *"That was fun. Let's do it again."*

CHAPTER 14

"**A**RE YOU SURE about this?" Camilla asked again, stopping to look Shaughnessy in the eye. Would she know if he were lying? Maybe.

"It's too close to sunrise to make the cave from here even if I were willing to chance the place again. You're starving, injured, and exhausted. This is our best option."

"All of that might be true, but you know it's not what I meant." She strained her ears for any sound that would hint at how close they were to the wolves' den. This wasn't safe. "The wolves hate Eirnen, and me by extension."

One of the male creatures pushed his head up under her hand. She was glad they'd survived the hunters, but it had been close. The other male was limping and had what Shaughnessy thought was a wound from an arrow at his flank. The caster boy was more skittish than ever and wouldn't come close enough for her to see if he'd been injured as well.

"At least tell me they like you."

"We've had our differences," he skirted. "Look," he said and stepped in front of her with both hands on her shoulders. "Like it or not, you are a Westwood. There's a reason the wolves give Eirnen a wide berth. They respect power and strength. If they test us, use both. You go in there acting like the meek little moppet I snatched up from those dungeons and it'll mean a bigger fight. Your weakness will be a lure to their animal. Wounded prey doesn't fare well with their kind, love."

She drew in a deep breath and blew it out slow, steadying herself. He let go of her shoulders and took her hand. He pulled her through woods where she still couldn't see much despite his argument about impending daylight. She was tired, more tired than she thought a person could be and still be walking. Her muscles ached and burned on top of the bruises and various wounds she still carried courtesy of Winston. Shaughnessy offered to let her drink from him to heal them. It was too soon, everything that happened too raw. When he'd offered, an image of Bosch squatting over that bowl flashed through her head.

The creatures' ears perked and they crept ahead, sniffing at the air. "No, wait for us," she said when they were more than two yards ahead and moving faster. They stopped but looked back at her expectantly. "You know them, they might not know you until it's too late."

"And they're additional leverage to make us appear friendlier." She didn't like the way it sounded, as if they were commodities, but she had to admit he was right. She could heal them. Though she'd be doing it for them, the other wolves might look at her favorably for it. It was underhanded, but they needed any advantage they could get to help them keep the lives they'd just won back.

She gripped Shaughnessy's hand harder at the first sounds from the pack. He gave her a sharp look and she let him go. She'd been single-minded and callous when she sank that blade in Bosch's throat. Now that Shaughnessy was here and brought with him enough physical strength to level the woods around them, she'd lost it. He made her feel safe and secure, but they were neither.

Besides, he wasn't her protector, and she wasn't his. They would take care of each other, but she couldn't do that if she was always hiding behind him.

She sent out her searching fingers until they brushed on the pack. *So many. Hundreds.*

"That's it, lass," Shaughnessy said as her own species-specific lust rose to the surface. Not blood, but power. It was tantalizing, intoxicating and she yearned to call it to her. It would be so easy. By the time they noticed, she'd have all she needed to overpower them and take the rest.

Just a little. In case they attack.

"There's something strange," she said, wrinkling her nose. She pulled in more energies, testing them. "Not just wolves," she said. "But I'm not sure what is with them. Not casters exactly."

The swirling energies filled her with warmth from head to foot. After many days of cold, it was delectable. She closed her eyes, soaking it in, savoring. She felt revived and strengthened, awash in delight and she'd barely scratched the surface of the bounty they held.

"Oh, Shaughnessy, you can't imagine," she said and smiled up at him.

"I can. But be of care. You don't want to rile them before we've given them a reason.

"Grayson," he said as a greeting and looked over his shoulder. She'd been too caught up in the wolves in front of her to notice the one coming in behind them.

Grayson was alone, for now, but he wouldn't be for long. He was just as he'd been that night at Westwood, though now his dark hair was tied back. His fingers wriggled at his side, the motion clicking his claws against one another. He looked her up and down. It was difficult to keep her hands free as she needed them to be and not cover herself. He was trying to make her uncomfortable, take away some of her shaky confidence and throw her off balance.

"Winston bore of you already, princess?" She didn't know how he knew, and it shot anger through her that he would use it against them. "What of you, Shaughnessy? I hear a thatch isn't a requirement as long as you're tight and screaming. Did you scream for him?"

Camilla snarled and threw her arm out, knocking Grayson back into the woods. "Stay here," Shaughnessy said and went in after Grayson.

There was the sound of snapping branches and then silence for seconds that stretched to minutes. When the silence ended, it was with a collective growl that seemed to vibrate the very ground beneath her feet.

She could see them now. The wolves were gathering, circling to trap her in the center. Some showed their teeth and dug their claws into the ground as if they wanted to lunge on her so badly, anchoring themselves to the earth was the only way they held control. She didn't know why they waited and she didn't care.

"Camilla," Shaughnessy shouted her name as Grayson slammed into the tree just ahead of her. In a blink, he was there, grabbing Grayson up by the neck to slam him back to the ground. "Show them who they're picking a fight with, love."

The two creatures who'd been wolves stood in front of her as if guarding her from their pack. The caster boy curled at her feet and dug his fingers into the ground over and over again as if the gesture was enough to calm him or give him something other than the surrounding enemy to think of.

"I won't allow them to harm you," she told him and began to draw energies from the pack.

Grayson did little more than protect himself against the trees and rocks Shaughnessy threw his body against. Though from the gashes marring Shaughnessy's chest and stomach, Grayson wasn't easy prey. The goal wasn't to kill him, just beat him until it was clear Shaughnessy chose to leave the alpha with his life. She was betting killing him was an easier task than subduing him.

As one, the pack moved forward, closing the distance. Camilla gathered their energies. Some fought her, but it was no contest. She raised a wall of fire between them and her. It scorched the new leaves and branches overhead and lit the circle inside like daylight. Some tried to run through but jerked back while others ran the perimeter, testing for weakness. They'd find none.

"Call them off, Grayson," Shaughnessy said, but the beaten and bloodied alpha only bared his teeth. "We didn't come here with the intention of harming your pack, but if you push us, we will win."

Camilla threw her hand out and knocked a brown wolf back into the flames before it could finish its leap. He landed on his side, legs tearing at the ground as he scrambled away from the fire. More leapt through. The two creatures who used to be wolves lunged to meet them.

They were going to wear her down if she kept trying to go at them one at a time or they'd overwhelm her with numbers. Much as she hated it, the thought *what would Eirnen do* came into her head. She knew exactly what he'd do. He'd make a spectacle. A large display of power, and if some of them died, more the better.

She dropped her hands to her sides, cupped toward the sky as if she could hold all the energies in her palms. Just as Eirnen had done on his tower, she pinpointed individuals until she had more than half the pack in her mind. She yanked energies from them, enough to stagger them and overwhelm her to the point of bursting, then let it go.

The ones she'd drained were disoriented. Her aim was the ones still trying to attack. She hit them, hard. Harder than intended, but it was too late to back down now. Those taken down by cast lay on the ground, some panting, some motionless. Those that were still on their feet—very few—stopped trying to attack. Shaughnessy held Grayson on his back by the throat.

"I am in no mood, Grayson," she called without pausing in

watching the others. "Winston Cleary is dead, as is his seeker. We're tired, hungry, and I am quickly losing patience."

"What does Henrik want with us bad enough to send you?" Grayson asked and finally looked at the creatures surrounding Camilla. "What is this? Do you mean to taunt me?"

"No," she said and though it was premature, she relaxed a bit. He was talking, asking questions she could answer and he'd know if she was lying. He'd smell it. "No one sent me here. Henrik still believes me to be at Gladen. I can give them back to your pack, but I need your help to do it," she said. "Call them off so we can have a true discussion."

"Do it," a voice came from the other side of the fire. "She's not with them any longer. I saw it for myself."

Shaughnessy gave her a tight nod and she let the fire die until they were ringed by angry wolves with one man at the front. She recognized him from the dungeons. He had seen for himself. He was there when Henrik sent her to Winston. That's how Grayson knew. "Henrik freed you."

"As a peace offering," Thomas said and came closer. "Can you really reverse this as you claim?"

"She can," Shaughnessy said before she could answer. "But it costs her much and the sun will rise in less than an hour. Your vow that we have food and shelter for the day and that there will be no further aggressions."

"Food for her," Grayson said. "My pack will not be donors for you."

"I'll do it," Camilla said. "I have no desire to make enemies of any of you. Nor does Shaughnessy."

"You have my word," Grayson said and led them through the woods. He was limping. He and Shaughnessy were covered in drying blood. The wolves separated to allow them passage without so much as a growl in their direction.

"Worry not," Shaughnessy said. "Grayson's vow is also theirs. As alpha, he speaks for them."

"They won't attack us?" she clarified and he nodded. Thomas kneeled by a wolf that wasn't moving. Had she killed it? The wolves let her pass, but she wasn't sure if it was because of her or the creatures that wandered in front of her.

They watched her, some warily, some with aggression, but none still in wolf form came any closer. Those in human form were nude and didn't seem bothered by it. Some were much younger than she thought they'd be. It made sense there would be young in the pack, but she'd always pictured the wolves as adult males. There were males, females, young, but very few old enough to be greying.

"Beckett?" A female voice came from somewhere to the right and the creature who'd been shot raised his head. A tall girl with jet hair, bronze skin, and long legs stood in the middle of a tight cluster of wolves. "Let me through," she said and pushed her way to the front. She stopped and stared, trying to see any similarities to the man she knew as Beckett. "Is it him?"

"I don't know," Camilla answered honestly, though she wanted to say yes. "But if it is, I'll give him back to you. I swear it." It was a few more steps to Thomas and she took them. "He's breathing," she said and relief washed through her. His hair was singed to the skin in places. He was the first to come through and had been hit twice.

"He's healing," Thomas said and cocked his head to the side. "You're bothered by this, though it was your doing."

There was nothing to say to that. She was bothered by his injuries, but she wouldn't apologize for protecting herself and she didn't expect them to apologize for defending against the trespass. Warm fingers brushed her shoulder and she turned in time to see the female pull her arm back. Tears streamed down her face and her mouth worked like she was trying to speak but couldn't. "Please," she rasped.

Shaughnessy stopped walking with Grayson long enough to

watch Camilla. She was harder than she'd been, but the softness was still there too. The way she held her breath while she waited to see if the wolf lying on the ground was still alive or if she'd killed it told him that.

"There are still meat and vegetables from our evening meal," Grayson said. "Camilla may have her fill."

"Thank you." Shaughnessy caught up with Grayson out of earshot of the others. "She can sense them," he said, leaning in close. "I tell you not to cause concern. She will do them no harm. She's a vicious little thing when it comes to retaliation but is slow to attack without due cause."

"Marion entrusted them with us," Grayson said.

"They aren't helpless children, Grayson. Marion sent them here to benefit you as much as you can be of benefit to them."

Those that made up the small group were powerful, though disregarded by much of the caster community. There was one remaining full fae, Gianna. She was the ruler of the outer creatures, as they called themselves. Halflings, mostly. Those ostracized or hunted found safety. Marion had brought them together, protected them. They'd hidden Shaughnessy from Eirnen's gaze until the time came for him to be caught. The nymphs and the fae mistress were the ones that placed the aversion spell on the cave.

"You cannot reveal them to a Westwood."

"I may have no choice," Shaughnessy said. "She is much more vigilant after her time at Gladen. She sensed them on the way here, though she shouldn't have been able to through their protective and concealment spells. If she fears we are in danger she will fight, Grayson. She will not attack them unprovoked. You have my word."

"Your word? You don't speak for her and I would not trust another's life on the word of a Westwood. That godsdamned family is the reason there are so few to be protected. You know this, Shaughnessy."

He was aware. The men of the Westwood family had a tradition. A hunt. Each year they mounted steeds and spent two days hunting those who refused to bend to the will of the Westwoods. They refused to add their power to the collective, refused to bow, refused to acknowledge a ruler who declared himself one. The family turned the hunt into a rite of passage for the males in their tenth year. The older males incapacitated the outer creature they'd run to exhaustion, but the first kill was saved for the youth.

Unfortunately, their hunts were so successful there was few prey left. Those hunted that remained were hidden here, behind a veil of collective magicks.

Camilla came toward him with a look of determination. She was about to be a pain in his arse over whatever it was she wanted. He had an idea she thought to fix the creatures now, but one look at her and anyone could tell she hadn't the strength. Her skin and eyes were dull, her hair blackened with dried blood in places. The circles under her eyes were as dark as the bruise on her jaw.

That ridiculous frock Winston insisted she wear was covered in filth and torn to tatters, allowing him to see the lashes both fresh and scarred. For there to have been scars this soon meant Winston had given her just enough vampire blood to seal the wounds but not heal them completely. He'd meant to mar her.

"No," he said before a sound came out of her open mouth. "Not this morning, Camilla. The day will be here in less than an hour. You're exhausted. Rest. Eat. They will be just as grateful tomorrow night."

"I can't, Shaughnessy. I can't leave them like that one more day if I can help them." He shook his head. Just like that, the pleading look that begged him to understand was gone, replaced with defiance and resolve.

"At least allow me to heal you," he said.

"No," she shook her head hard enough to make the hair bounce around her face. "I can do this, Shaughnessy. I'm going to do this." She turned to Grayson. "I need some wolves."

Grayson looked to Shaughnessy before turning back to Camilla. "Why?"

"I have to use the energies of wolves to heal these two. I can't do it on my own. I need help from the pack. Please."

"You intend to try to give us back these two now, this morning?"

"Not try. I will if you help me. I swear it."

Grayson looked to Shaughnessy again. Shaughnessy shrugged. He recognized the look on Grayson's face. Grayson was trying to figure out if she was serious and if she truly was a Westwood.

"I thank you, Lady Camilla, but Shaughnessy is right. Eat. Rest. If you are to do this thing, I need you to be at full strength."

"I am no longer in need of nor am I in search of more caretakers. Wolves, Grayson. What I need are wolves."

⌇

"Where's Riley?" *Henrik, oh, yes, Henrik, my son. Henrik!*

"Still missing," Marcus said.

"Find him. Get the wolves to track him if you have to." Eirnen listened to the sound of retreating feet and the groans of rope twisting around a tree branch. "Father, can you hear me?"

Yes, yes, please!

"Westwood's descent is imminent," Marion giggled and kicked her feet to swing higher. *"Did you hear that, Eirnen? Another rhyme, and I wasn't even trying."*

No, no, no! Henrik, keep talking. Don't leave me alone here.

"Still a mewling pup." Eirnen stared into the dark toward his father's voice, waiting for the man to appear. He was silhouetted in light, just as Marion always seemed to be, adorned in full battle gear. His broad sword sang through the air in an arc that took the head of a vampire before he thrust it through another's chest. He

gave the blade a vicious twist to destroy the heart then kicked the body from his blade.

"*Malachi,*" Marion squealed and ran to the big man who was always frightening to Eirnen as a child. She embraced him, wrapped her arms around his waist even as he glared at Eirnen and slung the blood of his slain to the ground. "*Your son has been most ungracious. Help me punish him.*" She put her fingers to her mouth and smiled at Eirnen.

"*Aye, child,*" Malachi said and came forward with his sword, his armor creaking with every purposeful stride. Marion clapped and skipped behind him, humming that awful rhyme.

Not real. They are not real.

"*Are too,*" Marion said darkly as the sword ran Eirnen through. The brass hilt hit tight against his belly. He wanted to scream but the searing agony stole the breath from his lungs. His father leaned closer to his face, jostling the blade that impaled him. His teeth clamped so hard he thought they'd shatter in his bloodied mouth.

"Father?" Eirnen's body slammed forward, his hands holding intestines in the abdominal cavity. "Father, look at me," Henrik said. Eirnen searched the dark again, this time for Henrik.

"*He's leaving us,*" Marion pouted.

"*Worry not, lassie, he'll be back,*" Malachi sneered and ripped the blade free.

Eirnen gasped, dragging air down a throat that was raw with screaming. "How long?" he croaked and was racked with violent, coughing spasms. Henrik brought water from the pitcher that Eirnen struggled to drink without choking.

"Not long this time. Hours," Henrik answered and refilled the glass.

"Camilla?" he asked and drained this glass with more ease.

"Not yet returned," Henrik answered. "The warriors Gabriel and Nox left shortly after your spell began to gather the rest of our family."

"Marcus, I heard him talking. What was Abel's answer?"

"Perhaps it would be best if you rested for a while. We can discuss this later."

"I don't have later!" The glass shattered against the wall, throwing shards back at the two of them. "Do you not understand what is happening to me? Or is it that you don't care? Camilla is the only way that I stay out of the pit and you sent her to Winston."

"Again, your suffering was not my intention."

"Perhaps, but it certainly was the result, wasn't it? Abel's answer, now."

"Marceline returned to him, and your head as proof you are no longer at the reins."

"Have Nikolai and Dorin located Camilla? Or did you forget to inquire before you sent my only means of communicating with them away as well?"

"They had not, but they will."

Eirnen went to the window and glared at Rowan's back tethered to the front gate. Camilla's lure and a warning to all in the village below who thought him weakened. He was no fool. His illness would not be kept secret. The whispers were already spreading and soon enough someone would try to take advantage. His vision narrowed, the darkness around him pulsed with laughter. *Not again, not this soon.*

"Henrik," he said, groping behind him for his son. "I heard you before. Don't hunt Riley." *Ooooh, he's coming, he's coming!* "Shut up!"

"Riley brought you out of this bef—"

"No, he will find her to save him," Eirnen panted. His body shook and he dropped to the floor. Henrik's shouts were muffled, as if from a distance like Camilla's words had been the day she condemned him to this. She'd built him a hell and it dragged him back under on a scream.

"Hell, you say? Yes, I think that's a delicious idea. I remember how much you enjoy fire."

~§~

Camilla sat up gasping, fresh out of a nightmare, rather a real memory turned nightmare. It was dark, so dark she couldn't see. Not Gladen's dungeons, the smell was wrong. She wasn't in the dungeons.

"Easy, love." Shaughnessy. She felt around until she found his hand and held it tight.

"Where are we?"

"In the tunnels—the wolf dens. I carried you here after your stubborn arse nearly got yourself killed again trying to save those creatures."

She remembered. "I didn't just try, I succeeded." She'd undone some of the evil Eirnen had imposed. It wasn't nearly enough, but it was something.

The male was Beckett. She'd returned him to his mate, Jasmine. They'd fallen on one another, kissing, crying, and touching. He was still very pale and weak, but he clutched at her as she did him. Camilla had missed this with Rissa. She watched, as moved as the rest of the pack, while the two lovers reunited.

The other's name was Jesse. He didn't have a mate or any blood relatives within the pack, but the rest of them treated him as if he were family. What struck Camilla was how young he looked, her age at most, and Eirnen had done that to him. Beckett looked to be in his late twenties or early thirties, which didn't make what was done to him any less despicable, but Jesse had barely started his life when Eirnen took it from him.

"It's still hours until dark. Why don't you go out into the sun, get something to eat?" She hesitated. "Camilla, the wolves are all but in love with you for what you did. They won't hurt you. Besides, if they try, knock them in the dirt," he said and nudged her playfully.

She turned to her side until she could lay her head on his

shoulder. "I don't want to let you out of my sight. I'm afraid I'll come back, you'll be gone, and I won't know what happened. Did you leave or were you taken?"

"Stop," he said and put his hand on her face. "You can't live your life attached to me like a wee tick. Besides, I need rest too and you snore."

"I do not." She pushed at him, but she did sit up. "Fine, I'll leave you to your rest if you promise me you will tell me goodbye before you go, should you decide to leave."

"My word of honor," he swore. "Now, it's time for you to get out of the dark. Go."

He told her how to get out of the tunnels, but it was a confusing labyrinth. The place he was given as a daytime retreat was deep within to protect him. She called blue fire to her hands to wind her way through the paths, getting lost twice in what ended as a false tunnel that went nowhere, until finally there was sunlight ahead.

The wolves were all out laughing, talking, and cooking. Children played in the field, hiding from one another in the tall grass. She closed her eyes and drew in a deep breath. The motion tugged at the healing skin at her back but filled her nose with clean woodland air and fresh grass. Finally, there was no master, no king, no warden. She had the freedom to do as she wished. What she wanted was to stand in the sun, eyes closed, letting the breeze wash across her skin, and breathe.

"Camilla."

She looked for the voice and found a petite girl with short, spiked black hair waving her over to a shaded area under the tall oak trees. Camilla didn't recognize her, but she was smiling and seemed friendly enough. There were other females with her. Camilla assessed them with suspicion as she approached. Smiles greeted her from all around.

"Are you hungry? Shaughnessy said you haven't eaten in a while," the girl said and handed Camilla a chunk of dried meat.

Her stomach chose that time to growl and cramp with hunger. The wolf grinned as if she'd heard it, pushing the offering closer. "And you must want to bathe and dress in more appropriate clothing," another of the women pointed out.

"I have no other clothing, appropriate or otherwise. I'm sorry, but I don't remember any of you." She took the food but didn't eat it.

"Oh, forgive me," the petite girl said. "I'm Sparrow. This is Layna." Layna had black hair as well, but hers hung down past her bottom in straight, sleek perfection that had Camilla trying to smooth her own tangled hair.

"And I'm Dee," another girl said, putting out a hand. Camilla took it and gave it a shake as she'd seen men do. The gesture made her smile and she pumped their joined hands more vigorously. "I'm closest to your size so I can give you some clothing. Do you prefer dresses or trousers?"

"She's a princess. Of course she doesn't wear trousers," Layna said.

"I am no princess." Camilla sniffed at the meat, which smelled delicious, and bit off a piece. After the first taste, she didn't hesitate to accept the second chunk Sparrow offered.

There were clothes draped over taut lines tied between trees in the sun. Dee walked over to them, running her fingers over the material. "I washed these and hung them this morning so they'd smell fresh. You may choose any you like."

When Camilla hesitated, Dee backed away as if space was what she needed to choose. She kept her eyes on the wolves, grabbed the first bit of material closest to her and offered the women a tentative smile. She wanted to trust them, she did, but she'd learned the hard way caution was best.

At their invitation, Camilla sat with the three women. After a few moments of awkward silence, they began talking amongst themselves and tried to include her in their conversations. Some of the others watched their small group with open suspicion and any child that came close to her was quickly called back. They were using caution as well. She couldn't blame them and took no offense.

What she really wanted was to bathe. To cleanse her body of Winston, of Bosch, and of Gladen. The filth that covered her from hair to feet was unspeakable. Bosch's blood yet lingered around her fingernails. "Do you have the means for me to cleanse myself, please?"

The women led Camilla to a small pool of water where they assured her none of the males would be nor would they be coming. She confessed she couldn't swim, but they explained the water got deeper the closer to the middle she went. All she had to do was stop walking forward when the water was as deep as she wanted it to be.

It was cold, but as it crept up her body with every step, the sensation was invigorating. She scrubbed at her hands and arms, watching the water run from her skin until finally it was clear. She dipped her head under and when she came up the women were staring at her.

Layna's gaze rose until she met Camilla's eyes. Camilla refused to look away or be made ashamed. She stared back at the she-wolf. Layna took the tail of her shirt and lifted. She threw it to the ground before meeting Camilla's eyes again. Camilla let her eyes wander to see what it was Layna wanted to show her. Scars. Her right shoulder was a mass of scar tissue, there were claw marks across her belly.

"I got these fighting for my pack. I am not ashamed of them, nor should you be of yours. Among the pack, scars are proof of battles fought and won. They are a reminder of strength, trials, and enemies conquered."

The other women nodded, then got into the water as well. Sparrow gave Camilla a tin filled with something that resembled jelly and smelled of rosemary and lavender. It was gritty, like it was mixed with sand. Sparrow confided sand was one of the ingredients, but the woman who made it, Mariella, wouldn't share the recipe—bad for business.

It smelled lovely and familiar, like something she'd used before. It was cold on her fingers, but she used it to wash her hair as instructed. The sand scraped at her scalp and worked to loosen the dried blood and filth. She was reminded she'd broken most of her fingernails off prying at the warded cuffs as she tried to scratch at the more resistant clumps.

"If you like, we've had Mariella make a calendula paste for you. It aids in healing. We can put it on your scars and fresh lashes."

"Why? Why are you helping me? What I did last night doesn't erase all my family has done to yours. Not by half, I'd imagine. Our bargain with Grayson was for food and shelter, yet you offer comforts we haven't negotiated. I swear, I will do you no harm without cause. If it's a promise of safety from Eirnen you want, I can't offer it to you. I have nothing to give you."

"What you did last night, it was miraculous. You did that. You. Our old alpha, Blacke, offered them to Eirnen. Eirnen used them up. You returned them. We will not hold you responsible for the actions of those who are also of the Westwood name. Just as we hope you will not judge us based on the actions of our previous alpha. He was alpha, father, leader, brother, yet he gave them over to be used as tools. As a pack, we have decided you are to be treated on your own merit."

Her own merit. Not by rumor or association, but her own words and deeds. How liberating. She washed her hair and scrubbed her body twice more as she thought this over. Never before had she been separate from the Westwoods, treated as her own person. How to begin?

The other girls had gotten out of the water and were drying in the sun. Within the pack, nudity was something that went unnoticed, it seemed. So far, there had been no leering or rude remarks, no unwanted touching or comments. She looked around again for anyone approaching, took a deep breath, then climbed from the water. The grass smelled sweet. She lay back and watched lazy clouds ease across the sky. The sun was warm, warmer still after light breezes coaxed goose bumps to raise on her skin.

Honesty wasn't a bad place to start, she decided. "I met him—Blacke—after he was a creature. I promised him I wouldn't leave him like that, but I've broken that promise. I think he's dead. I'm sorry."

"We know he's dead. Eirnen permitted Grayson and Thomas to end his suffering." Camilla turned her head, looking at Sparrow with what she was sure was a mix of confusion, pity, and anger. "We thought there was no hope of saving them."

After a moment, she nodded. She understood. But how must Grayson and Thomas feel now, after knowing she could've brought him back to them. Then again, Sparrow hadn't sounded as if the pack was happy with their previous alpha.

Before she dressed, the women did as they said and covered the scars and fresh lash marks Camilla couldn't reach with the ointment. They were gentle and moved slow as if they knew that was what she needed from them. The dress she'd chosen was pale green and much thinner than her gowns but covered more than the shift she'd been wearing. It was quite comfortable. Dee did up the ties in the back that left triangles of bare skin showing. She had nothing to tie or pin her hair up with. The feel of the damp strands brushing her lower back was a strange sensation.

In the camp, most were welcoming, some kept their distance, but none glared. She'd take it. They brought her a plate heaped high with more food than she could hope to eat. She was invited to sit with a group of men and women and though she did, she still felt separate from them. In their laughter, she heard screams echoing through Gladen. The meat in her mouth tasted like blood. The smell of late summer dissolved into the scent of choking stale air and human filth.

"What's wrong?"

"Jesse, you scared me," she sputtered.

"Sorry." He sat down next to her and watched the rest as if trying to figure out her thoughts by taking in the same view.

"How's Beckett?"

"Fine. Stronger, but Jazz won't let him away from her for a moment."

"And you? How are you?"

"I'm better, but you're not. I can tell, I can feel it. Your fear and anger? Beckett and I can feel it too." He put his hand on hers and waited until she looked him in the eye. "We won't hurt you. We won't let anyone else hurt you. You're safe here, Camilla."

"Jesse," Grayson called, walking toward the two of them. "Evening chores need to be done."

"Nice talking to you, Camilla," Jesse said and left her alone with Grayson.

Grayson sat beside her but didn't say anything. She waited for the silence to become awkward, but it didn't. They watched the children chasing each other, the women sitting under the shade trees laughing and talking. Some of the men and a few of the women were off hunting, others were scouting the perimeter of the camp.

She wondered if Eirnen knew about Gladen. If not, he would find out eventually. Then what? Would he hunt her? Maybe send his warriors to drag her back? Punish the wolves for giving aid? No matter what Jesse said, they couldn't protect her, not from Eirnen and his warriors. She was powerful, she knew that now. But Eirnen was more powerful still, even injured she couldn't match him and win. To fight him, the best hope was for her to drag him down to the grave with her. If they tried to save her, they'd die.

"Easy, girl," Grayson said. "Your heart is flying in your chest." He tapped his ear to let her know he'd heard it. "I've offered you no violence. There's no need for fear."

"But there is," she said and looked at him. His eyes were hazel and scrutinizing, she had the thought that not much escaped his attention. "They will look for me."

"The enemy of my enemy may offer a solution in Abel Lockley," he suggested.

"No. I'll not be in league with another would-be king."

"Do you mean to challenge Eirnen for Calame?"

"No. No, absolutely not," she said. "I don't know how I will find my way out of this calamity, but it will not be as a weapon, pawn, or a version of Eirnen Westwood."

What she wanted, was what they had here. They cared for one another, trusted one another and treated each other as family. She wanted community, something real and warm. Home.

"I'll be back," she said and set the plate of untouched food to the side.

"He's fine, Camilla. The vampire can take care of himself."

True. He was safe from the sun in the wolves' tunnels, but she still had to see. And she had to have a minute to herself. She watched the wolves interact and was envious. It was shameful, but it was there all the same. They weren't concerned that few of them were truly related by blood. The weakest weren't culled or abused, they were taught and protected, given roles that suited them to serve the pack. Grayson was a paternal figure, always ready to give or do anything in his power to help. The entire pack took her in and was kind, clothing, and feeding her.

Eirnen had no desire to live in peace in the sizable kingdom he already had. He wanted more. He wanted to take from others both their power and their homes so none had even the hope of coming close to being his equal. He had little interest teaching her much more than the basics of caster ability, until he thought her of value. Before the day they watched the heron fly through her illusion, he'd taught her just enough to make her an enticement to more powerful men who would wed and impregnate her in hopes of a stronger line in the future. A line Eirnen and eventually Henrik would continue to mold after themselves. She swore to the children she may never have that she'd do whatever it took to spare them that future.

The tunnels went all the way through to the other side of the hill, an escape if they were cornered in the valley. They had a lot of plans that involved defense or retreat and by letting her and Shaughnessy find sanctuary here, they'd placed trust upon her to not carry this information back to Eirnen and Henrik.

The complete darkness was unnerving. It made her seek out Shaughnessy's power as a way to feel him getting closer. Plus, it was helpful in not getting lost, again. He was there. His energies would be bright white if she could see them, but there was something else, something hazy in the periphery. She opened her power a little more, searching, probing at the energy sparking just out of reach. It didn't feel hostile or aggressive, just elusive.

She wandered past where she knew Shaughnessy was, but never seemed to get any closer to the other energy she was sensing. It was moving or camouflaged. She sent more power, seeking tendrils, more curious now. Enemy or friend?

"Camilla?"

"Shaughnessy, just a moment," she said. It wasn't one, it was many. A mixture of energies, beings. They conspired. "Someone watches," she whispered and threw another burst of energy out to join the hunt.

"Camilla." Shaughnessy's hands landed on her shoulders. "Please, stop."

"You know what this is, who this is," she said.

"Aye. They are no threat. They are hidden for good reason."

"From me?"

"In part," he confessed. "They are what is left of the creatures Eirnen, and his father before him, all but killed off. Halflings, fae, nymphs, harpies," he said and she turned to face him.

"You have a fae?"

"I do not have a fae. None of them are owned, Camilla. They are creatures in need of refuge. Marion gathered them together and gave it to them. They are hidden under a concealment spell much more powerful than the temporary one they placed on my cave. Please, do not continue to seek them out. They and the wolves help one another, live here together, protect each other. They will not like you knowing of their existence."

"I understand," she said and hung her head. "I will leave them to their peace. But you Shaughnessy, you know I would never hurt them without cause."

"I do, but I also know that they aren't weak. The fae are especially protective and angry. They will give you cause. It will be a fight if you were to breach their concealment and enter their village."

She nodded and walked back to where he slept. She sat, hugging her knees to her chest and felt the corresponding tug at her back.

"I'm jealous of them," she confessed. "I couldn't stand to watch them any longer."

"So you've come to sulk in the dark with me? Fitting. It smells like dog and death in here," he said. "I despise being underground, surrounded by fresh earth. This is a place for coffins and worms. It's below me, really."

"I came in here to be with someone more like me. Someone without a pack. I look at them and I can see everything I don't have but could if life were different. In the beginning, even after I was told and then saw for myself, I fear it would've taken little more than a skilled lie to let me see their side. I wanted so badly for Eirnen to be the grandfather I'd always thought him to be. He has complete control over his ability, he could've taught me how to wield my own, to help defend my family. The sad truth of it is, I would have. But now, there's nothing to defend."

"The other two paths Marion spoke of," he said. "Come here and I'll tell you a story," he said and raised his arm in invitation.

She curled into his side and laid her head on his chest, listening to the slow thumps of his heart while she waited.

"Marion has claimed to be born of the Moirai. To my knowledge, myth says there are three. She held to the claim that there were once more that were cast from the fold by the three more powerful sisters that rule all beings from creation to death. I first met her fresh from a battle I lost to Eirnen. I was alone, lamenting, and rageful. Yet this wisp of a girl sat next to me in the dirt and began speaking as if we were the oldest of friends. She ignored my attempts to frighten her away with threats. When I'd had enough and struck out to snap her neck, I found her inches from my grasp, though we'd been hip-to-hip the moment before.

"That was many, many years ago and I believed her ramblings those of a madwoman. She spoke of her immortality as if I couldn't smell the death that lingers close to all who aren't as I am. Then she happened in my path again a few months ago and she was unchanged. I was in Greece and there she appeared, telling me it was time to come back to Calame. She picked up our conversation as if I hadn't walked away twenty years before and then scolded me for making her late to another meeting. She told me of you, used my hatred of Eirnen Westwood to get me back here by telling me that for the first time, Eirnen cared for someone. A fragile someone it would destroy him to lose. But there was a window of time, 'soon,' she'd said, 'he will not hold her as precious and her death would be a grace.'"

"My death would be a grace? I don't understand," she admitted.

"I took it to mean that you would become an enemy of my enemy. My curiosity was piqued. Only those who are a threat to Eirnen or his kingdom are worthy of the title of enemy, others are merely inconvenience. It wasn't until I was already staked to a wall in the bowels of Westwood Castle, waiting until I would have the opportunity at your neck as she'd promised, that she revealed an alternate path."

"Instant gratification in killing me to watch Eirnen suffer while he still cared enough or wait for the day he'll wish for my death." Lovely.

"You, me, Eirnen, Henrik, Grayson, Winston—we're but a few of the pieces in Marion's game. What you said when you came in here, was your path. This ability would've blossomed under Eirnen's tutelage and you'd have adopted his philosophy just as his other children have. There was no reason for you to do otherwise. You're jealous of the unity of wolves now, but what did you believe about them before you came here? About me and all vampires? What you wish you had now would have led you to one day be worse than Eirnen himself."

She thought back to the visions Marion had given her. In the one with her on the golden throne, she now recognized the three warriors behind her as the ones Eirnen created, but there had been only three. Dorin wasn't among them. She knew, marrow deep, that in that future Eirnen had killed Dorin, then his brothers helped her level everything Eirnen built. In the visions, she loved Dorin and Eirnen taught her how dangerous it is to love in Westwood Castle.

The other vision was a future with James. It had to be. Dorin was her path, the one Marion said Camilla would have chosen for herself. James was the dying path Marion gave life. Joy swelled her chest as she remembered the laughter of the two children, her children. Was that warm place full of life and laughter truly meant for her? Loss was a very real presence as well. Dorin.

Realistically, she knew she couldn't have them both. Alone in her chambers, with no plausible hope that either of them were an option, she'd held tight to both of them. There were times that she was alone in her quarters for weeks on end before Callum came, long enough she'd thought she'd go mad if she didn't hear another's voice. Someone to say her name, remember she was there and a person. When Grandfather summoned her for a lesson, she felt he rescued her and did everything she could to please him so maybe he'd want to see her more often.

Then she had Dorin with his passion and playfulness. With him, she wasn't alone anymore and she came to wish for night and blessed sleep to be with him again. He looked at her as she'd never seen a man look at a woman, made her want it above all the promises of power an arranged marriage would wrought.

A short time later, James came. He was warmth, home and hearth, a comfortable place to land. He was a whole world away, farther than she'd ever have considered traveling on her own. But she wasn't on her own anymore now, was she? And Marion was the reason. She'd led Camilla to Shaughnessy and him to her.

"But she *died,*" Camilla said, thinking of what Marion had suffered just to see Eirnen fall. If she was a descendant of the Moirai, she was unprizable and it seemed a paltry thing for her to have given her life for when weighed against all else.

"Did she?" Shaughnessy said and Camilla couldn't help but scan the darkness for another ghost. "I'm not convinced. It's faint, but it's there. I can feel her in my blood. In my head. However, there's no doubt in my mind that Eirnen killed her, I felt that too."

"Do you never tire of this? Of the treachery and deceit, the fighting and loss?" His chest lifted with the deep breath that was his answer. "I only went back to Westwood Castle to try and keep Eirnen from making creatures of the gigantes and I couldn't leave Callum. The gigantes are made and Callum is gone. I'm finished. I want to leave, go far enough from here no one knows who I am. I don't want you to feel obligated to come with me, but I'd like it if you came, too."

"A fine menacing pair the two of us would make," he mused. "Prowling the streets of darkened cities, lavishing ourselves with the bounties of our take before we move to the next. Squander away the nights with pretty lasses and lads who would relinquish their very lives for just one more."

"My only condition is that we be out of Eirnen's reach. The rest is negotiable," she said. If he thought to put her off with talk of scandalous deeds, he was going to be disappointed. He stayed quiet and she thought it best to give him time to think it over. She was leaving, whether he went or not. But she trusted him and knew nothing of the world outside of Calame. His company would be as useful as it was pleasant. "Will you tell me about Cassandra?"

"I should have known Eirnen would use her," he said. "Let me guess. I seduced her, then threw her away as so much trash before I killed her."

"Close," she said and brought fire to her hands to see his face. He met her eyes and closed his hand over hers to put them back in the dark, but she'd already seen the sadness. "You don't have to tell me, but if you do, I'll not doubt your word."

"Cassandra Westwood was not only the most beautiful lass in Calame, she was the most beautiful girl I'd ever seen. She was also untouchable because of her lineage and by her choice. She didn't fear me. She laughed and ran from me as if daring me to chase her. And chase her I did. I could not help myself. It took time, but finally, she allowed me to catch her. I was lost. Completely, utterly, and exquisitely lost. When Eirnen killed the king and ascended the throne, she came to me and asked me to leave with her, much as you are now. I couldn't believe my fortune. This goddess could have had any man she deigned to crook her delicate finger at and yet, she wanted to be with me. She was also finished with the title of Westwood caster and all it entailed. *Her* condition for me was that we be together as equals. She asked me to make her as I am."

"She asked you to make her a vampire? She was willing to forsake all she was as a caster to get away from them?"

"Aye, and I told her that was not the way. She had to relinquish nothing. I swore to take her from this place, protect her and love her as she was, but she wouldn't hear of it. If they caught us, they would slay me and take her back. It wasn't a risk she was willing to take, and as a vampire she would be useless to them. I did it. I turned her and then I let her be killed not two nights out of transition. Eirnen brought the whole of his army on us. She begged me to save her, but I was too late. Eirnen took her head. A short time later Marion found me."

Camilla didn't know what to say. There wasn't anything to say. Nothing she could do would change what happened or make his hurt any less, but it did explain why he and Eirnen were set on destroying one another. Calame had more bad memories for him than it did her, but now she wasn't sure he would leave until he saw Eirnen dead.

"I'm not asking you to save me or be responsible for me. I'm asking my friend, someone I trust and value, to keep me company while I prowl, lavish, and squander." She raised to her elbows and kissed his cheek. "I'll leave so you can sleep."

"Wait," he said and she froze as he caught her wrist. "By the gods—" he spit and was on his feet "—if the pack doesn't kill him, I will."

"Who? Shaughnessy, what's happening?" She peeked around him as if she expected to see someone outside the alcove. Her name echoed down the tunnels. She recognized the voice. "Riley."

"Where are you going?" he snapped and kept a tight grip on her wrist. "He's Eirnen's. Do you forget he delivered you, bound and defenseless to Winston? Leave the pack to their fun. He and his brother have taken enough of their lives. They're owed some recompense."

"He didn't have a choice," she said and tugged against his hold. "Shaughnessy, let me go. You don't understand."

"It's another half hour to full dark, lass. I can't stop him if he means to return you to Eirnen." He let her go to make the choice.

"He won't. But if I'm wrong, how far can he really get in less than an hour? Come get me," she said, repeating his words to her in the cave back to him.

The voices were louder as she ran down the tunnel. "I will cut your pack down if you force me," Riley threatened just as she came out into the open.

He had his swords ready, his feet planted, and casts crackled the air around him. She'd seen him heal with his ability and she'd seen his skill with a sword in training, but she'd never witnessed him in an actual fight. The wolves were circling, trying to surround him. His eyes followed their every movement, but his body was fixed. His back was to a stone outcropping, but with this many wolves, it didn't matter how good he was with his swords.

According to Callum, Riley could disassemble as easily as he healed. He could see old wounds, sense them, and reopen them. If he used his ability, he might hinder a number of wolves. Even then, he was so outmatched, challenging them was a foolish endeavor committed by a sensible man.

There was only one reason she could think of that would make Riley take a risk like this—Rowan.

"Wait," she yelled and pushed her way through the wolves until she was in the semicircle of them with Riley. "Stop for a moment, Grayson, please."

Riley didn't change his stance, but his eyes flicked to her as often as the wolves. "He and his brother killed our kind for nothing more than speaking before Eirnen's ass was planted on his golden throne. And you ask me to spare him?"

"He didn't have a choice. You know how Eirnen gets what he wants, you know how he loves his leverage. One refuses, the other suffers the consequences. They're bound to Eirnen. They can't allow him to be harmed or harm him themselves. If they try to run, he can summon them back. What would you have them do? Defy Eirnen for you, knowing they condemn the other to be a toy for Henrik? How many scars have you seen that are as neat as those?" She pointed to the spiral carved onto Riley's left cheek, as if Henrik were bored and drawing lazy circles. "There are more under the clothing, I assure you."

"That's a difficult position to be sure. Still, you ask me to allow him to live and continue to be Eirnen's killer. For what they've done and for what they will do, I can't allow him to leave here with his life. Don't fight me on this, girl. The sun lingers and you still need my generosity."

"The sun you say?" She felt the darkness begin the seep over her. It was colder and thicker without Callum and the reminder only angered her further. For a moment, a bare flicker of time, Grayson's energy parted and the soul hidden beneath the skin was exposed to her. "Do you know that you're all dead?" she asked and tipped her head to study what she'd seen. "We all are, really. Me, you, Shaughnessy. These bodies are nothing more than casings that trap the soul inside."

"Camilla," Riley said, his voice steady even as he took the same step back from her as the wolves did. "You've made your point."

"I don't think I have, or Grayson would've known better than to threaten Shaughnessy with the sun." She blinked at the crowd around her as one-by-one their casings seemed to dissolve until the hidden was revealed. She clenched her fists and they stilled, hands at their sides. "Fascinating," she said and a smile stretched her lips. "You gave me your vow, Grayson. You gave Shaughnessy your vow. Is it now your choice to break it?"

She couldn't draw on the attached souls as she could with the lost ones like Callum and Tamara. She could free them. They'd no longer be attached to a body and everything that they were could be hers. Right now, they were puppets as the vampires had been, their bodies hers to command. Their wide-eyed fear let her know she didn't have their minds. Eirnen manipulated energies. She went deeper. A Westwood, through and through. She could see the other path now with perfect clarity, it was an easy one to walk and oddly comfortable. It made her stomach churn.

"It's true," Thomas gasped, stumbling back to clasp his chest once he was released.

She wanted to run or apologize, but she couldn't. The wolves would respect neither and if they knew how wicked and rotten she felt for what she'd done, they might think she'd hesitate to do the same or worse again. She'd done no permanent damage to any of them, but she'd made them vulnerable in a way they'd never felt before.

"Don't ever try to use someone I care about as leverage," she said and leveled her eyes on Grayson.

"Should've known better than to bluff her." Camilla whirled to see Shaughnessy propped with one shoulder against a tree in the woods where the shade was deepest. "He wouldn't have tried to force me into the sun, love. Wolves never break their vow. It's a fault of theirs."

There wasn't any way for him to have gotten in the shadows without first crossing through the sun. She went to him, trying to see any injuries without him catching her doing it. The right side of his face was pinker than the other and one of his hands was red and blistered as if he'd used it to shield his eyes. Riley was following behind her, but he hadn't put the swords away.

"Don't make me beg to not have to do that again," she said once she could whisper around the tightness in her throat. "Please, don't fight each other."

"Come on, lass. Let's take a walk." She fell in step next to Shaughnessy and they went deeper into the woods. She couldn't swallow enough times to clear her throat and she dared not blink though her eyes stung. She knew the moment they were out of sight of the pack because he stopped and folded his arms around her.

She pressed her face into his chest to stifle the sobs she couldn't let the pack hear. Eirnen had created monsters, but he bred them too. She condemned him yet she'd leveraged the wolves with their very souls. Marion was right, the Westwood line shouldn't continue. If power grew with age and each generation, what would her children be? Her grandchildren? What would she be in twenty, thirty years if someone didn't put her down like a rabid animal before then? His shirt grew damp under her face and he said nothing as she pulled away and wiped her eyes.

"I can't stay here, Shaughnessy," she said and dabbed her nose with her sleeve.

"I'm beginning to see that, lass."

"Camilla, I must speak with you," Riley pressed.

"Not now, twin," Shaughnessy said without looking from Camilla. "What did Thomas mean when he said, 'it's true?'"

"He was in the dungeons when I was. I guess he overheard what I did to Eirnen and Marceline," she said.

"He doesn't know," Riley said at Shaughnessy's look of confusion and sheathed his swords. "Marceline is dead but breathing and Eirnen is being driven mad by the caster Marion."

"Marion?" Shaughnessy said as Camilla looked up with her brows furrowed. She didn't know that part either.

"Yes. Henrik's doing what he can to keep him in his quarters out of sight, but there's no chance of not hearing him. When he isn't screaming or talking to Marion, he's singing a lullaby. Henrik took control, dispensed orders, but Eirnen comes back to himself for short periods of time and gives his own."

"Camilla, how about you start at the beginning?" Shaughnessy said and sat down next to her. She told him everything that Riley hadn't and he stayed quiet, though he did wipe his hand down his face a few times.

"And now Eirnen will do anything to get her back, to reverse what she's done," Riley said. "Rowan helped you. He kept the depth of your power from Eirnen and didn't let Bosch go after your vampire that night, though he could've and was ordered to. Eirnen figured out Rowan wasn't the one who broke Winston's bones and put him in the dungeons."

"He got caught. Why is she to answer for his lapse?" Shaughnessy asked.

"When Eirnen learned from the warriors that Gladen was burned and you were in the company of Shaughnessy, there was a chance he could lose you and never get his mind back. He's hung

Rowan on the front gate because he thinks it will lure you back of your own will to bargain for his life."

"He knows you will bring her to save your brother, you mean," Shaughnessy's voice held an edge of anger.

"Rowan is branded a traitor. Eirnen can punish him any way he sees fit, as is his right. There are whispers of his illness in the village and Rowan's displayed as a deterrent to any who think Eirnen has lost his nerve. Camilla, please, he's seen your power and he wants it. He's even talked of passing Henrik over as heir and giving it to you. He won't kill you, but he will let Rowan hang on the gate until he dies."

"If you think he won't kill her the moment he's convinced, bargained, or threatened her into repairing the damage she's done to him, you're a fool. He'd have no other choice unless he wants to live with the threat of going back."

"I can't leave Rowan like that, Shaughnessy. He wouldn't be there if he hadn't helped me."

"By the gods, girl," he said and ran a hand over his face again.

"She will be returned to Westwood one way or another. Two of the warriors still track her. Eirnen has decreed they can't kill you for fear of angering Camilla further, but that doesn't mean they can't stop you. Bones take time to heal, even for you, vampire. I expected to come here and find they'd taken her already."

Camilla couldn't help but cast her eyes around the trees for them. "Could they have followed you?"

"I was careful, but the pack is less than a day's walk from Gladen. After being with Winston, food, rest, and healing would've been necessary. It wasn't difficult to decide where to look for you first."

Shaughnessy got to his feet and started pulling her back toward the camp. "We need to go have a chat with your pets."

Shaughnessy's faster pace on the way back only made her feel more uneasy. His face was set in the neutral mask he wore when he was thinking through ideas that didn't have a pleasant end. She hoped she was wrong and he was trying to decide which location was an ideal first for squandering.

The pack was out and waiting. Grayson and Thomas sat at the fire as if nothing out of the ordinary happened, but others watched her with a wariness that hadn't been there before. She kept her eyes forward and her shoulders back, taking Shaughnessy's advice from the night they arrived. The three of them sat together on the log opposite the alpha and his second, the tension palpable.

"Let's finish this business with Riley before we move to other matters," Shaughnessy said. "He's not here to execute anyone and when we leave, we take him with us. We can leave now, but we leave with all the information we have regarding the king, his illness, and his warriors. Or we can call a truce for discussion's sake and talk as friends."

"You want something from me or you wouldn't make the offer," Grayson said and tossed what looked like a twig into the fire. "What is it?"

"For now, I need to speak with Jesse and Beckett," Grayson smirked, probably at the "for now" and called the two wolves over to the fire. "When the two of you were creatures, you tracked her to my cave despite a concealment ward and then again at Gladen. How?"

"Dunno," Jesse said and shrugged. "I didn't know where I was going or why, I just knew I had to follow."

"It was a call that was impossible to ignore," Beckett added. "I felt like something was missing and my instinct knew where to find it."

"And now?"

"It's still there but tempered. I can disregard it if I want when I couldn't before, but when she yelled for us to wait with Riley, I wanted to obey." He glanced at Grayson then Camilla before coming back to Shaughnessy. "I can get a vague sense of her emotions, but not the reasons behind them."

"Eirnen's warriors are tracking her to return her to Westwood. You saw a fraction of what she's capable of, enough that you know it's nothing you want in Eirnen's hands. Allow her and Riley to stay here with the pack until I return."

"Return?" Camilla squeaked and Shaughnessy held up a hand to silence her.

"They can't stop them," Riley said, his face falling with tiredness and defeat to match his voice. "I mean no offense to your pack, but you can't begin to understand what they are. The vampirism didn't strip them of what they were as it does with a bite. Not only do they possess the ability to cast, but it's Eirnen's power. They heal before you've finished making the cut, they have a vampire's cunning and their telepathy gives them the advantage to strategize like a pack."

"Telepathy," Shaughnessy said and let out a long breath. "They are the sons of Anthelian," he said. "She was a gigantes warrior, their equivalent of a queen," he added in answer to the confusion on the faces around him. "Don't worry," he said to Camilla. "They can only hear one another. No one else.

"You're no equal to them either, Shaughnessy. Rowan and I trained them ourselves with the long swords. They surpassed us in days and spend every waking moment training to avenge their clan. They have the sunlight," he said and Shaughnessy frowned deeper.

"What you're trying to get everyone to acknowledge is if they want to take me, the only thing any one of you can do about it is die. What about me? As you saw earlier, I've learned a few things about myself. I have more, I know it. I can feel it."

"I don't know. Eirnen was working with them with casts before his illness began, but I don't know how far he got or if they have any level of skill with it. They don't like to use it. They prefer to fight." He gave Shaughnessy a look of sympathy that was also a warning. "I do believe they've retained some of the foresight from that little female. Eirnen thinks it's because they're brothers, but I don't. They anticipate an attack and block too well for instinct or muscle movement giving away the angle."

"My request stands. Will you allow them to stay here or not?"

"If these warriors are as Riley says, I won't sacrifice my pack to keep her from them. It sounds like she'd have more of a chance against them as any and from what I saw earlier, I don't doubt it." Grayson glanced up at Jesse and then Beckett, who was looking across the clearing at Jasmine. "I'll allow them to stay and vow no harm under the condition that Camilla remember our kindness in the future."

"Agreed," Shaughnessy said and Camilla stuttered as she came to her feet when he did. "We must talk," he took her hand and started toward the tunnels. "Riley, you come as well."

"Shaughnessy," she snapped once they were inside the tunnels. He kept walking as if she hadn't spoken, winding through passages she'd not explored. He talked to Riley about strategic position-ing, any advantage they may have against the warriors, a weakness found during conversion or training since Riley was present from start to finish. "Enough," Camilla said. "Shaughnessy, where are you going?"

"Riley, if you could give us a moment," he said and they watched him go back the way they came. "If there are rumors about his illness, there could also be a few as to how he got to be that way. We need to find out what's being said and by whom."

"You think someone might get the idea to use me? It's already a rather long line, Shaughnessy."

"Not use you, put you down," he said and she fought a shudder. "No one will want someone who can do what you did to Eirnen roaming free. If you can do it to him, there's no one safe from you. As his granddaughter, they won't to listen to reason as to your difference from him. They won't take the risk. I wouldn't have. To others, you're nothing more than a Westwood with the potential to be worse than the last. And, if it's as bad as I think it's getting, this is the perfect time for Abel to attack. Two of Eirnen's warriors are gone from Westwood, Eirnen himself is incapable of defending it, and Henrik is a weakling."

"Then we can leave," she insisted, "right now. Tonight. Let Eirnen and Abel kill each other and be done with it."

"And Rowan? We'd be leaving him to his fate as well."

"Underhanded, Shaughnessy," she said and looked away from him. she'd forgotten about Rowan already. He didn't care if Rowan lived or died, but she did and he knew it.

"Sorry, love," he said and folded his arms around her shoulders in a loose hug. "I'm going anyway, but guilt seemed the most expedient route and I need all of what's left of the night if I'm to find Devlin and Rissa before morning. He will know all there is to know and who hunts us. If we are to have any hope of leaving Calame with our lives, we must have this information. I will need their help to arrange safe passage in secret."

"I'll go with you."

"Not only does this need to happen quickly, but with you and Riley in tow, fights are a certainty. Winston had other allies. We already know of the warriors. How many abused villagers are finding their bravery in Eirnen's weakness? The pack is a deterrent for most and when the warriors take you, they will serve the same purpose." She shivered and he squeezed her tighter. "Delay them as long as possible, in any way you safely can."

"You don't think I can kill them, do you?"

"No, but do feel free to prove me wrong."

"I can't lose you, too, Shaughnessy. My family is gone. Callum is gone. There's no one else."

"There is," he said and ran his hand through his hair. "If for some reason I'm unable to return, find your James." Camilla's mouth popped open, full of so many questions, objections, and arguments they tripped over each other across her tongue until they were nothing but a squeak of sound. "Two to choose, but one to keep. You ask for distance from Eirnen—"

"—With you," she interrupted.

"The warriors will take you back to Eirnen, but you must not heal him. No matter what he threatens, do you understand? He'll kill you to protect himself the moment it's done. When an opportunity presents itself, you take Riley with you for protection and you leave."

"You're not saying the catalyst for this," she said and jerked back from his hands. "Say it, Shaughnessy. Your death or perhaps you'll go back to Eirnen's dungeon. That's what you meant when you said no matter what he threatens isn't it? He'll have you so well hidden or locked away from me there would be no way of getting to you again and you expect me to just accept that and skip down Marion's chosen path. To hell with that, Shaughnessy, and to hell with her."

"Calm down, lass. I'm not imprisoned or dead now. I've managed to keep myself alive for a very long time. I may yet be able to do it again and this must be done." He pulled her into a hug. "Don't forget, I hope to also find a route of safe passage for us—all of us."

She shook her head and a treacherous part of her wanted to lock him inside the tunnels, effectively making him her prisoner. A near hysterical laugh dissolved to tears at the justification of it. For his own protection. "I love you, Shaughnessy," she said and let him go.

"Father, the warrior Gabriel has arrived," Henrik said, waking Eirnen.

Eirnen rose from the bed, his head clouded with deadly nightshade. So far the only one it had been deadly to, despite the name, was Marion. The constant fog left him muddled, slower, which he loathed, but his mind was his own for the brief periods he was awake. It wasn't ideal, but the alternative was horrifying. The room tilted. Henrik caught him by one arm and around the waist before he fell.

"I'm fine," he said, his tongue tacky in his mouth. "Water," he slurred and leaned heavily on the wall when Henrik's support was gone.

His arms were weighted until he was forced to use both hands to work the glass to his mouth. They shook, sloshing the moisture he desperately needed, waving the temptation of relief in his face. Henrik busied himself in a bid to preserve the dignity Eirnen was nearly stripped of. His knees buckled with pleasure at the first roll of sweetness over his tongue. It spilled out of the corners of his mouth, soaking his shirt, but some of it was making its way down his throat.

His arms gave out before he was sated, his breaths heavy and fast. "More?" Henrik whispered, taking the cup. Eirnen shook his head. He couldn't lift the glass again and he would not ask his son to do it for him.

"Bring him to my quarters," Eirnen said and waited until Henrik was gone to walk forward with his shoulder dragging across the wall to keep him upright.

It was humiliating, a man like him wary of six feet of distance. He gripped the doorframe with his eyes fixed on the armchair closest to him. There was nothing to use as a crutch, but he ground his teeth with anger and determination. He'd be seated in that chair, eyes open and alert by the time Gabriel came to him. As degrading as this was when he was alone or with Henrik, it would be an absolute affront to his pride to have it witnessed by a vital, powerful male like Gabriel. He let go and led with his hands stretched in front of him, more a controlled fall than actual steps, but he landed in the chair. It grated across the floor from the force of his body, but he'd made it on his own.

His mind was beginning to clear, marginally. Within the hour he would be walking the fine line where Marion would wake and come for him. He had to get another treatment before then. It was a razor's edge he tread. One mistake, one moment too late, and the nightshade would trap him under with her until the effects waned. When he was on time, he went into the deepest, dreamless sleep imaginable that locked her in chains in her pit. He very much wanted to keep her in chains. She lived in his head, knew his every thought and terror and brought them to life down there in the dark.

One of her cruelest tricks required no physical torment at all. She was fond of inflicting pain on his body and did so with frequency, but it was when she gave him everything that he broke. Calame and the Westwood line flourishing, generations ahead their power was without equal. She built a world around him, so real he could feel his great-grandchild, Camilla's child, warm and wriggling in his arms. She waited until he let himself believe it was real and then she yanked it back. The babe dead and decomposing in his lap, Westwood Castle in ruin, Calame burnt to ash. There were no Westwood casters, the numbers dwindled lower and lower with each passing generation until there were none. And then she'd sing the rhyme, asking if he understood now.

A boom of thunder shook the castle and rumbled long after the rattling stopped. *Marceline.* If he were a sentimental man, he'd allow himself to believe she was trying to get his attention. But he wasn't and it was a thunderstorm conjured up by Mother Nature, nothing more. Marceline was beyond his reach. He straightened at the sound of heavy boots thudding down the corridor. He couldn't hear Henrik's steps, not when they were pitted against Gabriel's, but he'd return as well. He'd expressed concern that Eirnen's control over the warriors weakened as he did, leaving him vulnerable to them. But if that were true, he'd have not been able to summon Gabriel here now.

"Your timing is less than opportune," Gabriel said. The male filled the doorway, his black eyes glittering with menace.

"As is your brothers'," Eirnen countered. "It would be wise to remember who it is you serve, warrior, and address me as such." The leather of his pauldrons and breastplate creaked as his back straightened him to maximum height. The iron cuffs around his biceps were visible and marked him as a man of significance within the clan, the son of a ruler. He wasn't accustomed to being brought to heel.

"Warrior, know your place," Henrik warned.

"Have you forgotten what that binding to me means? If I were so inclined, I could command you kill one of your own brothers. Your tenacity and hubris will not be enough to stay your sword, I promise you."

"That would be unwise, especially at the present time," he said with an air of smugness that set Eirnen on edge. "Your Majesty."

His anger was full and crystalline. He was running out of time. "Very well, tell me why you're confident enough in that to risk one of your brothers."

"Abel is moving, swiftly. He's split his army, which outnumbers ours by half. The one led by him is advancing on Calame. The other is working their way backward toward Gladen." A chill raced up Eirnen's spine. *No, no.* "Marcus told him of your madness, the cause, and the cure. He means to keep you from it."

"Marcus?" Eirnen rubbed his forehead that was beaded with sweat. Abel can't kill her, not if he wants Marceline. He would, however, leave Eirnen in this state. He'd have Eirnen bowing and scraping at his feet for a chance to beg Camilla to revoke this madness. "Niko and Dorin, have they Camilla?"

"You mean two of my brothers who you'd see me kill because of your pettiness?"

"Do not toy with me, Gabriel." He slammed his hand on the arm of the chair with bruising force. Moisture dripped onto his lips. He wiped it away and the back of his hand smeared red. Henrik produced a handkerchief and Eirnen held it to his nose. "Camilla," he panted.

"They have her in sight. An opportunity to separate her from the vampire presented itself and they chose to take it."

"Get Nox. Go get them. Keep her from Abel at all cost." Those few, short sentences caused him to breathe in an exhausted pant. Gabriel turned on his heel and Eirnen let his body slump when he heard him descending the stairs. "Marcus?"

"Went to meet the messenger with a counteroffer and didn't return. The guard was put on the ready once Marcus's body wasn't found at the meeting site. I guessed what he'd done, he'd been uneasy, questioning."

Betrayed once again, and again he was powerless to seek his vengeance. "My tonic," he said at the first whisper of a child's laughter.

CHAPTER 15

"WHERE DO YOU think you're going?" Grayson asked and stepped onto the path in front of Camilla. It was early, well before dawn, but apparently not early enough. "We had a bargain, and as I recall you have quite the temper when a bargain is broken. Why now are you sneaking away without taking the executioner with you?"

"Shaughnessy made the bargain. Track him down and take it up with him."

"Camilla," he said and blocked her path again. "You can stop feigning callousness, now. No one here but me and I know you were sickened by what you did to my pack. I don't think you meant to do it. Don't misunderstand, I believe you meant to flex, but it got away from you. That is something we understand well."

"You're right, but don't think I'll hesitate to do it again if you force me."

"I know that, too. We're not dissimilar, you and me. I've done unspeakable things to protect my pack, whatever was necessary, because I care about them more than I care about myself. Each time I commit an act I once thought too vile to contemplate, I feel myself sliding deeper. Every scream, every pleading gaze, and every word spoken to me by a mate or child to stay my hand is with me. I can live with those memories and the nightmares they wrought. I let the darkness pull me deeper toward a place that makes it easier to do the same again and again. I can live with that too, though it makes me unrecognizable to myself at times. I couldn't live with knowing even one of them suffered when I could've stopped it but didn't out of fear for myself."

"How many pieces do we lose until we're no different than Eirnen?" she asked. He shrugged and scanned the woods around them. "The warriors are close. They have a history with wolves. It's not a good one and I was worried Beckett and Jesse would interfere. Shaughnessy was right, there are others after me—what's left of Winston's wolves, I'd imagine. Four of them died less than an hour ago and I don't want to add any of your pack to that list. Go back, get your guard up. The warriors will follow me, but any remaining wolves will follow my scent to your camp." She didn't want to explain how she knew about the deaths or that she could feel the power of the warriors like a pressing weight.

His brow furrowed. "Riley?"

"Will catch up. He'd argue the benefits of staying with your pack, but I've been with you long enough to know that you would take offense to the warriors trespassing on your territory. The fight would be about the offense, not me, but I'd still be the cause. If I leave, there's no reason for them to be there and no reason for the pack to fight." She bowed her head to him in a sign of respect. "Thank you, for all you've done. You are a good man and a good alpha, Grayson Quinn. For what it's worth, I count you among my friends."

"After what I've seen of your loyalty to your friends, I accept it as an honor."

She lowered her head again and turned away from him to walk deeper into the wood. The cedars were thick. The sap clung to her skin and hair in sticky clumps. The warriors were close enough to be a hum over her skin, but when she tried to test them by pulling the energy she felt emanating from them, it was a hollow vacuum. A sucking that tried to pull hers from her. She cut off the connection. She wondered why they waited. She was walking away from Westwood, away from their master and king. They weren't following along behind her with no reason.

The four wolves that died at the hands of the warriors didn't belong to Grayson's pack and hadn't been close enough to alert the ones patrolling the boundary. She was sure Grayson raised an alert once back with his pack. Deaths were coming to her from greater distances. They had to be, since Grayson kept a wide perimeter. She'd done something, set something free in the fight for Callum, but would it be enough to hold the warriors at bay?

She didn't know. She had only Riley's words to go by. The things she knew of Dorin were the intimacies of lovers, shared stories and confessions. She didn't recall him having any abilities in her memories of him other than those of a man in love with his woman. She'd wondered, in her waking hours, what he might be and hadn't gotten any answers. Power, casting, none of those things entered into their time together. It was him and her, nothing more and nothing that would aid her in keeping outside of Westwood walls.

With the limited library in her quarters, she'd searched to learn more about him. This was another area Grandfather held control, the tomes selected or approved by him alone. However, one tutor, a woman by the name of Magdaline, had smuggled a forbidden book called *Convergence* inside. She had left it, knowing how Camilla coveted it when Eirnen discovered what Magdaline's lessons entailed and sent her away.

She smiled at how doing nothing more than holding that book had made her feel wicked. It was contraband. Eirnen wouldn't approve and she'd known it. How innocent she had been to have a book flutter her heart with excitement at the rebellion of it all.

She now knew Dorin was a gigantes but knew little of their history. Her lessons had taught her they were dullards, lumbering brutes that loved to war with surrounding villages to steal resources. They were stronger than the wolf or the vampire but easily tricked and outmaneuvered as they were much slower. Dorin had been none of those things in the corridor. Another thing nagging at her was his size. He was very large, yes, but the gigantes didn't reach full physical maturation until thirty years of age. In her dreams of him, he'd been just as she saw him at the castle with the exception of the eyes.

Was it possible this was how she met the gigantes male? Was his becoming a warrior the path that led him to her and she to him? After all, what purpose had she to venture to the valley where they resided? None. Say some fluke, some turn of fortune, led her there and she met him, how then did she continue to meet him given the long distance between them? It made more sense that her visions of Dorin were possible futures provided by a seeress who was already meddling in the affairs of the Westwoods.

The remaining creature appeared at her side and she let out a surprised yip before she collected herself. He'd kept to the tunnels during their time with the wolves, only allowing her close enough to give him some food. Jesse and Beckett tried to make the caster boy feel safe in the dens, but he preferred solitude to company.

"I'll do my best," she assured him but didn't reach to touch him. He was a pitiful sight, small and dirty, the bones of his bent spine stretched the skin of his back. "Just try not to get killed, okay?"

Dark eyes flashed to her and she saw hatred in them. She'd given the rest their lives back and he'd had to watch it all while he was stuck. If she could do it on her own, she would've already. She told him as much and hoped he understood, but after only a few sentences he sprinted ahead of her. He was angry. She let him go. The warriors had no fight with him and they wouldn't hurt her.

The last thing Eirnen Westwood wanted right now was to give her more reason to leave him as he was. They both knew it, which meant she now possessed leverage of her own.

She stopped and was proud of herself when she didn't allow the rush of fear and anxiety show at seeing Dorin and one of his brothers in her path. They both wore their hair tied back in a tight braid that fell more than halfway down their backs. They'd traded their training clothes for battle gear and she could see the hilts of their swords peeking up over their shoulders. Dorin's hair was the same sandy shade she remembered so well. The other's was pale enough it was as light as her own.

"It's time to come with us now, Lady Camilla," Dorin said.

The village was in turmoil. Houses and shops burned, cheering crowds lit more ablaze while the owners begged them to stop. It appeared Eirnen had used Winston's ability at some point because a wall surrounded the castle inside the gates. Villagers beat on the wall of earth with their fists, with pickaxes or clubs, any tool they could find on the way. Casting flashes flared through the darkness both in the streets and around the wall. Those that remained with much power were few, they'd long been killed or recruited as guards by their king. The result was men using their fists to beat one another. Some were lucky enough to have found a knife. One woman was slashing at a man's gut with what looked to be a shard of glass with a strip of her dress wrapped around it to protect her hand.

Shaughnessy stayed out of view as best he could, watching, listening as he made his way to the wrought iron fence that wrapped the perimeter of Westwood grounds. Rowan was bound on the bars where he'd be in sight of the village, which helped shorten the search area. Whether he still survived was another matter. Large sections of the fence were open, the bars missing to allow entry to the castle. The people there weren't calling for Eirnen's head, they were demanding Henrik face them.

Had Eirnen expired? It wouldn't be such a hard thing to scale the wall of earth to see what was transpiring inside. Minutes. If he lived, perhaps Eirnen was wandering alone, defenseless, an easy kill. Were the warriors inside? Could they sense him this close to their king even now?

All around him were shouted curses, the names of people who'd been lost to make Eirnen's warriors. Men, women, children, old and young, he hadn't discriminated. He'd searched for the greatest energy, those who burned brightest, and stripped them of everything. Devlin was a vampire of power, enough to entice Eirnen that night for sure. Did he live or had he fallen victim? What about Rissa? She had some of Camilla's essence now, just as those two wolves did. Had Eirnen found her? Did he know what she could do?

A bottle whistled in front of his face and shattered against the wall. He looked for the thrower, but no one was advancing on him. He hadn't been targeted, just in the right place. There was glass breaking everywhere, so no one paid the sound any mind. Broken shop windows had people crawling out of openings with their arms laden with bread and cheeses, fabrics, and anything else they could carry.

The closer he got to the fence, the more bodies he saw. The trail of them thickened at the wall around the castle. He didn't see any of the guards, but he could now see that something was burning a high fire on the grounds. He searched the length of the fence as far as he could see until he saw Rowan. He was several yards away and tethered high for all to see. There were a few people around him, beating at the bars to get him down and within reach, but none of them were guards awaiting a rescue attempt. He'd not seen one guard since his arrival. Sloppy, very much so, another testament to how far Eirnen had fallen.

Shaughnessy slipped through a wide space in the bars and ran inside on Westwood grounds. There was so much blood in the air coupled with smoke and bowel it was impossible to pinpoint one person from another. Rowan wasn't moving. From the way his arms and legs were stretched wide, secured at the wrists and ankles, he probably wasn't able to move even if he was alive.

This time it was a stone that flew past his face and he was the target. Six men and two women had turned their efforts from getting at Rowan to Shaughnessy. "I have no fight with you," Shaughnessy said. "Not yet."

"If you mean to take the executioner, then we have a fight with you, vampire." The man spoke, the others shouted agreement. Tedious.

"Very well." He reached through the bars and jerked the talkative prick toward him. His skull connected with the iron with a crunch and opened a gash in his forehead. One small adjustment and he was through the opening until his shoulders stopped him from going farther. One thing he'd learned from the Westwoods, a gruesome enough display and the rest would scatter.

Shaughnessy kept his eyes on the rest and pulled slow but steady on the man's head. Vertebrae let loose with one dull pop after another, then went the snap of tendons and the wet tear of muscle. Blood rushed over Shaughnessy's feet. He opened his mouth and bared his fangs at the seven who remained. They jumped as if startled by that as opposed to a manual beheading, but they did turn and run. He tossed the head over his shoulder and climbed the bars to Rowan.

"Are we...finally...to have our day...vampire," Rowan said, gasping between words, his peeling lips cracked and bled with the motion.

His head was back, face to the sky because of a collar around his neck with two thick spikes on opposite ends of one another. The tip of one pressed into the soft skin under his chin tight enough a thin, but steady, trail of blood leaked down his neck. The other was resting against the exposed skin of his chest.

"Do not even swallow," Shaughnessy warned.

If he broke the collar in back, it would push the stake deeper under his skin. He had to rid the collar of the top spike first. He wedged his hand in the small space between the metal and Rowan's neck, clasped it tight, wished Rowan could tilt his head back further, and wrenched downward. The metal groaned, then broke. Rowan's head dropped as if the spike had been the only thing holding it up. It wasn't, the tip was too sharp to have been used as a chinrest.

The collar was next. He dropped it to the ground and looked over the binds on Rowan's wrists and ankles. He held much of Rowan's weight to keep from severing his hands with the cables that tied his wrists. Rowan was all but draped over Shaughnessy's shoulder, the sun blistered skin leaking heat and fluids onto him.

"Last one," Shaughnessy warned. He braced with his free hand and both feet on the bars, centered Rowan on his shoulder and popped the cable free.

He released his hold on the fence, taking them to the ground. Though he landed on his feet, it wasn't an easy stop for Rowan. He groaned pain and immediately curled his arms and legs in close to his body as soon as he was on the ground. The muscles were knotting hard enough Shaughnessy could watch them bunching under the skin. He was covered in blisters, bruises, and knots. Some of the thrown stones had found their target.

Shaughnessy growled a curse and bit into his own wrist. Doing this for Camilla, Marion or another vampire was one thing, but Rowan—it infuriated and disgusted him. Camilla knew Rowan did things he was forced to do under Eirnen's command, but Shaughnessy knew *what* he and his brother had done. He'd seen it. But he hadn't time to be choosy. He intended Rowan and his brother assist him in taking Camilla from Calame. He trusted them to not hurt her if left to choose for themselves. To do that, Rowan had to be able to walk.

Rowan twisted his head to keep from drinking, but again, no time. Shaughnessy gripped his jaw and dug his fingers into the muscle until his mouth opened. "You will swallow it or I'll break your teeth out and we start again." He gave him enough to get him moving and no more.

"Riley?" Rowan tried to sit up but failed. He breathed as though the small action exhausted him, but he'd gain more strength shortly.

"Begged Camilla to save your arse," Shaughnessy said and pulled Rowan up by the arm. "Let there be no mistaking, as of this moment you are no longer Eirnen's executioner."

"If he calls me—"

"Then I will kill you before you've taken the steps to return." He pushed Rowan forward. Rowan stumbled but stayed up and walking. "One honorable action and the word of Callum Dunn was enough to sway Camilla. She accepts you as one of hers because of it. I do not."

"Callum Dunn is dead. My brother and I performed his rites ourselves. We watched him burn. Camilla was mistaken."

"Your ignorance on the matter is not a problem of mine. She trusts me. If I return to her with news of your death before my arrival, she will believe me without question. You are a liability to me. I will have to argue against killing you where we go. One hint that you aren't to be trusted and Camilla will see your twin through the mourning of your death. Understand?"

"Yes."

They walked on in silence, following the fence as far as it went to remain on the outer limits of the village and out of sight. The burning structures on the grounds had once been the stables and the guards' quarters. No guards in sight, but horses scattered, running headlong for the wood. The villagers were still smashing and cutting at the wall to get to the castle, chunks wide enough for a child to sit in were taken out already. If they kept at it, they'd get inside.

"Is Eirnen dead?"

"No," Rowan said with a shake of his head. "Though many seem to think he's as good as. They started taking the village apart early in the day. Those—" he said and nodded back toward the people on the ground "—they're the ones that went to the wall and called for asylum. Shifters mostly, but not only. The others killed them as traitors."

Yes, well, not many cared for shifters on the best of days. They fought with anyone who wasn't a shifter and with one another. They were physically weaker than wolves or vampires, but stronger than casters. They took their grievances out on anyone who hadn't the power to stop them. Cowards and bullies.

The crowds of people thinned the farther they walked. They could still hear the roaring of fires, the breaking of glass and the cheering in the main section of the village. It didn't sound as if it would wind down anytime soon. The home Devlin currently occupied was set back in the trees far enough he may have missed the riotous behaviors. Shaughnessy hoped so. Dawn would be soon and he wanted to be nowhere near the village when it came.

"She be a death wraith."

Shaughnessy twisted his head toward the distant voice.

"Tis true, I seen it with my own eyes. A soul eatin' banshee, she be."

"If we stay north—"

"Shh," Shaughnessy warned and turned toward the bodiless voice, hoping to hear more. No words came. Either the man had nothing more to say on the subject or had walked beyond hearing range. "Who do they think is a death wraith?" he asked Rowan. He'd been on that fence with nothing to do but listen for days.

"Camilla," Rowan said. "They believe her to be making a move for the throne."

❧

"You know I'm not going to just follow you back."

"Aye," Dorin said and dropped his head in a nod.

Neither of them looked worried about the prospect of her attacking them. It made her nervous. Dorin was the one who stopped her before she could kill Eirnen. He'd seen what she was capable of and there wasn't the slightest hint of apprehension. Confidence like that meant he had reason to have it. If what happened when she tried to pull their energies was any indication, they were entitled.

"You might change your mind about that," the blond one said.

"Niko," Dorin admonished, confusing her more. Did he want to fight? "Well, let's be done with this, woman."

Apparently so, she thought as he took a few steps ahead of his brother and stopped, waiting for her to make the first strike.

Dorin's gaze was steady on hers, challenging but not as aggressive as it had been that day in the corridor. It was resigned. As if he was sure of his victory but wasn't pleased by it. Niko leaned against one of the cedar trunks, his arms crossed over his wide chest as if he were bored. Over Dorin's shoulder, she marked a clear path through the trees where there weren't bushes or creeping vines to snare her. All she needed now was for them to move.

She smiled at Dorin and he stood taller, bracing himself. She spread her arms and then brought them together with a clap of her hands. Niko bounced to the side as the tree he was using as a resting post was felled only to end up in the way of another. Dorin grabbed his brother by the collar and jerked him backward before a third could crush him. She ran, leaving them to dodge cedars, taking more down as she passed. She didn't dare stop or look behind her. The woods echoed with the sounds of the mighty trunks splitting and crashing to the ground.

Every boulder she passed, she launched blindly behind her.

They landed with great thuds that shook the ground, but she'd yet to hear one pained sound from the warriors. They had the speed of a vampire and should've caught her by now, the thought that they were letting her wear herself out wasn't one she could discount. It was working. Her legs burned and her energies were beginning to wane. They had none she could steal. She had to think. Delay, as long as possible. That was the best outcome she could hope for at present. The farther she ran, the farther they had to walk back. More time.

She could feel them on both sides of her and groaned with effort as she threw her arms out to push against the thick stands of trees they were running through. Sweat dripped from her face and she was nearing exhaustion, but a sense of satisfaction rose at a shouted oath from one of the warriors.

"Enough," an arm coiled her waist from behind and popped her feet off the ground. She kicked as he turned to face the way she came. He dropped her but kept her wrist.

She dug her heels in, but it did no good. Neither did her nails raking against Dorin's hand while she tried to pry his fingers loose. He kept his eyes straight ahead and acted as if she weren't there. She gathered her power, what she'd saved for the opportune moment, and hit Dorin only to have it…fizzle. She stumbled along beside him and stared stupidly. He'd paid it as much attention as he had her nails. His energies weren't there, instead there was a tar-like lacquer that absorbed what she'd thrown at him. How did she fight someone who, for all appearances, devoured anything she hit him with?

The trees she'd knocked down and the boulders she'd thrown littered the way. They came to a place where the broken branches were tangled until he couldn't drag her over or under them. Without word or warning, he picked her up as if he had every right in the world to do so. Her hand snapped out and slapped him across the face. He was betraying her, whether he knew it or not. He stopped and stared at her as if he were surprised by that above everything else. She slapped him again.

"Don't you touch me," she hissed and scrambled from his arms, and this time, he let her. He reached for her wrist again to keep dragging her along, but she pulled away. "I said keep your hands off me, Dorin."

"How do you know my name?" he asked as he glowered down at her. "Twice you've used it as if we were known to one another. Tell me why."

She stood on her toes and still didn't get close to meeting his face even as he leaned over her. "No."

The masculine smell of him that she remembered mingled with the scent of leather. Her body wanted to sway into him, fall against him and inhale deep. Which was absolutely ludicrous. Instead, she lowered from her toes and marched forward on her own.

She passed the blond one, Niko, who was grinning as if there was nothing in this world or the next that could trouble him. She certainly hadn't. She couldn't use casts against them, couldn't pull energies from them, couldn't outrun or fight them, but there had to be a way to keep from going back to Westwood Castle.

"Is Riley not still with you?" Niko asked.

"And it matters to you, why? You didn't care enough to free Rowan from the gate, so why would you now concern yourself with his brother?"

"Think what you want about us, but Riley and Rowan are good men. Riley shouldn't be out on his own right now. If you know where he is, you need to tell us for his sake," Dorin said from behind her.

"Did Eirnen think of a new way he's to be used and you need to deliver him as well?"

Riley was only this far from Westwood because he was trying to save his brother. Now that Eirnen knew what Rowan did to aid Camilla, he'd never be safe from Eirnen and the binds wouldn't allow him to defend himself. As close as Rowan and Riley were, Eirnen knew as well as she did that Riley had been in on the secrets, too.

For now, there was nothing she could think of to get away from the two of them. She'd wait and watch for an opportunity. Shaughnessy would be fine and he'd come back for her. She believed that. If she was cooperative, didn't try to run again, maybe Dorin and Niko wouldn't watch her as closely after a time and she could sneak away with him. Shaughnessy fighting them was not an option, not to her mind, but if they became complacent, he might not have to.

"You knew Riley was with me," she clarified and looked to Niko. "You said still, 'is Riley not *still* with you.' Which means you know we were both with the wolves. The four you killed, they were Winston's?"

"The twenty-three we killed were Winston's," Niko said and that smile came back. "Those four were the scouts that ran ahead of the rest in hopes of finding a larger pack to join. You burn Gladen?"

"I did," she answered.

"Did you kill Winston?" Dorin demanded with more heat than the conversation dictated.

"Get to like him during his time at Westwood, did you, Dorin?"

The two of them looked at each other over her head and then Dorin jerked her to a stop while Niko kept walking. "I would've let you kill him had I been capable," he said and released the hold on her.

"What are you talking about?" She crossed her arms over her chest and looked away as if she couldn't be bothered. It was a habit of Henrik's. One she knew well how goading it could be.

"Eirnen. I assume me stopping you is why you insist on antagonizing me."

"I know you had no choice. I heard you apologize when you did it," she admitted. "As far as being antagonizing, one would have to care enough to make an effort and I can assure you I do not."

"You are and you know it, woman. Do not lie. You can't claim it's because of what I am because you spoke civilly enough to my brother. That means it's something about me specifically."

It bothered him, she realized. Though he didn't know how betrayed she felt or why, she wanted to punish him. Unfair, but too tempting to resist.

"Perhaps so," she said and began to follow Niko's back in the distance.

"You know nothing about me," Dorin growled and she smiled to herself.

"I know plenty about you," she said and laughed. "You have a scar down your right side from a fight you lost when you were eight. You killed your first man when you were thirteen. And when you were twenty, you and your brothers traded everything you were to become monsters for Eirnen."

He stopped, but she kept walking. *Let him puzzle over that for a while.*

He followed again but stayed behind and kept his distance. She did her best to catch Niko, but his stride was much longer and he easily scaled the fallen trees that she had to crawl under, around or through, sometimes all three at a single pile. It might not have stopped them from chasing her, but she had to admit she was impressed with what she'd done. No energies to pull to fuel her, it'd been all on her own power.

Ahead, Niko unsheathed his sword and she lost the self-congratulatory feeling. She scanned the ridge for what caused him to be on the ready and saw a flash of pale skin.

"Niko, don't," she shouted. He looked back at her over his shoulder. She began to run, stumbling over roots and tall tangles of weeds. "He won't hurt anyone," she said.

Niko didn't sheathe the sword, but he didn't attack. He reminded her of Riley in the way he watched, never taking his eyes off the creature as it ducked behind trees and rocks to get out of his sight. She got to his side and laid her hand on the tight forearm that's hand still held the sword on the ready.

"Niko, please. He isn't a threat to you. He just needs to be near me, that's all." He looked down at her and then at Dorin, who gave a nod. She let out a long breath.

"What is it?" Niko asked and replaced the sword at his back.

"Do you think the four of you are the first warriors Eirnen tried to make? He's what can happen when the process fails."

Both of them locked their eyes on the slinking creature that glanced at them with fear at frequent intervals. She had to help him, soon. It wasn't fair to leave him this way all alone. He didn't have the wolves and vampires that fought anything that threatened them anymore. She started walking before they did as they watched the creature with unreadable expressions upon their faces.

She'd come close to telling them why their clan had been killed but stopped the words from spilling. For a moment, she'd forgotten it was more than a desire for vengeance against Abel that drove the warriors. It wasn't as simple as them seeing Eirnen for what he was and coming to her side. They were bound. Eirnen had seen to it they couldn't kill him for his treachery, it would be cruel of her to give them information they could do nothing about and then leave them tied to him.

Taking small jabs at Dorin was one thing, but to hurt him like that was out of the question. In truth, he didn't even deserve the prodding she'd given him, but she didn't want to soften toward him. If what Marion showed her really was to be their path, she would condemn them both. She wanted to, gods did she want to. He moved the same, spoke the same, smelled the same, she could only surmise that the way he'd touch her and look at her would be the same as well.

"Camilla." She looked up to see Riley barreling over the terrain toward her. He didn't slow until he was in front of her and that was to take both her shoulders and shake her. "What were you thinking leaving without me?"

Riley looked up and narrowed his eyes as Dorin moved closer. "Riley, we must speak," Dorin said.

"Are you alright?" Riley asked, ignoring Dorin to look her over.

"I'm fine, thank you," she said.

"Riley. Now."

Riley didn't appear to appreciate the order, but he did walk a short distance away to speak with Niko and Dorin. She took the opportunity rest her legs and sat on one of the stone ledges to watch them. Riley's expression went from annoyed to shocked and then his eyes kept returning to her. After a moment longer, Riley was the one doing the talking and he was animated about it. He was angry and she wished she could hear why.

He moved to come over to her, but Dorin stepped in his path and they were talking again. Niko was watching the same as she was, no longer involved in what the other two were discussing now. Finally, they reached some type of agreement and Camilla got to her feet as Riley came back to her.

"What's happening, Riley? Is there news of Rowan? Has Shaughnessy freed him?"

"Nothing of Rowan, but Henrik has orders for the wolves and it's best that I deliver them. Stay close to the warriors. I'll be back as quickly as I can."

The way they were leading her was an odd and zig-zagging path with no obvious direction. Granted she was lost out here, but even she knew the fastest route was a straight line. They didn't go straight, not for long anyway. One moment they were trekking north toward Westwood Castle, the next they were backtracking to go west and she was beginning to wonder if they weren't lost as well. She doubted it but couldn't help being hopeful.

Riley found them again, though, so perhaps this aimless wandering was premeditated and not aimless at all, but still the reasoning was a mystery. Riley's explanation was to make it more difficult for them to be tracked. He must think her as naïve as she once was. Wolves and vampires alike could still track them by scent, regardless of how many hills and valleys they scaled or which turns they took.

It was dusk and they hadn't stopped. Riley's mouth was set in a determined line, but the glean of sweat on his skin and the harsh breaths through his nose belied his weariness. Camilla had given up not panting her breaths long ago and she was sure her bare feet were no more than a collection of blisters and thorns. The warriors appeared as fresh as when they began.

"I can't walk any farther," Camilla said and held onto a tree to keep from falling. The muscles in her legs were hard knots that refused to loosen, her mouth was so dry her cracked lips stuck to her teeth. "I need rest and water," she said and shivered despite the heat of the sun that dampened her skin and hair.

"You'll kill her before she makes it to Westwood, warrior," Riley said and laid his hand on her forehead. "I can take her pain, but I can't conjure water and without it she'll die."

Dorin's brow furrowed and he tipped her head back to see her face. She hadn't the energy left to bat him away. As it was, his finger under her chin felt as if he'd relieved her of a heavy weight.

"Why did you not tell me how to care for you sooner?" he asked as he stroked her jaw with his thumb. His expression was soft, gentle, full of concern and it was for her. Her eyes slid closed. How foolish she was. "Niko," he said, then caught her under the knees and across the back to pick her up.

"Put me down," she cried as the material abraded her skin.

"Warrior," Riley said to get Dorin's attention as he looked at her with confusion. "Set her on the ground."

"No," she protested and twisted away as Riley moved behind her. "Water. Rest. Nothing more."

"There's blood," Dorin said and looked at his own hands though there was nothing there.

"I suspect this wasn't of your doing," Riley said. "Camilla." He scooched around until he was crouched in front of her. "You must let me see so I can help you."

She shook her head and pushed to her feet. "I don't need it," she said and put her hand against a cedar trunk to wait until the dizziness passed. She didn't want anyone to see, but especially not Dorin.

"Niko will find suitable cover for the night," Dorin said. He looked at her again and let out a long breath. "I'm sorry, Camilla," he said and before she had a chance to wonder which offense he was apologizing for, sleep took her at his command.

CHAPTER 16

THE SMELL OF molding straw and dust irritated Camilla's nose and throat, making her cough and bringing her fully awake. She was lying on her stomach on a bed of old linens on a dirt floor. Her back was exposed and worse, Dorin was sitting against the wall with an unfathomable expression on his face.

She stayed quiet while she sorted through the scattered and varying feelings assaulting her. She was embarrassed, furious, touched, vulnerable, and tired. Part of her wanted to try again to strike at him, hurt him, the other wanted nothing more than to let go and cry and beg him to be her Dorin if only for a moment. She wanted, needed, for it all to stop or she feared she would be as mad as Eirnen soon.

There was no getting around it. He'd seen them all, every mark from her time with Winston. Vanity made her small and compared to all the other happenings of these last weeks, it was nothing. But still she felt it now. With him. Despite everything, she wanted him to think her beautiful. Shame added itself to the tangled knot of emotions. People had died, were still dying all around her, whether Dorin found her beautiful shouldn't be a thought or concern.

"Say something," she said and picked at the blanket that resembled the one she'd put across the horse's back.

He stood and went to a pail, then knelt in front of her with a dipper full of water. "There's a well," he said and put it to her lips. With the first taste, she pushed herself up to get more, to drink faster. She put her arm across her chest to hold up the dress and gulped. It was cool and delicious and once she drained the first dipper, he got another.

"Thank you," she said and lowered back to the makeshift bed.

"Niko and Riley are hunting," he said after her stomach rumbled.

Riley had healed the few remaining lashes and even the blisters on her feet, given that she could move and wiggle her toes without pain. There wasn't anything he could do about the scars. She hadn't seen them for herself, but she felt them. They were raised ridges, more sensitive than the rest of her skin, that she felt each time she dressed or lay on her back to sleep. Each time they made themselves known, Winston Cleary was alive and waiting again until she convinced her thumping heart and shaking hands otherwise.

The reminder made her desperate to see Shaughnessy and know he wasn't in pain. It wasn't as easy as following a tunnel to his alcove now. She didn't know where he was or when he'd come back. She didn't have Callum's ability anymore so she couldn't look for him either. It was night, he'd be traveling, maybe on his way to her now. She fixed her eyes on the gaps in the slats of wood that made up a rickety barn door and waited for his approach to ease and occupy her mind.

"Do you love him, your vampire?" Dorin asked from his place against the wall.

"Shaughnessy is none of your concern."

"I disagree," he mumbled and let his head roll to the side until he wasn't looking at her anymore.

The silence grew tense and she wondered if he was struggling as much as she was. She had so many things she wanted to say but didn't know where to start or even if she should. It was disheartening. She missed him and she had the idea that if they began to talk, they'd fall into it with ease. He tried, many times throughout the day, and she either ignored him or addressed him with hostility.

She pulled her hands up to use them as a barrier between her face and the scratchy material and built her nerve.

"Shaughnessy means more to me than I can begin to describe. Saying he's my friend hardly does the depth of my feelings for him justice." He was guarded, but he was looking at her now. "I do love him but allowing you or anyone else to believe it's a romantic love is a falsehood that has already cost us much."

"A falsehood," he repeated, wary once again.

"I know what you must've heard about him and me once I was returned to Westwood. It was a misconception I allowed to continue as a means to put off Winston Cleary."

His eyes closed and he swallowed hard. His hands squeezed into fists at his sides. "I didn't know," he said, his voice low and rough. "Please, Camilla, give me this one thing. Please answer me without taunt. Were you—" He started and stopped to swallow hard. "Did he—"

"No," she said as fast as she could as his frame began to shake. "No, he didn't."

"I was coming for you. I felt you begging me, pleading me to help you. I didn't know," he said again.

"What do you mean, you felt me?" she asked and said a silent prayer that she didn't already know the answer.

"They put you in the dungeons. Eirnen was displeased that I didn't protect his queen. It was days before he weakened enough for me to free myself and by then you were gone from the castle. I had a conversation with Henrik and then Riley to learn where you'd been taken. I was coming, I was on my way to you, I swear it." He stopped talking, the anxiety drained from his features as if it had never been. "How did you know my name?"

If some of Marion's essence was inside Dorin and his brothers, and it must be since she was used in their conversion, perhaps Dorin had some of her foresight as Riley suspected. What had he seen and how much? Had he seen her? Seen them together as she had?

"I'm not another means to trap you as you accused," she said. "The caster, Marion, she was a powerful seeress and part of her essence is now in you. I think that's the why of your feelings." She pushed herself up to sit with one hand while the other kept the dress in place. "I'll tell you how I know your name if you tell me what you and Riley were whispering about. It's something bad, something you feel I shouldn't know, but that's not your decision."

He shifted, stretching one leg out in front of him. The other stayed bent at the knee. He was glorious. She took her time appraising him, skipping over the blackness of his eyes to focus on lips she knew were soft, but consuming. She'd spent hours lost in this man from nothing more than his kisses. And he knew none of it.

"And what's the why of yours?" he asked, rather than answer her question. "You look at me now with either sadness or softness and I don't know why. You desire me."

She watched him, tears pricking her eyes and she couldn't think of a lie. She didn't want to lie. Not to him. "I," she began and didn't dare blink for fear tears would fall. "I don't want to tell you," she managed to whisper.

"She warned me that you weren't mine to keep," he said and tapped his head. "So why does she torment me with you? How can you not be mine when I know that I belong to you? I saw you when I awoke as this. Never before the transition, but now, after, I see you, hear you, smell you. I've even felt your touch as if it were real. I know you called out for me from Gladen. I know it, without question, but only me, not my brothers. Why, Camilla? My sanity hinges on answers only you seem to possess. Tell me why I crave you as I've craved nothing else."

୶

Leave it to the young and naïve to find a way to make a rickety, stinking old barn into an opportunity for romance. Tenderness was plain in Camilla's voice. She was softening toward the warrior. He should tell her. If Marion was right, Camilla was going to find out the visions of Dorin were future. Not present. Not past. The life she saw was one she could still have, but it also led to his death, which in turn led to her corruption. Even with Eirnen dead, the man would die if he was her lover. Eirnen Westwood wasn't the only being who used the heart as a weapon.

Calame was a place where the ground had soaked up too much blood to build a house of peace. There was no happiness to be found here except by those who found joy in suffering. If the rest perished and Camilla ascended the golden throne, she would be challenged swiftly and savagely. There would be constant wars and battles to keep her life and her title. So much so, there would be no time to rule justly and fairly as she'd like. In one of these battles, Dorin would die. He would die and her fury would be unmatched.

She'll have to choose, Marion said. The more time she was around Dorin, the more likely it was she'd convince herself or allow him to convince her they could overcome any obstacle together. A load of foolishness. Regardless of what they believed, love did not conquer anything but the those who become victims to it.

The warrior was on his feet before the door completed its fall. His sword was out and ready. Camilla sat up, a look of guilt on her face. She dipped her head and used this time of distraction to replace the ties to her dress. By the time she lifted her head again, he couldn't discern if she was happy to see him or irritated at the interruption. Likely both.

"They're coming for her," he warned, though if Shaughnessy could hear the fighting, Dorin could as well.

"Who?" Camilla asked and got to her feet. "Grandfather? Henrik?"

"We don't have time," Shaughnessy said. "We must leave," he said as he scooped Camila up into his arms.

"She does not leave my sight," Dorin ground out, teeth bared.

"More than fifty wolves, casters, and vampires are even now charging in your direction with the sole purpose of terminating *her*. Not to capture or leverage. Kill."

"It's true," Rowan said as he ran through the open doorway. "Dorin, our only hope is to run."

"The safest place for her is behind Westwood walls," Dorin insisted.

"Agreed," Shaughnessy said. "No matter how powerful you and your brothers fancy yourselves, are you willing to bet her life on your ability to keep from being overwhelmed by numbers and the seconds it would take one of them to tear out her throat?"

"Nox and Gabriel are fighting now on the north ridge. Niko has gone to help them, but they will not be able to contain them all. Minutes, Dorin. We have minutes to make an escape." Riley glanced back at frequent intervals, watching for the moment their time would run out.

"Go," Dorin said. "My brothers and I will buy you time, but know I will find her before dawn comes, vampire." Dorin ran one finger down Camilla's cheek and then he vanished into the darkness.

Shaughnessy ran as fast as he could run, but it wouldn't be fast enough. Rowan wouldn't leave Riley behind and so it was once again just him and Camilla. This time, they weren't racing the dawn, they were being chased by more enemies than they could hope to beat. Their goal of Westwood was farther away than he could run in what was left of the night.

"We haven't much time," he said. "Listen closely." She turned her face into the crook of his neck, protecting herself from the rain that stung like tiny flames against her skin with his speed. "Rissa,

Devlin, and Mischa await us. I will leave you with them. I have told Rowan where to find you. The warriors and Abel's army, with any luck at all, will believe I still carry you and follow my scent toward Westwood."

"No. Dorin can sense me somehow. Something in Marion's magick. He will not be fooled."

There was no luck to be found when it came to this lass. He kept running, set on the plan they had because he had none better. Dorin would do as he was commanded and take her back to Westwood Castle and Eirnen if he found her. Since he had the daylight and they did not, it seemed likely he would find and take her while the others were trapped by the sun.

The battle was still raging in the distance, he could hear it, but it was getting fainter. The footsteps weren't. "No casts. They'll see the lights," he said and sat her on the ground just before he was knocked off his feet. A wolf, not of Grayson's pack. It was faster but wouldn't be alone. He crouched and met its lunge. One hard punch to the back where spine met skull and the animal was finished.

Another leapt out of the dark. He hadn't heard its approach. He twisted, hitting its stomach with his hands to toss it from him. It landed on its feet and came again. It jumped. He connected with a backhanded fist across the jaw and heard the corresponding snap followed by a howl of pain he was quick to silence with a twist of the beast's neck.

Camilla couldn't keep up with what was happening. It was too dark, the rain too heavy and the fighters too fast, but she was certain that more continued to join the fray. Shaughnessy couldn't best them all, not if they kept coming. She lifted her hands, then was grabbed around the waist, pinning her arms.

"No casts." It wasn't Shaughnessy who held her, but before she could attack, his voice was there.

"Remember, this must be done," he said and kissed her cheek.

She hadn't a chance to speak before they were running away

from Shaughnessy. She stretched her hand up and felt facial hair. "Devlin?"

"Yes."

He said nothing more as they ran. Thunder and lightning joined the rain, and in the brief flashes, she saw two other figures running through the night with them. It had to be Rissa and Mischa. Fear made her want to start gathering energies from them in anticipation of an attack, but they'd feel her doing it and wouldn't be happy about it. He said this must be done. If Shaughnessy trusted them, she'd try as well.

They were running in the opposite direction of Westwood Castle and, hopefully, toward a way to leave Calame for good. Perhaps before dawn she would be on her way to somewhere else. Somewhere thick with trees and hidden fields, a lovely manor house and warm days full of peace. She closed her eyes, remembering the sun on her skin and the smell of earth under her feet as she walked through her own flower garden.

"Hold tight," Devlin said. There was a sensation of being propelled upward. He stopped for a moment and then he was jumping again. She looked down in a flash of lightning and saw the tops of trees far below them.

They took a winding path until, finally, the rain stopped. A cave. They'd taken her to a cave in the top of the cliffs she'd seen in the distance.

"We are to stay here until nightfall, then we depart for the ship that will take you from here."

"What about Shaughnessy and Rowan and Riley?"

"They know where to meet us."

It was too dark to see Rissa, which was a small disappointment given the current situation, but still a disappointment. "Thank you for helping."

"I am drawn to you," Rissa said. "I can find you. Shaughnessy gave me the choice of staying with you or leaving Calame, out of reach of anyone who may get clever enough to use me to find you."

"I feel as if I should apologize, but I don't know what I've done," Camilla said.

"Rissa is my sister," Micha said. "Where she goes, I go. Devlin is my mate. Where I go, he goes."

"And you love living in Calame so much that leaving it is a hardship?"

"In a manner of speaking, yes. The human habitations are expanding while ours are shrinking. Calame is a safe haven from the humans. They do not tarry here."

"But, they're humans. They have no power. They're mortal. For you, they're food. Why would you fear humans?"

"They also learn. They study our weaknesses. It matters not how much stronger we are if they find our daytime resting place and expose us to the sun or burn us where we lie. There are those among the humans who spend their whole lives hunting beings not of their own kind. They teach their children who teach their children. Each generation learns more and more about us."

Admittedly, Camilla's lessons had had very little to teach with regard to humans. Perhaps Eirnen discounted them to his detriment? If vampires were wary of these creatures, she would be as well.

"Camilla," Micha said quietly. "Thank you, for giving me back my sister."

"You are welcome."

The sky outside began to lighten, but the rain continued. The vampires retreated deeper into the cave. There was a slight turn where a rock protruded into the path, blocking the sun from a small alcove barely big enough for the three of them to lie down. Camilla reached up and traced marks in the mud of the wall and realized they'd dug out this place to hide before they'd brought her here.

"Keep away from the entryway," Devlin advised.

She did as he asked, but it would do no good. Dorin was coming, she could feel it. She sat with her back to the wall and wondered how long it would be until he arrived. She worried about Shaughnessy and Rowan and Riley. She wondered if the creature survived. None of these things she could do anything about, which left a feeling of helplessness. All this power, yet none of it was of any help to anyone now.

Devlin mentioned a ship, one that would presumably take her to James. Shaughnessy meant her to take Riley and Rowan with her, but it was their choice. She wouldn't force them. There was also the matter of Eirnen's binding within them. He could call them back to him at any time and she didn't know if distance had any bearing on the potency of his beckoning. Could she free them? Was it possible to unravel the binding on them as she had the wards on her chambers? If she could, did that mean she could also free the gigantes?

Dorin could be free from Eirnen's reach.

A smile spread across her face at the possibility. It wasn't a future Marion had seen. How could she have seen it? Until now, Camilla hadn't thought of undoing a binding Eirnen placed. The idea she could challenge Eirnen Westwood had once been unfathomable, but that was no longer the case.

She could kill Eirnen, or she thought the two of them would at least end in a draw in which they killed one another. She couldn't best him and Henrik together. It was highly probable Henrik or Eirnen had called the rest of the family home to Westwood Castle for protection as well as a combined power that was, admittedly, difficult to match. Also, if she managed to defeat Eirnen—murdered her own grandfather—one of the warriors would kill her as their final bonded act. They'd no longer have to obey Eirnen's every order, but she'd be dead unless she could free them.

The sound of falling gravel brought her attention to the entrance a moment before Dorin filled the opening in the cliffside wall. He was wild-eyed and panting. There was a snarl from the vampires behind her that he matched, baring his teeth and reaching for his sword.

"Stop," she said and got to her feet.

He was covered in blood, though how much was his she had no way of knowing if what Riley said of their healing ability was true. His face and hands were coated in the thick, drying gore of the fight. He hadn't stopped to clean himself on his way to her. She stood beside him to look over the edge, the tree tops she'd glimpsed last night were nothing more than green specks within a green canvas below them.

"I won't let you fall," he rumbled and held his hand out to her.

"I know."

⇜

Eirnen could hear the sounds of his children. They'd come seeking the safety of Westwood Castle. Apparently, there was an uprising. The shifters—weres who weren't of the lycan strain—casters, and any other rogue species who yet survived decided to join together with the express intention of killing any Westwood they saw. How quaint.

His children seeking asylum did have the benefit of bringing their own guard to add to his as well as their collective power. The numbers lost by death or defection were replaced plus some. Henrik had been ordering the guard, placing them around the grounds, seeing to it that those not of this household's training were up to par or placed as pawns. He was practically running Westwood Castle now.

Henrik had enlightened all his siblings and their spouses as to Eirnen's and Marceline's conditions as well as the cause. At present, they debated the best strategy to *deal* with him. They were as a pack of vultures, wondering how to divvy up the wealth Eirnen had amassed. Their survival instinct was intact as far as Camilla. They feared her now. Not him. Her. HER! She was a pathetic, mewling pup who'd no doubt done this by accident in a time of distress and likely couldn't replicate it. If she couldn't replicate it, she couldn't undo it, either, which meant she was useless as a cure.

Rowan was gone. Saved by Camilla or dragged from his tether by the raging villagers below? Eirnen thought it was Shaughnessy who'd done the freeing at Camilla's request. Eirnen had seen enough of Shaughnessy's kills in the past to recognize his flare. They were together against him. This had been the master vampire's plan when he took her. He'd turned her against her own family with half-truths, out and out lies, and seduction of the body and mind. He no doubt promised her a kingdom of her own, perhaps Calame.

Marceline showed no sign of improving. She lay in their chambers in an eternal sleep. He could imagine her suffering. At least he was capable of surfacing from his hell on occasion. He believed Marion allowed him to have his mind more often now for the sole purpose of showing him the fall of his kingdom. The village was on fire. The lawns were scattered with bodies. The shouting outside the walls was near constant and called for his head. There was little doubt they would join Abel when he mounted his attack. The rumors were that Abel was not trying to capture Camilla, he was going to kill her. No tormenting Eirnen with something he needed and someone he loved, he'd not get the opportunity to win her trust and affection back. She was to be exterminated on sight.

For this reason, he didn't regret sending all four of his warriors to bring her back to Westwood. They wouldn't fail him. He refused to entertain the idea of this torment as his future. Camilla would be returned. She could and would reverse what she had done. If she did not, Abel would take Westwood Castle and kill everyone within. Surely Camilla still held a soft spot in her heart for one of the servants or her cousins if not him. Some of her family that these walls guarded were toddlers, innocents in every sense of the word. Abel would dispose of them as well. He'd not risk allowing them to grow to seek vengeance.

He stood on the balcony and looked out over his crumpling kingdom. It was truly falling. Winston's wall crumbled under the assault of those villagers left still determined enough to breach the walls to take their revenge. The stables had been burnt to the ground, the horses gone. Even Marceline's beloved steeds were no longer on Westwood grounds waiting for her return. A cloud of thick smoke blanketed the village. Blood, bone, and severed body parts scattered the lawns. The flower garden, however, was as lovely as ever.

One last look and one last deep breath. There was work to do.

His children and their spouses gathered together in the dining hall. His daughter, Adelaine, and Henrik were the only ones who weren't speaking of him as if he were a sick animal in need of a hammer to the skull to end its misery. Adelaine's husband, Jolie, would do as Adelaine said to do.

"Children," he greeted and they fell silent. Adelaine rested her chin in her delicate hand and grinned as she did when they were younger and her siblings were about to get a thrashing. "The rumors regarding my health and power are numerous. Some are true. Today, I will tell you the whole of it because if we are to win this coming battle we must fight together."

"You want our help?" Durbin asked, taking his wife's hand. She was pregnant, again, nearing the end of the pregnancy by the look of it.

"I want you to help yourselves, Durbin. Do you think Abel will content himself with killing me?"

"Of course, we will all fight against any who thinks to challenge a Westwood," Adelaine said, glaring at Durbin. "Father, if I may, is it not a possibility that it will also be a Westwood we fight against?"

"No. Camilla and I will finish this between ourselves. I do not believe her to be in league with Abel. She is, however, aligned with the master Shaughnessy, which means the vampires of Calame now follow her as well. She was among the pack. I've been informed they think fondly of her and are refusing the orders Henrik gave them to come to defend the castle walls. They may well be her beasts now."

"Father," Henrik said and stood, offering a bow.

"Finally, a show of respect from my own children."

"Father, I believe the warrior Dorin to have some level of empathy for Camilla. He stopped her from attacking you, but in such a manner as to not harm her. The opposite, he apologized for taking the opportunity to finish you from her. While you were indisposed and she at Gladen, it was again the warrior Dorin who came to me, demanding to know where Camilla was taken and when. He was obstinate and unreasonable."

"Interesting." He paced, remembering watching Dorin's body twitch on the floor and knowing that caster Marion was responsible. Had she said something to him? Implanted some thought regarding Camilla? Could the warrior truly care for her with nothing more than a few whispers from that insipid caster?

He continued to pace and think. Camilla was young and impressionable. Dorin was also young and a warrior, handsome, he supposed. The journey back to Calame was a lengthy one. Was it possible Camilla could develop a fondness for the warrior? Could it really be that simple? He rushed off to the servants' quarters. Servants hear everything, know all the secrets. Perhaps a bit of gossip slipped into their ears regarding Dorin and Camilla.

Camilla had to admit, the fall was unlike anything she'd ever felt. It was exhilarating and freeing simultaneously. She was laughing by the time they finally made it all the way to the bottom. Dorin was smiling down at her with such affection she reached up to trace his lips. She stopped herself before contact was made, but not before he saw her intention.

The lightheartedness of the moment now gone, she cast her eyes from his face and scrambled to get back to the ground on her own two feet. He went to a small creek and began washing the blood from his hands and splashing the cold water on his face. A few strands of his hair had come undone from the tight braid. The untidiness of it made him seem younger and less harsh.

"Your jaunt with the vampires has put us behind. We must go," he said, rising to his full height.

It wasn't just Niko who awaited them. The other two brothers were also there now, and untidy or not, they were intimidating. Their black eyes and severe expressions were made more vivid by the blood speckled across their faces. Though only inches separated their size from Dorin and Niko's, they seemed so much larger. There was no way she could escape all four of them and Shaughnessy was as pinned down by the daylight as the rest.

Eirnen had forfeited the power and protection of all four of his warriors. It spoke to his desperation. Desperation was weakness, vulnerability, the feeling of a victory slipping away. Even tethering Rowan to the fence was a desperate act. Desperate men were also dangerous men. Shaughnessy was right. If he was willing to relinquish all his warriors to retrieve her, he would never allow himself to be placed in such a position of weakness again. Even the threat of it would be unacceptable. If she healed him, she would die.

As they walked, Dorin asked about her wellbeing often and insisted they stop for breaks. He had water he'd collected from the well at the barn where she'd woke. He stayed by her side, kept pace with her, but didn't speak though she found him looking at her often. While the others were in the lead, she took the opportunity to analyze the shell, the tarry power that kept her from casting against them. There was no light, no clue to the essence below. She reached out searching fingers and found no power to use. She kept probing at the layer, trying to strip it away, until Nox spun and snarled.

"Stop trying me, woman," he warned.

"Or what? What will you do, Nox? Nothing. There is nothing you can do but endure me. Harm me and I will blame a portion of my anger at Eirnen on his allowing his dog maul me."

"I am no one's dog!"

"You're certainly demonstrating fetch as a skill," she said and smirked at him.

He stomped back toward her, his face twisted in fury. Gabriel grabbed for him. She crossed her arms and smiled, daring him. What made it easier to maintain the challenging stance was that there had been no sign stripping pieces of their protective shell was within her capability. Perhaps, they must relinquish control to her as they did Eirnen?

Nox was still coming and Gabriel was still trying to stop him. She waited for fear to rise up at the sight of him stalking toward her. She couldn't cast against him, forget physical violence as a solution, but she had a come-what-may attitude about it. She stood taller and lifted her chin, managing to take a posture of looking down on him even though she was feet shorter than him. The next moment, she was staring at Dorin's wide back. There was a roar of rage and then she was looking up into Dorin's solemn face.

"Is that how you see me—a dog?"

"A pet. A weapon. A thing to be used. That is what you asked Eirnen to make you and so he has," she said.

"You lie," he said, shaking his head. "I can smell the deceit. You don't believe your own words."

"Or perhaps you're not as astute at telling truth from lie as you'd like to believe."

He snorted a laugh at her and she couldn't keep the surprise from her face. "You are quite fierce, aren't you?" He shook his head and, unbelievably, the look on his face was pride. For her? "It's the rare creature who would challenge Nox as you did. Niko and I dared not irritate him since childhood."

346

The others were getting farther away. Gabriel still had a hand on Nox's elbow and was leaned in close talking to him. She glanced up at Dorin and saw he was staring after them.

"Did you send them away?"

"Yes."

"You did so by telepathy and you could because you are the sons of Anthelian."

"How do you know this?"

She smiled up at him but didn't give him an answer. In truth, it was no longer spite that motivated her to continue needling him. She was quite amused by it in a playful sort of way. These last weeks had been so filled with anything but laughter, it was the only excuse she had for the utterly unladylike snort that escaped her when she tried to refrain from laughing at his perplexed expression.

"Now you laugh at me," he said, but he looked as if he were fighting a smile of his own. "Since you won't share with me all you know about me and how you came by this knowledge, perhaps you will answer my questions about you."

"You can ask."

"But will you answer?" She gave him another smile and shrugged. "You enjoy teasing me this way."

"That was not a question. But, yes, I do," she confessed and felt her smile widen with his.

He'd asked permission to ask questions but remained silent as they walked. Along the way his expression stopped being playful and friendly, instead his face was tense, serious. She stayed quiet as well, letting him sort through whatever it was that caused his features to harden.

Her own thoughts began to darken. Where was Shaughnessy? Did he get out of the sun? Did Abel's army capture him, is he now a prisoner? She shook her head. Shaughnessy was clever. He didn't get captured by Abel or the sun.

"I want to know everything about you, which makes me want to ask you why I do. Have you put a spell upon me, caster?"

"I swear, I have not."

"Do you know who did?"

"I don't think it's as simple as a spell," she said and pushed her hair out of her face. "The short of it is, I believe the caster Marion to be a far greater power than I or Eirnen realized and taking her life had consequences none were able to see save for her."

"What I feel, it isn't real? I've been bespelled, deceived."

"No," she said sharply and stopped to take a breath. "I don't know how you feel, so how am I speak of what is real and what is fallacy?"

"I've told you. I woke to this new life with you as my first thoughts. I dream of you. I can feel you. The more I'm near you the stronger it becomes. I could feel you call out to me from Gladen. I could feel your fear and pain, but there was no path to follow. To find you this morning was the easiest thing in the world."

"Can you tell how I feel right now?"

"Vague impressions," he said, then he was back to grinning as if he'd heard her sigh of relief.

"He's going to kill me," she said.

"No, he needs you."

"I do not believe that and, I suspect, nor do you." She closed her arms around herself against the sudden chill.

Did she believe he would kill her on sight? No, but they could no longer trust one another and had both gone too far to earn or win it back. She couldn't contend with him and the whole of the Westwood family, which was likely within the castle walls. To survive, she had to leave. She looked up at Dorin and held herself tighter.

"I can't let you go," he said so low it was just above a whisper.

Ahead, his brothers stopped to wait for the two of them to catch up. Niko smiled and winked at her, but Nox and Gabriel both glared as if she were the cause of all the world's evils. Dorin moved until he was more in front of her than at her side, as if he'd noticed their hostility and meant to protect her from even a harsh look.

"Why are you immune to my casts?" she asked, stepping back to Dorin's side. They looked to one another, Nox and Gabriel with matching expressions of confusion. "You didn't know. Does Eirnen know about your immunity?"

"We aren't immune to him," Niko said.

"Someone approaches," Nox said in a voice so deep it sounded like a growl. The brothers drew their weapons simultaneously. Dorin used one arm to usher her behind him.

All she could see were their wide backs and even straining she could hear nothing. Was it the caster boy, the last creature? "Please don't hurt him," she whispered.

"Easy."

She recognized Riley's voice and pushed through them to see for herself he was unharmed. Rowan stood at his side. Both had new bruises and cuts, but they were on their feet under their own power. Blood dripped from the ends of Rowan's fingers from a laceration high on his right arm. He didn't have his glaive, but they each had one of Riley's short swords.

Rowan's expression was hard as he came toward her. She began to take a step back from him but forced herself to hold steady. Dorin moved as if to block her again and she laid a hand on his forearm to stop him. He looked down at her quizzically, but she kept her eyes on Rowan. She would no longer cower. She would not hide behind Dorin, or Shaughnessy, or anyone else.

Rowan stopped and dropped to one knee before her, his head bowed. "Mistress, my life is yours."

"As is mine," Riley said and went to one knee beside his brother. "We will defend you, fight for you, protect you with our own lives should that be the price."

"Pretty words, but you are Eirnen's just as we are," Gabriel said and sheathed his sword.

Rowan and Riley both lifted their eyes to her as if seeking an answer she didn't have, then lowered their heads again. "If Eirnen summons, we ask that you stop us from answering his call."

"That is hardly necessary given that Eirnen's warriors are soon to deliver me back to him as if I were within his thrall as well. If it is me you follow, you must enter Westwood walls with me. From there, I fear for you should you deny Eirnen in my favor."

Riley gave her a scrutinizing look. He and his brother were part of the plan that entailed her boarding a ship that night and fleeing Calame. She gave him a slight nod and bid he and Rowan to rise. The end of the plan was unchanged. It was the execution that had come into question.

They began walking once more. The pace set by Gabriel and Nox was not one she could keep up with and rather than asking them to slow, Dorin lingered behind with her, Rowan and Riley just ahead of her, Niko behind to guard their back.

"Earlier, you said please don't kill him. Who did you mean?"

"The last creature. He has to stay close to me. He wants me to repair him as I did the others, but I get the sense he hates me too. I can't blame him for his feelings. He's been left in such a state for so long and has had to watch as the others have been made whole."

"His condition is not your doing and not your fault."

"Nice to think so," she said and her eyes landed on Rowan and Riley. "Wait. Stop."

Everyone was on guard in an instant, but she ignored them and went to stand before Rowan and Riley. Two casters. No blood exchange needed. Would the three of them together be enough?

"What is it?" someone behind her asked. She didn't know who and didn't care. She put a hand out in an attempt to silence them.

She looked over the twins, trying to get a sense of their energies. They were strong, both of them. Of course they were. Eirnen would accept nothing less. This could work. "I need you to help me save a life."

"We haven't time for this," Gabriel said. "Eirnen will summon soon. He is not a man of patience."

"We will make the time," she snapped and looked around to find the caster boy. "Where are you?" She took a few steps into the tree line, but he wasn't there. "Have you seen him? I haven't seen him this morning."

"No, but it's likely he just hasn't caught up to us yet."

She kept walking, deeper into the woods and Dorin stayed at her side. He was there, he had to be, she thought, ducking under another branch. Her feet were still bare, the occasional sharp stone hidden under the fallen leaves dug into her skin.

Dorin caught her upper arm to pull her to a stop. "I smell blood."

"It's nothing. I think a stone cut my foot."

"It's not your scent," he said and moved ahead and off to the left.

She trailed after him until she saw a pale figure lying in the leaves. It was him. He rose to his arms and tried to crawl away when he saw Dorin coming. There was blood on his back and one of his hind legs wasn't moving as he tried to drag himself to safety.

"Riley," she cried and knelt next to the boy. She ran her hands over his face and head, trying to soothe him. He made a hissing sound between his teeth and snapped at her. His hands pushed at her until she moved away. "I'm sorry," she said.

Riley and Rowan came to her side. The boy cowered and hissed at anyone who came near him. He was badly hurt, but no matter how much she tried to convince him Riley was only trying to help, the more he reacted like a caged animal. He was terrified. They had to do this now.

"Rowan. Riley. I need you to help me. To help me, you have to trust me. I can strip you of your guards, but that requires energy and I need all I can muster to fix him."

"You can't fix him, Camilla. What's done is done."

"You swear your life but not your trust?" She narrowed her eyes at them and they dropped to bended knee once more. "I repaired two of the wolves and one vampire already. He's the last. Please," she said and knelt with them to take one their hands in hers. "Please, help me make him whole."

They agreed to do anything she asked, the obstacle was the warriors who argued it wasn't safe to linger. They couldn't move him lest they risk him hurting himself more trying to fight away from them. She stood and faced the warriors, refused to back down or give an inch. She'd made a promise. Gabriel grabbed for her to force her to go and Dorin shoved him away. They both seemed surprised at Dorin's behavior, but he didn't back down. He stood between her and his brother and wouldn't force her from the creature.

In the end, it was decided all the warriors would patrol a perimeter. Riley and Rowan stayed with Camilla and the creature. They opened themselves up to her completely, enough so she could see Eirnen's energy wound in and through theirs. The design was not dissimilar to the wards that sealed her inside her chambers. Ideally, there would be at least one more caster to pull from, but there wasn't. It was the three of them and it had to be enough.

"Don't try to block me out," she said and held her hands out, one facing the creature and one facing the twins. "Here we go."

She started pulling from the twins and felt the power build. They widened their eyes at her as if she'd done something shocking, but they'd had energies pulled before. It wasn't an unfamiliar feeling, but perhaps they were surprised she'd gained this skill. In truth, she wasn't the best at it, but she was better than she'd been thanks to Eirnen and Henrik's lessons, enough to not kill Rowan and Riley.

She could feel their heartbeat in the energy, could feel it begin to slow. She started pouring what she'd collected into the creature. He arched and let loose an animalistic scream unlike anything she'd heard. It was a cry of pain and it was piteous, but she didn't stop. She couldn't if he had any chance at being made whole.

The twins swayed on their feet and their eyes began to close. That was it, that was all they had to give. She stopped pulling from them and turned all her attention to the creature. This was it. If she didn't finish this now, she may never get the chance to make things right. She opened her own energies and pushed them into him. She was a caster and her energies could heal him as well. She just had to hold on to consciousness long enough for it to be complete. She was strong enough to do it. She had to be.

The caster boy's body straightened with a sickening snap as his spine was forced back into proper position. He fell face first on the ground, fingers clawing at the dirt, trying to find purchase to get away as he screamed. She stopped feeling sorry for him. To do so was to risk guilt and guilt would lead to her not doing what needed to be done because it was causing him pain. His face turned to her, his lips were bleeding as if he'd bitten them, his eyes squeezed tight.

"Keep him back," she said when she felt Dorin approaching but didn't look to see if Rowan and Riley obeyed.

The world swam. She drew in a deep breath and hit the boy harder with a bigger jolt of energy. She wasn't going to make it. The boy's eyes and mouth opened wide but no sound came out. His eyes were the loveliest shade of dark green. His skin was still pale but not deathly, a flush crept over his cheeks. Camilla staggered, grit her teeth and let loose another wave of energy on a scream.

"Please, no more," she heard from an unfamiliar voice as darkness swallowed her.

⌁

Camilla inhaled deep and smiled as she breathed in the familiar scent of Dorin. She was warm and dry and he was here. Everything was right. She snuggled in closer, splaying her hand across his chest. The feel of him was something to be appreciated, lingered over, savored. He stroked her hair, then traced lazy circles on her back. She was being pulled from sleep, but she didn't want to go. She liked it here. But fight it as she might, wakefulness loomed closer and closer.

"Callum?" She blinked open her eyes and searched for Callum to tell him of her newest adventure with her Dorin. She sat up. She was under a rock ledge and Dorin was there, which meant Callum wasn't. Her chin quivered and her eyes burned.

"Camilla?" He pushed her hair back and she covered her face with her hands.

"I'm sorry," she sobbed. Dorin lifted her onto his lap and it only made her cry harder. She turned her face to his neck as his arms closed around her, sheltering her, making it okay to cry as she needed.

She hadn't cried over Callum. She'd not given Winston one tear, but now there was no stopping it. She sobbed and hiccupped apologies to Dorin, telling him of Callum and how she'd failed him.

"That boy, he was yours?" She nodded against his chest. If he was part vampire now, he would've seen Callum just as Shaughnessy had. He'd played witness to what she allowed to happen. "You fought like a Valkyrie for him. He saw that, but he didn't want it."

"He was just trying to protect me," she sniffed. He'd been in pain, whether he wanted to be free of Westwood or not, he shouldn't have been taken like that. He'd suffered enough.

"That boy, he knew my face. He called me by name to stop you before you were killed, as if he was certain I would. He begged for your life, not his. Why, Camilla? Please, tell me why there was recognition and relief in that boy's eyes when he saw me, though I'd never seen him?"

She took a deep breath and felt tired. Selfish or not, she told him how Callum came into her life, and he listened without interrupting. She wanted him to know her as she knew him. She wanted to give him the answers he sought. She wanted him to look at her the way he had when she dreamed of him. She wanted to allow herself to be truly lost in him, even if it was just once.

"Callum looked at you like he knew you because, in a way, he did." She swallowed hard and told him the truth. "Just before he came to Westwood about a year ago, I had my first dream. The dreams were so real, as if I were living another life while I was asleep. I could smell the woods and the grass we walked through on my skin when I woke.

"The man with me there was rough and brutish, but at the same time he could be gentle and there was a vulnerability in him that I wanted to know. My ability, the lesser one, is to recreate things that I've seen with my own eyes. Callum was my only confidant, and I used my ability to show him."

She steeled her nerve. He'd stayed quiet and let her explain as best she could. Now it was time to show him as well.

The small space they were in was overtaken with the image of an ancient oak with low hanging, twisted branches. It sat in an overgrown field all alone, surrounded by waist-high sun-browned tufts of grass. But in the shade of the leaves, the grass under the tree was shorter and deep jade. It was soft and sweet-smelling and dotted with lovely purple flowers. Dorin sat with his back to the trunk, his eyes following the swaying grass as if searching for something.

A wide smile stretched his face, sensing Camilla sneaking up behind him. She leaped to scare him and he twisted around at the same time, catching her around the waist to pull her down with him. She lay across his legs, cradled by his arms and didn't look like she minded being caught. "I knew you'd come," he said and brushed his thumb across her lips.

"And how do you know I'm not here to tell you goodbye once and for all?" she asked as she threaded the hair falling around his face through her fingers.

"I suppose you'd mean it this time, just as you did every other," he said and leaned down to tease her mouth with his. She nodded weakly and clasped the nape of his neck for more. "Say it, Camilla. Tell me you want me to kiss you until you quiver."

"Kiss me, Dorin," she said and raised to flick her tongue across his bottom lip. "Until you quiver." His deep laugh was a half growl of satisfaction as his lips claimed hers with no sense of teasing.

She dropped her hand and let the image go. They both stayed quiet. He probably trying to decide if this was some caster trick and she trying to stave off the depression that was threatening to drag her under. She wanted him to stay. She wished he would leave. Having him sitting this close was painful and what she really wanted was to curl up on this floor and give up for a while. Not forever, but to break alone in silence. She wanted to cry some more, scream if she had to, thrash her weakness to try and reclaim her strength and she didn't want an audience. Then she was going to get up and think of some brilliant way to make the right choice.

"That day by the training room, it was the man you just showed me that you were grieving, wasn't it?"

"Yes." She sat on the cold stones, huddling around herself for warmth.

"I am still that same man," he said, stroking the tears from her cheek.

"You're not," she said and lifted her hand toward his face but stopped. "You weren't touched by Eirnen's evil there. You weren't tethered so tightly to him that you would follow his every command. You haven't known him long, but in the short time you've been near him, you had to have noticed the lengths to which he will go to get his own way. You can deny him nothing. If he were to know my feelings for you, you will be his perfect leverage."

"Your feelings for me?"

"All those awful things I said and those are the words you focus upon?"

"Yes. Eirnen is not here now. You and I are."

"But he is here, don't you see? You said Marion warned you that I was not yours to keep. I can't keep you either, no matter how much I may want to. The vision of us in that field was not the only one given to me," she said and waved her hand to fill the space with an altogether different kind of image.

She didn't look at the ash- and blood-covered landscape, nor the golden throne or the slivery white dress she wore that had by some miracle been untouched by the ruin around her. She looked at her face. The expression she wore was blank. Her eyes were cold and empty. There was no spark of liveliness or joy. There was nothing.

"Do you see what is missing?" she asked and left the image in front of them as if he needed to study it to see he was not there beside his brothers. "In that future I showed you—the two of us—we were happy. I loved you with everything that I am or would ever be. I would have done anything, given anything, sacrificed anyone to spare you pain, to save you from Eirnen's wrath. My power, it's strong and getting stronger. It can be dangerous if in the wrong hands. If Eirnen controls me, he controls my ability."

"What is your ability, exactly?"

"No," she shook her head, "I cannot be sure if Eirnen commands you to tell him all you know you will be able to keep my secrets. If we stay, if we fight to be together, if Eirnen even suspects I am fond of you, he will use you to hurt me. He will use me if he thinks it will gain your compliance. This is the result."

"Fair enough, even we are unsure how far-reaching is Eirnen's compulsion. My brother, Gabriel, tells me Eirnen used the threat of forcing us to fight against one another for naught more than a displeasing comment."

"He requires nothing less than perfect allegiance. A displeasing comment, to question a course of action, anything he may perceive as a show of disrespect is also disloyalty and punishable by death. Already he used the threat he knew would cut the deepest to force your brother into submission. To his way of reasoning, if he forced three of you to kill one, those still alive will have learned a lesson and therefore never falter again."

"He needs all four of us," Dorin said. "We would be able to resist such a thing, surely."

She let him sit and mull over what she'd said, but he still doubted Eirnen's ability and his cruelty, she could see it. He wasn't nearly fearful or angry enough to have found the depths of Eirnen's depravity.

"Dorin, how did you and your brothers survive the attack on your clan?"

"The lengths you will go to change the topic from you and I and our future together," he said, shaking his head. Little did he know, she hadn't changed the subject at all, not really.

"I really do want to know how you did it. By all accounts, it was an assault which should have netted no survivors."

"Niko and I survived because we weren't there. Nox and Gabriel fought the day of Abel's raid. Nox was alive by sheer force of will when we returned from a hunt to find our homeland burning. We saw the smoke and smelled the stench from the hilltop. We dropped our game and ran down into the ravine and up the next hill that showed us the valley where we lived.

"There was no movement save for the dancing of flames that still burned high enough we knew we'd missed the enemy by mere hours. Bodies were strewn on the ground and the smell of blood and bowel was choking. Some of the gigantes they had taken time to position as if on display. Our mother and father were both hung for all to witness, their bloodied bodies impaled onto long poles side-by-side. Someone had even run a spike through their hands to join them together. Their iron crowns rested atop their heads that were stripped clean of their warrior braids.

"My sisters, our beautiful sisters who were warriors by their own right, as all gigantes women are, had been mauled by claws and teeth before being laid out at father's feet. We sifted through bodies, praying to Great Mother Gaia our brothers survived. We found Gabriel first, anchored to a slick rock face with thick chains around his neck and arms. They'd cut strips of flesh from his body, beaten him until he was nearing unrecognizable. The twin iron bands around his biceps marked him as one of the sons born to the gigantes king. They hadn't taken those, but his hair fell around his face in jagged pieces as if they'd taken a dull blade to his braid.

"Niko and I, we yanked the anchors free of the rock and lowered him to the ground. He was barely breathing, but even then he tried to crawl, his arm stretched out in front of him as if to urge himself a little farther. Niko tried to stop him while I searched for Nox. That was what Gabriel fought so hard to reach, it had to be, and I was desperate to find our last brother. It was a matter of moments that I saw the shock of black hair.

"Nox hadn't been tied. He'd fought, viscously from the looks of the bodies around him. He lay on his back, his chest and belly flayed open by wolves' claws, but his chest rose and fell in shallow waves. We dared not move him for fear the contents of his abdomen would spill to the ground. Still Gabriel struggled to get to him. We took Gabriel where he wanted to go. We dressed the wounds as best we could and then went about to bury the dead, hoping we wouldn't be digging two more holes before the day's end. Nightfall came and Henrik found us. He offered his aid."

Tears streaked Camilla's face. It wasn't just an attack, it was torture. Abel and his men had tormented the gigantes clan and she'd wager anything he'd been all the more vicious in his attack because they were something Eirnen coveted.

"I'm so sorry, Dorin."

He pulled her into his side, trying to soothe her, make her feel better when the loss was his. She lay there, again, letting herself be comforted by him, again.

It was the perfect opportunity to tell him the truth of the attack, to show him once and for all what Eirnen Westwood was, and she just couldn't do it. He needed to understand, but to leave him tied to the monster responsible that way was just as cruel, maybe more so since she'd be telling him to prove a point. She let her body relax into his and closed her eyes, just a moment more.

When she opened her eyes, he had her folded in his arms, his cheek resting against the top of her head. It felt as if hours had passed. Maybe they had, but they'd stayed locked together even after the tears stopped.

Enough. Enough crying. Get up.

She stood, brushed the wrinkles from a dress that was beyond saving, pulled her shoulders back, and went out onto the ledge. The sky was cloudless and full of stars, the air still smelled of last night's rain. There was movement on the rocks below. She tried to sense who it was without alerting them, but no sooner had she sent out those seeking fingers that the figure looked up at her. It wasn't Shaughnessy, of that she was certain. It was too small, too thin, the hair too dark. Just as she was about to alert Dorin, he appeared at her side.

"Do you not recognize him?" he asked and smiled down at her. "That was an extraordinary thing you did for him."

"The creature," she gasped and covered her mouth with her hand. He was walking upright, his skin no longer glowed in the night like newly laid snow. "What's his name?"

"Merrick is the only name he will give."

"Merrick," she tested the name and smiled. It suited him somehow. He was getting closer, a few more steps and she could reach out her hand to help him make the step up onto the ledge should he need it. He stopped as if he heard her speak his name and looked up at her. He was much changed, but she recognized the hatred she saw there.

"They have made the shelter suitable," he said to Dorin and turned to leave again.

"Shelter?"

"An abandoned cottage. The others have been preparing it while you recovered. You and I both know your vampires are going to come for you sometime in the night."

"You can't kill them," she said and stepped away from him so she could look up into his face.

"I assume you are referring to Master Shaughnessy and the three of his horde I found you with. I have no intention of harming them unless they give me cause." He stepped off the ledge onto the rocks below, then reached back up for her. "We must go, Camilla. Do not forget, not all who seek you out this night are friends."

She took his hand and allowed him to help her navigate the steep hill and loose rocks. Merrick was gone. She watched his back as he hurried for the cottage. She could understand why he'd be upset with the whole of the Westwood family, but she'd hoped to speak with him, ask him where he came from, who he was, how he felt. Perhaps once he recovered more? Did he have friends or family in the village? Had they survived the magicks that made the gigantes into warriors? Had Eirnen taken more from Merrick he'd yet to discover?

It was clear she would not be boarding a boat tonight as planned, but would Merrick want to leave Calame with her? If he didn't talk to her, she couldn't know what he wanted, not that she knew much herself. She didn't know where they were or how far they were from Westwood Castle or the river where she was to board the vessel. Once she was at the bottom, Dorin kept her hand in his and she didn't try to pull away.

"We will stay here the night," Dorin said. "And travel through the day."

Of course, while the vampires who were allies were trapped. Out in the open, travelling, it would be too easy for an ambush, then they would fight and someone would be hurt. If she had the vampires to draw energies from, would it be enough to slow the gigantes? Maybe. It would be difficult, but maybe. Even if she bought them time enough to run, Dorin could find her. How far did this compulsion reach? Was there anywhere far enough? She looked up at Dorin's face and eased her hand out of his.

"I need to see Riley and Rowan." She walked faster, moving toward the stone cottage they'd chosen.

He didn't try to stop her and didn't match the faster pace. This was getting out of hand. They'd been wandering through the dewy grass, under the stars, hand-in-hand as if they were lovers and for a moment, she'd forgotten they weren't. She'd begun to strategize against the gigantes, all the while forgetting or willfully ignoring Dorin was with them, not her. He was an asset of Eirnen's, not hers.

The forest was trying to reclaim the cottage. The only part visible until she was within several feet of the front door was a portion of the second level. Overhanging trees, vines, and tall grass obscured most of it from sight. The door was open with broken vines dangling in the space. Though there was plenty of room, she ducked her head and eased inside.

A few short candles burned, just enough to keep from tripping over the broken furniture scattered around and the bracken that had blown in from outside. Dorin shut the door once he was inside and dropped a wooden beam that spanned the width of the door as a barricade. It was hardly a deterrent for anything they were up against.

Rowan and Riley were in one corner, sitting with their backs to the wall. Camilla sat with them and drew her knees up to her chest. It was cold tonight, but a fire would give away their location from a distance. A light rain had started to fall again, the pattering of it against the old cottage accompanied by the relentless chirping of crickets was lolling her toward sleep. There were things to be done, but sleep was not among them.

Dorin was speaking with his brothers. They were occupied with who would guard which section of the perimeter and escape strategies for Camilla should they be attacked. It left her free to speak with Rowan and Riley.

"First, thank you for helping me free Merrick."

"With regards to Merrick"—Rowan whispered and leaned in close—"I can't get a read on his abilities, which is unusual. He has them, he isn't latent, but there is no sense as to what he can do. I warn you, he stares at you with malice and Eirnen was not in the habit of choosing lower-level casters to take part in his experiments for his warriors."

Camilla glanced over her shoulder to see Merrick watching them, the look on his face blank. There was no expression for her to read, but even the emptiness of his gaze caused her skin to prick with warning. She wondered why he stayed with them if he hated her that much? Did he believe he wasn't free to go as he wished? If that was the case, she needed to reassure him that he wasn't expected to stay with her.

"Thank you, Rowan. I will take care in his company. I wanted to speak to the two of you regarding your binding to Eirnen. When you opened yourselves to me to cure Merrick, I could see it wound through your energies. I think I can unravel it if you would permit me. It is your choice."

"Yes. Please. However, we would ask that whatever you do to one of us, you replicate with the other. Even if it becomes clear during the process the unbinding cannot be undone."

"Certainly."

It didn't take long for them to decide Rowan would go first so Riley could heal any injuries the unbinding might cause. Rowan sat perfectly still, breath slow and shallow as he concentrated on dropping his guard and opening himself. She could see it there, pulsing through his essence, a glowing thread wound in, through, and around in complicated patterns.

"Riley, help me follow the pattern. It's like a maze. We have to follow the thread to its end and there is only one possible solution."

"I can't, Lady Camilla," he said, looking at her with his brows furrowed. "I don't see what you describe. Eirnen has the ability, as it seems you do. What I see are the places of injury both old and new."

"Old and new?"

"Yes, I can heal a wound. I can also see where there once was injury no matter how long healed. I can then reverse the healing, should I choose."

"So a long-healed broken bone, it would become broken once more at your command?"

"Yes."

She held her hands above Rowan, using her fingers to pick through the thread, and thanked Callum for making her practice the wards on her chambers, because this wasn't dissimilar. She followed the path Eirnen's binding made, unraveling as she went. It was intricate and she'd be lying if she said she wasn't impressed. Another tug of the thread she couldn't feel and Rowan groaned as she screamed, jerking back from the pain, falling onto her backside.

Dorin and Nox were leaning over her and Rowan. Riley was beside his brother searching for the cause of his pain. Rowan was breathing hard, his face still screwed up and teeth clamped tight. Her arm throbbed from fingertips to shoulder. She cradled it to her chest as she slid closer to Rowan.

"Are you okay?"

"What was that?" Dorin asked

"A deterrent, I think." The bite of Eirnen's power wasn't something easily forgotten. "Rowan, can you hear me?"

"Yes," he wheezed, curling in on himself.

"I'm sorry. I followed the wrong path with the binding, this is the consequence. We can stop if you like."

"No," Rowan said with force, his jaws tightened as he clenched his teeth. "I will be free of Eirnen Westwood. I will be my own man."

She nodded and settled back at his side to start again. Her

breath was still unsteady and her hands shook. Dorin and Nox loomed over them and it was making her nervous.

"If you will excuse us," she said, looking up at them. "I have to concentrate and I can't with the two of you standing there."

It was nearing dawn by the time she finished with both of them and the three of them were exhausted. She and Rowan had been hit with Eirnen's power three more times before the pattern revealed itself. When it was Riley's turn. She'd learned a few things—markers to see false paths and Eirnen's tricks were more evident. She and Riley were only hit twice. Six times total, six times she was hit by the king's magicks and she was still standing. Not steadily, but standing all the same. Her hands felt bruised and burned at the same time, her back ached from being knocked to the floor, but she'd done it. Riley and Rowan belonged to themselves.

Eirnen emerged from yet another battle with Marion to find Camilla and his warriors were still not in Westwood Castle. Unacceptable. However, he now knew there was something the little witch wanted from him, something he and only he could give her—information. It seemed some years ago, a distant Westwood relative had imprisoned a caster female who was Marion's sister. Marion wished a reunion. She was now at a place of disadvantage.

Even now, he carefully kept his thoughts turned from the information Marion coveted. She could probably dig it from his memory, but how long would that take? Would he go mad before she found what she needed? He agreed to tell her, but not until after they'd reached a bargain and he refused to entertain a discussion until after this war with Abel. He'd found a way to wrap her in chains and gag her.

There were still moments he found himself wandering through the castle with no destination. He wasn't cured. He'd wake, staring at his children over breakfast service and not recall how he'd gotten there or what they'd been discussing, but the screaming in his head had lessened until he was able to function.

He stood on his tower, high above all he ruled, and watched the rain douse the last of the embers glowing in the village below. There were a few shops still standing, more homes were left untouched, but where there were usually streets full of villagers and caravans for the marketplace, there were but a few stragglers left behind.

During his most recent episode, Henrik and Adelaine had put in place some defenses against Abel's army. Adelaine was more mastered at illusion than Camilla. Her ability wasn't dependent upon seeing an image beforehand, though it helped. Somehow, Henrik had managed to get her to use it for something more than her own vanity. Trenches eight feet wide and as many feet deep now dotted the landscape between the castle walls and the field beyond. However to any looking or charging ahead to attack, all they would see was a smooth field, thanks to Adelaine. Inside each of the dozen or more holes in the earth were poles sharpened on the end, waiting to impale those who fell inside.

She'd also conjured a pack of wolves, sitting on guard, pacing, waiting and snarling for a fight. This was what he was forced to show Abel's scouts since his actual pack had refused his orders. Refused him. His warriors would exterminate the entire pack, down to the last pup, once this was finished with Abel. Durbin's power, like Henrik's, was more physical. He would be of great help once the fighting began. He could crush and mangle even the sturdiest of enemies with a squeeze of his hand. With arms spread wide, bring them together on a clap. He could crush a whole line of men. He burned through his energies quickly, then would be of no more use. They'd have to strategize to use him to their greatest advantage.

There was smoke in the distance. More destruction caused by agitated townspeople or a warning of Abel's impending attack? It didn't matter. He'd gathered and reformed his guard. He and Henrik were to discuss battle strategy once he returned from gathering those still loyal in the village below. There would be few, but every match needed pawns.

Eirnen closed his eyes and found the tie with his warriors. It was comforting to feel that line of power and know it was all his. He reached down the line to them and gave a jerk, a summons for them to come to him now. To deny him was impossible, to try meant pain. In the end, he would have his way anyway.

Rowan and Riley were not there. He searched harder, added more power, but it didn't matter, they were lost. Dead? He had his doubts. The only other answer was Camilla learning more of her power and using it. He needed Camilla here now. She needed to be brought to heel.

⤍

The warriors had taken turns watching her with the twins through-out the night. They stayed quiet, but she wondered how long it would be before one of them asked if she could free them as well. If she could, if they were freed of Eirnen's bond, it opened possibilities she dare not hope for, not yet.

Her stomach growled and her body ached, but she didn't argue when Gabriel said it was time to move. The twins stayed close to her side, on guard, but the way they were with her had changed. If it wasn't yet friendship, there was definitely affection and trust. They spoke with her about Callum. It was sad at first, but they were soon laughing as the men described their many mischievous adventures. She recounted to them the story he told her. Grieving him, talking, and laughing about the person he'd been, felt like he was close again.

The rain started falling harder around mid-morning. They were all soaked and shaking cold. Well, not the warriors. So far it seemed as if very little bothered them. None of them had slept during the night, but neither had she and the twins. The day was grey, the clouds overhead thick, but other than an occasional squint, the light didn't appear to cause them problems, either. They hadn't cast that she'd seen, but since they didn't have cause to defend themselves from casts, it didn't matter if they were skilled or not. They had the best defense she'd encountered or read about.

Merrick was still with them, but he stayed deeper in the woods, out of sight for the most part. He spoke little. She'd told him he was free to do as he pleased back at the cottage, he'd given a tight nod, then looked away. During times they were least likely to be overheard, she asked the twins if they recognized him from the village or if he'd been one of the guard. They didn't remember him.

The warriors didn't leave them long enough to speak about their departure from Calame. She hoped Shaughnessy was coming up with an escape plan. She had none unless she could free the gigantes. Even then, she could only hope when left to make their own choices they would choose to disobey their king. But he wasn't their king, was he? Not really. According to what she'd learned from Dorin, they were the children of a gigantes king. It stood to reason the oldest of them was now king of the Fagaras gigantes clan. Because of Eirnen and Abel, they made up the entirety of that clan, but still one of them had as much right to the title of king as Eirnen. More so.

Eirnen's father, grandfather, men as far back as stories could recall, were warlords and conquerors. They moved from area to area, warring until there was submission or death from those who lived there. Their surname, Westwood, was adopted by Eirnen's grandfather. The story went, as she'd been told it, that there was a western wood near the keep they'd built on a newly taken territory. They were warned to leave it and the beasts within, as they were deadly and had never lost the wood to any aggressors over millennia. None had even come close to taking it.

That set the course for Eirnen's grandfather, whose name was Laird. Laird and his army laid waste to the western wood, burning it to the ground and killing its keepers. Their victory was so great, stories were told of Laird and the western wood. Laird decided he would call this new place Calame to honor his peasant mother, as that was her surname. Laird, however, was too proud to carry the name of a peasant. He'd risen above it and adopted his greatest victory as his new moniker. Laird Westwood.

Great grandfather Malachi held disdain for the title of king. He ruled because he'd earned his place. His men respected and followed him. He answered each challenge and defeated his opponent to continue holding leadership of his men. Eirnen had a throne fashioned, sat upon it, and declared himself a king. Eirnen used his guard to execute all challengers to his rule rather than face them himself. No matter how this ended, it would not be with Camilla declaring herself queen.

It was well after noon that she saw a lovely flat rock sticking out from the hillside like a shelf, a seat just begging to cradle a weary traveler. She climbed up and lay down on the cool stone. The heavy-laden boughs overhead shielded her from the majority of the rain until enough gathered in the leaves to dump fat drops on and around her.

"I have to stop, just for a while," she said when she could almost feel the displeasure radiating from one of the gigantes, probably Gabriel. He seemed quite the rule follower. She lifted her head to see, now that curiosity had her. Sure enough, he was standing in front of her. "Are you always so serious, Gabriel?"

"Yes," he said and walked away.

"Camilla, I will carry you if you will allow it, but we must keep moving." Dorin had taken Gabriel's place, his expression tense, almost pained. "Eirnen summons."

He leaned down as if to lift her and she slid out of reach. "I will walk."

The first step was a stumble, but she righted herself. Her arms and legs felt weighted down, her stomach a cold knot. She shuffled forward with Rowan and Riley at her side. The warriors kept a much faster pace. Dorin glanced back over his shoulder at her often, his expression unreadable.

"They have to come when called," she said. "I do not."

"Nor do we," Riley said with a smile.

"Don't be so prideful, brother," Rowan warned. "We know more than most what it is to try and deny Eirnen's summons."

"Is it painful?" she asked, both curious and determined to keep her mind on anything other than the heaviness and pain of her own body.

"Yes," they said at the same time. "It's as if the yarn of power you unraveled within us is trying to get back to its owner, to Eirnen. If making progress toward the goal, it is but a tugging sensation. But if you stop, the yarn tries to pull free of your body, to keep going. It's as if you are being turned inside out."

Camilla trudged on, feet scraping the ground more often than taking full steps, but she was moving forward. She noticed the twins weren't quite as full of pep as they had been. They were tiring too.

"Devil this," Gabriel said and then she was over his shoulder. She walked her hands up his back, but they gave out, her upper half flopping against him.

"Put her down, Gabriel." Dorin's voice was low, even, but still full of warning.

"She is too tired to continue. We cannot stop. You will not force her. What option have you left me?"

"I will not ask again, brother. Put her down."

Camilla could hear her heart pounding in her ears. She couldn't see what was happening, but the tension was palpable. "Dorin, use your sense," Nox barked and then there was the sound of movement. "Stop this," Nox said.

"Gabriel, put her down," Niko shouted over the sounds of groans, grunts and yells both of anger and pain. "He'll stop if you put her down."

"Gods dammit, this female," Gabriel growled. He flipped her onto her feet too fast to find her footing on the ground that was now heaving. Her knees buckled and she landed hard on her backside.

Before she could move, Dorin was standing over her and he'd shoved Gabriel back. He crouched, facing his brothers and the twins. His fangs were longer, his expression dangerous. His reaction startled her, but it would be a lie to say it also didn't affect her in other, more pleasant ways. "She is mine! No one touches her. Anyone who handles her roughly will fight or take a beating."

"That is a vow you cannot keep," came a voice from the darkness. "Eirnen will kill her, warrior. You cart her to her death."

"Shaughnessy," she breathed and found she couldn't stand on her own. Dorin helped her to her feet, but she hadn't had food, water, or sleep in days and couldn't keep herself up.

"As it appears, you're to do his work for him," Shaughnessy said lifting her face.

"We are but a few kilometers from the Westwood boundary," Nikolai said. "There will be more of Abel's creatures out patrolling, trying to catch her before she gets inside the walls."

"I brought friends of my own," Shaughnessy said, then faced the woods. The warriors were at full attention, waiting. One-by-one they stiffened as they sensed what was coming. It was the whole pack.

Seeing them all spaced between the trees, the occasional glow of eyes and flashes of teeth would have been frightening had she not gotten to know them as people. There was an occasional growl and yip which she interpreted as caution or a warning to the warriors. Grayson and Thomas walked from the woods in human form. Neither of them so much as glanced at the warriors as if they refused to acknowledge their presence.

Grayson handed her a leather bag full of dried meat and fruit. She sat in the grass, uncaring how it would be perceived and started devouring the food. Someone pushed a canister of water toward her, probably Dorin. She turned it up for a sip before shoving more of the sweetest fruit she'd ever tasted into her mouth.

After one hunger was sated, another came to the fore. The wolves and Shaughnessy were a power source, a way to get back the energy she'd been expending these last few days. Fighting against the gigantes, fixing Merrick, unbinding the twins, it had taken its toll, more than she'd realized. She closed her eyes and skimmed the surface of their energies, not enough to weaken or harm them. There were so many she could spread out what she took. Muscles loosened, the fog cleared from her head. She was so languid all she could do was lie back in the dew-soaked grass and bask.

"Jealous you've never put that expression on her face, Dorin?"

"Shaughnessy, please. Not now," she said without opening her eyes. "If you take this feeling from me, I'm going to scream."

"Well, lass, start shrieking," he said and poked her in the ribs. She rolled her head to the side and saw him kneeling next to her. "We have to be at Westwood tonight." He narrowed his eyes, willing her to understand. The boat.

Her eyes went to Dorin, who was watching her with a blank expression, an expression that said he didn't want to show how he was really feeling. She stood, facing Grayson before he could read more in hers than she should. "Thank you, Grayson. Thank you for the food and for allowing me to take energies from your pack. I'm feeling much improved."

"We must go."

"Of course, Gabriel. Let's," she said and stifled a smirk.

She needed to speak with Shaughnessy privately, but there was no way to do so as surrounded by those of superior hearing as they were. She filled him in on the twins and their release, pointed out Merrick to him. He gave a slight nod. He understood, Rowan and Riley were free to come with her and Merrick could if he so chose.

"Ahead," Nox said, drawing his sword.

"Catch them," Shaughnessy said and at least ten of the pack

sprang forward. "Scouts," he explained. "We can't let them report back no matter who they belong to, Abel or Eirnen."

"If they are Eirnen's they are our allies," Dorin said.

"Yours, not ours," Shaughnessy corrected. "Have you not figured out yet, you and she are not on the same side of this war."

Dorin's brow furrowed. He didn't understand. "I fight for her."

"You fight for Eirnen and wish you could fight for her. She is not yours, warrior. How can she be when you are not your own?" Shaughnessy held up a finger before Dorin could speak. "If you believe you belong to yourself and no one else, stop walking. Stop obeying the command of your master."

He looked so stricken she almost took his hand but didn't. She was leaving here. Leaving him. "Strip my binding," he said. "You have the strength of the pack, free me as you did Rowan and Riley."

"We haven't the time," Shaughnessy said.

"We will make the time," Camilla bit out. The other warriors came back to her, no doubt having heard Dorin's request.

"Can you do this?"

"I can try," she answered. "But you have to lower your guard, open yourself to me completely, which means you have to trust me."

The others looked to each other, but Dorin never looked from her face. "We do this now."

Dorin trusted her and his brothers to be with him while his guard was down, but no one else. Rowan and Riley stayed close, the pack and Shaughnessy spread out to pick off more scouts if they found them. It was difficult for him to do it, to lower his guard. The twins coached him, since as a gigantes, he'd never had to. He'd never had this protective layer, none of them had, it was given to them the night they were made warriors. Gigantes had no casting ability. They had clan healers Nikolai described as what Camilla thought of as a witch. Those with little innate magical ability but could practice and develop varying levels of skill in healing or tracking. Their ability was generally taught by an elder, their spells dependent upon poultices and trinkets. Of course what she knew of witches came from the same lessons that taught her about wolves and vampires.

"It's not the same," she muttered, feeling defeated. "I can see it, but it's not a thread like with Rowan and Riley. It hasn't been woven through your energies in a pattern I can unravel. It's like a glue, binding you to Eirnen but also holding the vampire and gigantes together. Your energies are there but large pieces have been replaced with Eirnen's."

"What's that mean?" Nox asked. It was impossible to not know him from his voice alone.

"I wish you could see it, that I could show you to help you understand. Even if I could take away the pieces of Eirnen's energy, there will be blank spaces. Your energies will be fractured, perhaps not to the same extent as Merrick's was to make you become a creature, but enough to change you. Maybe kill you."

"Perhaps is not certain."

"No, Dorin, it is not. However, I am certain that unbinding you will change you irrevocably. You will not return to your former selves. You will not remain as you are. You cannot be whole with fractured energies."

There was the white of vampire, the vibrant orange of the gigantes, but fusing them together was the green of caster. To undo the binding was to undo the cast, undo the cast, unmake the warriors. With the missing pieces, they wouldn't survive or worse—go mad and have to be put down.

"I am truly sorry," she said and stood, turning her back to wipe the tears tracking her cheeks before Dorin could see them. Luckily, the dreadful rain was there to mask them.

Shaughnessy watched her. As if he could read her thoughts, he shook his head. She turned back again to face Dorin. His expression was one of defeat. She hadn't understood how much hope she'd put in her ability to free him as she had Rowan and Riley until it was taken. She stepped in closer to him, reaching up to put her hand on his cheek. He leaned forward until his forehead rested against hers and then his lips brushed hers.

This was goodbye.

CHAPTER 17

THE RAIN WAS relentless. Thunder shook the ground and lightning lit the fields around Westwood Castle for moments at a time. In those strobing precious seconds, the extent of their opposition was clear and terrifying. Hundreds of wolves and men came over the knolls like a wave. The wolves howled in signals to command and instruct the pack.

Camilla slipped again and again in the sucking mud but stayed upright and moving forward by the grace of Dorin's steadying hand. The rain was cold and coming faster until everything was a nondescript, wavy blur. Their goal was to make it inside Westwood walls. Everyone but her thought it the safest place in the short term. For now, they said. As if Eirnen would release her once the threat of Abel's army was gone.

They were in the shadow of Westwood Castle when her heart began to race. She grabbed Dorin by the elbow, "I'm not going back inside that place."

"You have no choice," he said and wiped water from his face. "They want nothing more than to kill you. Eirnen cannot. Not if he wants to be whole again."

"I disagree." Camilla whirled and swallowed a scream. Eirnen sat upon his horse, looking down on them, a picture of health and vitality.

"How," she snarled as fear turned to fury. Dorin's hand on her arm tightened as he pulled her in closer to his side, a gesture Eirnen didn't miss as he looked from one to the other of them. This was it, he knew. In those few moments, he knew.

"My dearest granddaughter, have you not learned by now that I cannot be defeated? Not by my father, not by Shaughnessy, not by Abel and his army, and most certainly not by you." Henrik and her uncles Durbin and Jolie flanked Eirnen. "My warriors, it would be proper to take your place at my side."

Gabriel, Nox, and Niko went to him as commanded with a look of resignation. Dorin resisted. Eirnen sat up straighter in his saddle, a smile crossing his face.

"Dorin," he said, with more power behind the command. A groan slipped through Dorin's teeth with the effort and he was propelled forward as if pulled by a rope. "I see you have stolen Riley and Rowan from me, but not my warriors. That in itself, your inability to undo my binding, should tell you that you are no match for me, Camilla. You attacked me. You weakened me, yes. Your strike against me was quite impressive. However, as I sit here now, once again besting you and commanding them, is it not clear that you are not yet ready to go against me?"

Eirnen slid off his horse and walked toward her. Shaughnessy bared his fangs, the twins readied their weapons. "I could force you back to Westwood Castle, but I won't. Instead, I will stand here in the rain and mud and ask you to return first and foremost as an ally. You will one day be unstoppable, Camilla. I can see that. All your hardships have molded you into a woman who is capable of great deeds. I ask for you to return to train as my successor."

Camilla's eyes slid to Henrik of their own volition, his widened then narrowed with hatred. "And if I refuse to cure you and

Marceline, what then happens to your extended hand of peace and tutelage?"

"I think I have demonstrated sufficiently that I do not require your aid any longer." The look on his face was smug.

"You're lying," she said with confidence as she stared not at him, but the aura pulsating around him. "I don't know the why of your respite, but Marion will have you once more."

The army was so close now their footsteps were a rumble to rival the thunder. There was no way to make it into Westwood Castle before the first wave was on them. Eirnen raised his arm and dropped it fast, slicing the air and his army ran toward the other with a battle cry.

Eirnen watched the defeat spread over Camilla's face. She was learning there was no beating Eirnen Westwood. In the distance, the armies clashed. Metal and screams mingled with howls of pain and growls of savagery. "Gabriel, Nox, Nikolai, go do your duty," he said as he mounted his steed.

"What of Dorin?" Gabriel asked.

"Stays. You do not interfere," he commanded and the brothers snarled at him. "Go. Win me my war."

They loped across the field, swords already in hand, towering over every other fighter. Let Camilla have her rogue vampire and the pack would pay a hefty penalty in good time. For their defection, their mutiny, their utter disregard for his orders, their pack would be cut by half, at least. A staggering power loss for him, yes, but in his loss was a lesson they wouldn't forget.

He watched with pride as his warriors struck down one enemy after another without breaking their stride as they ran headlong into the melee.

"Dorin, since you seem to enjoy serving as escort for Lady Camilla, see her to the safety of the castle."

"No," Camilla said as Dorin went toward her.

"The choice is not yours," Eirnen said and turned his horse until his back was to her.

Camilla realized, though she'd tried to tell Dorin he didn't understand the hold Eirnen had on him, she didn't fully understand it herself. As he kept coming at her, despite her protests, she knew she still harbored the hopes of a foolish child. Love would conquer all, he'd be able to resist because his love for her was stronger than any compulsion placed by Eirnen. She was still living in daydreams and fairy tales.

"I'm sorry," he said as he took her wrist and began pulling her forward behind Eirnen's horse. His head hung in shame and defeat, while Eirnen sat tall in his saddle, back to her as if she weren't an enemy. As if she hadn't struck out at him once and would do so again.

She threw out a hard line of power that hit him mid-back and knocked him to the ground. Dorin pinned both hands before she could launch another attack. The sight of the great Eirnen Westwood wriggling in the mud filled her with satisfaction.

A sharp sting sliced across her face.

"Let me widen that smile for you," Henrik called. As warmth mingled with the cold rain to drip red from her jaw, Dorin released her hands and drew his sword.

The moment her hands were freed, she took aim at Eirnen once more. He raised his hands in defense, but to her astonishment, she hit him before he could make a strike. He bowed in the mud, screaming and flailing his limbs. Henrik slashed at her again. Dorin stepped in front of her, taking the hit from Henrik and her as he saved Eirnen.

"Dorin, move," she shouted, knowing he couldn't.

"Jolie, get your king to the castle! Now!" Henrik shouted.

"No!" Dorin was a wall in front of her, no matter what she did she couldn't get around him. Where the hell was Shaughnessy? Why weren't they attacking? Eirnen wasn't dead. Hurt, yes, but injured wasn't dead. Injured didn't end this.

She looked around and found an answer. Shaughnessy was fighting Durbin. Rowan and Riley were attacking Henrik. Jolie was now riding toward the castle on horseback with Eirnen in tow. He was going to get away. A scream brought her attention back to the fighting in front of her. Henrik was gawking at his chest where he'd been impaled by one of Riley's short swords, but the scream hadn't been Henrik's. It was Riley. Rowan lay in the wet grass, hand to his throat. Riley was above him, no doubt trying to heal him. Camilla scrambled to his side, but there was no saving Rowan.

"Be free, my brother," he gasped, reaching for Riley's face. The light left his eyes and his arm fell limp across his body. The sound of pain that erupted from Riley was unlike any sound she'd ever heard and hoped to never hear again.

Eirnen was almost to safety, almost inside Westwood walls. Henrick removed the short sword from his own chest and used it to cut open Devlin's throat where he then bent to drink from the wound to heal. Mischa's scream clawed through her ears. Henrik rose, wiped his bloody lips with the back of his hand and smiled at her before gutting Dorin like an animal with a swipe of his hand.

Mischa and Rissa launched themselves at Henrik, another swipe of his hand sent them reeling and bloodied to the ground. They were moving, but only just, when he turned his attention back to Dorin and began cutting him up one slice at a time.

That was it, the snap inside that opened the doors of nothingness. Her pain and rage so great, the only escape was into numbness. Camilla stood in the middle of the killing field, the rain falling all around her, Rowan's blood mingling with the puddles and absorbed the power of those who had been slain.

Shaughnessy was taking a beating at the hands of one of Eirnen's sons. He believed the man's name was Durbin and he apparently had the ability to put casting energies into his every punch. It was like fighting a vampire his own age. Durbin came at him in a rush, Shaughnessy braced and struck out to meet him with both hands to Durbin's chest. Bones cracked, the caster flew back, landing hard before rolling over the embankment to be swallowed up by the swollen creek. Hopefully he'd drown and there would be one less Westwood breathing in this world.

Thunder or a rush of power that cracked just the same, Shaughnessy didn't know, but he felt it when Camilla set her power free. He spun to see her crouching over Dorin, her disfigured face twisted in a rabid snarl. The catalyst for Camilla's loss of control knelt not four feet away. Dorin's intestines had been spilled onto the ground, his face unrecognizable and shrouded in blood and flaps of meat. At her feet lay Rowan with Riley bent over him as if protecting him from the rain.

Eirnen wanted unstoppable warriors. Camilla raised an unbeatable army. Every life lost in the battle rose to her command though their bodies lay broken. The vampires could see them coming but could do nothing to stop them as they flew across the ground, shrieking like wraiths. The smoky images twisted through those still fighting, slicing with jagged claws but leaving those who were still untouched. They didn't discriminate between either army, Eirnen's men fell as quickly as Abel's. The singular smoky beings joined as a wave. Shaughnessy followed their trajectory to see Eirnen being rushed inside on horseback.

Gabriel stopped, watching, then he and two of his brothers ran toward Eirnen. For moments, everyone on this side was motionless, watching. The casters saw nothing but men and wolves falling dead to the ground from no cause they could see. Shaughnessy watched as Henrik looked from the battlefield to Camilla then back again until realization lit his face. Camilla was standing stock still but her hair moved around her as if she floated in water. She appeared paler, her face hollowed and deep in shadow.

The door to the castle closed a moment before the wraiths hit the castle walls with a scream. They circled, as if looking for a way inside, but they were beginning to dissipate as the spirits moved on to their afterlife. Still, casting flares were firing off within the castle which let him hope some had made it inside and Eirnen was being torn apart under the claws of death.

Shaughnessy was at Camilla's side in a second. She'd fallen to her knees, covering Dorin with her own body to protect him from Henrik. Her back and arms bore the slashes that said Henrik hit his mark. Riley was crouched, ready to attack Henrik. Rowan lay dead, eyes peeled wide, throat opened like a scream. Riley hadn't been able to heal his twin.

Riley, wide-eyed and crazed, threw himself at Henrik. Henrik turned in time to wrap his arms around Riley and ease his fall to the ground. After some grappling, Riley was atop, his fists pummeling the larger man. He was screaming, an agonizing sound, that quieted to a snarl as he sat up, straddling Henrik's waist.

"I know every injury," he said just loud enough for Shaughnessy to hear. Then one-by-one, wounds bloomed over Henrik's body. "I healed most of these," he said and watched skin separate into fissures over Henrik's face and chest. Blood poured from the male, faster and faster as each old wound was opened anew. A snap twisted Henrik's right arm at a sickening angle, dragging a scream from the man.

When Riley rose from his victim, Henrik was pale, wide-eyed, his mouth working like a fish out of water.

The other warriors would be coming and they still had orders to deliver Camilla to the castle. As did Dorin. Shaughnessy approached cautiously, hoping the male could fight the order long enough to get Camilla from his reach. Camilla rose from the warrior whose body was healed beyond anything Shaughnessy would have believed had he not witnessed it for himself. There was barely any bleeding at all as the skin knit itself back together.

Camilla, on the other hand, was sliced open across her face and back. Shaughnessy tried to hide his shock when she turned her head and he saw her teeth through the gaping wound on her cheek. He bit into his wrist and put it to her lips. She slapped him away, eyes fixed on the castle.

"Camilla, we're done. You're done. Drink."

"Not until he's dead," she said in a deadened voice.

"He's gone, love. Beyond your reach. You go in there, you die." He took her shoulders and shook her hard, harder than he intended. "Stop."

She looked at him as if he were the enemy for a second before she blinked, eyes glittering as she came back to him. "Oh, gods, Rowan."

"There will be time for mourning, but now, drink." He shoved his wrist into her opened mouth, then pinned her to him when she struggled. "Sorry, love, but we haven't the time." He picked her up with all intentions of running for the ship, but Dorin stepped in front of them before he could take a step. "Dorin, surely now you see," Shaughnessy pleaded.

She stumbled forward as Shaughnessy released her. She was angry, but Dorin whole and unharmed distracted her. She ran the short distance and leapt into the male's arms. She all but disappeared in his embrace and the warrior, with his eyes closed, looked the picture of peace for those brief moments.

Finally, Dorin lowered her to the ground. He cupped her face and leaned in for a gentle kiss. "If I love you the way I claim, I'll let you go where you can be safe. And if you love me, you'll give me that peace."

She began to sob and shake her head. He pushed her back by the arms, then commanded her to sleep. She drooped against him. He studied her face for another long moment then laid her in Shaughnessy's arms.

"She is mine, vampire. I will come for her one day. Let no harm come to her. Do as you must to keep me from pursuing."

He'd heard their plan after all. Shaughnessy lowered his head once, a show of respect he never thought he'd be paying to one of Eirnen's creatures. "Riley, do it now."

As the first of Dorin's bones snapped, Shaughnessy began to run, hoping he would be fast enough, hoping the broken bones in Dorin's leg and arm would heal slowly enough to let them escape. He had his doubts, but perhaps since Eirnen hadn't put a when to his last order of delivering Camilla, they had a loophole to work through. Grayson and the pack were waiting to escort them to the boat, but he sent them back to the dens with a warning that Eirnen would be coming for them.

Riley had the location of the boat and would meet them there before dawn. Shaughnessy had to get Camilla on the boat and himself hidden from the sun. This was it, their one chance. They would make it.

EPILOGUE

EIRNEN CLUTCHED AT his chest, trying to find the air to speak. Where was Camilla? She'd wounded him further, he could feel the emptiness sucking at him, trying to pull him under. Henrik was at his side. He stared hard at his son, willing him to understand the questions he couldn't speak but needed the answers to desperately.

"I'm here, Father," Henrik soothed and gripped Eirnen's hand.

"Camilla," he wheezed out past the stricture in his throat.

Henrik dropped his head and drew in a great breath before meeting Eirnen's eyes again. "Father, do you not recall our previous talks?"

Talks? Talks! He shook his head, fear speeding his heart and panting his breaths. "How. Long."

"Camilla is gone. We search for her still, but there is no trace. Riley has gone with her. Abel Lockley is still in the dungeons as you commanded, awaiting the day you may give Marceline her revenge as you promised. We will not allow him to die, I swear it to you."

"How long?" he asked again and closed his eyes.

"Six months."

❧

The journey was longer than anticipated, but she and Riley relished the extra time to mourn their losses. The two of them had grown closer, but she was hardly a substitution for Rowan. Merrick hadn't been in the fighting but had been waiting on the ship for them. He didn't speak a word to any of them. Camilla thought he'd disappear at one of the many ports they stopped on their trip, but he did not. He waited until they were nearing the foothills of what Shaughnessy called the Appalachian Mountains that was to be their new home before he vanished.

The land was mountainous indeed. It was rough and beautiful in equal measure. Though it appeared to be heavily wilderness, Shaughnessy insisted she arrive as if she were still royalty. A black carriage outfitted with black horses carried her and Riley over treacherous paths with long drops until, finally, one afternoon they stopped at the bottom of a knoll. Atop it was the frame of a simple home. A man with sun-kissed skin stopped his work to look at his unexpected and uninvited guests.

James.